Timbrel arrived and dropped her pack on the ground next to the other exiles in the rescue party. Krys stood next to a large pack, Sarin wore the same faded robe, and Von arrived.

Marahir emerged from the Council Tree still dressed in his official robes, wearing a large hat as garish as Von's tunic. "Greetings. Your mounts will be here shortly, as will your provisions."

The horses arrived. The lead horse limped on three legs. Thin to the point of near-starvation, the horse shivered. The last horse in the group gave a quiet "Whuff" and lay down on the ground.

"This is some sort of joke." Kryslandir's deep voice cut like a knife.

Marahir looked at his feet. "The Council supplies your provisions." A servant brought a weathered crate. Inside lay a few moldy loaves of bread, a half-bag of grain with maggots crawling out the top, and a worn pouch with three gold coins. Four nearly empty waterskins leaked over the rest.

Krys spat on the road. He tucked the coins into his belt and waved away the crate. Checking the saddlebags next, the tall historian put his hand into one... and out slashes in the bottom. "These are useless." Krys stripped the saddles and saddlebags from the horses and discarded them in the roadway.

Sarin spoke for the first time. "A map would be useful on our journey, as would directions to where Lady Lostaria was taken."

Marahir opened his mouth, shut it with a puzzled look, and dropped his gaze to the ground. His voice strained. "I cannot tell you anything."

Krys turned on his heel, face twitching in disbelief. "Not even where to start? How do you expect us to succeed?"

Marahir closed his eyes.

"I see." Krys frowned. "And I suppose we must leave before sunset."

Marahir stood directly in front of Krys. "You are a most perceptive elf." He swept off his hat in a grand bow. Kryslandir

1

answered with a bow nearly as deep, sweeping the edge of his cloak across the Councilman's hat.

Timbrel wondered if anyone else noticed Krys pluck the folded parchment out of the Councilman's hat.

Books by Colleen H. Robbins

THE DARAGA SERIES
Daraga's Quest (forthcoming August 2018)
Daraga's Children (forthcoming 2019)

COLLECTIONS
Stories of a Sheltered Suburbanite (forthcoming 2019)

ANTHOLOGIES
Bombshells: Stories and Poems by Women on the Homefront (ed. M. Martin, J. Loren)
Krampusnacht: 12 Nights of Krampus (ed. Kate Wolford)
Eldritch Embraces: Putting the Love Back in Lovecraft (Micheal Cieslak)
Write Where We Are: 2017 (Write On! Joliet)
Write Where We Are: 2018 (forthcoming November 2018)

Colleen H. Robbins

# Daraga's Quest

Daraga Flight Publishing

2018  Daraga Flight Publishing

Published in the United States of America by Daraga Flight Publishing.

ISBN  978-1-7320803-0-0

Cover Art copyright Rafael Ramos
Printed in the United States of America

Visit www.DaragaFlight.weebly.com

Dedicated to my husband,

my children,

and especially to my mother,
who never stopped encouraging me.

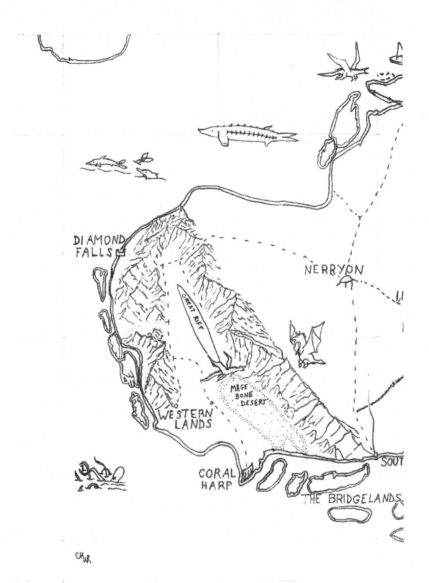

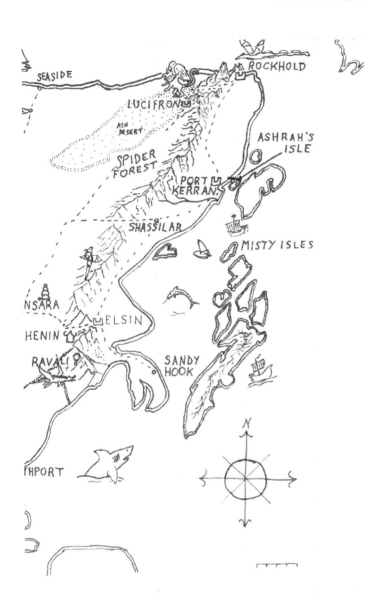

COLLEEN H. ROBBINS

# DARAGA'S QUEST

## BY COLLEEN H. ROBBINS

# Chapter One

*A mountain near the Dragon Valley*

Nayev scrambled up the mountain, hands grasping at protrusions and cracks in the granite. He slid once, skinning his hands and knees, before catching himself and continuing upward. He pulled himself up onto a ledge and rested for a moment.

He could see the dragon slowly gaining altitude. Its wings gleamed golden in the sunlight as the beast swooped around the granite face. Its wings beat as quickly as a hummingbird's as it tried to land on the sheer rock face.

Nayev continued climbing as the dragon struggled to dig its claws into the rock below him. He followed a crack upward, then clung by the fingertips of his left hand as he reached for another fissure. He swung himself across and skinned his fingers again as he gained a final handhold. From there, he dragged himself up over the lip of the mountain and settled safely on the ridge at its peak.

The dragon's head popped up over the edge, followed by nearly fifty feet of body and tail. It turned slowly and stretched its length along the ridge, long snout pointed toward the man.

*You cheated.* The dragon's voice echoed in his mind against a low growl. It half opened its wings, then closed them again carefully . *It was difficult to climb past that rockfall.*

"Not my rockfall. You were just in the wrong place..."

*... At the wrong time. Like you with your elf? Back on our Journey?*

Nayev half closed his eyes. "Oh, I remember her..." Memories of his yearlong stay with Allison made him smile. "Pretty, fun..."

*And an elf.* The dragon's jaws snapped shut on the last word. *Totally forbidden.* The crest at the top of its head flattened. *You really are a pervert. And to think of all the fights I got into defending you, brother.*

"Novich, I..."

*Don't explain. What is it that the humans say? All the wizards went mad? You are a perfect example. I don't even know why the Council wants you to breed.*

"What do you mean?" Nayev tilted his head and frowned at Novich.

*They want you to breed with Anyana. After you hunt down your elven offspring-- and no, I did not tell them.*

Nayev backed up and slid off the edge of the ridge. As he scrambled for purchase, Novich plucked him off the steep slope and set him back down on top.

*Anyana is not so terrible. Her daughter Sasha leaves for the Journey in a month.* A touch of wistfulness colored Novich's mind voice.

Nayev waved his hand. "I don't care about Anyana. What do you mean by *offspring?*"

### 

*Ravali elf territory*
*Three months later*

*One more week before the treaty is signed,* Timbrel thought. *Then it will be safe to return to the Human lands.* She bent back to the moist clay of the swollen riverbank, her fingers groping along the oak's roots to find the round swellings of the bloodroot fungi. Her fingers circled a walnut sized globe, expertly twisting the nodule loose. A few more bloodroots and some silvergrass and she would be ready.

The air pressure changed and an arrow whistled past, pinning a half dozen strands of her sun gold hair to the oak's trunk. A second knocked her basket of bloodroot fungi aside. She flattened herself into the muddy bank before turning her head to look. She glimpsed movement just as the deep chuckle of her tormentor reached her. Von.

For a moment, the girl remembered the torments of her

childhood. Five years older than Timbrel, Eevonhay had been as victimized by the older children as Timbrel. Quiet and without friends, the full-blooded Ravali elf seemed to blossom when he devised fresh torments for her. "Round ears! Human spawn! Half blood!" The insults still rang in her memory, along with the beatings she had taken. More than once she'd bled in mud puddles, only to be punished again at home for arriving in less than pristine condition.

Von stole her jewelry on feast days and locked it away, at least until she learned to open the locks and retrieve the precious heirlooms. Von chased her and dragged her by the hair, until she learned to run fleetly. Von stalked her like a beast even now.

A branch snapped under his foot and she looked up.

He sneered down at her from five feet away. "Your knees are muddy, Half Blood. Kneeling in the mud like the slave you ought to be. Better pick up your precious weeds."

Timbrel scooped the bloodroot nodules back into her basket. "It is a shame you cannot understand about herbs and healing." *Von might have mastered his weapons*, she thought, *but he did not yet have a true warrior's respect for healers.*

"A healer," Von scoffed. "The Genjin created us healthy. We are strong, we never catch disease, our injuries heal quickly... What makes you think that you have any use?"

"The Ravali are not the *only* people in this land." Timbrel stood and wiped the thick mud from her chest and belly. Von's jaw went slack as his eyes widened. Timbrel inhaled, enhancing the effect. Von stood staring. His pale face, prominent cheekbones, and ice blue almond-shaped eyes might have been termed handsome if he didn't scowl so often. "So is this a social visit, or did you just want target practice?"

The warrior's jaw snapped shut with an audible click. He glared at the girl, then glanced at the sun high in the sky and smiled. "Actually," he began in a honey-sweet voice, "I carry a message for you."

"Go on."

"The Ravali High Council requests your presence." Von's

smile broadened. "I am to escort you."

"Tomorrow?" she asked.

The smile became an evil grin. "Today, when the sun is high. I have been searching for you *all* morning."

Timbrel glanced at the sky. If she left now and ran, she would barely make it to the Council on time, with no chance to clean up. Yet another way to torment her. She did not show her anger, instead lifting her hand toward the warrior. "Since you have delayed me already, do you think you might help me up the bank?"

When he reached down with a smug expression, she planted a muddy hand on his shoulder, pulled his arm, and kicked sharply backward against the bank. Von overbalanced and landed under Timbrel as they hit the mud. She wiggled against him, then scrambled up and onto high ground before he could react.

"See you at the Council." She tucked a cloth over the nodules in her basket, gathered her muddy skirts scandalously high, and ran straight for the Council meeting.

### 

*The Ravali Elven Council*

Marahir, the Voice of the Ravali Council, watched from the third balcony of the Council Tree. The other nine councilors waited on the second balcony, discussing the morning's business. The meeting would continue when all the Summoned arrived. He did not understand why Soliari insisted that her half-blood daughter be included in the group to be exiled.

The girl had committed no crime, save embarrassing her mother by developing early and petitioning the Council to allow her to visit her father in the human lands. She left when she turned twelve and did not return until her twenty-first birthday, long after her Nameday. She refused to acknowledge her mother as a relative, and instead apprenticed herself to Allowei, a traditional healer. In the last year, the girl spent most of her time in the fields and forests of Ravali.

14

*Soliari does nothing that does not advance her cause,* he thought. *Why send her daughter off with criminals?* Marahir frowned.

The first two criminals waited below: Kryslandir who learned forbidden magic, and Sarin the historian who encouraged Krys in his crimes. The Voice chuckled at the irony of the third criminal. That young man, implicated in an outlawed society, had not yet been told anything except to summon the girl and return.

Soliari's motives still disturbed him. Related to the royal house of Urramach, the elven noble could not serve on the Council. Lacking the royal birthmark, she was not eligible to rule. Instead, she played with politics, gaining immense power through astute decisions that bordered on foreknowledge. Marahir knew that he was not her only influence on the Council, though he might be the only one trying to understand her actions.

With only an inch or two left for the Council Tree's shadow to shrink, Marahir scanned the horizon for the two missing among the Summoned. The girl ran with gathered skirts, coated in mud. The warrior followed at a distance. The innocent girl would clearly be on time, while the implicated one would not. Yes, the meeting would start on time. Let the young warrior come in late. It would be easier to hide the true reason for his inclusion. The longer Marahir could keep the other outlaws from realizing that they were hunted, the better.

The girl stopped just outside the Council Tree and squeezed muddy water from her skirt. Two other running figures appeared in the distance, both wearing white. *Messengers.* He would listen to them when they arrived. It would do the criminals good to wait and worry. *But first, to start the meeting.*

The Voice entered the hollow part of the tree and descended the living stairwell. The others joined him as he passed and they filed into the Council chamber just as the wide door set flush in the tree's living wood swung open and the girl entered. She walked in and stood under one of the crystals set into the trunk wood that scattered sunlight inside the hollow.

The councilors seated themselves, and the meeting began

15

with the obligatory speech from the Herald. Marahir ignored the well-known ritual words and concentrated on the Summoned instead.

Kryslandir dominated the room with his presence. Nearly seven feet tall, taller by a head than most elves, his moon-silver hair and storm-gray eyes glittered in the crystal-reflected sunlight. He wore dark blue robes, a style fitting for a historian, personalized with silver embroidery. Sarin stood next to him like a pale shadow, dark green historian's robes as faded with age as the white-haired elder elf.

Lanieli Lady Urramach, who called herself Timbrel since her return from the Human lands, stood to one side. The half-elven girl had made some attempt to wipe her face and squeeze the mud from her hair, but her wet clothes clung to her like a second skin. She stood proudly, still beautiful in spite of the mess. *It is as well that Soliari is banned from the Council*, Marahir thought. *She would hate her daughter even more if she saw the girl's pride.*

The Herald finished the opening ritual.

A councilwoman sprang to her feet and pointed at the mud-covered girl. "Explain yourself." The girl looked up just as the young warrior slipped into the room. The councilwoman's eyebrows rose. The young man dripped more mud than the girl did.

Timbrel looked contritely at the councilwoman. "I was... delayed." Timbrel's eyes slid toward the young warrior. He met her glance and turned red. Timbrel flashed him a quick smile before making her face carefully neutral.

"I see," said the councilwoman. Her tone left no doubt as to what she thought had occurred. The warrior looked furious. Timbrel looked momentarily triumphant.

*A true daughter of Soliari*, Marahir thought. *There is more intelligence behind that beautiful face then one would expect. Perhaps the mother does have a reason for including the daughter.*

A ruckus in the outer room interrupted the meeting. The Herald walked out and returned after a moment, visibly upset. "Council members, I beg a special audience in the back chamber

16

for these two messengers."

"Now?" asked Marahir. At the Herald's nod, he stood. "Very well." He started across the room, the rest of the Council falling in place behind him. He stopped and looked directly at the young warrior standing by the door, then waved his hand toward the three Summoned. "Stand with the others. You are joining them." Leaving the shocked warrior in his wake, he led the Council from the room.

#

As Marahir reached the back chamber, the first messenger's words tumbled out.

"A forest fire swept across the Besra province, trapping and killing eight Urramachi among the thirty elves present."

The second messenger looked as shocked as the council members. "Nine Urramachi were among those killed on a ship attacked by pirates off of Port Kerran."

Marahir nodded. "Send guards to the palace of the Urramach Matriarch." The messengers took off running. The Voice of the Council turned to his fellows. "Seventeen Urramachi dead."

"We should dismiss the Summoned," suggested the councilwoman. "Their exile is unimp..."

A third messenger arrived, wheezing with effort. Slim strips of paper dangled from his fist. He stretched one between his hands.

"Messages by hawk: Ambassador Lostaria has been taken in the night, stolen as she traveled to the temple." He fumbled with the second strip. "The Matriarch is dead, poisoned at her midday meal."

Marahir dismissed the messengers with a wave of his hand. As soon as the white-cloaked men left, the room broke into chaos.

"Are there any others left?"

"We must send a rescue party."

"Should we send for Soliari?"

"Is Lostaria still alive?"

"Dismiss the Summoned."

17

Marahir's voice rose above the others. "Our original task now takes on much more weight. Instead of exiling the Summoned, we shall task them with the rescue." He raised his hands to quiet the room again. "Think. We have four family lines within the group. Traditionally, that is sufficient."

"But we must send a relative!"

"We have one. The girl is an Urramach." Stunned silence descended on the room.

"But she is a half blood."

"Which makes her ineligible to become an heir. She remains a relative: Soliari's daughter, a direct Urramach descent line, and cousin-kin to the kidnapped heir. The group remains as it has been chosen." Marahir turned back toward the main Council room.

"We should send another." The counselor who had mentioned six survivors spoke.

"Who can we send? The only others of proper descent are Soliari and her four older children. Would you remove any of those five from their most important tasks? This youngest child is the one who will go."

### 

Timbrel waited in the Council chamber, enjoying the look of dismay on Von's face as he joined them. He inched past Timbrel, then looked up at Kryslandir and took a step back. In the end, he quivered between them as though both were poisonous.

Krys brushed past the young warrior and bent to her ear. "Timbrel, you did not..." He let the question trail off.

She glanced at the overdressed noble now standing on the far side of Sarin. "Of course not. I have better taste." She looked at Krys's finery. "Apparently you had some warning about this."

Krys shook his head. "I only know that I will be leaving the Valley today. Are you ready to travel?" He winked.

Timbrel wrinkled her nose at Krys. Only two elves in the Valley knew of her plan to leave before the next full moon: the healer Allowei and Krys. She only stayed this long to gather a last few plants. The silvergrass wouldn't be ripe for another week; her bloodroot basket was hidden nearby. Her pack had otherwise been ready for over a month.

"It shouldn't take long to throw a few things together." She glanced again at Von. Timbrel suppressed a giggle at the idea of the fashion-conscious young noble trying to choose the color and decoration of his pack, much less what he might place inside it.

Raised voices in the next room interrupted her thoughts. "All dead?" "But how?" "Coordinated attack." "The heir, too?" "One remains." The voices quieted.

Timbrel wished her ears were as tall as a full Ravali, but even Krys seemed to be having trouble hearing.

The door opened as the councilors filed back in. They settled into their seats uneasily, drumming their fingers on the table and twitching their ears.

The Voice of the Council rose and waved away the startled Herald before he could begin. "The four of you have been summoned for a rescue. Lostaria Heir Urramach has been taken while on a diplomatic mission. You are charged with her rescue, and may not return to Ravali until that rescue is complete."

Timbrel stood, frozen in place. Beside her, Sarin wavered and dropped to his knees. Von's mouth worked furiously, but only a hissing noise escaped.

Krys' voice broke the stillness. "Heir Urramach? Lostaria's name neared the bottom of the list the last time that I checked."

"Heir Urramach," the Councilman repeated.

"But a rescue has to include a relative," protested Von. "Tradition requires it."

"Lostaria is my mother's cousin." Timbrel's voice could barely be heard over the echoes of the warrior's protests.

"Yes, Lanieli Lady Urramach is indeed a relative." Marahir's voice took on a more formal tone. "I see four houses among you: Urramach, Illisiden, Persican, and Unjewel. I see before me strength, knowledge, and power; as a warrior, a historian, and a healer. I see nobles and commoners. I see a relative

19

of the captive. The four posts of tradition have been met." Marahir's voice hung in the air like the note of a gong. He waved at the door and an ink-stained scribe scuttled in.

"Lanieli Lady Urramach, Eevonhay Lord Illisiden, Kryslandir of the line of Persican, and Sarinjir of the line of Unjewel, you are sent on a rescue as tradition demands. Let it be so noted."

"No." Timbrel's voice rang out. The Council turned and stared at her.

"You refuse tradition?" Marahir blinked twice, unable to understand.

"You have named me wrongly. I am called Timbrel."

The Council broke out in excited babbling. No one ever corrected the Voice of the Council during an official pronouncement.

"Lanieli Lady Urramach, called Timbrel. Let it be so noted." He paused as if waiting for another objection. "You will assemble here at sundown. Mounts and provisions will be provided, though you may bring a personal pack." The Voice of the Council dismissed them with a wave, leaving the four standing dumbfounded as the Council filed out of the chamber.

Krys glanced around at the others. "Time to pack." He strode away, Sarin shuffling along in the wake of the taller elf.

Von sneered at Timbrel. "*My* mounts will far exceed the Council's quality."

Timbrel ignored the boast, instead retrieving her basket of bloodroots and walking toward the ancient tree that she shared with the healer. Von continued to walk near her, boasting endlessly of his family's great wealth and quality horses.

She neared the lightning blasted tree she called home before Timbrel finally had enough. "You will not have anything unless you go and pack." Von glanced at the sky, blanched, and scrambled off toward his family grove.

With a sigh of relief, she stepped through the soft moss surrounding her home. She would miss the old tree. The jagged stump left behind when lightning blasted the tree two centuries before stood barely three stories high, and gapped where it crumbled on one side of its base. Timbrel ran up the steps of the living stairwell that spiraled inside the trunk to her room on the third level, and took her pack from the branch-peg closest to the door. She reached into the rafters and took down bundles of drying herbs. She attached them carefully to the rings sewn to the outside of her pack. When the herbs were completely dry, she would place them inside her smaller bag, the one that held her medicinal plants.

###

*The Ravali stables*

The stable master wrung his hat in his hands. "But, Lady Soliari," he protested, "these horses are unfit to ride. The rescuers must have better horses."

"Do not argue. The so-called rescuers are nothing but criminals. I need the better horses for my messengers while I call together a proper rescue party." Soliari stared directly at the stable master, her unblinking eyes the blue of the hottest flame.

He became uncomfortably aware of the difference in their status. He mentally compared her rich red gown with his own homespun tunic and winced. "But the Council will be displeased. My reputation..."

"Let me handle the Council. Just make certain you supply these horses and the worst equipment possible." She sauntered to the stable wall, pulling a pair of cracked saddlebags from a pile awaiting repair. Her knife flashed, carving a long rent in the bottom of the leather bags. "The damage will not matter. They will have little to carry in any case."

"Why can't I send just one good horse with them?"

Soliari turned her head, mouth open. "I might wish to ride. If there are no horses left, I could perhaps become bored." Her voice dripped with menace. "I suppose I could entertain myself with gossip. There *was* that question about your cousin's parentage."

21

The stable master nearly tore his hat in frustration. "Lord Estin acknowledged my cousin as his son. My cousin is noble, and about to be married."

"And Lord Estin never questioned this? I really *must* have a talk with him, perhaps after the ceremony that places me as Regent over the Ravali."

"Regent?" The stable master dropped to his knees. "It will be as you say, my lady Regent."

Soliari muttered to herself as she rode back to her home tree. "What is it about these servants? Stable boy, mercenary, they all try to alter my plans."

###

*Two months earlier, Shassilar*

She thought back to her meeting months before with that mercenary captain--Kadeesh, that was it--and her surprise at his advanced age. She used him once before to arrange an attack on the human village that her daughter visited.

The inn still looked like it would fall down in a stiff breeze, and the smell. Soliari shuddered. She slipped through an unlocked door with her hood up and her cloak tightly closed, moved across the room as easily as water flowing, and slipped into an empty seat at a crumb-dotted table. "So..." she said in a rasping whisper, "you still live."

Kadeesh squinted across the table. "It *is* you, isn't it. Fifteen years and you sound just the same. What's the job this time?" He scratched his ample belly and pushed himself slightly back from the table.

"Kidnap a single girl. Keep her captive for a few months, then dispose of her."

"That sounds easier than last time. Is this one surrounded by former soldiers? Or girls with knives? Do you want me to attack again on a festival night? What *aren't* you telling me?" He rubbed his leg, fingering a slender dagger in a concealed sheath.

"Calm thyself, Kadeesh. One elf girl, barely into

22

womanhood, has been sent as an ambassador for secret talks of alliance." Soliari held out her arm, the cloak slipping enough to reveal pale skin and long slender fingers with no calluses. "She will have guards, but must be captured before she reaches the shrine of Ashrah on the night of the full moon, when negotiations begin."

"This isn't the same girl who escaped from Fafar village?"

"No, but there is a resemblance. This one has a birthmark behind her left shoulder." A harsh piping began, accompanied by a young human girl dancing on a makeshift stage. Soliari's pale finger absently traced a looping flower in the crumbs.

Kadeesh froze. "That flower," he stammered. "That... that flower is an elven royal symbol. Elves and humans are trying to ally? That cannot be allowed to happen."

"They would throw away the memory of those lost in the wars. The last twenty years of truce have been bad enough. True peace is intolerable." The hooded figure swept the crumbs from the table.

The crowd urged the dancing girl on with crude comments. Someone added a drum to the music and a handful of copper coins littered the stage as the dance changed.

"Won't they send another ambassador?"

"There are other disruptions planned." Soliari glanced at the stage. Three men dragged the shrieking girl off to a corner. A full minute passed. Soliari pulled her cloak tighter.

The battered dancer crawled back to the stage and collected her coins before withdrawing to the kitchen. Soliari shuddered.

"I'll do it," Kadeesh announced. "Payment up front."

"Half-payment now, and the rest after a month." Soliari stared out from under her hood. "Dispose of her any way that you like, so long as she does not return to the elves." The figure tossed three small leather bags decorated with finely stitched vines onto the table and watched as Kadeesh struggled to move them. *Humans were such a weak species.*

*So were the servant class of elves. Practically a sub-species.* She shook the memories away and let out a peal of

23

genuine laughter. With Lostaria taken and her death unproven, the Council would appoint a regent. Six of the councilors already belonged to her. Who would have thought her snooping would provide so much blackmail material? *The regency will be mine*, she thought. *Birthmark or not, I will rule the Ravali.*

###

It was an hour before sundown when Soliari tapped on Marahir's door. He answered on the fourth tap.

"I've been expecting you. What mischief are you up to this time?" He stood in the doorway, blocking her way.

"Marahir, please. I only have the best interests of the Ravali in mind. Won't you invite me in? I've brought wine." She held the bottle up carefully. "Four hundred year old Grentrer."

"You know I can't take a bribe." Marahir started to close the door.

"I wasn't giving it to you. I thought we could share a drink together like old friends." He stepped back from the door when she pushed at his shoulder. "Here, let me find some glasses while you clear the table."

Soliari slipped a vial out of her sleeve hem while the councilman was busy and shook its contents into one glass. Tucking the vial away, she twisted the stone on her ring, revealing a small pill that she discretely swallowed. It might make her feel a little high, but it would protect her if she sipped from the wrong glass. She decanted the wine and swirled the liquid in both glasses. The powder dissolved immediately.

She walked into the main room and handed Marahir a glass before seating herself. "I'd like to talk about the exiles."

"You know I'm not permitted to tell you anything." He raised his glass halfway to his lips and frowned. "Wait, I think you've given me more than my fair share of wine. Let me level them out."

Taking the untouched glass from Soliari's hand, he poured an inch of wine from his glass into hers. "Oh, now I've made them uneven." He poured some wine back, leaving her with the larger portion.

She reached for her glass. "Now you're just being silly. Shall we drink to old friends?" She took a long sip of the highly spiced wine and was gratified when he did the same. She could barely detect the undertaste. She set her glass aside and leaned forward. "I've made all the arrangements for you: horses, saddles, supplies. Everything's ready for the exiles except a map."

"I've already prepared one." Marahir's words slurred.

Soliari took his hand. His pulse was slowing, or perhaps hers was speeding from the pill she'd taken. Better to wait a few minutes more. "May I see it? I'm told you're quite the artist."

"You know better than that, my lady." The last word drew out twice as long as normal.

She moved closer to Marahir, leaning into him and whispering in his ear. "The exiles don't really need a map. In fact, Lostaria's mission was so secret that you shouldn't tell them anything about it. They're smart. They can figure it out for themselves. Don't make it easy on them." She kissed him on the cheek. "Remember, the longer they are gone, the more time we will have together."

### 

*Celiar's Garden, Ravali*

Soliari shuddered as she swept through Celiar's garden. Some after-effect of the drug, she thought, or perhaps revulsion from kissing Marahir. She shuddered again, ran the last few steps, and knocked sharply on the door.

"Soliari, darling, come inside. I am just finishing with some of my students." Four young Ravali climbed unsteadily to their feet, their eyes as dark as Marahir's had been after drinking the wine.

She wondered what her own eyes looked like, whether the dark centers overwhelmed the flame blue that so many Ravali admired. She shuddered again, this time with excitement. Her

25

senses had never been so sharp. She could practically smell how much Celiar wanted her. When the door closed behind the last student, she threw herself into his arms.

After a kiss that ran down her nerves like lightning and left her thrilled to her toes, Celiar guided her to a chair. "Has everything been arranged?"

Soliari perched on the edge of her chair. "Yes, everything. Marahir will not be able to speak of Lostaria's mission. They will believe him mad."

"My dear, I cannot tell you how much I appreciate your help, especially your financial help. With luck and skilled pushing, the humans will act against us first in a weak attack. Once that happens, we can destroy them for good."

### 

*The Ravali Council Tree*

Krys and Sarin waited under the Council Tree when Timbrel returned. Sarin shouldered an ill-balanced and too-heavy pack made of untooled leather. Krys' pack was larger, and Timbrel judged it to be well within his capabilities. Krys regularly traveled to find historical volumes for Sarin. As far as she knew, Sarin had never left the valley.

Timbrel dropped her pack on the ground and sat next to it. Her full brown skirt, ankle-length and split on the sides for riding, went well with her loose wheat-colored blouse. Her hooded cloak of woven deer fur, dyed green and waterproofed with plant oils, made a comfortable seat. The skirt fell just below the strap on her ankle that she used to conceal her ugly birthmark. Beneath her skirt, her daggers, balanced for throwing, lay safely in their sheaths just inside the top of each mid-thigh leather boot. She had already decided that her aim needed improvement before she would throw away her weapons.

Krys now wore a blue tunic and dark green trousers, far more acceptable than robes when traveling in the human lands.

Sarin wore the same faded green robe. Each of them carried matching black cloaks. *A gift from Krys,* Timbrel thought.

With a clatter of hooves, Von arrived. His crimson velvet tunic embroidered in gold could be seen for miles. He waved his white-plumed hat to the quickly assembling crowd from the back of a white horse with red ribbons braided into its mane and tail. Three cream-colored pack horses piled high with baggage followed. As if sensing the dramatic moment, the white horse reared. Von threw both hands around the horse's neck and clung tight. Snickers rose from the crowd.

Timbrel suppressed a giggle of her own. She, Krys, and Sarin all sensibly braided their hair for travel, but Von spent time curling his hair into loose ringlets. While the style certainly looked good, Timbrel knew that his honey-colored hair would be horribly tangled within hours. She made that mistake once herself, allowing her hair to be styled in curls for the journey to her father's village of Fafar. After two hours in the sun, her sweat-drenched hair hung in limp tangles around her face. The twisted mess embarrassed her horribly when she arrived three days later.

Marahir emerged from the Council Tree. Still dressed in his official robes, Marahir wore a large hat almost as garish as Von's tunic. "Greetings. I am glad to see that you are all on time. Your mounts will be here shortly, as will your provisions."

"I brought my own horses," volunteered Von.

"And we will be glad to take them in trade for the mounts you are being supplied with. I suggest you pare your belongings down to a single pack. You are only allotted *one* horse for the journey."

The young warrior started to protest, but Timbrel's attention focused on the arriving horses.

Her shoulders tensed in horror. Saddled without blankets or padding of any sort, the reins were bound around the four horses' mouths, making it impossible for them to graze along the journey. Loosely strapped on, the cracked leather saddlebags visibly shifted when the horses moved.

The lead horse limped on three legs. Thin to the point of

near-starvation, the horse shivered. The last horse in the group gave a quiet "Whuff" and lay down on the ground.

"This is some sort of joke." Kryslandir's deep voice cut through Von's continuing litany of protests like a knife slicing through curds.

Marahir's cheeks colored slightly and he looked at his feet. "The Council has decided to supply you with provisions, as well." He waved his hand to a servant with a weathered crate. The lifted lid revealed a few moldy loaves of bread, a half-bag of grain with maggots crawling out the top, and a worn pouch with three gold coins. The four nearly empty waterskins leaked over the rest of the crate's contents.

Krys spat on the road. He tucked the soggy coin pouch into his belt and waved away the rest. Checking the saddlebags next, the tall historian put his hand into one... and out the slashes in the bottom. "These are useless." Krys stripped the saddlebags from the horses and discarded them in the roadway.

Timbrel inspected the half-starved horses. Their legs and hooves showed bruises and unhealed scrapes on their legs, and all four bristled with thorns and stones in their unshod hooves. Beneath the injuries, the beasts showed promise. "We'll take the horses with us," she announced.

Krys raised an eyebrow and shrugged before turning to Von. "Which pack contains your bedding?" The young warrior pointed to the last pack horse. Krys pulled out a dagger and sliced the ropes along one side of the frame. The entire pack spilled across the ground. Krys rooted through the various bags, discarding clothing, a large feathered fan, and a sunshade in his wake. One bag finally produced half a dozen blankets. Krys chose four. "We will use these for the horses. Use the others for your bedroll." He threw two blankets to the young warrior, then stripped the saddles from the horses.

Timbrel folded the blankets and set them on the horses before replacing the saddles. She noted which straps needed mending before they would hold properly, but knew the horses wouldn't be ridden anytime soon. She chose several light cloaks among the discarded clothing to cut into bandages later for the horses.

"Von, you have to condense your packs." The young warrior looked up at Timbrel's words, but made no other move. "Do you even know what you have?"

"I will make it easy for him," Krys offered. He cut the rest of the young warrior's baggage from the remaining two pack frames and dumped everything on the ground. The framework for a personal cot spilled from one bag; a complete pig spit and props came from another. Von stood unmoving in the midst of the growing pile.

"You have never been camping before, have you." Timbrel shook her head.

"Of course I have. I brought everything I need."

Timbrel picked up a silk lounging robe between two fingers. "Everything you need." She flicked the useless piece of clothing aside and shook her head again in dismay. After rooting around for a minute, she found a bag of suitable size and thrust it at Von. "Here. Use this for your pack. I will sew straps on it tonight."

Von looked at the limp sack. "This is too small. How can I pack everything in here?"

"That is exactly the point," said Krys. "You do *not* pack everything." He looked at Von's blank face. "Here, hold the sack wide and I will toss in what you need." Ignoring the warrior's protests, Krys rooted through the clothing to find a serviceable change of clothes, then added a second. After a moment's thought he added one copper pot from a matching set of eight, a few eating utensils, and various other items.

"Where is your fire kit?"

"Fire kit? What do you mean?"

"How do you expect to start the evening fire when your turn comes?"

"Start the fire?" Von shifted uncomfortably.

"Do you at least have a waterskin?" Krys dumped out another bag.

"Why should I drink water? I have brought fruit juices and

wine."

Krys stomped away, muttering under his breath. "... too stupid to live... ... must never have been out of the city before... ...cannot really be this useless... ...no understanding..."

Timbrel tossed the skins of fruit juice to Von. "I hope you are planning to drink all the fruit juice in the next two days. It spoils easily. Save the skins afterwards,we can wash them out and carry extra water." Von opened his mouth and she held up one finger. "Do not ask me why you need to carry water. Just accept that Krys and I have done this before."

Marahir stood watching them, his garish hat shadowing his face. Timbrel thought she saw a fleeting look of approval. She chose two of the discarded copper pots to dedicate to horse medicines and tied them to one of the rings on her pack.

"At least Krys puts everything inside his pack." Von sneered at her. "You have as much on the outside of your pack as within it."

Timbrel snickered. "And where do you plan to put your weapons?"

Von's face paled.

"He will wear them," growled Krys.

"I cannot possibly wear all of them at once. Even my pack will not hold all my weapons." Von darted to the impressive stack of weapons tossed to one side.

"First, strap on your main weapon," Krys suggested in a slow voice as if instructing a child. Von pulled five swords from the pile. Krys looked disgusted. "You cannot use five swords at once. You do not have enough hands."

"What do you know about it? You are nothing but a historian."

Sarin spoke for the first time. "Krys specializes in the weapons, tactics, and strategy of ancient warriors, just as I specialize in ancient maps." He turned to Marahir. "A map would be useful on our journey, as would directions. Perhaps even some information about where Lady Lostaria was taken."

Marahir opened his mouth, shut it with a puzzled look, and

dropped his gaze to the ground. His voice strained when he spoke. "I have my instructions. I may not tell you anything that might jeopardize Lostaria's mission. I cannot tell you anything."

Krys turned on his heel with a look of disbelief. "You cannot even tell us where to start looking? How do you expect us to succeed?"

Marahir closed his eyes and touched his chin to his chest.

"I see." Krys studied his face before continuing. "And I suppose we must leave by the time the sun sets completely, like most exiles."

The Voice of the Council stepped directly in front of Krys. "You are a most perceptive elf. I take my hat off to you." Marahir swept off his hat in a bow that easily exceeded Von's posturing in its grandeur. Kryslandir answered with a bow nearly as grand, sweeping the edge of his cloak across the Councilman's hat.

Watching the display from the side, Timbrel wondered if anyone else noticed Krys pluck the folded parchment out of the Councilman's hat.

###

# Chapter Two

*The Edge of Ravali Lands*

Von's protests at leaving most of his equipment behind were only eclipsed by his outrage at being forced to walk. Timbrel refused to allow him to ride, much less place his pack on a horse.

"Who put you in charge of the rescue?"

"Lady Timbrel is Lostaria's relative." Sarin wagged a withered finger in front of Von's nose. "Even you know enough about tradition to understand how that works."

"She doesn't have the right to make us walk to the Northern Seas."

Krys pounced on Von's words. "The Northern Seas? What made you say that? Do you know where they kidnapped Lostaria? Do you know *who* kidnapped Lostaria?"

Von made a face. "I'm tired and my feet hurt. When are we stopping?"

Krys shook his head. "Is this what the new generation of would-be warriors are like? My feet hurt? We will stop a little beyond the barrier stones." He gestured at the crest of the next hill.

Twenty foot tall obelisks of pale stone carved with ancient runes glittered in the starlight. The barrier stones ran for miles around the outer perimeter of the Ravali lands, spaced a hundred feet apart. Tradition held that even dragons would shy from the stones. The last nearby sighting dated to almost a thousand years before, with the only survivor reputed to have been thrown back inside the stones' protection. Timbrel wondered what really happened.

Less than an hour later, Sarin dropped his pack. "I cannot go beyond the stones." The elder Ravali shivered. "I have not left Ravali lands since my youth. I cannot go any farther."

Timbrel took the elder's hand. Sarin's skin was clammy and cold. "We have been charged with..." She shook off the words repeating in her mind. If she had not been brought up in the Ravali's magic-hating culture, she would have suspected a spell had been cast over the group. "If we have not left Ravali lands by sunrise, they will hunt us down and kill us."

"If I go outside the barrier, the dragons..."

Timbrel squeezed his hand. "The dragons are long gone, Sarin. We will protect you from them.

The elder Ravali struggled into his pack. "I will try."

The road paralleled the stones for a few hundred feet, then turned sharply to pass between two huge boulders. Sarin sank to the ground with a cry. Timbrel and Krys rushed to help him.

"He's just unconscious. He'll be all right." Timbrel struggled to remove Sarin's pack.

Krys threw a pebble at Von. "Bring him to the other side of the barrier. Help me, now."

Von edged over to Sarin. Between them, Krys and Von carried the elder elf across the barrier and a hundred feet beyond. Timbrel brought the extra pack and led the horses between the boulders.

They made a quick camp, and started again at mid-day.

### ###

*Outside the barrier*

By evening, after cresting several hills and dipping into a second large valley, Timbrel was ready to stuff Von into his own pack.

"My feet are so swollen I can barely walk. You cannot make me do this."

Krys sneered at the young warrior. "You are right. We will stop and make camp right now. When we start in the morning, you can stay here. The quiet will be a nice change."

The young warrior gaped. "We are stopping?"

"For the horses' sake," answered Timbrel. "I need to treat their injuries or they won't have a chance to heal."

"As if you know anything about horses."

"Humans have horses, too."

"Humans should be exterminated. Your mother should never have birthed you." Von tilted his head up, nose in the air.

"Even Soliari would never kill a child."

"No, but having you around as a permanent reminder of her shame doesn't do anyone any good."

Krys returned from scouting the area and recommended a spot beneath well-leafed trees. Timbrel, Sarin, and Krys tied their horses to trees, while Von took his to an open meadow nearby.

"The grass is better over here."

Krys followed him and took the reins. "The night sky is dangerous in this valley. We need the cover of the trees."

Timbrel busied herself choosing herbs from her pack to make a horse liniment. She bent in sudden pain, her stomach trying to twist itself from her body. Nausea threatened to overwhelm her. Just as suddenly, the feeling left. Timbrel took a few deep breaths, measured water into two copper pots, and then rejoined Krys. "I need to boil water, so we need to start a fire..."

Krys fed a branch into the small fire that burned as brightly as his smile.

For the next few minutes, Timbrel busied herself adding herbs to the pots. When the first had changed color twice, she set it aside to cool, followed shortly by the second pot.

Sarin tried to help her with the horses. The animals snorted and shifted away from the old elf. When two of the horses laid back their ears, Timbrel sent him to help Von.

The horses settled as soon as Sarin left, allowing her to dig out the worst of the stones and thorns from their hooves. One particularly deep thorn released a gush of milky fluid. Timbrel shuddered and worried that the horse might lose its leg. After working on each horse's hooves, she rubbed their legs with liniment and then cut bandages to soak in the second pot. Before an hour had passed, each horse had its lower legs wrapped in medicine soaked stockings. The stockings had the added benefit of silencing the horses' hooves.

### 

In the pre-dawn light, Timbrel stretched her shoulders again and packed her things. She'd taken the last watch fully expecting to find Von asleep on the midnight watch. He did not disappoint her. Krys and Sarin breathed quietly from their bedrolls. Von's rasping snores echoed so loudly they could not be real, though they quieted some when she kicked him.

The horses slept standing, occasionally waking to graze. They seemed content beneath the trees. Timbrel walked to the edge of the meadow and scanned the skies. She squinted. Had she just seen something silhouetted against the night sky? She spotted a second silhouette a few minutes later. The stars remained clear afterward.

The rising sun, still hidden beneath the edge of the world, tinted the meadow pink and purple. Movement and the glint of light caught her attention.

At the far end of the valley, six dragons rose into the sky. Their wings and scales reflected the golden sunlight as they lazily spiraled upward. The six stopped simultaneously, frantically beating their wings like golden hummingbirds. Beneath them, the early sun reflected off of dozens more dragons leaping into the sky and racing after the first group. A few of the dragons flew off to the side, their darting flight like robins fighting for mates in the springtime.

When the chasing dragons reached the stationary ones, they were buffeted by the beating wings and turned away. The first six dragons rose higher before returning to their hummingbird-like wing beats. The chasing dragons circled the six originals.

"They are dancing the skies," Timbrel whispered. The great circling dance continued as the sun rose. Not wanting to leave, Timbrel called out to wake the others.

By now the furious circling slowed and many of the dragons glided away. The six original dragons continued their hummingbird beating, though two struggled and dropped to a lower level. Dragons darted from the circle toward the six, striking poses with their wings stretched above their heads and their tails pointing to the ground. After falling for a distance, the posed dragons snapped their wings into a more normal position and rejoined the circle.

Timbrel watched in fascination as a hummingbird dragon took an answering pose and glided away. The chasing dragon gripped the other by the shoulders and completely supported its body. The joined dragons glided slowly downward, twining necks and tails.

The sixth and last hummingbird dragon chose its partner just as Krys cleared his throat next to her. "Are you packed?"

"I packed earlier. They are beautiful." The gliding descent of the last pair of dragons turned toward the rescue group. "I hope they get close enough to see clearly."

Krys looked toward the fast approaching pair. "I think they will. We should get the horses untied before they get here."

Krys and Timbrel dashed to the horses, frantically untying the animals. Krys had already saddled them, and Sarin gave Timbrel her makeshift bandages to save for reuse. Von struggled with his pack, sliding his arms through the makeshift straps with great difficulty.

The horses screamed, plunging on their tethers. Timbrel looked up between the trees. The dragon pair glided past, the female's belly nearly scraping the treetops, the base of her tail faintly striped with red. Timbrel drank in every detail as the pair hung in the air for long minutes. The female rubbed her head along the mail's chin. The membranous wings stretched over bone fingers. The separate forelegs. The male's front talons grasping the female's shoulders deeply enough to draw blood. The curl of the male's body aganst the female during their glide. The blood on the female's rear talons. The corresponding gashes on the male's rear legs. The twined tails.

Timbrel turned her head as they passed, wondering at their grace. "They dance the skies," she whispered again. "So beautiful."

###

Timbrel stretched and twirled as she walked the next morning, working the stiffness out of her muscles. When they stopped to rest the horses, she foraged for food and practiced her dance moves out of sight. She had not missed a day of practice since returning to her mother's people, though she kept it secret. Timbrel could only imagine the scandal if her mother knew that she learned the human dances.

Soliari was not known for her tolerance of humans and their ways. Timbrel could attest to that, her mother reminding her every day about the shameful circumstances of her conception.

Because Soliari was an Urramach, she gave Timbrel the best education possible. Because Soliari hated the human lines of her daughter's face, she provided it entirely through tutors. Because Soliari was Soliari, she employed only tutors who hated the sight of humans.

Timbrel learned early to focus on memorizing her lessons. Most of her tutors found relief in her academic excellence, or perhaps relief when quickly out of her presence.

Soliari provided such a slanted version of human behavior that Timbrel expected to be grabbed and mauled when she arrived at her father's village. She thought that humans spent most of their time waging war on each other, and breeding the rest of the time. She was relieved to be wrong.

### 

*Fafar village*
*19 years before*

The carriage jounced along the road. Twelve year old Lanieli Urramach wished that the elven driver would slow down so she could see something outside the window other than tree trunks rushing past. Her hair dripped with sweat, so tangled that she might never brush it out, not that the driver gave her a chance to retrieve a hairbrush from any of her trunks. Her sweat-stiffened brocade dress smelled after three days of constant wear, and the few humans she saw as the carriage barreled through the villages along the road did not show them wearing any such thing.

At last the carriage slowed and came to a halt. She heard loud thumps as the driver dropped her ten trunks to the ground. Voices--human voices--surrounded the carriage by the time the driver opened the door for her. She stepped down.

The humans gathered around her. The men wore tunics and trousers, and a few wore thick leather vests. Everyone carried knives, and a few carried swords as well.

"Who is she?" "What is she doing here?" "Is that an elf?" "She's just a girl." The human voices tumbled over one another.

Lanieli took a step forward, her face warming with embarrassment. "I look to find the soldier Wayen of Fafar."

"Soldier? You mean the... ah... merchant Wayen." The man turned to the crowd and shouted. "Someone drag Wayen out of the tavern. He has a high class visitor." Laughter rippled through the crowd.

The men stepped back and the women and children came forward. The women wore simple skirts with shirts. The children dressed similarly to the adults.

While she waited for the humans to find her father, Lanieli opened the first chest and rummaged through the clothing her mother packed. She chose two underskirts from the first chest, three shirts from the second chest, and a few items from the rest. The last chest, filled with fancy dresses that she had never seen before, she closed without removing anything.

"Driver, take thou the rest of this back."

"No. I do not take orders from a half- elf." He climbed back up in the front of the carriage and left in such a hurry that a dust cloud obscured the road.

When it cleared, two more people had joined the crowd. A shortish man--well, tall for a human--with brown hair and slightly better dressed than most gathered here stood next to a young woman with fawn-colored skin and dark hair. "I am Wayen, and this is Katrina. Who are you?"

"I am Lanieli, thy daughter."

"I have no daughter," he scoffed.

"Thirteen years ago, thou caught my mother spying outside of Shassilar. Thou took her unwilling in an alley. I *am* thy daughter."

The woman Katrina reached out a hand. "You are welcome among us, Lani... Lani... We'll find a nickname for you. I'm not certain how much room we have for your clothing."

Lanieli thrust the bundle of clothes in her arms forward. "This is all I have. Give away the rest."

Katrina patted her on the arm. "Let's get you inside and cleaned up."

### 

*Fafar Village*
*5 days later*

Black smoke billowed across the Inn's kitchen. Flames peeked from inside the kettle where it hung over the coals in the hearth.

"Lan... Lani... Elf Girl!" The cook stumbled over her name. "You've boiled the tubers dry! Get over here."

Lanieli ran to the cook's side, overly conscious of the dozen other children watching in the kitchen. She lowered her head and hunched her shoulders.

"Stand up straight, girl. I'm not going to beat you." The cook swung the kettle stand out from the flames with a carved wooden hook and tossed a damp towel over it. "Don't just stand there, get me some water."

The half elf ran across the kitchen and dragged the full water bucket back to the hearthside. She scooped a cup of water and poured it on the towel. The kettle sizzled and popped.

"Too fast, too fast. You'll crack the kettle." The cook sprinkled water through, guiding Lanieli, until the kettle no longer sizzled. "When it cools completely, you'll be scrubbing it clean." The cook gave the girl a menacing look, and Timbrel cringed.

39

Music and laughter rang out in the common room. Timbrel crept from the kitchen to see.

On the other side of the curtain, a few of the older children played instruments. The younger children whirled with their arms out near the wall, falling over and laughing. Strangest of all, Katrina stood like a statue in the middle of the room, back bent gracefully and arms held out before her.

A moment later the woman swayed upright and continued her dance. Hips rolling in circular patterns, arms swaying like tree branches and then undulating like snakes, Katrina floated across the floor with her feet barely visibly beneath translucent skirts.

Lanieli stood open-mouthed. Katrina was dancing? Publicly?

A few of the people who lived at the inn watched with open approval. Katrina threw her arms out and spun, somehow moving across the floor at the same time. As she reached the center again, she dropped to the floor in a final pose, then sprang up and swayed her way toward the stairs to a scattering of applause.

Humans approved? Lanieli blinked in disbelief. Certain elvish celebrations involved dancing with partners in a group, but each intricate step must be performed exactly to avoid shame. Individual dancing... Lanieli had never heard of such a thing.

*It is a human thing*, she decided. One that she would embrace.

The music continued, as did the children's play. She crept out and joined them, trying to copy Katrina's dance. Lanieli almost fell when she bent backwards to pose, and she tripped more than once while trying to roll her hips and walk. She halted in place, rolling her hips slowly, trying to remember the movements she had seen.

The clapping startled her. All of the children stood nearby, clapping out a rhythm. She tried to match it and stumbled again. The children laughed.

"Now you have to spin and spin, like this!" A small girl, perhaps five summers, turned in place with her arms out and fell dizzily to the floor.

Lanieli threw her arms to the sky and spun like a top. She lasted several turns longer than the younger child, but soon joined her on the floor. The half-elven girl tried to stand and fell twice more before giving up and resting on the floor. "How does she *do* it?" She joined the children as they giggled, her bell-like laugh soaring above theirs.

"You laugh like a timbrel." Katrina said.

Lanieli felt the heat across her cheeks. "I was attempting to dance as thee," she explained.

"As you," Katrina corrected. "And doing a fine job of it. Why didn't you tell me you've had lessons?"

"Lessons? In the dance?" Her jaw sagged for a moment in her confusion. Soliari warned her that the dancers were the worst of the humans, breeding constantly. Katrina had no children. Lanieli asked the night she arrived, just to learn where she stood in her father's hierarchy. The silence lengthened.

"You haven't had lessons?" Katrina stepped back and looked at Lanieli from head to toe.

The heat in her face grew worse. Words tumbled out. "I tried the best I could but it was my first time. The elves dance differently, and never alone. Their dances are different than thine. Show me what I lack and I will repair my errors." Timbrel bowed her head and hunched her shoulders again, expecting punishment.

Katrina shook her head and frowned. "You're telling me you've never had a lesson, this was your first attempt to dance like this, and you would like me to teach you. Is that right?"

Lanieli continued to look at the ground. "You, or any suitable tutor. I learn quickly, truly I do, so you won't have to look at me for long." She hunched her shoulders further as she heard the pleading note in her own voice.

"There is no reason not to look at you. In fact, I think some of the young men already look."

"Have I done something wrong so quickly?" She thought her fresh start had been going so well.

"You did nothing wrong. Men watch women when they like what they see. You are growing into a beautiful young woman,

Lani... Lani... We still need to find you a name."

"What is a *timbrel*?"

Katrina waved to the musicians. "Bring out a timbrel."

The drummer pulled a flat drum with bells around the edges from his bag. He tapped it in the middle, then shook it sharply to ring the bells. It did sound like her laugh.

"Can I be called Timbrel?"

"Of course. We'll start your lessons tomorrow morning, Timbrel, after breakfast clean-up."

Timbrel threw her hand across her mouth. "I have to go clean up the kettle!"

### 

*The Meadow of Dragons*
*Present time*

Krys watched Timbrel as she came out of a spin. He marveled at her balance.

"So this is what you have been doing. Are you any good at human dancing?"

"Enough to earn my own coin." Timbrel watched his face closely for signs of disapproval. The older elf kept a neutral expression.

"With the wonderful provisions they gave us, you may have to earn coin in the Human lands. Has your time in the human world made you comfortable with bargaining?"

Timbrel nodded, using the human gesture instead of the elven hand slash of assent. "Where did the Voice's note say we should begin searching?"

Krys lost control of his features enough to blink twice.

"Don't worry, I won't say anything."

"I'll explain our route after we reach Henin. The elves there are a different line, and I plan to ask for a warrior to help us."

Timbrel giggled like a child. "You don't think Von can make it through either, do you. He really *is* skilled with his

42

weapons, but you're right. We need someone who is seasoned by war who will act, not stand around and worry about his clothes." She chewed on her lip. "It could all be an act. He's too good a hunter to be as indecisive as he seems."

"You are perceptive, Lady Timbrel." One more family trait. "It is hard to remember that you are only thirty-one. You remind me of your mother before she became so bitter." With the exception of her more horizontal eyes and the human roundness that sculpted her high cheekbones into a heart-shaped face, Timbrel bore the distinct look of the Urramachi elves, just like her mother Soliari.

Looks aside, mother and daughter could not be more different. Timbrel had returned from her time among the humans with an open honesty, and an odd code of honor that often sparked bizarre behavior. Instead of hiding her human blood, as Soliari continually insisted, Timbrel flaunted it. Krys approved, if only because it disturbed Soliari.

"Once, just after they acknowledged me a Master Historian, I thought she might accept a seven-year marriage to me. Foolish thoughts for a commoner, I know." Krys waved his hand dismissively. "Everything about the ancients interested her, especially their politics. She even convinced me to search hundreds of ruins for old records about the elves."

Armed with a copy of Sarin's oldest map, Krys set out to explore the ruins of an elven city with Soliari's blessing. What he discovered in the ancient records changed his life.

Krys left his Ravali home for the first time with his illusions: magic, invented by the Hinjin-spawned humans, caused madness and death; the Mage-Wars of the past wiped out nearly all of the wizards, as well as a significant portion of the planet's population; and the Genjin-created elves had been hit hard, though the humans were knocked back into barbarism by the conflict. The elves retreated to their hidden mountain valleys to recover in peace.

During his two year intensive search, Krys became aware of an unhealthy faint green glow that overlaid the city. When he

43

rubbed his eyes, he could see it clearly before they focused again. He avoided the brighter areas, and finally found the record he searched for.

The ancient scroll, paper brown and crumbling around the edges, claimed to be a copy of an even more ancient human copy of a Genjin document. Elvish comments dotted the margins in several different handwritings. Krys translated the few unfaded lines:

#

"We have discovered the gen. link to ambition. This dna [denied?] link will mask the birthmark sites, as will certain other factors... possible to select the best leaders... those who do not want the power or responsibility... placed in power and advised by a Council of ambitious [energetic?]... The birthmark line will obviously be excluded from any such Council... If a birthmark line should vanish, a new leader should be chosen from a competing birthmark line until such time as the original birthmark resurfaces, usually in a generation or two, at which time the foreign birthmark ruler should return to her former home."

#

Soliari's very ambition prevented the family birthmark from appearing, like a Genjin curse. Krys understood now why Soliari financed this journey, though it would do her no good. He copied the last two readable sentences and returned the document to its stack. As he turned, his sleeve brushed another stack of documents, scattering them on the floor. The faded magenta mark on the corner of one fragment caught his attention.

The triangular fragment showed the original Genjin script, each small, neat letter precisely the same as those before. "We have continued to manipulate the gen. structure to provide resistance to nuclear expos... three best efforts give limited storage capacity within the body to handle excess gamma energies... Periodic discharge has considerable side effects such as... e manner of incremental discharge must be w... seems like magic to the uninitiated. A good qu..."

Krys paged through the stack of crumbling fragments,

44

finding several more that spoke of gamma and magic traits. He started to shake. The Genjin had somehow created the ability to use magic as a solution to some terrible problem. The Genjin had created magic. Krys felt the conflict spinning in his mind. The elves hated magic. The Genjin created elves. The Genjin created magic. Centuries of indoctrination against magic crumbled. The opposing ideas suddenly melted together into a question. Could elves use magic?

"What did you find? Krys?"

Krys shook his head. "Not what she hoped for. She never forgave me."

"I thought she hated you for learning magic." Timbrel chewed her lip again.

"It's all part of the same thing." He shouldered his pack. "Time to go."

### 

*South of Ravali*

Nayev approached the southern entrance to Ravali. The road, wider now than during his Journey, almost touched the bases of the two ancient trees that marked the Barrier. It seemed dustier than before, as if hardly used. He dusted his robes off, and passed into the Elven lands. Even with new roads lacing the meadows and forest, he could still find Allison's tree. The massive redwood was taller than before and nearly twice as wide. He wondered how the internal stairwell that wound around the inside of the trunk adjusted to the extra size or if it remained the same as when the tree was younger.

As he paused at the redwood, the door opened and a young elf barely out of her childhood walked towards him. She had the same golden hair and blue eyes as Allison.

She greeted him with a shy smile. Nayev returned the greeting, very conscious that his ears formed no points.

"Do you live here?" Nayev asked in elvish..

"Yes, with my mother and grandmother."

"Is your grandmother's name Allison?" He wondered if Allison still lived there, and if she would remember him. Then again, it had been a thousand years.

"No, silly man. *I* am Allison. I was named for my grandmother's grandmother."

"And a very nice name it is. It's been nice speaking with you, young Allison."

He walked on past the tree, sniffing the air. He did not detect the odor of a dragon. If his Allison had birthed his children, they no longer lived here. The little girl smelled of pure elf.

After several hours of walking, Nayev approached the Council Tree. His nose twitched. There, that was the scent of a dragon. The open area in front of the Council Tree was deserted. Except for some moldy grain mixed into the sand, some discarded clothes, and a few hoof and footprints in the sand, no sign showed that anyone had been here in the past few days. The scent hovered near the moldy grain. Nayev followed it as far as he could, but it was mixed with the scents of several others as well as horses. Nayev knew he could track the group better if he changed shape, but he did not dare do so in the center of an elven city. Particularly this one. The high-pitched sounds from the barrier... Besides, many of the Ravali elves disliked magic in all its forms. Once it had even served as the center of Yarite activity, though that magic-hating sect had long ago been wiped out.

Nayev considered his choices. He could try to track down Allison and see if she or any of her descendents lived. He could follow the road that he had lost the scent on and shift forms outside of the territory to pick up the trail again. Thirdly, he could head for Shassilar and reestablish himself there. He periodically spent many months in Shassilar, where he was known as a wizard. Since many of the roads in the eastern kingdoms passed through Shassilar, he felt confident that the group would come to him.

Before he left Ravali, however, he would check to see if Allison still lived.

When he found the newest building that housed the records,

he was surprised and saddened by what he learned. Allison's twin sons were well-known as warriors. Twins or perhaps triplets, the accounts varied. As they approached their naming day--twenty-one among the elves--the twins rode outside of the Ravali protections along with several friends. They had the misfortune to encounter three dragons lying in wait. The twins did not survive the ensuing battle.Two of their friends, severely wounded, returned and told of their bravery in trying to keep the dragons away from the rest of the group. A party of warriors sent out to retrieve the bodies returned to find that the two survivors from the initial group had died in their absence.

I had sons, thought Nayev. He double checked the records to see if either of the twins had children, with no success. Who is the half blood that I am smelling? Nayev asked himself. And who does this person belong to, if not me?

### 

When they stopped to make camp that evening, Timbrel helped Krys with his pack. The tall elf had been lost in his thoughts ever since learning that she could dance. At every branch in the path, Krys stopped in a daze until Sarin roused him with a touch. Timbrel concentrated on grinding the ingredients for the horse medicines, then collected wood and arranged it for a small fire.

As she reached for her flint and steel, Krys bent over the wood and touched it with his finger. He whispered a *word* that slid right past her understanding. She shuddered at its strangeness, then bent double with wrenching stomach cramps as severe as the night before. The cramps stopped as a fire sprang to life.

"I'm getting better at this," Krys whispered. Timbrel looked around the camp. Sarin dozed nearby. Von glared from the far side of the camp. Nothing out of the ordinary except a burning fire that no one started.

"What did you do?" she asked, shifting into the human tongue to keep her words from Von.

Krys smiled. "Just performing a public service."

Timbrel backed away in horror. "You used *magic*. You're tainted." She backed away another step. "Soliari was right about you."

Krys glanced down. "I'm sorry. I'll put it out and let you build another if you want. I just thought to save you some time like yesterday."

*Yesterday?* Timbrel eyed the fire from a safe distance. It seemed normal enough. The flames flickered in the right colors. The wood blackened predictably. The horses grazed near a trickle of water, unhurt by yesterday's medicine, medicine prepared when she hadn't known about the fire. She decided to chance it.

Keeping Krys in sight, half-expecting him to turn into living flames, she prepared the horse medicines and left to treat them. On her way back, she tripped on a root and sprawled.

Her hand landed in mud. A trickle of water bubbled to the surface: a small spring. Cattail shoots rose through the mud, slender leaves striped yellow and pale green. Digging carefully with a branch, she uncovered a cluster of starchy tubers. Closer to the center of camp, she found a single small wild garlic bulb growing just off the path, and a few early lionflower leaves.

Refusing to trust the magical fire any farther than she had to, Timbrel filled her own iron cooking pot with water and started a second small fire. She added a few pinches of herbs from her bag, and before long the smell of boiling vegetable stew floated across the camp. Sarin woke at the smell, and even Von came across to peer into the pot.

"There's no meat in it," he complained.

"I would rather eat without meat than not eat at all." Sarin patted her shouder.

Krys was more practical. "You're the hunter of the group. Go catch something."

Von stomped off across the camp, frowning. He returned when Timbrel started serving, taking his filled bowl back across the campsite to eat.

Krys and Sarin praised her ingenuity, if not the bland taste of the meal. A flush of embarrassment warmed Timbrel's cheeks.

As she scrubbed out her pot with gravel, she resolved to watch for more cattails the next day.

### 

Krys watched as Timbrel spread her bedroll and settled down to sleep. Her reaction to his firestarting had surprised him. He felt a small knot of cramping when he cast a spell, but not as severely as she obviously did. Sarin seemed unaffected, and Von hadn't complained. Was Timbrel a potential wizard herself?

Krys looked at her with unfocused eyes, looking for a source of magic. The girl herself gave off no glow, but several glowing patches of ground appeared to be moving in her direction. Krys gave a wordless cry and plucked Timbrel bodily from the ground.

She struggled in his grasp. "What's wrong, Krys? I just got comfortable."

Krys couldn't explain. "Choose a different spot. I have a bad feeling about this one."

Timbrel moved about fifteen feet away. "Is this better?" She snuggled down on the hard, lumpy ground. The green glows closed in.

He scooped her up immediately. The hard ground now had smoothly contoured hollows that fit her. Krys put her down again and watched as the green patch appeared again, readjusting the ground beneath the girl.

"What is it *this* time?" she asked.

"Just checking again to make certain you are safe."

"I'm safe. Now let me sleep." Timbrel rolled over, and the contours of the ground adjusted yet again. Her soft breathing soon matched the sound of the breeze in the trees.

The silver hair on the back of Krys' neck rose. The forested slopes of this valley had been windless all day. Krys looked at the trees across camp, their leaves still. Overhead, the leaves rustled faintly. Unfocusing his eyes, he detected two air beings chasing each other through the branches above Timbrel's head. He looked

49

again at the girl sleeping peacefully. Just who–or what–was this daughter of Soliari?

###

*Near Ravali lands*

Nayev leaned against an old stone wall while Novich stalked back and forth in front of him, tail lashing and claws gouging the rock.

Novich whirled and stuck his snout in Nayev's face. "You didn't rise to mate. Do you know how angry the Elders are?" Rearing up, Novich flapped his wings and blew dust in his brother's face. "Only Belina and Reyalla mated successfully. Anyana's tail is still stripey, though the other three have passed their fertility for the season. You should have mated."

"Why me? Anyana is not worth mating. She's so lazy and arrogant that no one wants her."

"She's fertile. So are you. Everyone knows you're a shifter, and everyone remembers the population explosion the last time a shifter lived among us."

"Jocen, Father of Dragons, was no shifter. As I recall, he killed most of the shifter's offspring." He leaned over, grabbed a handful of gravel, and pitched it at his brother. "If you feel so strongly about it, *you* mate with her. You're as much a shifter as I am." *Even if the Elders don't know it*, he added in mindspeech.

"I haven't taken human form since... since our Journeys. I don't live among them like you do.*" I haven't mated with them either. Are you sure your surviving hatchling among the elves never had offspring of his own?*

"What surviving hatchling? I found no evidence." Nayev kicked a few dry leaves over the edge.

"There are so many rumors, and one of the mated pairs claimed they smelled dragon when they passed over a group of elves north of the elven city."

"Why didn't they do anything about it?"

"They were busy. In any case, the Elders are going to force

you to mate with Anyana."

"I'll pick my own mate when the time comes."

"You're over a thousand years old, Nayev. When will you get around to it? Not your perversions, but a real mating?"

"Don't worry, brother. I was barely out of adolescence when I left that elf. I doubt she could even lay an egg. It would take a lot more than a pretty face to bring on a mating urge now. Unless you think a human can manage a mating flight?" Nayev pushed his brother's snout aside. "I'll be back next year, after I find any wayward offspring. Give the Elders my greetings."

###

# Chapter Three

*On the road north of Ravali*

Von glared across the clearing at the other travelers, particularly the girl. His interrupted training was *her* fault. The Council thought they had been together. As if he would taint himself with a half-blood.

Master Celiar would have been teaching him the tricks to root out the last of the wizards and kill them. He already mastered the art of walking silently. *I hide my skills well*, Von thought. *Soon I will detect wizards before they can throw a spell, like Arlis.*

The older apprentice, not as skilled with his weapons as Von, had chosen to learn the magic-detecting skills first. Von chose the opposite path, honing his weapon skills and mastering a weapon from each of the seven types. He gained his seventh mastery just a few days before the exile.

*And I felt so honored when the Council recognized my skills and asked me to escort Timbrel to the Summoning.*

Such a betrayal! He should never have been among the Summoned. Why didn't Master Celiar prevent this? The Master had powerful friends with influence on the Council. Or was Celiar angry with him for choosing the path of weapons first? Did the Master even know that Von had been included? Or did the Voice of the Council include Von on the spur of the moment because of his supposed transgression with that half-blood whore? What a waste of his precious time, saving an elf who actually wanted the alliance. Maybe he could arrange an accident on the way back. He'd done so before, paired with Arlis.

Von's anger spilled over and he glared at the girl again. Instead of resting while the horses grazed, she spun and twirled in a human dance. The intermittent breeze swirled leaves in a mini-whirlwind. She danced with the swirl of leaves like a living partner, matching her spins to the speed of the swirls. Revolting human behavior. He felt nauseous just thinking about it.

The old historian Sarin sat silently near the restless horses. Rumor said Sarin encouraged Krys to travel. Darker rumors said that Krys gathered ancient magical knowledge from the ruins he visited, and that he gave it to Sarin. So far, Sarin cast no spells. The old Ravali even ignored the books in his pack since they passed the Border stones. Von glanced through them during his watch. The books contained maps. Nothing of interest.

Krys gave the signal, and Von grabbed his pack. He watched Timbrel carefully, in part because he loosened the knot that held the pots to the ring on her pack. The knot unravelled and the pots fell to the ground with a satisfying *clank* as they hit some rocks.

The girl bent to retrieve the pots. The smallest was badly dented, nearly unusable. She waved the pot at Krys. "How soon will we pass a settlement? I need to find a smith to fix this."

"Let me see." Krys caught the tossed pot and smoothed his hand across the crushed area, whispering.

Von's guts cramped with fear. As Krys stroked the pot, the dent slowly rounded out.

"Will this work better?" The pot Krys tossed back barely showed a dent.

The young warrior ground his teeth. After he wasted almost a full week, Sarin was not the wizard; Krys was. Like blood welling from a scratch, understanding seeped across Von's mind. Celiar suspected Krys. No wonder Von had been included. It was a test.

Still averting his eyes from the others, Von began his usual litany of complaints about the too short break. The more useless he appeared, the less the others would expect him to do anything. But how long could he keep up his act while waiting for the opportunity to kill Krys?

###

*The Cat's Claw Tavern, Shassilar*

Nayev landed in a rocky meadow near the northern edge of Shassilar. He stretched and folded his wings, then leaned against a tumble of small boulders with his forepaws. He let his power flow through him, reveling in the feel. A moment later he pushed away from a much larger rock slab and dusted off his hands.

Double-checking his now-human appearance, Nayev adjusted his robe and tied his left boot. A few miles walk brought him into the edge of town. Horses in a fenced pasture snorted and edged toward the far side as he walked past.

The clapboard sign swung in the breeze, creaking against its rusted chains. The faded picture of a cat surrounded by claw marks loomed over even more faded words.

"The Cat's Claw Tavern," Nayev read, pleased with himself. "This sounds like a good place to start."

The front door hung open, propped with a rusty short sword. He strode in as though he owned the place.

His eyes adjusted almost instantly to the dim light inside, though he stopped a few feet inside and blinked for several minutes. He scanned the room before the occupants thought he could see. A thin man with a curled beard moved something from the table in the corner and hid it under the edge of his cloak. Two others at the same table dropped small items –rings, perhaps?— into their belt pouches. A few others around the room reached for weapons, all relaxing after a moment except for those furtively moving at the table. Others glanced up but otherwise ignored him.

Making a show of looking around after his pause, Nayev headed directly for the man with the curling beard and sat next to him. "Good morning, gentleman," he called cheerily. "You don't mind if I share the table, do you? Of course not. What's good for breakfast?"

"You're sitting in my friend's seat." Curling Beard glowered.

"How nice. We're friends already. Thank you, friend." Nayev smiled back. He could smell the man's discomfort. *Just a*

54

*little more pushing should do it.*

"You should move."

"Oh, is your other friend coming? Certainly." Nayev scooted along the bench closer to Curling Beard, knocking the cloak off of a lumpy sack in the process. "What do we have here?"

Curling Beard snatched away the sack and rose to his feet. "Enough! Olon, Jenk, take him outside." Two of his companions jumped up and grabbed Nayev by the shoulders.

Nayev continued to smile as they dragged him out the door and halfway around the building. He let a trickle of power run through his feet and into the ground.

The hardpacked dirt dissolved into fine dust a foot deep beneath Olon and Jenk. They let go of Nayev and flailed their arms for balance. Nayev stepped away and sent a second trickle, firming the dirt around their lower legs and feet.

"Nice talking with you, gentlemen. Beware of wizards." Nayev gave them a jaunty salute and returned inside for breakfast.

###

*Kerran Castle, Port Kerran*

Ragnar, Prince of Kerran, brooded in his office. He walked back and forth, running his fingers along the many books shelved along one wall. The elven ambassador--Ravali, he corrected himself--had arrived in Port Kerran almost two weeks before. He had not even met her when she went to the Shrine of Ashrah and disappeared before the treaty could be signed. Broken furniture and bloodstains on the floor were all that remained of the Ambassador, her retinue of guards, and the women that cared for the Shrine. Had another elvish race decided against the formal alliance? Or could humans be responsible?

Prejudice between the races still ran deep after the last war. Questions tumbled across his mind. Without the signatures on the formal agreement, would the elves reject the alliance entirely? Did the original truce, first signed by Ragnar's father, still hold? If not, when would the elves move in to attack?

A mouse-like scratching came from the center bookcase. After hearing a second scratch, Ragnar walked to the side bookcase and removed a thick volume of poetry. He slid his hand into the empty space and flipped the lower of two levers. With a click, the lower section of the central bookcase swung out like a door.

The prince cautiously peeked around the edge of the shelf. His spymaster knelt within the tunnel.

"Any word on the elf?"

"Nothing yet, my Prince. We found a survivor of the attack. She's being escorted in."

"I'll wait for her." Ragnar pushed the bookcase back into place and flipped the lever again, locking the hidden door. Slinging a formal half-cloak across his shoulders and then picking up his seal of office, he headed for his public chamber. His guards fell into place around him as he walked down the hallway, and his assistant Magda met him near that door.

"You have a supplicant today, Highness." Magda's thin, reedy voice set his nerves on edge, but there was no better scribe at keeping accounts.

"I only hear supplicants at the end of the month." Ragnar plumped up the thinning cushion on his chair.

"This supplicant is a priestess from Ashrah."

*The witness. Nicely timed.* "Very well, send her in."

The priestess entered, clutching Magda's hand in a death grip. Her wide eyes darted around the room, as if to search out every hiding place. With a cry, the girl pulled her hand from Magda's and darted under a chair.

Ragnar, already standing to greet the priestess, walked halfway across the room and bent over. "How old are you, child?"

Her wide eyes gazed at the Prince from beneath the chair. "Seven years in this world, Sire." Her body might have been seven, but her eyes looked old enough to have seen the beginning of the world.

Ragnar tried not to shudder. "You wished to ask a boon?"

56

No wonder this child was sent to serve the gods.

"I want you to protect me. The bad men know I'm here. They killed all the men, and all the sisters, and took the beautiful lady."

Ragnar's blood chilled. "Tell me more."

The child's voice became faint, as though she spoke from a dream world. "I was playing in the Shrine of Ashrah. The men came in with the lady, and she went to talk to the big sisters. The lady knelt to pray, even though she had long ears like a cat. The men knelt behind the lady and turned into porcupine-birds. Feathers flew everywhere, feathers with points attached. They turned red and the red ran on the floor like water. The sisters screamed and tried to take the lady away, but the bad men came in and the sisters all fell down with red mouths." The girl gestured vaguely toward her neck, her eyes unfocused. "The sisters told me I would get in trouble for playing in the shrine. I didn't mean to. Now I'm hungry because the bad men took all the men and all the sisters away and there's no one to make supper."

"Do you remember what the bad men looked like? Did they have cat ears?" Ragnar fought to keep the horror out of his voice.

"No, the lady's men had cat ears. The bad men had arrows."

"What color did they wear?"

"Color? What is color? Everything was red, even their shells. Except the fat man, he was too big for a shell so he just told everyone what to do. The lady didn't like him. She screamed when he took her away. Like this." The girl let out an ear-piercing scream a full minute long.

When she stopped, her eyes focused on Ragnar. "I'm hungry. Is it time for supper, Sire?"

### 

Von watched Krys carefully over the next few days. The wizard would be a formidable opponent even without his magic. Extremely tall, the silver-haired elf wore a serviceable broadsword in a worn sheath at his side, which he practiced with in the evenings. With Krys' long reach, Von would have to close quickly and deal with the tall elf's powerful arms. Arrows might be warded off by magic.

Perhaps at night, during Sarin's watch. *No*, he thought. *Sarin could still be a wizard too.* Tonight, then.

The afternoon passed far slower than most. When the sun neared the horizon, three rabbits streaked out of the brush practically beneath their feet. His mind focused on planning, Von pulled his bow from its sheath and strung it in one smooth motion. He shot two of the rabbits before the third vanished from sight.

*What did I just do?* Mentally kicking himself for the slip, he threw the bloody carcasses at the girl's head. She snatched them out of the air with a twirl, ruining half of his pleasure. The rest evaporated when she tied them to her pack without a single sign of disgust.

When Krys called a halt a few minutes later, Von set his bedroll across the camp from the others. This time, he did not miss Krys' fire spell, nor the girl cooking his rabbits – *his* rabbits – over that same fire. His resolve hardened.

"Are you going to eat? The rabbits are ready." The girl waved him over.

Von wanted to say no, but that would break his act again. He stomped over and grabbed half a rabbit, then returned to his bedroll where he forced himself to eat a few bites.

"You overcooked it, half-blood. Who taught you how to cook? Someone should execute them."

Timbrel paled and burst into tears, then ran into the brush.

*Really? Of everything I've said to her over the years, she breaks because I complain about her cooking?* He stomped into the brush on his side of camp, buried the uneaten portion of rabbit, and forced himself to throw up the few bites he'd taken. Better to go without than to eat something cooked by magic.

Von returned to his bedroll and tried to sleep. The anticipation of his planned kill kept him uncomfortably awake. He had agreed to his usual third watch, determined to attack Krys as soon as Sarin fell asleep. He would be long gone before the girl woke on her own, if she even came back. Von spent the first two watches going over his plans in his mind, adjusting for every possible contingency. He would set the horses free when he left, slowing the others. Perhaps he would kill Sarin after he eliminated Krys, just to be certain. And the girl...

Sarin shook him from his reverie of tortures. "Time for your watch."

Von stretched and paced the perimeter of their camp, waiting for Sarin to settle down and sleep. By his third circuit, the old elf's breathing settled into a slow, shallow rhythm. Krys' breathing was deeper, but just as slow. Watching both for signs of movement, Von drew a slender blade with a stained edge. He circled wide and crept silently toward Krys from the darkness. He reached out with the blade.

"Krys, look out!" The girl's voice shattered the silence.

Krys' eyes snapped open as Von lunged. In a blur of speed, Krys reached up and closed his fingers around the young warrior's wrist.

Von struggled to move the blade. The stained edge glinted in the firelight. One scratch and Krys would die. Von shifted his weight, bringing the blade an inch closer to Krys' throat.

"Die, wizard." Von's words hissed. "Purify the elven race with your death." Von twisted to the side. "Yara be avenged!" he shouted, threw his weight forward...

...and stopped, suspended in mid-air as Krys caught him with the other hand. He struggled to turn the blade. "You. Must. Die."

Krys threw him into a tree. The slender dagger spun off into the brush beyond.

Von scrambled to his feet, pain tearing through his shoulder. He pulled another dagger and launched himself at Krys.

The tall elf captured both of Von's wrists this time. "Stop this madness."

"You are the mad one, wizard. Yara help me purify the elves from your taint."

Krys shook his head, then frowned and whispered a *word*

59

that echoed through the darkness.

A drop of liquid fell on Von's back, then another. He wondered how he felt them through his clothing just before they started to burn. The pain in his shoulder paled in comparison to the fire spreading across his back.

Still unable to move in Krys' grip, Von could just see the girl in his peripheral vision, vomiting in the dirt near the fire.

*How badly am I injured?* He wondered. *It can't be too bad. It doesn't hurt any more.* He shivered, the edges of his vision darkening.

The last thing Von heard was Krys' voice dripping with disgust. "I didn't think there were any of you left. You caused the Mage Wars a millennium ago. Your fanaticism nearly destroyed the world."

Von tried to protest the importance of killing wizards. He could not seem to form the words. *Master Celiar will be disappointed that I failed his test...*

### 

Timbrel stood in the rising sun, watching as Sarin prodded Von's body with a stick to roll it over. She stared at the scorched oval of ground beneath, dotted with black and withered moss. The moss nearby stood as green as ever, save for the patches damaged during the scuffle between the two elves. She touched a finger to the scorched moss.

"Lady Timbrel, no!" Krys ran from where he saddled the horses.

Her finger started to burn. Not waiting for Krys, she ran for the stream as the affected skin blackened and crumbled away. The water soothed her finger, cooler water washing the last of the pain away. Timbrel looked closely at her finger. Blood seeped from the wound.

Krys laid his hand on her arm. "It is an acid. It must be neutralized before the wound is treated."

She thought for a moment, then searched the bank of the

stream for Purple Trill and gathered an armload. She crushed a few of the leaves from the first plant and let the juice run across the wound. The juice fizzed and bubbles rose like the froth on ale. The second application of the juice washed away the bubbles. A moment later, Timbrel had bandaged her finger and picked up the rest of the Trill. She mashed the plants between two rocks, dropping their mangled stems on the blackened oval.

The ground fizzed, and froth erupted until it covered the oval almost two inches deep. She continued adding plants until the frothing subsided. She glared at Krys. "You would have left it like that," she accused. The first rain would have killed all of these trees." Timbrel swept her arm out to include a nearby stand of saplings growing in the scar left behind by a recently fallen tree. She stormed over to her horse and checked the saddle.

Horrified by Krys' use of deadly magic, she grew angrier as they packed. No wonder magic was outlawed. It *did* seem to damage the mind of the user.

"How could you be so careless?" She scolded the tall elf.

Sarin looked up in surprise. Krys blushed.

"Staying alive seemed a priority at the time. I did not think about the leftover acid. It would have vanished by sunset." Krys actually looked contrite.

Timbrel's anger wavered. Curiosity filled the void. "Why did Von attack you? I haven't seen you do anything evil with your magic, at least until now."

"I think I know." Sarin pointed at Von's hip. A fingertip-sized mark that looked like the human letter 'Y' had been burned into the flesh. "He has the Yarite mark."

"He yelled something about Yara when you fought. What is that?" Timbrel cocked her head to the side.

Krys sighed. "Before the Mage Wars, the wizards wielded immense power, running governments through puppet rulers. Yara stopped some of the worst--some that had gone mad--and about a century later a group called itself the Yarites. They believed that all wizards were evil and must be slain."

Timbrel backed up a step, uncomfortably aware that the

entire philosophy of the Ravali elves held similar beliefs. They exiled wizards, though. They did not kill them.

"I know what you're thinking," Krys said quietly. "Our people supported the Yarites at first. At least until they showed their true colors. Yarite spies and infiltrators worked their way close to the ruling wizards, then slew many of them on a particular day. The more paranoid wizards who survived blamed the near extinction on the other wizards and went to war."

Sarin stepped up. "When we found out, we tried to get them to leave. They promptly tried to execute the Council. Some of our people still supported them, and the struggle got bloody. The Yarites tried to exterminate all those not under their sway. The Council declared them illegal and subversive."

"Did you study the war?" Timbrel asked.

"My brothers fought in it. I was too sickly." Sarin looked up and trained his eyes on the horizon. "We need to leave now. We need to reach the border stones of the Henin lands before the sun sets."

"What about Von's body?"

"I'll take care of it." Krys raised his arms.

Timbrel's stomach clenched as the ground seemed to soften and Von's body sank beneath the surface. Krys gestured again and the ground firmed.

Timbrel picked up her pack and started a faster pace, worried about Krys and wondering if Sarin had lost his mind. Ravali only lived five centuries, six if they were lucky.

### 

*The Henin Lands*

As they crested the hill and wound their way between the rune-carved Henin border stones, Timbrel felt nervous. This would be her first time among foreign elves, and her stomach felt like she had eaten a handful of live bees. She looked back over her shoulder as the sun slipped below the horizon.

A flicker sprang up on the border stone nearest the road, then spread along the top of the stones as far as the eye could see.

"Krys, look at that." The girl pointed at the glowing hilltop. Krys frowned.

Sarin gave a strangled cry and collapsed. Timbrel ran to his side. The old elf already stirred.

"Stop throwing stuff at the barrier, Krys. And stop with the spells. Your magic is making me sick again,"

"It's not *my* magic. I think we should move carefully down this trail before we make camp."

### 

*Inside the Henin Border*

Timbrel woke to the nudge of a boot against her foot. She opened her eyes a tiny bit and peered through her lashes. Sarin's watch, by the length of the moonlit shadows. She resisted the urge to move. The old Ravali wore sandals.

"This one sleeps hard." A male voice speaking Ravali with a slight lilt. Timbrel's lips twitched into a ghost of a smile. Her captor had an accent. The smile vanished as cold metal pressed against her throat. "Stop pretending and get up."

"Move the blade first." When the metal retreated, Timbrel opened her eyes. A dozen elves wearing identical brown tunics with green cuffs stood near their fire. Sarin hung between two of them. Krys stood with his hands behind his back, one sword pointed at his throat and another at his belly. A third elf held Krys' sword. Timbrel felt her sheathed knives pressing against her thighs, but made no move toward the blades. She sat up, two other elves assisting her to her feet. They kept a grip on her shoulders and arms.

"What do you want with us?" Krys glowered at his closest captor.

The elf who woke Timbrel answered. "Why are you in our

valley? We seldom find unknown visitors at night." As tall as Krys, he towered over the others in his unit. His pointed ears rose as tall as a Ravali, but through dark brown hair. He motioned with a hand and Timbrel was forced closer to Krys and Sarin.

"We arrived near sundown," Timbrel blurted out. "We camped here to wait until morning."

Timbrel's outburst provoked murmuring from their captors. Krys glared at her through narrowed eyes, but she ignored him.

"You passed over the glowing hills in the dark?"

"Of course not. Krys led us over them as the sun set, just before they lit up. Should we have camped on the other side of the hill? There were animal tracks everywhere."

"Krys." The leader said it slowly, as if rolling it around in his mouth and tasting it. "That would be you, I presume?"

Still glaring at Timbrel, Krys nodded.

Their captor addressed the old Ravali next. "And you would be?"

"Sarin." His voice came out a harsh whisper.

The leader looked at the girl.

"I'm Timbrel," she said proudly.

"An uncommon name, Timbrel." The leader's gaze dropped from her face.

Krys spoke up. "*Lady* Timbrel."

Timbrel frowned at Krys. Why did he have to bring *that* up?

Her questioner's eyebrows rose and he switched into the complex Court dialect. "Lady Timbrel you are?"

Timbrel suppressed a smile at his imprecise grammar. "Jherik of the Ninth House I am." He bowed deeply to Timbrel. "Your bond may I have?"

"You may," she replied slowly in the same dialect. "I would extend my bond to these men as well, Jherik of the Ninth House."

"I accept your bond for all." Jherik bowed, then switched back to Ravali. "They will remain peaceful. You can release them.

Krys rubbed his wrists, slightly raw from the rope that restrained them. "Can we sleep in peace now?"

Jherik smiled. "We will all stay until morning. The town is much prettier in the rising sun."

### 

The winding trail quickly became a well-traveled road. Although Jherik's guards completely surrounded them, Timbrel felt safe.

Jherik walked with them, pointing out places of interest like a tour guide.

Timbrel took in the sights with childlike glee. During her first and only other trip outside of Ravali, she had never seen another elven city. She laughed easily, drawing Jherik's attention to details in the rocky landscape. "Look at the way the rooftops curl. They look almost like the mountains and high valleys." She looped her fingers through the air in exaggerated mimicry of the first scattered houses. The roofs *did* curl upward, at least the corner extensions did. They reminded her of an ancient skeleton with massive tusks curled competely around until they nearly touched the animal's face,

The closer they approached to the city center, the more disoriented Timbrel became. Ghostlike visions overlaid the horses, visions that pulsed and wavered as the air tinged with blood. She resisted the growing urge to look over her shoulder, afraid of what she might see. She stumbled suddenly, grabbing at her horse for support. Jherik looked into her eyes as he helped her regain her balance. Her vision flickered to strange rhythms. Timbrel's sense of dread grew.

Jherik drew back from her as if slapped. "You have *human* blood?"

Timbrel nodded, then waved assent. Jherik touched her shoulder. She heard someone muttering. Her stomach clenched and released. Her vision cleared and the nagging sense of dread left her.

Krys narrowed his eyes. "Lady Timbrel, are you well?"

Timbrel brushed dust from her skirt and cloak. "Of course I am. If you'd stop your little tricks, I'd be even better." She wrinkled her nose at Krys.

The city center contained the largest stone building Timbrel had ever seen. Five stories high, the stones changed color twice in its height. Jherik entered first, then motioned for the group to join him.

An official in a nubbly tunic almost buried beneath brightly colored sashes and badges of office waited for them. He quickly masked his sneer of distaste. "Lady Timbrel, is it? You and your retainers must attend tonight's festivities. Jherik, you will escort our guests tonight after they clean up. Make certain they are presented properly. Tomorrow they can speak to the Council."

"Sir?" Jherik hesitated. "I was to escort my betrothed tonight."

"Your duties come before your love life, Guardsman. Will the Ninth House be run by a woman's whims? Bring our guests to Mistress Marya for rooms and appropriate attire."

### 

*Ravali*

Soliari rode up to the Council Tree, tossing the reins of her horse to a startled guard as she swept past him. She quelled the second guard's challenge with a look--his family owed its precarious position to her good graces--and pushed open the doors of the Council Chamber.

Marahir, the Voice of the Council, looked up. "We are meeting right now, Soliari. You cannot stay."

A murmur of assent rose from the other councilors, many of whom had the dark-rimmed eyes and drawn faces of those not sleeping well. With the mass funeral for the Urramachi heirs and the much larger funeral for the Ravali Matriarch so close together, the city had been rocked to the core. Soliari wondered which drug Celiar used to poison the nasty old woman.

"I bring news that may affect your decisions." The murmuring ceased. Most of the council looked up at her, though

66

two glanced guiltily around. Soliari decided to check further into their affairs. Perhaps she would arrange for their replacement. The silence lengthened.

"Let her speak." Other councilors echoed the first to speak. Marahir rapped his knuckles on the tabletop for silence.

"Give us your news, Soliari." Marahir drooped with exhaustion.

"My riders have just returned from Port Kerran, after a fruitless journey to bring news to the rescue party. Instead, they found and questioned a witness to Lostaria's disappearance. The heir has been kidnapped."

The council members all tried to speak at once. Marahir pounded on the table until they quieted. "What was learned? When can we question this witness for ourselves?"

Soliari looked down at the floor and slumped her shoulders slightly. When she spoke, a note of apology tinged her words. "The witness died while being questioned. My riders learned that the kidnappers plan to ask for ransom but they are uncertain of the heir's worth. We should expect to hear from them in the next several                                                                                  months.

The murmurs of the Council rose and fell like wind sighing through the trees. "If she lives, there is no need to call for an outside birthmark to rule for a generation."

"It might be best to keep her kidnapping quiet. If word leaks out that Lostaria is the heir, the ransom demand is likely to increase."

Soliari kept a concerned expression on her face, masking her inner glee. The last comment came from one of the few councilors she did not yet have influence over.

The Voice stood and the room quieted. "If we need not choose a generational Matriarch, then we should choose a Regent to stand until the heir's return." Marahir looked at Soliari. "If you will excuse us, it is best that you leave now."

Soliari withdrew from the chamber with a curtsey and then walked slowly through the antechamber. Before she left the tree, she overheard her own name mentioned twice.

She was still wrapping the reins around her hand when a messenger from the Council ran up and asked her to return. She feigned surprise.

The guards were solicitous this time, greeting her by name and escorting her inside. Soliari stood silently before the Council, waiting.

"Soliari Lady Urramach, as Lostaria's closest living relative, we charge you with the responsibility of Regent, expecting you to act in the Matriarch's stead until the heir can be reclaimed and crowned. You will be expected to work with the Council as you rule the Ravali." Marahir paused.

Soliari looked suitably stunned, glad she had practiced for hours in front of a mirror.

The Voice continued. "You will be granted a small stipend to partially compensate you for the extra responsibility."

The Ravali woman made a show of regaining her composure. "I thank the Council for their great confidence in me. The stipend will be welcome. It prevents me from having to call some small loans due." Soliari noted the look of relief that flashed across a councilman's face. "Please notify me of the appropriate time for the induction ceremony." She curtseyed low and left the building.

### 

*Henin Castle*

A Henin maid led Timbrel to an undecorated room crowded by a small bed and a washstand. The Ravali girl poured water from the chipped ceramic pitcher to the washbowl and sniffed at it. The water had the stale smell of an old puddle, and she could see tiny worms wiggling about in the bowl. She poured the water back into the pitcher and held it out.

"Take this away. I require a tub, hot water enough to fill it, and some soap and shampoo."

The maid hesitated for a moment longer than she should

68

have. Timbrel was pacing the floor for quite some time before the maid returned with an armful of clothing, followed by servants carrying a tub and buckets of water.

Timbrel settled into the water, not surprised to find it lukewarm.

The maid handed her a rough bar of brown laundry soap and then withdrew to the side, vigorously brushing the travel dust from Timbrel's cloak into the air.

"Please do that somewhere else. You're muddying the water."

"Won't matter much, lady." The maid drew the last word out into a taunt. "Lady Kareni is going to *hate* you if you show up with *him* tonight." She brushed another layer of dust into the room. "I'll lay out your clothes and take these for cleaning. I think you'll look proper in the red dress if I tie ribbons in your hair."

"I can manage my own hair. Bring me some towels and you can go on about your normal duties." The towels appeared in record time.

Timbrel fussed with her hair, washing it with sweet-smelling herbs from her pack instead of the strong-smelling laundry soap. She finally elected to pull it back from her face.

Three dresses and a pile of ribbons were laid out on the bed for her inspection. The first gown consisted of overlapping white lace and hundreds of buttons. *A funeral dress*, Timbrel thought. *Completely inappropriate.* The second glowed with the deep red of falling leaves, laid out with a wide golden scarf and black velvet slippers. When she held it up, the sleeves drooped almost to the floor. The third dress was sapphire blue, with a thin belt and a heavily embroidered vest that would barely have covered her breasts. She held the dress up. If only she had a mirror.

She searched the room, finally propping up the polished copper plate beneath the water pitcher against the bed. The dress fell straight from her shoulders to her waist before flaring out into a wide skirt and short train. Timbrel found the fingerloop easily, but elected to leave the back of the dress touching the floor until she saw how others wore their dresses. Leaving the vest and belt to the side, Timbrel tied the golden scarf around her waist to shape the dress to her figure. As an afterthought, Timbrel strapped on one of her thigh-sheathed daggers, ready to protect herself if it became necessary.

She reached for her boots and cursed under her breath. The maid had taken them for cleaning. The slippers would have to do. She slid matching ribbons beneath the soles and braided them to just below her knee. It gave her the look of fancy boots, as well as obscuring the birthmark on her ankle.

She sighed as she brushed her hair again and found another tangle. She didn't trust the maid's advice, not after recognizing the look of superiority that servants seemed to feel over a half-blood. Better to trust her own training and good sense to get her through the evening. She might never have set foot in a palace before, but court custom and behavior before royalty had been drilled into her by her tutors. She could easily adapt to any small differences.

Jherik had promised to call for her at the sixth hour. She applied a tiny bit of cosmetics while she waited.

The touch of the brush brought memories flooding back. The elaborate court make-up that Soliari wore always seemed too thick, hiding any trace of emotion. Katrina's make-up was much subtler. The human dancer showed Timbrel how a few strokes of the lightest color could freshen her face without changing it, highlighting her best features. Timbrel chose to follow Katrina's teaching.

She replaced the plate and empty pitcher just before Jherik arrived. His knock coincided with the first stroke of the great bell. By the second stroke she opened the door.

Jherik stood at the door, dressed for court in a tight fitting pair of black trousers, a loose white shirt, and a matching black vest with silver trim. His sword, tied into its sheath with a bright red cord, hung on a polished black belt with silver studs that matched the finely polished black boots. Even his brown hair was pulled back and fastened with a silver clip at the nape of his neck.

*Von could have taken a lesson in taste from this warrior*, Timbrel thought.

70

"Are you re..." Jherik's voice trailed off into silence. Timbrel searched his chestnut brown eyes for any sign of disapproval. She saw none.

Tossing her head so that a lock of golden hair fell across her shoulder, Timbrel reached for the silent warrior's right arm. Jherik turned smoothly at her touch, transferred her hands to his left arm, and smiled gently as he escorted her down the hallway.

They stopped twice for Jherik to chat with various guards before continuing to the Grand Ballroom. The steward waited for them in the antechamber, so wrapped in sashes and badges of office that he looked like an insect wrapped in a spider's web. The steward motioned for Timbrel to sit. Instead, she stood near the double doors and listened to the presentations. There were apparently several antechambers feeding participants inside. She could hear both Krys and Sarin being presented, as well as others of low rank. A few lower nobles passed through the room next, and Timbrel stepped aside to allow a higher noble to pass through.

"My lady," the Steward protested, "the introductions are made in ascending order of rank."

Timbrel smiled. "I am aware of this." The Ravali elves presented the highest ranks first, but she figured out the changed pattern quickly.

The steward frowned. Timbrel was now the last person in the anteroom except for Jherik. Snubbing her, the steward gathered the various cards left in a basket, and began polishing a platter as if to hurry her from his sight. Timbrel listened for the noise generated by the last nobleman's entrance to die down before stepping up to the door.

She slipped through the door on Jherik's arm. He bent to speak with the herald. "Announce her as Lady Timbrel."

Timbrel immediately corrected him. "I am Lanieli Lady Urramach, called Lady Timbrel."

Jherik inhaled sharply.

The herald's voice echoed around the large chamber. "Presenting Lanieli Lady Urramach, and escort." Something crashed to the ground in the room behind them.

The whispers began almost immediately. "She's beautiful." "What's an Urramach doing here?" "She's a half-blood."

Timbrel strolled down the aisle at a leisurely pace, nodding and smiling at those who met her eyes. As she approached the front of the room, she looked for an angry woman.

Wearing jade green, a red-haired woman with too much make-up and far too many pieces of jewelry watched Timbrel's approach with narrowing eyes.

Pulling Jherik with her, the half-blood girl stepped up to the angry woman. "You *must* be Kareni. I've heard *so* much about you."

Kareni blinked in surprise. "You have?" She smiled gratefully at Jherik.

Based on Kareni's original look and the gush of emotions the woman showed now, Timbrel knew she chose correctly using politeness. Better to disarm those who might believe themselves your enemies. Timbrel had learned Soliari's lessons well.

### 

Timbrel kicked off her borrowed velvet slippers, twisted past the tub, and flopped onto the bed. Dust puffed up and clung to her skin. Exhaustion made every muscle tense. Stripping quickly out of the blue gown, Timbrel stretched. As she loosened, she stepped rhythmically around the room and hummed to herself. She was caught up in the dance within minutes. She danced out her frustration with the entire court. The hostile neutrality of her meeting with Kareni, the shocked disbelief at the existence of an Urramach half-blood, the byplay of insult couched in politeness; all of this and more the girl expressed in her dance.

An onlooker would have noticed the balanced tension of the girl's posture, the sweeping arm motions that distracted the eye from the quite different rhythm of her hips, and even the occasional sweeping leg as the girl spun in her dance. A warrior might notiice the occasional martial stance as she posed for a heartbeat, each pose signifying a slight change in the next part of the dance. Her body's movements would have mesmerized an onlooker. It is unlikely that they would have noticed her face and its lack of happiness.

For nearly an hour the girl pounded the polished oak floor with her bare feet, spinning until her golden hair stood out like a yardwide fancy ruffled collar, swaying until the sweat streamed down her naked body and splashed on the wood. Slowing, nearing her finish, her mind completely at peace in the meditative trance the dance could bring, she crashed back to more worldly sensibilities when a sharp knock sounded at the door.

Timbrel caught up the golden scarf from the floor and tied it around her hips while leaning forward so that her hair covered her breasts. The door opened as she finished the knot.

Jherik stood there, mouth agape. He made a strangled noise.

"I was about to bathe," announced Timbrel, trying to sound aristocratic. "The maidservant forgot to leave a towel and a robe. Would you be so kind?"

Jherik turned and fled down the hallway, leaving the door open.

Timbrel stuck her head out to watch him run. She heard giggling behind her. Whirling, the girl saw two young maids giggling nervously. "So there you are. What are you waiting for? I require a robe and a towel for my bath."

Startled, the girls ran down the hall. Timbrel leaned out to yell behind them. "And bring me hot water."

Less than a quarter of an hour later the servants returned, a dozen buckets of hot water on a small cart. Timbrel allowed them to empty and refill the tub. A clean robe and a towel lay on the bed, along with her freshly cleaned traveling clothes. Timbrel luxuriated in the hot water when another knock sounded.

The door opened only a tiny bit this time. "Timbrel? Are you ready for a tour?"

The girl giggled at Jherik's embarrassed whisper. "I'm almost finished with my bath. I can be ready in a few minutes. Would you care to come in and wait while I dry off?"

73

The door shut hurriedly, and she heard Jherik's footsteps pacing back and forth. Timbrel quickly dressed and checked her pack. While it had been obviously searched, the contents were intact. She shouldered the pack and opened the door.

Jherik looked at her with surprise. "You won't need that today."

Timbrel smiled. "Perhaps not, but I've grown accustomed to having it nearby."

Jherik made an impressive tour guide for an equally impressive city. The homes closest to the grand palace stood four and five stories in height, built of stone lined with wooden paneling. Farther away, the homes were built of wood and stood three stories and less. The smaller homes were scattered to the rims of the valley, some built into the side of the mountain. Large and small, though, the homes all had the same curling room decoration that she'd noticed in the early morning.

"Why are the roofs like that?" she finally asked.

Jherik looked confused. "To support the net."

Timbrel stared upward. "What net?"

"That net." Jherik pointed up to the empty sky.

She glanced around. "I don't see anything."

"Use your other sight." Jherik's voice slowed, as if explaining something to a child. "Your magic sight."

Timbrel looked directly at the tall warrior. "You can see magic?" At his assenting gesture, she continued. "How?"

"How do you tell the magical power in one of your Councilmen?" Jherik countered.

"We don't," she answered matter-of-factly. "No wizard would be allowed to stay in Ravali, much less be allowed on the Council. We don't condone evil in our leaders."

Jherik's jaw dropped. After a few more minutes of conversation, it became apparent to both of them that one of the fundamental differences between their cultures was the Henin use of magic as an everyday tool.

Timbrel openly shuddered at the thought of so much magic flying around.

74

"There is no need to fear. Even the youngest children learn to see the magic so they can avoid the spells." At Timbrel's confused look, Jherik continued. "I could teach you how to see it."

"I do not have to learn any spells, do I?" Timbrel backed away, alarmed.

"Of course not. It's just a different way of seeing. Now, you start like this..."

After ten minutes, Timbrel managed to unfocus her eyes, contort her face, and squint... and still saw nothing. An hour later she managed the tiniest flash out of the corner of her eye.

"Are you... are you magical?" Timbrel was horrified at the thought. She was fond of her guide.

"Of course. Part of my warrior's training. Magic augments my shield and armor, as well as my combat skills." He turned a vaguely unfocused stare at Timbrel. "You have no magic at all? What did you train in?"

"Healing, though most consider it a waste of time. It will be far more useful when we reach the human lands."

As they returned to the Henin city center, Timbrel tried to see magic again with no result. She just didn't have the talent for it.

### 

They were summoned to the Henin council in the morning. Thirteen Council members seated themselves and chatted while the herald droned through the formalities necessary to begin the meeting, leaving a fourteenth chair empty at the far end of the table. A muffled gong rang as the herald finished. the Council's door opened and a fourteenth Henin slipped through. Still in his early adolescence, the brown-haired son of the Henin Matriarch seated himself in the empty chair.

Timbrel was horrified. Expressly forbidden in the documents that reinforced ancient tradition, royal blood should never be seated on the Council. She could only imagine what havoc Soliari would wreak in the same position, and fought to keep her face under control.

The lead Councilwoman glanced at the prince and stood. Jherik, Timbrel's assigned guard for the session, nudged her to stand. Sarin's guard assisted the ailing old elf. Krys gave an icy glare at his guard, who immediately stepped back from the wizard without touching him.

The Councilwoman motioned for the Council to sit, though a servant removed the three chairs behind the Ravali elves and left them standing. "It seems we were remiss in not offering better quarters to your group."

"Half-blood should have been locked in the cellars," muttered one councilman. His fellow murmured assent.

Timbrel spoke up. "While inadequate, at least they were clean."

The Councilwoman ignored the girl's comment and continued. "You are on a rescue quest. By tradition, you may ask us for three boons to aid that quest. What are those boons?"

Timbrel nearly clenched her fists, furious at the snub. Would her requests be ignored as well? She turned her head and met Krys' eyes. His lips were pressed into a thin line. He was just as angry, she thought. She nodded at him, then pointedly looked away from the proceedings and inspected her fingernails.

Krys looked directly at the Councilwoman. "We require adequate food and water for a month's journey, a pack animal to carry it with, and a warrior to replace the one who died on the way here." When the shocked murmuring of the Henin Council subsided, he continued. "We require these things to be ready by sunrise tomorrow. You have delayed us long enough."

The Council broke out in open argument. Timbrel stared upward, fascinated by the crystal chandelier. In her peripheral vision, the young prince frowned in thought before an admiring glance stole across his face.

The young prince stood. "Cousin Urramach," he called out. Silence dropped like a broken branch. Timbrel turned her head to look at him, her body still in an attitude of utter boredom. "Cousin, it shall be as you request. Let us take a walk in the garden while our underlings determine the details."

Before anyone could stop her, Timbrel crossed the room and took the prince's arm, Jherik trailing helplessly in her wake.

The prince opened the door and escorted Timbrel through, firmly closing it before Jherik could enter. He remained quiet until they reached a bench in the center of the garden. He sat down, then sprang up again as the words tumbled out. "You certainly put them in their place. I have so many questions for you. Are you really on a rescue mission? I've never been anywhere else. Did you ever meet a human?"

Timbrel laughed. "Ask them one at a time, Cousin, or you won't give me a chance to answer."

Hours later, she sipped tea to soothe her throat. The Henin prince--he'd never told her his name--had questions about everything.

### 

*Beyond Henin Lands*

The sun had been up for two hours and Timbrel already felt hot. Krys led the way down from the mountain valleys and toward the human lands. Sarin's horse nervously flicked its ears. Jherik brought his own horses, one to ride and one to carry his armor and spare weapons. Timbrel held the horses to a walk, unwilling to overtax them for a few days yet. The beasts still needed shoeing, but that could wait until the first human town with a blacksmith or farrier.

Jherik slumped in his saddle almost as much as Sarin. After her third unsuccessful attempt to cheer him up, Krys took her aside.

"The Henin Council accused him of having a relationship with you. The question of his betrothal's validity is being decided while he is gone."

"Of having a..." Timbrel's voice trailed off in disbelief. "We did nothing. He walked into the room while I was taking a bath. The servants that brought my towels saw him leave."

Krys nodded, copying the human gesture from Timbrel. "It will take him some time to grow comfortable near you."

Timbrel understood. Since her return from her father's destroyed village, the same accusations came up over and over. None of them were true. Admittedly, she did use people's propensity to believe the worst as a weapon against those who wronged her. She never intended the resulting rumors to harm those she liked. Jherik was off-limits to her, anyway. Kareni already claimed him.

Katrina taught her long ago that a man could only belong to one woman at a time. It was best to avoid entanglements. The dark-haired dancer knew much about men, for she had spent time with hundreds.

Timbrel remembered the first time she'd seen Katrina dance, only a few days after her arrival in Fafar. The dancer spun and twirled her way around the Inn's common room before returning to the cleared "stage" and slowing her dance. She locked eyes with a traveler during a pause, returning to dance for him time and again as the song progressed. When the music stopped, she knelt on the floor at his feet.

Timbrel's father did not try to stop his woman from going upstairs with another man. If anything, he encouraged it. Later he left on a short trading trip with his partners just a few hours before the traveler did. When he returned the same night laden with coins and jewelry from his successful venture, he and Katrina spent two days together.

Katrina never chose any of the Fafar villagers except Timbrel's father, but when strangers traveled through the village she often chose a different companion. More than once she sent her chosen back to the common room with his pants in his arms when she found out about a wife elsewhere. Timbrel swore never to be involved with a man who loved another.

While traveling back to Ravali after Fafar's destruction, Timbrel saw many fights between men over a woman unclear about her choice. Worse, she saw two women fight over a man. One was his wife, the other his lover. Somehow the three had come to the same inn at the same time. The fight got bloody, with fingernail gouges and hair ripped from each other's skulls.

The wife left the building with the local constable. The husband and his lover remained until the gravedigger arrived.

Timbrel came back to the present as Krys called a halt by the side of a trickling stream. While the three men discussed directions over one of Sarin's maps, Timbrel stretched and wandered by the streamside, foraging for plants that she could add to dinner. The pack pony the Henin prince granted to them staggered under the weight of their provisions, but Timbrel remained certain that Krys had indicated a longer journey was necessary. Why else would he insist that the warrior be fluent in the human tongue?

She wandered along the tiny stream until she heard Krys' call. She returned, her basket full of tubers and berries to supplement their evening meal, as well as a few medicinal herbs she tied on the outside of her pack to dry. Just before leaving, she refilled all the waterskins.

While there, she shook a stone out of her boot and glanced down at her ankle. The mud caked over her birthmark had cracked and crumbled during their morning ride. She quickly slid the boot back on, remembering her nurse's insistance that she cover up the ugly mark. A tangle of loops, it almost looked like a flower drawn by a child. Her nurse insisted the mark was a terrible flaw. Timbrel suffered recurring nightmares for almost a year that the loops would cover her body and strangle her to death. The nightmare still haunted her, usually after she dealt with her mother. The last few days the dreams troubled her again, so she took care to obscure the mark with mud each morning and evening.

One more reason she wished to return to the human world. Her dance bells covered the birthmark nicely.

###

*Elsin Pass*

The last of the high mountain valleys behind them, the group descended to a mountain pass. A vertical slash through the solid rock, great gashes and broken tunnels interrupted the sheer drop. Gravel and fine sand spilled across the narrow floor of the pass like a dry riverbed. Halfway through, Jherik stopped to refill his waterskins at one of the tiny trickling waterfalls dripping from creases in the sheer walls. Small rounded ponds at the base of each trickle testified to the power of the water when the mountain snows melted in the late spring. Tiny frogs hopped about, catching tinier insects.

Jherik poked his head inside one of the lower tunnels. Nearly circular, the tunnel bored through solid rock with smoothly scraped edges. It dipped and curved at the limits of his sight.

"Krys, you are a scholar. What made these tunnels?"

Krys shook his head. "I have no idea. There were no tunnels here the last time I used this pass."

"How many centuries ago was that?"

"Five years."

Jherik loosened his longest sword in its sheath. "Years?"

That was less than a human life-span. Less than the thirty years since the war between the land-grabbing humans and the elves. Henin and Ravali remained sacrosanct only because of ancient protective magics.

Jherik shuddered. Soon they would be surrounded by thousands of humans, all ready to continue the fight even though the truce had been in place for thirty years. He remembered his battles vividly. How many humans did the same?

Krys called a halt.

The Henin elf scanned the area. The tunnels were smaller here, barely two feet across, though gouges in the gravel now accompanied them. There were signs of human wagons passing through, the tracks in the gravel cut by the gouges.

After a short break, they continued picking their way over gouges and past tunnels. The horses shied twice when the breeze

80

blew, but the Henin did not detect any immediate threats.

The entire group was tense by the time the pass opened out into a lush green valley. The road followed its curve downward toward the foothills, water glinting in small spring-fed streams. Fields spread out on both sides of the road, and herds of sheep dotted the higher slopes. A cluster of small huts rose where fields of different colors touched. Jherik thought it looked peaceful, but remained ready to defend the group.

Timbrel rode ahead with a clatter of hooves. Jherik leaned forward, using his knees to guide his horse as he caught up with the girl.

"Have a care, Lady Timbrel. We do not know if these humans are friend or foe to us."

Timbrel gave him a look of disbelief. "Foe? What are you talking about? Don't ride in the fields and we'll be welcome at the Elsin Inn. It's a great place to stop."

Jherik looked at Krys. The Ravali shrugged, another annoying human gesture. Jherik tried to shrug back, pulling his shoulders up to touch his ears. The gesture felt unnatural. The three men caught up with the girl, allowing her to lead the way.

Broken and burned stone foundations left over from the war were overgrown with tangles of vines. Boulders disturbed the neat lines of plants in the fields, boulders with bones and bits of armor still pinned beneath. Several perfectly circular ponds caught his eye, the water hiding the ugly scars in the land from other attacks.

The regular lines of an intact stone fortress stood against the mountainside. Jherik took some comfort when he realized that the path between the fortress and the main road showed little signs of use.

As they rounded the next curve, the human city came into view. Wooden structures, stone buildings, thatched and tiled roofs, and dozens of smaller roads and alleys sprawled on both sides of the road. In the midst of the general chaos, one stone building dominated. Its wooden roof extended out from the building on two sides, supported with numerous poles. Several horses stood with their reins tied to the poles, while others wandered a fenced pasture across the road. A small stable stood in the far corner of the pasture.

"There's the Elsin Inn," Timbrel said, pointing at the singular structure. As they rode closer, Jherik made out a sign depicting a wine goblet and a knife, as well as a sketch of the mountain itself. Human letters decorated the sign beneath the picture.

Timbrel slid from her horse in front of the Inn. Two human boys dashed toward her. Jherik's sword was out of its sheath in an instant.

"Hold," Krys shouted out. "They're just stable hands."

Jherik resheathed his sword slowly. The two boys edged around the warrior, then took the reins of Timbrel's horse, as well as Sarin's and Krys' horses.

"He won't bite," Timbrel assured them.

"I'm not worried about his teeth, lady, just his blade."

"He'll be good. He's not going to attack anyone." Krys took the reins of Jherik's horse as the Henin slid from his saddle, and then handed them to the boys.

Timbrel grabbed Jherik's hand and pulled him toward the Inn. Krys and Sarin stood with the boys, instructing them on the horse's care.

Jherik pulled his hand back from the girl's grip. "My sword hand."

"You won't need it." She grabbed his hand again.

Steeling himself for what might be ahead, Jherik walked with the girl and entered his first human building.

###

# Chapter Four

*The Elsin Inn*

Timbrel felt like she had just come home. The heady odor of baking bread and the smell of spices, cooked vegetables, and roasting meat rolled out as she opened the door to the Elsin Inn. Inside, the huge common room took up almost two-thirds of the ground floor. Wooden trestle tables stood around the room, some set up next to the pillars supporting the hewn oak beams. Two small fires burned away the evening chill, one in a hearth built into the wall shared between the common room and the kitchen, and the other in a larger fireplace on the far wall.

Travelers filled every bench, while others sat on the floor beneath the wall pegs holding their packs and weapons. A small group gathered in a circle near a pair of minstrels playing the lute and pipes. Half a dozen serving girls ran back and forth from the kitchen, their platters heaped high with food, mugs, and pitchers.

Jherik stood next to the girl, mouth gaping and body immobile.

"Come on, don't block the door." She pulled him into the room. Krys and Sarin followed. Timbrel moved toward the music, her long fingers still wrapped around Jherik's wrist.

Waiting for the minstrels to take a break, Timbrel noticed that the doorway to the kitchen, curtains pulled back for the serving girl's ease, stood next to a narrow staircase winding upwards. Two patrons stumbled down the stairs, their mugs clasped to their chests.

Krys strode to a small table of humans just finishing their meal. Before Timbrel could stop him, he tipped the drunken customers out of their chairs and swept the table off with one arm. Mugs and plates crashed to the floor. Mortified, Timbrel tried to ignore the wizard as he and Sarin seated themselves. As soon as she let go of Jherik to cover her face, he joined Krys and took a seat.

The music trailed off, and Timbrel saw the lute player placing his instrument in a carefully padded case. She reached out to the piper. "Can you play for a dancer?"

The piper glanced around the room. "I could if there were a dancer here, and if she wanted to dance to *The Greensward*."

Timbrel smiled. The piper named a popular folk tune that she danced to many times at Summerfest in Fafar. "*The Greensward* would be wonderful. Is payment by acclaim, here?" Timbrel wondered if the patrons would be permitted to toss coins freely or if she needed to haggle with the innkeeper for a set price.

"Acclaim. What's our portion?" The piper indicated his partner, now unpacking a small drum.

"You earn the first ten silver bits, and everything after is split evenly between the dance and the music." It was a more than generous offer. The pipers nodded their acceptance. "Begin in five minutes. The dancer will begin by the second line of the long version."

Before they could object, Timbrel dashed to the kitchen. Quickly explaining to the head cook, she hired an ash-smudged child to collect the coins that would be tossed onto the floor. She rummaged in her pack for a moment, pulling out a silken blouse and pants, as well as a sturdier skirt. To the amazement of the kitchen boys, Timbrel stripped and changed into her dancing clothes on the spot. As the music started up in the common room, she wiped her face and hands with a wet rag to remove the worst of the travel dust.

Just as the second line began, Timbrel spun into the common room from the kitchen. Head snapping around, her spinning walk took her to a spot near the minstrels. The patrons pulled back to give her room. She continued to spin for a moment, her golden hair flashing in the torchlight, and then dropped into perfect synchronization with the drum. The drumbeats carried her forward, her body swaying and twisting in time with the changing

84

rhythm. The piper nodded, and she matched her head and arm movements to the melody of the pipes.

The music grew more complex as both minstrels experimented with the song, adding small flourishes. Timbrel's gleeful laugh was an instrument in itself as the music changed and she rose to the challenge. The drumbeat suddenly slowed. Timbrel took advantage of the new rhythms to mix poses into her dance, swirling her hips in a slow circle before freezing in place for an impossibly long measure, then continuing as if she had never stopped. When she leaned back and dropped into a standing backbend, the music halted for a terrifying second, forcing her to hold a pose that seemed on the edge of disaster.

She heard the intake of the watchers' collective breath. Turning her head to the side to catch a glimpse of a much larger crowd, she noticed that those in the rear surged forward for a better look. When the music began again she gracefully arched out of the pose and began a slow circle, her index finger swaying in time with the pipes. The girl twitched her finger faster and sprang into a spin as the piper increased in speed. A heartbeat later the drummer responded as well and the half-elf finished the dance as she had begun, spinning through the crowd and back into the kitchen. Thunderous applause followed her as the hired child dashed out into the common room

By the time she had changed back to her traveling clothes, the child staggered back dragging a full apron on the floor. Timbrel flipped it open. Copper chits, silver bits from various towns, and gold mountains spilled out across the floor. Timbrel carefully chose a large silver coin stamped with a dragon for the child. She pressed it on the head cook when the child shyly hid behind the large woman.

"Shush, child, and come say Thank you," instructed the cook. "You've a dowry now, thanks to this kind woman." A tiny sound escaped the child, muffled by the cook's skirts. The cook looked at Timbrel. "Thank you."

Timbrel knelt beside the little girl. "Honest pay for honest work," she whispered. The dancer was rewarded with a shy smile before the child hid again.

Smiling herself, Timbrel sorted the coins into two stacks, and transferred a gold mountain from one to the other. She poured most of the smaller stack into a large pouch, fixing it inside her pack. She placed the last few coins from her stack in a smaller pouch, which she tied onto her belt. She wrapped the second stack of coins in the bottom edge of her cloak and sought out the minstrels. They looked overjoyed at the sudden bounty, and tried to press several coins back on Timbrel. She refused.

Her passage across the floor was met with appreciative comments and colorful suggestions. She avoided reaching hands by spinning and twisting as she wove her way through the crowd. Only once did she slap away an insistent grip. The heavyset man followed her across the room until she neared Krys, then faded back into the crowd.

Krys was furious. "I thought the idea was to keep a low profile," he hissed in Ravali.

"Provisions come first, she answered.

"We already have an entire packhorse of provisions."

"And a long journey ahead." Timbrel carefully laid three gold mountains on the table. "This should be enough to feed us, take care of the horses, and perhaps even rent a room for the night."

Krys stopped in mid-whisper, staring at the coins. He laid a finger on one coin, pushing it toward the girl. "This is more than enough."

Timbrel waved her hand at the coin in dismissal. "Keep it. I'll give you the others later." She looked up as the innkeeper arrived at their table, bearing a heavily laden tray.

The innkeeper looked at Krys. "Are you with her? Your coins'll come back later. Bed and board is on the house tonight. Well, as long as ye don't mind sharing a room together. Only one left in the place."

Krys choked out a strangled-sounding "Thank you."

Timbrel smiled, mostly in amusement.

"Will ye be staying with us another night? I've not seen anyone dance like that since I was a boy."

"You flatter me, sir. I wish that we could stay, but we must leave in the morning. You know how relatives are." She winked at the man. "Perhaps on our return journey?"

"Certainly. You are always welcome here, lady."

"Timbrel," supplied Jherik. "She is Lady Timbrel."

Krys' answering wince would long be remembered.

### 

As they traveled north through the human lands, Krys grew increasingly frustrated. Sarin became quieter with each mile they traveled. The old historian spent hours staring at the sky, his shoulders hunched over, but the old elf refused to speak of his fears.

Timbrel was a problem as well. She insisted on dancing at each inn they stopped at, leaving a trail childishly easy to follow. They no longer needed the money: they purchased a third packhorse with months of dried provisions, and Krys' own horse carried a leather sack bulging with silver bits inside each saddlebag. Not only did she dance, but she insisted on sitting and drinking with every man in the inn. Each evening she would weave her way drunkenly up to their room before Krys and the others. Krys doubted that she was as drunk as she seemed, but could not be certain.

And Jherik's problem with the human language. Although fluent in the words, he completely missed the gestures and tonal shadings that humans used. He could not tell a question from an accusation, and too often responded to the literal meaning of the words in colloquial phrases. In the process, he gave out too much information. Unfortunately, the lands ahead were seldom at peace, and the warrior's presence would be vital.

Krys consulted his map again. Though crudely drawn, the map contained information from several of Sarin's maps as well as a human one that Timbrel obtained for them. Some of the ruined cities lay close to the roads, but he may have made a mistake by following this one.

The last three days they had passed only a scattering of human huts, many abandoned, and the great swamp grew closer to the road with every step. The promised ruin had not been found, though if they made it through the swampy road they would cut days off their travel time.

*Camping in the cool damp was hard on Sarin*, thought Krys. His teacher moved with painful slowness in the morning, in spite of Timbrel's best efforts. Her odd-smelling potions did seem to help, however, and lately she joined Sarin in a ritual of morning teas.

Krys refused to join them. While Timbrel sweetened Sarin's tea with honey from a comb she found, her own drink was dark, opaque, and bitter, based on the face she made with the first sip each morning. He didn't ask. Her behavior, like that of most women, remained a mystery to him.

Jherik had confided to Krys about his worries, as well. Twice he saw Timbrel leave the rooms of other patrons, and he worried that she might conceive a child.

Krys knew that Timbrel was probably sterile as a half-blood, but even if not, she understood the difficulty of their task. Then again, Jherik might just be jealous of the attention the girl gave to others, particularly because she ignored Jherik as thoroughly as she ignored Krys in that fashion. In fact, Jherik watched the girl much more than he should.

Only a day more of this swamp and they should return to firmer ground.

###

*The Cat's Claw Tavern, Shassilar*

As the four reached the drier ground of an open plain, signs of human habitation appeared more often. A cluster of thin smoke trails rose in the distance. Timbrel looked forward to reaching the next human town and staying at an inn. Or at least stopping for a meal. When she stayed at Fafar Village with her father, she tasted her first cheese and loved it. After returning to the elves, cheese remained unavailable to her.

The last few human towns they passed through had little or no cheese for sale. The grasses of these open plains should support cattle and goats, she thought. Plenty of milk for cheese.

The sun beat down on the group of elves before they found the first shack. Unlike the simple but clean homes in the forest villages, this town was in a state of disrepair. The few ramshackle homes looked abandoned. Furtive movements behind shuttered windows and tiled rooftops with as many gaps as a child's grin worried her further. Her mother Soliari and the dead warrior Von might have used this town as an example of everything wrong with humans, right down to the dirty child skulking near the trash heaps that sprouted like mushrooms near the doors of every building.

Krys flipped the hood of his cloak up to shade his face. "We don't want them to see our ears." Jherik and Sarin followed suit.

Timbrel pulled her hood up as well, carefully tucking her hair underneath. They rode through the town slowly until they finally located a tavern on the far side. The poorly chinked log building, rough hewn and visibly splintered, looked unstable enough to fall in the next windstorm. An unsavory smell hung in the air, part piss, part rotted food, and part greasy smoke that rolled down from the damaged roof and clung to the sides of the building.

The girl shuddered. She clearly heard the low muttering of the patrons inside, a sort of angry growl. Some of the gaps in the walls seemed darker than before, as though heads clustered to watch her from inside. Timbrel lifted her hand to wave them on when the door opened and a man staggered out.

89

As greasy as the tavern itself, he wove his way around the end of the building. Timbrel smelled the fumes of strong ale even at such a distance. With a glance at the sun's height to reassure her, she thought the man must have started drinking at breakfast.

She tempered her own drinking among the humans with the knowledge that she was immune to the worst effects of alcohol, metabolizing each drink in a double handful of minutes. She learned in Fafar to mimic the behavior of others to avoid being singled out; that counted twice when among those who drank heavily.

The breeze swirled, bringing the man's full scent to the girl. Her eyes watered from the alcohol fumes and body odor. Underneath the alcohol, however, was the scent of cheese. Good cheese. Cheese that made her mouth water.

"I'm going in. Wait here." Tucking her money pouch into the waistband of her riding skirt, she slipped from her horse, threw the reins to Krys, and strode inside.

Stepping to the right, she waited as her eyes adjusted. The scent of unwashed bodies, alcohol, and the sharp scents of anger and fear mixed with the smell of food. Knife-scarred tables with ancient stains sat near soot-blackened walls, a few sputtering torches adding another layer to the grime. Many of the patrons wore hoods, the unhooded ones all men, and every one of them stared at her except the motionless bodies lying on filthy rushes caked with grease and mud beneath the tables. Timbrel eyed what she thought were dead men. relieved when one took a slow breath.

Some of the cloaked patrons resettled themselves, and her eyes strayed to the bulges of concealed weapons.

### 

Nayev sat near the back wall. He loved watching the humans interact. This particular group often entertained him with fights and loud thoughts of grandiose plans. Thieves, former soldiers, and occasional murderers all; they met for whispered deals, celebrated their few successes, and drank away their many failures.

A few roughly pushed through to his table, grabbing spots on the benches and stools. He smiled beneath his hood. They would be quite horrified if they realized who they sat with. He had shown his magic once when he first entered the town, creating a dust pit just deep enough to capture the feet of the three men who threatened him, then solidifying the dust into rock around their ankles. He let them go after they pissed themselves. He took some time as he recreated the normal rocky soil again once they scrambled out. Most avoided him afterward.

He heard the horses first, then the mention of cheese. Those nearest the front clustered against the gaps in the walls to see who approached. The door opened and a cloaked figure stepped inside and to the right. Average height, slender... the stranger could have been any of the usual patrons.

The stranger waved off the frightened barmaid and headed straight for the barkeep.

Nayev leaned his chair back and sniffed. Ah, the scent of horses--he liked horses--and travel dust from the south. He heard no anger or fear in her thoughts. A woman?

"How much for a small wheel of cheese?" The woman's lilting voice rang with confidence. She had Nayev's full attention. Everyone else's, too, judging by the immediate silence.

The barkeep looked her up and down. "Two copper wheats for the size of your hand, a silver bit for a wheel the length of your arm."

"The larger, if you will." Coins clinked as she produced a silver dragon.

Nayev heard the hiss and scrape of drawn weapons, heard aggression rise in the patrons' thoughts. The comments started before the innkeeper even left the room.

"C'mon, girlie, I can take really good care of you."

"Sweetheart, come back to me."

"You're not walking out of here without kissing me first."

One rose to his feet. "I want to see who you are." The man stumbled toward the woman. Nayev recognized him as one of the ankle men.

"Who is she? Who is she? Grab her."

Encouraged by the crowd, Ankle man lunged for the mystery woman.

She leaned back at the last minute, just enough for his hand to miss her and crash into the bar.

Roaring with pain, Ankle man charged. The woman spun out of his path. As he passed her, she kicked out one foot and let the force of her spin assist him across the room. He crashed into the wall by the door and slumped to the ground.

His two friends sprang forward, punching at her.

She dodged again, twisting. Her hood fell back, revealing pale skin, slightly pointed ears, and a braid down her back as blonde as Nayev's own hair. She could have been anywhere from sixteen to a few hundred years of age; with elves it was nearly impossible to tell.

"It's an elf! What's an elf doing here?" The sound of the crowd turned ugly.

"No elf is going to buy my wife's good cheese. Get out of here, elf, before I clip your ears."

The barkeep returned, bearing a wheel of cheese covered in beeswax. Several men jumped the counter and grabbed him. "You're not selling anything to a magic-slimed elf."

The barkeep shook himself free. "I'll sell to whoever can pay the price I set."

His attackers swung. The barkeep reeled backward as his nose gushed blood. The second man yanked the cheese away and held it up like a prize.

"That's mine." The elf-woman slipped past her last attacker, leaving the others groaning on the floor, and caught hold of the wheel. She pulled, the human man visibly struggling to hang onto the cheese.

*Serves him right for underestimating an elf.* Nayev snickered.

92

The door burst open, knocking aside Ankle man as he tried to rise. Two tall warriors entered the room with weapons drawn, hoods back to show their tall, sharply pointed ears. More patrons stood to enter the fray. The girl pulled the cheese free and cradled it in her arms.

The thoughts in the room turned murderous.

Nayev took a deep breath. "Stop!" His clear tenor voice rang out above the shouts of the patrons. The word echoed around the walls much longer than it should have, fading only when the room quieted. "Let the woman have her cheese."

One voice, lost in the crowd, shouted back. "We don't need no money from a slimy elf!"

"Very well, then. *I'll* buy the cheese." Nayev stood.

The nearby patrons blanched and leapt away from his table, leaving their meals and drink behind as they scrambled for the far side of the inn. They crowded onto benches and pushed other patrons from stools, and some edged their way along the walls to the door.

Alone now at his table, Nayev pushed his hood back to reveal hair as golden as the woman's. "Come, friends. I'll buy you a drink." He sat back on his stool.

The warriors pushed across the room to stand by the woman. She cradled her cheese and carefully paid the innkeeper. "I'll pay for my own cheese." She glanced at Nayev, revealing sapphire blue eyes. "But I think we will join you for a drink."

As they turned, ready to push through the crowd, the patrons melted away from their path like water receding from the shore. The warriors waited until the woman seated herself across the table before sitting down on either side.

"Nayev of the Mountains, at your service." He stood again and bowed slightly, smiling at the woman.

The taller warrior, with silver-white hair and an unlined face, answered in kind. "I am Krys, he is Jherik, and she is Lady Timbrel."

Jherik nodded, his brown braid pulling free of his cloak.

Timbrel blushed from her cheeks to her ears, then as quickly paled.

Nayev studied her. She used a human name. Her thoughts flitted about from interest in him to sorrow at a village of dead bodies, to anticipation of the taste of cheese. He blinked and sat back. Her mind voice sounded as strong as that of most dragons.

As he thought of dragons, he noticed a faint scent of dragon clung to the woman. He tried to look deeper into her thoughts, but they whirled so quickly his head hurt trying to follow them. In self-defense, he shielded his mind. It left him vulnerable to surprise, but allowed him to get to know these travelers better, especially this elf-woman.

*Half-elf*, he corrected himself. How had that happened?

He signaled the barmaid. "My friends and I will have some Forest wine."

Timbrel spoke up. "Forest wine for them, I'll have an ale."

After the barmaid set down the light brown ale and the bright green wine, Jherik stood. "Lady Timbrel, I will pack your cheese. Sarin no doubt needs help with the horses anyway. Nayev, good to meet you."

As a patron slipped out the door, a horse neighed, nearly drowning out Sarin's pleas to settle down.

The barmaid walked by with a tray of bread and meat. "Can I bring you something?"

Jherik stepped over to her tray and grabbed a round loaf and two pieces of meat in a long-fingered hand. "These will do." He hefted the cheese in his other arm and left.

Nayev burst out laughing at the girl's confused expression and tossed two copper bits to her. "You can bring us a similar tray..."

"With cheese," Timbrel added.

"...with cheese and meat both, after you refill your tray and bring it to that other table. I apologize for my friend."

The barmaid scampered off to the kitchens.

They shared pleasant small talk over their meal. Krys asked leading questions, but Nayev played the conversation game well. He gave Krys information, but never what was asked.

He caught Timbrel staring at him more than once, an odd expression on her face. He smiled back. She blushed again.

"They don't like elves very much here, do they?" Krys glanced back across the room where the other patrons clustered.

"You are the first they have seen in many years. Too many of the old men remember the war, and they've brought their sons and grandsons up to feel the same."

"Grandsons? It's only been thirty years since the war ended."

A drunk patron walked toward their table. He blinked a few times, then spun on his heel and joined the crowd across the room.

Krys' voice suddenly softened. "You seem popular with your fellows. What is it you said you do?"

Nayev leaned forward and dropped his voice to a whisper. "I didn't say. I'm a wizard."

Timbrel squeaked and nearly dropped her mug. "A wizard?" She frowned for a moment, then brightened. "I don't believe it. You're no more a wizard than my father was a merchant."

She looked directly at Krys. "I think it's time we returned to the road. Jherik and Sarin must be thirsty by now."

Krys went to the bar and purchased a skin of wine.

Nayev bowed. "We'll talk together again some time, Lady Timbrel."

Timbrel reached out as if to touch Nayev's arm, then pulled her hand back. She stood, smiled at him, and walked away.

Unable to resist, Nayev lowered his mental shields and listened as she left the room.

Timbrel's mental voice rang with confidence. *Oh, I know what you are, sweet Nayev.*

He sat motionless as the sounds of their horses faded into the distance. How had she discovered his secret? Was she distantly related to him? He certainly hoped not; he was quite attracted to her.

*It is time to move on*, he thought. *I wonder where she's going next?*

### 

Jherik, ever quick to notice the actions of those around him, continued to be confused by Timbrel. Since leaving the tavern, she remained quiet. He missed her normal annoying chatter.

He watched her openly. Her human blood gave her an exotic look, broadening her cheekbones and creating a heart-shape instead of the usual near-triangular face of elves. Her waist length golden-blonde hair intrigued him. Krys assured him that the color was within the normal range for Ravali elves, but Jherek felt more comfortable with the browns and reds of the Henin. Her ears stood a bit shorter than most, though nicely pointed.

The breeze blew, showering Timbrel with loose leaves from the last storm. She threw her head back and laughed.

As her hair fell away from her ears, Jherik gasped. She had *earlobes*! And true to form, she pierced them to hang short strings of beads in the human style.

"Timbrel, you have earrings."

"I do. You've seen me in earrings before, every time I dance." She pursed her lips.

Jherik covered his eyes with his hand for a moment. He had thought the palm-sized hoops dangling at the sides of her head were attached to the thin chain she sometimes wore in her hair. Why did she have to be so human? If only she acted more elven, she would be extremely attractive. *Far more so than my fiancee...*

He forced himself to think about the tavern. Granted, every inn they stopped at before this was filled with such well-behaved humans that Jherik started to doubt the tales of bad humans. His stereotypes about humans and inns took a beating with kindness, at least until he rescued Timbrel from the mob inhabiting this last place. He felt justified in his paranoia of humans now.

From Timbrel's startled reaction this time--one she hid well--she had expected the kind behavior.

He tried to shake the confusion from his mind, nearly bumping Sarin's horse as he did. The old elf moved behind him on what passed for a road here. Women were... well, women.

"Krys, what is up with that girl? She makes faces at you when you start the fire, she wouldn't talk to *me* for two days when I enhanced the edge of my sword... and she comes out joking around with a wizard? Did he cast a spell on her? Where's the respect? Where's the fear?"

Krys reined his horse to a halt. "Wait. How did you know that Nayev was a wizard? I didn't tell you."

"You didn't need to. He glowed."

"You can *see* magic? You'll have to teach me that trick."

"You can't either? She can't." Jherik pointed his chin toward Timbrel.

"No Ravali can. Or at least none that I've ever heard of. Wizards are not looked upon too fondly there."

*That explained a lot.* "What did she do when she found out about Nayev?"

Timbrel galloped up and stopped her horse between them. "I didn't believe him," she announced. "He's no more a wizard than my father was a merchant."

Krys tilted his head. "You said that inside. What do you mean?"

"My father met with merchants time and again, but never made any deals until after they left Fafar. Then he and his men would go out to meet the merchants along the road, and return with many fine things." She sighed and shook her head slowly.

Jherik frowned. "It sounds like he made good deals."

"The merchandise sometimes had blood spots on it." She looked Jherik directly in the face. "He was a thief, a brigand, and a murderer. He robbed people, and no one ever spoke of it."

"Are you calling Nayev a thief? Is he dangerous?" Jherik's hand stole to the hilt of his sword.

"No, but he does have a secret. He's not a wizard." Her words hung in the air for a moment.

"This is a good place to stop," Krys announced. "Jherik, help Sarin with the horses."

Jherik slid from his saddle. Why had Krys brought the old elf on this journey? Sarin could barely ride a horse. Except for showing Krys a few maps, Sarin had spent most of his time watching the skies and cringing at every cloud. His fear seemed to infect the horses, who acted up whenever he neared. Sharing a room with him at inns became difficult. Sarin tossed and turned with nightmares, denying any problem. His heart beat loud enough for half the inn to hear. The sour musk of his nightmare sweat woke Jherik every time.

Jherik tossed his reins to Sarin. "Only thing you're good for," he muttered under his breath. *And not much good at that, either.*

It took only a few minutes to set up camp. Jherik set his tarp and blankets in a pile, then gathered firewood. Sarin staked the horses and arranged his bedroll as unobtrusively as possible, laying long grass over his blankets to conceal them. The horses shuffled to the far end of their tethers. The girl poked around in the bushes, digging up her dinner surprises. She cooked well enough, but they carried dried stores. She must be a fan of fresh food. And cheese.

Krys had his tarp set up as the girl laid wood for the fire. She wrinkled her nose at Krys as he lit the fire with a wave of his hand, practically an evening ritual between them. Timbrel pulled out her cooking pot, and placed two small copper pots nearby.

"You aren't cooking up more horse medicine tonight, are you?"

Timbrel put her hands on her hips. "The horses need to be healthy."

"So do we." Jherik chewed on his lip. "Did you ever think about how far the smell of your medicines--and your cooking--

follows the wind? We've been lucky so far that nothing has attacked."

Krys broke in. "It doesn't matter. Nothing will attack us tonight."

"Fine." Jherek stood. "I'll do a perimeter check." He stalked off across the meadow, stopping in the shadow of a small clump of trees. If only Krys had served with one of the elven armies during the last war, Jherek would have felt more comfortable with his answers.

The food smells drew him back to camp. Timbrel dished up some porcupine stew and handed him a twist of bread, still coiled around the roasting stick.

We carry enough dry food to feed a battalion, he thought. Why not use it?
###

Timbrel approached Sarin by the horses while Krys and Jherik argued yet again about the best path.

"Do you think he likes me?" She chewed on her bottom lip and felt heat rising in her face.

"Who, child, the Henin?" Sarin frowned. "He is betrothed to another. It should not matter whether he likes you or not."

"I know that, and I didn't mean Jherik. Do you think *Nayev* likes me. The man we met when I bought the cheese."

Sarin nodded. "I didn't meet him, child. The horses broke loose and dragged me into the pasture before you came out of the inn. They never liked me, you know, the horses. But one saved me once..."

"Sarin, what do I do? I just met him, and my heart... I haven't felt this way since my first love. I want to see him again." She shuffled her feet in the long grass at the side of the road. "The others are just friends, or a few nights of fun. He feels different. It's as if he understands me."

"Child, keep your heart. You might never see this man again. Perhaps you should discuss this with Krys. He has had many lovers over the years. Surely he could better advise you."

They both glanced at Krys as the argument got louder.

Krys pointed ahead. "All the tracks go straight down the road, but none come back. There's some hazard up there."

"Fine, Krys. I'll double-check your tracking." Jherik stomped up the road.

Timbrel touched the old elf's sleeve. "No, Krys doesn't understand my feelings."

"I would hate to see you pine away for this man. My mother knew a man like that, long ago."

"What happened?"

"He charmed her and stayed with her for a year before he left. She never saw him again. She never even knew his real name. When she sent out searchers, they found no trace of his existence. She never forgot him, not for her entire life."

"How sad." Timbrel wiped a tear from her eye. "You don't think Nayev is like that, do you? I know he's hiding something, but I just don't know what."

Sarin patted her on the shoulder. "If he likes you, maybe he'll find you again on our journey. If he does, I'd like to meet him."

Krys walked past them to the horses. "Time to go. We're circling off of the road for a while."

### 

*Sweetwater, near Port Kerran*

The road ended at the docks of Sweetwater. Timbrel shaded her eyes and looked eastward across the choppy grey water towards a distant island. According to Krys' map, Lostaria's destination was there, at the Shrine of Ashrah.

"We should check the local inns and taverns," she suggested.

Sarin, still shaking after a small grey dragon flew overhead with an overlarge insect that morning, frowned. "They wouldn't have stayed here, not with the Shrine so close."

"Maybe not, but they still needed to hire a boat and crew to take them across the water."

"And sailors talk," Krys added. "We can check a tavern or two along the way."

They stopped at the first tavern, its door painted with a spilling cup. Timbrel stayed outside with Sarin, wincing at Krys and Jherik's heavy handed style of questioning. She hoped the inn, when they found it, would be friendlier than the last. While Timbrel enjoyed Nayev's company, and the cheese tasted like paradise, she had never been glared at by humans before. Elves, yes, but humans? She always considered humans the more tolerant of the two races.

### 

*Ravali, during Timbrel's childhood*

She would never forget the torments directed at her by the other young elves, or the glares and noses wrinkled in distaste from many of the adults. Only her nurse seemed to actually care for her, and Soliari sent the woman away after the nurse stood up against some maltreatment of the girl. The nurse's final words seared themselves into Timbrel's mind. "Lady Soliari, you only hate your daughter because you hate everything that is not purely elven. Her human blood doesn't taint her. If anything, it improves her."

Years later, when she reached puberty at the unexpectedly early age of twelve, she begged to be sent to her father.

"You don't want me here," she told Soliari. "I remind you of the humans every time you see me. My tutoring is complete, and the tutors are anxious to leave for the same reason. You have completed all the requirements of care; neither of us holds much love for the other."

"You know nothing of the requirements. If you were properly sired, I would present you to Elven Society on your nameday. You are barely half that old, and know *nothing*. I doubt you could survive a day in a human court, much less an hour in the elven court."

"If you send me to the humans, you would be free to return to your beloved elven court." When Soliari did not answer, the girl continued. "If I stay among the humans, you need never trouble yourself explaining me to the elven court."

"And if they reject you?"

"Then I will plant my own trees and grow a house in the human forest."

She arrived at Fafar village a full month later, her hair pinned up in sodden, dust-muddied ringlets. With a glance at the village children--so many children!--she rummaged through the ten packed cases of clothing. After removing the few items that seemed similar to village wear, she tried to send nine cases back with the driver, then gave them away to some of the slightly older girls in the village when he refused to take therm.

Life in the human village suited her. With Summerfest only a few days away, the people welcomed strangers and invited her to help with preparations. She even had time to play with the other children, where she quickly learned the cardinal rule: never show your physical superiority to the humans.

After an easily won foot race, the half-elven girl waited at the finish line. Tall skinny Eric the blacksmith's son came in next, then the others all at once.

Instead of the expected praise, accusations flew.

"No one could run that fast!"

"You musta cheated!"

"You didn't follow the trail!"

"Eric really won." Cheers followed this announcement, and the girl walked slowly away.

Eric caught up to her. "I know *you* really won. I could just barely see you ahead of me."

"Why did thee not tell of it?" She knew her words did not always match those of the village, but they were usually understood.

102

"No one would believe me. You are already strange, with those ears."

Timbrel winced and fingered the tips.

Eric caught her hands. "I like your ears. They make you different and pretty. But don't win any more races. They'll forget soon enough about this one, and things will be better for you."

Eric's words proved true. She became an expert at blending in and helping out.

When her father learned that she helped someone open a lock after they lost the key, he pulled her aside to test her. Determined not to stand out, she only opened the simplest of locks. His attempts to teach her to open other locks, including many that were far easier than those Von used to lock away her jewelry, met with failure. She pretended such difficulty that he gave up after a few weeks.

The iron manacles fascinated her. Designed to keep short-fingered humans immobile, she found that her long, slender fingers could easily reach the lock, and her strong fingernails worked as well as any metal picks to unlock the double-pin mechanism. Before long she could open them with her eyes closed, or behind her back. She continued to practice when no one could see, afraid to be too good at anything.

"These people just won't talk to us." Krys' voice jarred Timbrel from her memories. She eyed the faded mermaids under the lettering on the inn's sign.

### 

*Sweetwater Docks*

The Siren's Call was not the best-kept inn that the group visited. The patrons were men of the sea, seasoned sailors with weathered faces and calloused hands. Some wore bits of finery: a fancy jacket, a double handful of necklaces and rings, a jewel-hilted sword. It seemed they would not turn down a little piracy on the side. Many had tell-tale signs of goblin blood: the wide, square jaw and a bit of webbing between their fingers.

Timbrel leaned over and whispered in Krys' ear. "Just pay for the room tonight."

Krys looked at her, surprised. This was their first evening stop at an inn where the girl did not insist on dancing. More significantly, she used the elven tongue.

After paying for the room, Krys, Jherik, and Sarin wandered the common room, asking questions.

"Have you seen any other elves recently? Any blonde girls with guards? A group of travelers looking for a boat to the island?" They got the same answers here that the men in the taverns supplied: a glower, a shifted glance, a shuffling of feet, before each turned back to their meals in silence.

Timbrel fell back into old habits, however. She flitted between tables like a butterfly, sharing an ale or a piece of cheese at each one.

Jherik finally lost his temper, pinning a human against the wall by his throat and shouting, "Where did she go?" The man's mouth moved, but no sound came out. Krys moved to intercede when the man turned blue.

Prying Jherik's fingers from the man's throat, Krys caught only three words before the man slumped into unconsciousness.

"Ne'er yon market." It made no sense at all.

Krys sent the frustrated warrior out to check on the horses. He tried to rouse the unconscious man, then sat him in a corner. He spent the rest of the evening questioning patrons. Surprisingly, a few men talked to him after Jherik left the room.

He vaguely noted Timbrel climbing the stairs arm and arm with a drunken sailor. Oh well, Krys thought. At least her evening's entertainment seemed reasonably clean and better dressed than most.

The Henin elf's return heralded the return of childlike silence.

*These people aren't ignorant, just uncooperative.* Frustrated again, Krys ascended the stairs to the room he had rented, closely followed by Jherik and Sarin.

Timbrel was not there. Krys and Sarin nodded to each other, but Jherik seemed perturbed. *He spends too much time watching the girl, and not enough on the problem at hand.* "Never yon market. That's the only piece of solid information we have. A few thought Lostaria was moved there."

"Yon market? How does that narrow anything down?" Jherik's frustration sent his voice up the register. "There must be hundreds of market places in the human lands. Telling us to look anywhere but here is not helpful."

Sarin's soft voice was barely audible. "Perhaps we are supposed to look at *this* market? It does indicate never the yon, so this market is the only one that remains."

No one had a better idea, so they agreed to discuss it further in the morning and investigate the local market when it opened for the day.

The sun was rising when Timbrel slipped into the room.

Krys glanced at her, then leaned over and stabbed a long finger at the map. "It has to be the island. The harbormaster said her group bought passage."

"The island? We wouldn't want to go there." Timbrel's voice cut right across Krys'.

"Why not?" asked Jherik. The Henin warrior glowered at the girl as though she'd personally insulted him.

"Well, because of what Reniu said."

"Reni-who?" Jherik stepped forward.

Krys frowned. "What did Reniu say?"

Timbrel frowned a little, thinking hard. When she opened her mouth, her voice took on the accents and tones of the original speaker, presumably Reniu. "A golden treasure like you should stay away from the island, love. The fat man rules there what takes all the golden treasures in the land, and ye'd be lost."

Krys gave the girl a puzzled look. "What does that have to do with Lostaria?"

"With my mother's cousin? Oh, lots. Everyone was talking about her last night."

Krys lifted a silver-white eyebrow. "Everyone? What were they saying?"

Timbrel launched into a rapid-fire mimicry of accents and tones, close enough that Krys could identify the speech of some of the same men he'd tried to question.

"A golden treasure like you should stay away from the island, love. The fat man rules there what takes all the golden treasures in the land, and ye'd be lost."

"No, not lost. Send her north and west by ship, trade the golden treasure for good gold."

"You look just like t'other, sweetie, just like her. Would you be kin? She went with the fat man, he took her right from the island, then stopped at our docks. Fat man's gone 'round the world, you know. 'Round the world." Timbrel circled her arm overhead.

"Prince Ragnar was damn pissed. Sent his people all over the island and the docks. I hid my cargo under the ballast so's they wouldn't find it. Ruined a whole box what wasn't watertight. Next ship over had to dump theirs, didn't want to get caught with no con-tra-band in these waters. Wisht I'da known what they was looking for."

"It wasn't a what, it was a who. I was sitting in the Whalebone's Pisser and they came in and took everyone's hoods off. Uggh. Some of them hooded types shouldn'ta never taken them off. They's like to make people sick through ugly-power, like them goblin-types over there. Don't look, pretty thing."

"Fat man was waiting for her there, sweetie, even 'fore she got here. His people took the other four down, used poison I think 'cause they went down so fast. They knew what they was looking for. Took down her guards and then grabbed her, he did. She didn't get two words out before they stuffed something into her mouth. Took her 'round the world."

Jherik jumped up. "What did they put in her mouth?"

Krys shushed him. "Let her finish"

106

Timbrel frowned for a moment, then continued, each voice a good mimicry of the original speakers.

"Grabbed her and took her, that's right, love. Brought her right across to our docks, almost knocked me over. Big old sack, kicking and wiggling so bad she slipped away from him. Almost got away, too. She wiggled out and you could just see that golden hair like yours shinin' in the moonlight. It was the hair that got her, too. She got too close to a sharknet, got her hair tangled in all those little hooks. Almost like she didn't know they were there, love. 'Fore she could get untangled, they caught her again, dragged her right out to the big ship, love. Didn't even try to hide that hair of hers."

"Never saw a ship put out to sea after dark like that afore. Most dangerous thing, runnin' at night. Gotta know the reefs, gotta hope the monsters ain't hungry, gotta hope you don't drop nothin' overboard because you ain't gonna see it in that dark water, sweetie. Couldn't see where he was a'goin."

"Don't need to see. Everyone knows the fat man runs north and west. He don't wait for no ransom, not even if they's rich and there's people what're looking fer 'em. Goes off and sells 'em for shiny copper. Or more likely good gold."

"Yup, he said sells 'em. There's a whole wide world out there, pretty thing, and lotsa bad men in it. Don't just want a night o' fun, like us. They want to buy their fun and keep it forever. Nope, you don't want to go anywhere near that island, pretty thing, and you don't want anyone to know yer friends are asking about it. Not a healthy thing, that asking. Yer friends need to learn to keep their pointy ears open and their big mouths shut."

Timbrel stopped suddenly, grabbed a waterskin from her pack, and took a long drink.

Jherik's jaw sagged as he blinked rapidly. Krys felt dumbfounded, too.

"Timbrel?" Krys reached out and touched the girl's arm. "When did you learn all this?"

"Last night when I was having a few drinks. Why? I thought you already knew all this stuff." She took a second drink from her waterskin and wiped her mouth on the back of her hand. "Are we ready to go?"

Krys and Jherik exchanged glances. "We did know some of it," explained Krys, unwilling to let the girl know how little they had uncovered. "It's just...well...you learned the same information so much faster."

"Did I? I was just talking to people. Well, mostly listening. I just remember what they said. It makes more sense when you switch it around and say it all together like that, doesn't it?" The girl seemed pleased with her discovery.

Krys was stunned. In just a few hours, Timbrel had gathered more information than the other three combined, and somehow sensed the order in which the quotes gave the most information. Krys stood and faced Timbrel, then bowed deeply. "Lady, I have underestimated you."

###

# Chapter Five

*Kadeesh's Compound*

The light-haired elf rolled over, rubbing her manacles as she lay in dirty straw. The close-set bars of her cage could not be squeezed between, though Kadeesh had watched her try the day before.

The elf staggered to her feet. "Where are the others?" She waved at the two empty cages set near her own in the fenced yard of the compound.

The fence kept out prying eyes. Kadeesh only let buyers and his employees inside the gate.

"Others? You are mistaken." He enjoyed the look of confusion on her face. She wore the square of cloth he allowed her for a garment knotted over her shoulder and left the birthmark on the other open to view. He circled the elf's cage until he had a good view of the gap in the cloth, admiring her slender figure. As he began to react, she turned to face him.

She waved her hand at the two empty cages. "What happened to the other two captives?" She had an imperious note in her voice that he didn't like.

"Captives? There are no captives, only slaves like you."

A scuffling noise outside the yard muffled any protest she might have made. One of his guards dragged a bruised and battered woman through the gate. Pale skin showed between the bruises. Kadeesh unlocked an empty cage long enough for the guard to toss the woman within. The woman crawled to the far corner of her cage, whimpering and pressing her knees together. Blood soaked the straw beneath her.

"Can't bring t'other one back. Stupid cow got the soldiers angry, wouldna do what they wanted. Well, they did it anyway, after they slit her throat. Sell'er for monster food?"

"Yeah, sell her for monster food. Rockhold is always buying, trying to keep that dragon fed so he doesn't attack the city.

And make the soldiers pay a fair price for her. They broke her, they bought her. In fact, charge them for the disposal, too. Just don't tell them where. It'll be a nice bit of extra profit, and a bonus to your pay." Kadeesh turned back to watch the elf, enjoying her horrified expression.

The injured woman muttered to herself, the whites of her eyes showing all around the iris while she rocked herself. Kadeesh nodded. He hoped she would subside into a quiet madness, tractable and subservient. Maybe an extra beating or two before feeding time. Maybe not. He'd have to see how she developed.

"You don't know who I am." The elf used that same imperious tone, accompanied with an unladylike glare. "I'm worth more to you as a hostage than as a slave."

"I know exactly what you're worth as a hostage. I've already received my first and second payments. After the third one. . . well, I already have a buyer interested in you. He's just fascinated with elves, the paler the better. Later in the year I'll keep you indoors, let you lose the little color you have. He'll like that."

"You can't sell me. My people will find me. They'll send out a rescue party."

Kadeesh leaned back against the fence, his ample belly shaking with laughter. Stopping to scratch himself, he laughed again at the thought of the rescue party. He had received his bonus pay not two days before, along with details about the four misfits sent to rescue his captive: A tall elven scholar, an old elf - that would be a sight - a halfblood girl, and a dandy so full of himself that he tried to bring a servant along. Some rescue party. Easy to spot. Not too many elves walking around this far north.

I'd better send a message, thought Kadeesh. Let my confederates in Sweetwater know who to watch for. Just in case they make it that far.

###

110

*Sweetwater Docks*

Krys came back to the room at the Siren's Call, his cloak white-spotted and stiffening with salt. "I've managed to arrange passage on a ship."

Timbrel looked alarmed. "You didn't tell them I would be there, did you? They believe women are bad luck on ships."

"Ah, no wonder most of them warned me of the current storm season even though there is not a cloud in the sky. In any case, passage is arranged for the four of us, as well as for the horses. We leave in the early afternoon."

Timbrel spent the rest of the morning with the horses, repacking the loads and wrapping portions in oilskin against the sea spray. The skies filled with grey clouds, completely hiding the sun.

Shortly after midday, Krys suggested they board the ship early. They collected the horses, tying them together with a long lead line. The horses, usually easy to lead, grew balky as they walked down the docks. The smell of tarred ropes warred with the salt tang in the air, almost but not quite obscuring the scent of blood.

The girl looked around in alarm. Reddish-brown clots of blood hung between the stained, half-scrubbed boards of the dock, making a trail to the water's edge. The boards closest to the water were slimed with moisture. Timbrel glanced into the dark water and moved a little faster.

The ship stood by itself, tied to the end of the dock. A weather-beaten hulk with patched sails, its figurehead seemed to be a carving of a woman, but the chipped and peeling paint obscured any details. Timbrel managed to make out the faded words "Lady Elizabeth" painted on the transom. A short, stocky boy pushed a mop around the deck and grinned at them with a wide goblin face. A large wooden cage stood on deck, tied down near the cargo hatch. On the opposite end of the ship, a small upper deck with an even smaller cabin helped support the single mast. The space between the two decks remained open to the air on one side. Hammocks and netted sea chests swung from the rafters.

A heavily bearded man climbed down from the cabin and headed for the group. "Well, hurry it up. Beasts go in the cage, and ye bed down near the beasts. Stay out of the way of my crew and we'll get along just fine." They led the horses up the gangplank one at a time, settling them inside the cage. Coils of rope, barrels, and crates covered the entire deck.

"Are you still loading?" Jherik asked. Timbrel looked at the locked cargo hatch, then at the Henin warrior with disgust.

"Everything's stowed. She's full up to the brim and ready for a run up to Rockhold. Last run of the season. Storms been bad this year. I know a lot of ships haven't made the run at all. Those Northers always need food and supplies to get them through the winter. They should be happy to see us."

"And the storms?" Krys commented dryly. "I thought the journey would last two weeks."

"Me father had the weathersense, and his father before him. It runs in the Overton line, you see."

"Very well, Captain Overton, we'll trust your heritage and settle in." Krys seemed perfectly content.

Timbrel, on the other hand, paced. She'd been careful to remain silent in her voluminous cloak, wearing trousers instead of a skirt to further disguise her sex. Captain Overton's father and grandfather might have possessed the weathersense, but the Captain never claimed it for himself. As they cast off and headed out to sea, Timbrel became more certain than ever that the Captain was not telling them everything.

Dark wavelets smacked against the ship, and the breeze changed direction every few minutes. As far as Timbrel could tell, it blew most often straight from the north, making their progress difficult. The overloaded ship wallowed in the waves; water swept across the deck regularly. Krys moved their packs to the top of the cargo hatch, the driest spot on the lower deck. The horses whinnied when the water touched their hooves, occasionally stamping their displeasure.

In spite of the adverse conditions, the *Lady Elizabeth* seemed to be making steady progress. The leaden clouds broke apart to reveal patchy sunlight. Timbrel walked to the front of the ship, dodging the sailors that ran back and forth to adjust the large triangular sail. The breeze filled her hood, trying to blow it back. She caught it in time, still worried about the sailors' reaction to a woman.

Krys, Jherik, and Sarin sat on the hatch cover, busy planning their next step. Timbrel would ask Krys about their decisions later. She needed to know what she should listen for when they reached dry land again.

Suddenly nauseous, Timbrel clutched the ship's railing. The wind changed direction, freshened, and the *Lady Elizabeth* leapt forward, slicing through the waves. Timbrel was furious. She stalked over to the cargo hatch and swung her hand at Krys.

"How dare you!" she began, then squawked as Jherik caught her arm before the intended slap could land on Krys' cheek. Krys looked up at her, confused. Timbrel jerked her arm free from Jherik and ran for the rail as her belly convulsed. She could hear Jherik's laughter behind her as he poked fun at Krys.

"She blames you for her seasickness? What does she think you are?"

Krys' mumbled answer was lost as Timbrel threw up again. The ship moved faster than ever. She wove her way back to the cargo hatch, quieter this time.

"Seasick, Lady Timbrel?" Jherik said with a chuckle.

"Magic-sick, I think." She glared at Krys.

Krys spread his hands in front of him. "It's not me."

The knot in Timbrel's belly tightened, and she wobbled as she grew paler. Suddenly concerned, Jherik sketched a quick spell in the air. Immediately the pain and nausea eased and the girl sank down with a grateful sigh.

Krys raised an eyebrow. "Magic it is, then." The wizard scanned the deck of the ship, looking for the source of the spell. At last his eyes focused on the Captain's small cabin. "I'll return in a few minutes. I think I need a word with the Captain." He stood in

113

one smooth motion, crisply clean historian's robes swirling around his ankles.

Timbrel watched his progress as he climbed the ladder to the upper deck and knocked on the Captain's door. The wind immediately died down and Timbrel felt all traces of the nausea vanish. The Captain's door opened and Krys went in as the grinning goblin boy came out and took up his mop. A few minutes later, Krys exited the cabin. He stopped long enough to send the mopping boy scurrying back to the Captain. By the time Krys reached the cargo hatch, the ship was increasing in speed again and Timbrel could feel edges of the nausea beneath Jherik's protective spell.

The wizard sat down on the cargo hatch, shaking his head. Try as she might, Timbrel could not get him to say a word.

### 

The journey took ten days, most of which Timbrel spent at the rail. In spite of Jherik's protections, the nausea grew stronger each day as if the magic behind it gained in strength. At night, the magic eased and the ship rocked in the normal winds and breezes, and dealt with the nightly flying fish invasion. More than once Timbrel woke to find herself sharing the bed roll with flying fish, and the goblin boy sleeping curled at her back. Those were particularly bad days for her stomach.

They spent the last day of the journey battling uncooperative winds again. The sailors not involved with the actual sails scrubbed and mopped the ship, readying it for visitors. Timbrel stood by the railing, watching the water roil and surge as if large creatures moved beneath the waves. Patches of seaweed appeared, floating on the surface like tangles of leafy ropes. The girl noticed one patch that seemed to be staying ahead of the ship. Disturbed, she walked along the railing toward the back, only to find that the patch moved with her. After it followed her to the front again, she fled to the safety of the cargo hatch, huddling between Jherik, Krys, and Sarin. She avoided the railing until they docked and, while disembarking, glanced at the water to be certain the seaweed patch was gone before stepping on the gangplank.

Captain Overton timed his entry to Rockhold's natural harbor well. A three-quarters full tide lifted the *Lady Elizabeth* and slid her smoothly next to the floating wooden dock at the base of a tall cliff. The horses scrambled off the gangplank, Jherik's mount jumping from the top of the narrow plank to the middle of the first wide section of rafted dock. The horses eagerly transversed the dozen floating docks, scampered up the wide ramp to the more permanent stone dock, and tried to enter the warehouse-style cave where sailors stacked supplies. Another crew piled select crates onto flat wagons and pulled them into a second cave. Ropes dropped from above and hooked onto the wagon corners. The horse was unhitched and removed. At a signal, a work crew above smoothly pulled the wagonload of supplies into the air, bringing it back to a second opening in the rock where another horse presumably waited.

At the far end of the stone dock, workers placed small loads on mules, then led them on a switch-backed trail up the imposing cliff. Timbrel counted eight separate turns in the path before she lost sight of them. She sighed when Krys signaled her to use the trail.

Closer, the trail did not seem quite so bad. Each turn of the switchback had a level area suitable for resting, and two of the rest areas funneled natural springs into wooden horse troughs. In spite of the design, the group was exhausted when they reached the opening through the cliff wall.

The large opening quickly narrowed, forcing the group to move the horses in single file. The cave suddenly opened out into a large flat area, where several guards met the group. "Welcome to Rockhold."

The opposite side of the cave opened to the air. Timbrel looked down and saw a steep walled circular valley, becoming bowl-shaped at the bottom. Terraced fields lined the sides of the bowl, and stone houses clustered together in the center. Caves pocked the inner walls of the valley, many with cloths hung across the entrances. Small streams trickled down from springs throughout the valley, meeting together into a river that vanished at the base of the cliffs on the southern side. A circular road ran around the central settlement, with smaller roads branching off in various directions. Two cobblestone roads lead to openings in the southern cliff, while another two connected with the sea cliff entrances. From this side, Timbrel could see that both men and horses accomplished the lifting of the wagons, using winches similar to those that the sailors used on the Lady Elizabeth.

As she led her horse down the road, Timbrel could see two fortresses, almost palace-sized, built into the upper slopes of the valley. One overlooked the sea almost directly over the docks, but the road winding up to it was covered with scattered brush growing between the cobblestones. The second palace perched on the opposite rim of the valley, centered between the two roads to the interior. Bright pennons of cloth snapped in the wind from clustered flagpoles.

Wide swaths of cloth suddenly unrolled beneath each window of the palace, striping the grey stone with bright green. The new color provoked a flurry of activity below. The roads emptied and Timbrel saw a few men run to concealed stone shelters built along each road. Frowning, she turned to ask Krys.

The road behind them was clear, the bustle of mule-drivers silenced. A single green stripe of cloth hung down from the cave at the top of the trail. If she didn't know better, Timbrel thought, she could easily imagine their small traveling party as the only inhabitants in the entire valley.

Sarin looked up and fell off of his horse, scrabbling at the stones beside the trail. His horse reared and then galloped down the trail at top speed, ears flat to its head. Krys grabbed the reins of the other horses, murmuring a spell to keep them calm. Timbrel glared at him, tired of feeling nauseous. She looked back at Sarin's horse and winced as the beast turned too quickly and skidded on gravel.

The horse screamed as huge bone claws snatched it up from above. Timbrel's heart jumped into her throat as her eyes traveled upward. Four claws, each as long as the horse was tall, attached to

116

a pale greenish-white foot at the end of an immense leg. As the dragon flew further off, she saw that its color deepened to dark green on top, almost the color of the sea. The wings of the green dragon beat more quickly than those of the mating gold dragons, and when the creature banked for a smooth turn she understood why. The smaller wings of the dragon were cupped slightly, reminding Timbrel of the wing-fins on the flying fish that had sacrificed themselves daily on the deck of the *Lady Elizabeth*. The dragon struggled as it climbed, finally catching the breeze from the valley to lift it up over the cliffs. The breeze that followed the dragon brought a mix of fishy scents and a sharp odor that made Timbrel's eyes burn and her nose itch. The half-elf sneezed twice and rubbed her nose, then spun to join the others in scanning the skies directly above.

They looked around for cover. A single white stripe unrolled in the midst of the green hanging from the newer palace. As if on cue, people reappeared on the road below. The green stripes slowly disappeared back into their original windows. Timbrel found Sarin hiding beneath the edge of a raised wooden sidewalk. She helped him up, prying his bloody hands loose from the cobblestones.

"My maps," he moaned. "It took my maps."

"Nice of them to warn us," Krys commented dryly.

### 

*Sweetwater Docks*

Nayev landed after dark, before the moon rose. Not that it would have given much light--the storm clouds covered everything in the sky. The inns and taverns overflowed with sailors, their ships anchored out in the harbor, and their long boats piled and tied to the horse posts on the lee side of the inns.

Nayev stopped at the first tavern. "I'm looking for a girl."

The bartender smiled. "I can certainly help you with that. What sort of girl?"

"Hair like mine, and very friendly." Nayev nodded to himself.

"I know exactly who you mean. Come with me." The bartender signaled another man, then led Nayev into the back and up a set of stairs. They stopped at the second door on the left in the upper hallway.

The bartender knocked twice, then opened the door. "My friend, I'd like you to meet Salana."

Inside, a girl with straw-blonde hair beckoned. "I'll take care of you," she said in a deep, whispery voice.

Nayev backed away. "That's not the girl I am looking for."

The bartender nodded. "It will cost you more for a specific girl."

"Cost? She never mentioned a cost when I met her before." Curious now, Nayev listened to the man's mind. The mind-voice was so weak he could barely hear the thoughts.

*If I ask him enough times, he will try one of our girls.*

Nayev turned and left without a word.

He tried the Inn next. Again he questioned the bartender. "There's a girl I'm looking for, part elven. She travels with several men."

"A girl like that passed through about a week ago. They took the last ship north before the storm hit. By now they're on the way to Rockhold, or at the bottom of the sea."

*Bottom of the sea!* Nayev set off for Rockhold, hoping to find Timbrel there in one piece.

### 

Rockhold's marketplace, a huge round cave filled with individual cloth stalls, was surprisingly large. Almost the entire crew of the *Lady Elizabeth* strolled around, sampling local delicacies and looking at the displays. Timbrel bought some dried mushrooms to add to her medicines, then moved on to look at the jewelry.

Crystals and polished gemstones sparkled everywhere. Jewelers hand-forged chains and settings of gold and silver, and

Timbrel found a matching trio of stones for considerably less than she expected. The most surprising thing, however, was their size. Fist-sized clear crystals that appeared perfect or only slightly flawed to her eye lay next to a ruby the size of a large walnut.

Timbrel remembered watching the blacksmith in her father's village work with gemstones. She would watch for hours as he removed large gemstones from their settings, carefully cut them into smaller matching stones, and placed them in different settings, saving the leftover gold to be melted down and reshaped later. At the time, Timbrel had been uncertain as to the stones' origins, either a trade from merchants who recently passed through the village, or a purchase made during one of her father's trips that always followed such visits.

Of course, she had another reason to visit the blacksmith. Eric. He would always stop his own work to talk to her, or sometimes beckon her closer. On one trip, he surprised her with her own long leather apron and gloves and allowed her to hold a piece of iron for him. They met regularly, Timbrel helping Eric and then the two of them running off to the fields.

Eric encouraged her to run whenever they could find time together. The only one who remembered her speed after the first few months of pretending, the blacksmith's son sought to keep up with the half-elf's stride, increasing his own speed in the process. Long after Eric lay exhausted in the sweet-smelling grasses, Timbrel would continue running, stretching her legs and pumping her arms as she raced the wind. When she finally tired, the blacksmith's son would make a place for her to lie next to him and they would talk. It was possible that Eric knew everything about the elves that Timbrel did. Or he would have, if the village hadn't been attacked.

Timbrel shook her head, driving away the thoughts of the attack that destroyed her life. The ruby merchant looked at her strangely. "Is there a problem with the stone?"

The girl looked up, startled. "No, no problem," she assured him. "The color of the stone brought back memories, that's all."

"It is a particularly rich red, very unusual even for our mines."

"Almost like clotting blood." Timbrel shoved the stone's tray back and staggered away. Suddenly tired of shopping, she returned to the Crystal Inn.

Krys stalked back and forth by one of the rearmost tables, his arms sweeping in grand gestures as he spoke with a table full of men. Whatever his point, they did not agree with a tall elf. Timbrel could read their hostility from across the room. The man closest to Krys, a warrior by his uniform, leaned back in the chair with his arms tightly crossed. The next man at the table appeared to be an older sailor, scowling openly. The third man, his back to Timbrel, hunched his shoulders.

The girl looked around the room. Neither Jherik nor Sarin were present. Near the opposite wall, a young officer sat alone at a table. Timbrel bought herself an ale and went to join him.

In his mid-twenties, with the thick brown hair and bushy eyebrows common to the men of Rockhold and a neatly mended uniform tunic, he stood out. Timbrel noticed how his biceps strained against the fabric. His square-jawed face was unlined, different from most soldiers she'd met. A very attractive man.

The officer was attracted as well, his brown eyes dilating when Timbrel seated herself. He half rose out of his chair. "Captain Harnek, my lady. And you are. . .?"

Timbrel let the question hang in the air for a moment. She liked this captain. He continued to look her in the eye, unlike most men. "I am Timbrel."

It took Timbrel only a few minutes to learn why the captain seemed so calm. Rockhold had not been attacked since the Mage Wars, being too far off the beaten track and inhospitable for most armies to bother with.

"Our biggest problem," Harnek explained, "is the dragon that moved into the old palace a few hundred years ago. It takes a sheep or a mule once in a while, but usually feeds from the ocean."

"Hasn't anyone tried to kill it?"

120

"We've had our share of monster-hunters. For the most part the dragon just picks them off and eats them. We try not to encourage that, though. The dragon might develop a taste for people."

"Don't you have any kind of defense plan? What if there is another war?"

"Warriors won't come here, we're not worth the effort. We pull up the supply elevator, station a few archers on the seawall to pick off anyone using the trail, and wait for a storm to pound on them. Nothing to it."

The officer's attitude horrified Timbrel. "Don't you train your troops?"

"Of course. Every week they report for an hour of marching and weapons practice. We're practicing this afternoon if you'd like to watch. I'm sure the men will appreciate an audience with the Baron away." Harnek nodded to himself and stood, his lunch finished. "We'll expect you in an hour, lady. I'll see you at the city square."

Harnek strode out the door just as the men near Krys raised their voices. No one drew weapons, so Timbrel scurried up the stairs to find Jherik. It would be interesting to get the warrior's appraisal of the city's readiness.

### 

Jherik was jogging along the southern road when Timbrel caught up to him. The girl started babbling immediately. Only when he heard the words 'local weapons practice' did he start to listen.

"Weapons practice, you say?" The Henin warrior flexed his shoulders; partly to stretch them and partly to see what effect the move would have on Timbrel. The girl confused him terribly. She seemed attracted to every warrior they met, yet would not give him a second glance. The women in Henin constantly wooed him, trying to convince him to dissolve his betrothal with Kareni and indulge his freedom of choice. The half-elven girl, while clearly the sexiest creature he had ever encountered, treated him like a younger brother. She did not even seem conscious of her effect on him.

"They should be starting any minute. Come on!" Timbrel wrapped her fingers around his wrist with the surprisingly strong grip she had used during the Henin court presentation. Knowing it would do no good to pull away–she was amazingly tenacious–the Henin warrior allowed her to tow him to the city square.

An actual square area of greenery surrounded by artistically carved stone benches, the practice field sat open to the sky. Jherik scanned for magic. With the exception of weak glows from two or three weapons, he detected nothing at all. With no protective nets across the sky and the surrounding rock walls, the elf felt oddly exposed, particularly knowing that a green dragon lived on the lip of the valley.

The local militia marched in, accompanied by a small drum and a set of pipes. Three-dozen soldiers followed their five officers, only two of whom appeared efficient at command. The group turned and saluted, ragged in their timing. Jherik saw Timbrel wince from the corner of his eye.

The Captain put the group through its paces. Jherik snorted. Any group of teenaged elven girls with a half hour's training could do as well. While each soldier carried his weapons easily enough, they had absolutely no unity on the field. The musicians laid aside their instruments before practicing. Jherik frowned. Didn't these humans understand the use of music on the battlefield?

Jherik made up his mind and walked out onto the practice field to confront the Captain. As he pushed through the center of the group, the soldiers stopped their practice and milled about in disarray. Jherik noticed a few new onlookers seating themselves on the benches.

"I challenge you and your unit to a practice bout." Jherik's spoke with an intentionally loud voice. He wanted Timbrel to hear him.

The Captain stepped forward. "Certainly. We'll alternate choosing warriors for our sides. You may choose first."

122

Jherik dipped his head and drew a deep breath. "You miss my point, Captain. I have challenged your entire group."

The Captain looked horrified. Jherik glanced at the sidelines where Timbrel watched, fascinated. "I will start by the benches at that end. You and your group must prevent me from reaching the benches at the opposite end. Fair enough?"

"But that would be uneven and unfair."

"Don't worry about it. Just give the signal." Jherik took his starting position. At the Captain's signal, he ran directly at the first soldier. The man retreated a half step and Jherik rushed by. A minute and a half and three individual fights later, the Henin elf reached his goal.

A wail of protest rose up from the soldiers. "He didn't stop to fight with me."

"He just pushed past me."

"Running around isn't fighting."

Only three of the soldiers remained quiet, two because they were unconscious from Jherik's blows. The third soldier, bruised and bloody, joined Jherik and the Captain.

"Nice fight," offered the battered soldier. The words sounded a little strange and Jherik realized the soldiers jaw was broken. With a wave, the Henin elf called Timbrel over to treat the soldier. She led the man off to the side, opening the small bag of medicines she carried with her constantly.

With Timbrel otherwise occupied, Jherik scolded the Captain for his unit's lack of tactics. Frustrated, the elf outlined some basic tactics for delaying an enemy. The injured soldier rejoined them during Jherik's impromptu lecture.

Jherik took the field a second time. This time, two others joined the second soldier he faced, the three protecting each other while also forcing Jherik to protect himself. They successfully landed two blows on the elf's arm before he beat them away. Jherik continued up the field with one hand tucked into his belt, simulating the crippling of his arm from the two strikes. Ten yards before his goal, three more soldiers formed a group, delaying him long enough for a fourth to attack from behind. Jherik wheeled and struck with such speed that the trailing soldier did not have time to guard himself. A second wheeling strike took out two more. The final soldier stood his ground, delaying Jherik almost long enough. Almost. Jherik disarmed the man, swept inside, and leapt to the top of the bench just as the next group of warriors reached him. It had taken the warrior almost five minutes to traverse the field.

Untucking his hand, the elf stretched leisurely. Timbrel responded to a wave from the captain and ran about the field, treating small cuts and checking for broken bones. The only major injury was a broken shoulder on the soldier that attacked Jherik from behind.

The man laughed at Jherik's apology. "Next time I'll remember you can see behind you. Won't catch me by surprise, then."

Jherik congratulated the man on his attitude, remembering at the last minute not to clap him on the shoulder. The third bout took Jherik a full ten minutes to traverse the field.

"Now that we have this unit warmed up," the elf observed, "I'm ready to take on the next one." He was dumbfounded to learn that the entire Rockhold militia consisted of a single unit.

###

Two days after Captain Overton departed for the South, the sun rose against a bloody sky. The clouds darkened and mounded up as the wind picked up. Swirls of gravel and leaves skittered across the ground. The crash of the waves into the cliffs protecting the city sent plumes of spray high enough to blow through the upper cave entrances. The trickling springs became raging rivers as rainwater sheeted off the heights and flooded the lower end of the valley.

The wind turned cold, and swirls of snow and sleet mixed with the driving rain. The few travelers at the Crystal Inn huddled around the central hearth. The dampness increased the chill of the stone. Timbrel found herself wishing for the warmth of wooden walls and the gleam of sunlight. Ravali storms quickly blew over, the trees sucking up excess moisture as the sun reappeared.

Rockhold storms, on the other hand, lasted for days. The sky remained leaden gray and showed no sign that the sun would ever rise again. The innkeeper lit torches and hung crystal screens that scattered the light around the room.

Timbrel shivered again, feeling the chill settle inside her mind. Dark days like this brought back dark memories. Like the storm after the final Summerfest in Fafar.

### 

*Summerfest, ten years before*
*Fafar*

That day had dawned brightly. Timbrel ran about doubly excited. Not only was Summerfest her favorite holiday, but this year Eric came home. Five years before, just as Timbrel turned sixteen, Eric confided in her that he was chosen for warrior training by the Rangers of Garent Forest. The two teens, blacksmith's son and merchant's daughter, spent the night together in the edge of Fafar's forest, exploring their bodies and sharing newfound pleasures. When Eric left for his training the next morning, he left as a man complete. They planned to marry on his return.

The usual crowds arrived the morning of this special Summerfest. Timbrel's father rushed about welcoming everyone. Decorated tables lined the pasture. The crowd cheered Eric as a local hero. Wine and ale ran freely between the holiday and the upcoming wedding. Timbrel couldn't wait for the moon to rise. They would be released then to begin their lives together.

In their minds, they had been married for five years, but the vows would make it official. Eric towered over everyone in the village as he ran in and swept Timbrel up in arms twice the size of his father's brawny thighs. The descendent of a line of towering blacksmiths, Eric's warrior training increased his chest and biceps until he looked like there might be giant's blood in his ancestry.

Awe-stricken, Timbrel could barely whisper her vows during the sun's midday height.

Per custom, friends separated the two young people, not to be reunited until the sun dipped below the horizon and the moon rose in all of its pale glory. Twice the girl tried to sneak away and find Eric early, but her friends knew all the same tricks and urges.

Actually, they had not known, thought Timbrel. The old priestess-healer of Fafar had asked Timbrel and Eric if they would consent to a few drops of *likshas*, a powerful aphrodisiac, in the marriage wine since Timbrel's elven blood would nullify much of the alcohol. They agreed. When the time came to drink the marriage cup, it smelled of licorice and tasted terrible, but they both drank it down.

The partial dose affected Timbrel so much that she began to unconsciously seduce those around her. More than one of the girls reached out to touch the half-elf before stopping, their arms awkwardly hanging in the air. For her part, Timbrel barely noticed. Instead, she struggled against her friends, trying to run and find Eric. The feeling of the other girls' restraining hands only inflamed Timbrel's desire for the blacksmith's son.

It didn't help that she could hear Eric's struggles in the distance, his friends actively ganging up on the young warrior to restrain him. More than one of the young men crashed into the brush as Eric sought to escape them. The sun sank behind a bank of grey clouds as she anxiously awaited moonrise.

Arrows hissed from the edge of the woods, falling around Timbrel and her friends in a deadly rain. Timbrel, her drugged mind focused on Eric, only vaguely remembered flowers of red blooming on the chests and abdomens of those around her. The girl shook herself free of restraining hands and ran through the woods in search of her husband.

It seemed she searched for hours, though the moon had not yet risen. She returned to the Inn's pasture, hoping to find Eric at the tables. As the silver disk of the moon finally slid above the clouds, its pale light illuminated a nightmare landscape. Tables and benches lay overturned. Wine still dripped from open casks, pooling beneath the bodies of those who had been drinking. Red wine, red blood. The silver light made the wine-blood glow red

126

with life, fading as a cloud partially obscured the moon. Timbrel was on her knees, unable to stand, crawling between the bodies, looking at each face, searching for Eric, wanting to find him, not-wanting to find him.

She crawled to a tree trunk and pulled herself up, the rough bark of the tree making her drug-heightened senses scream with desire. She staggered across the grass as she saw movement ahead. "Eric!"

The man turned, a stranger, not Eric. Timbrel screamed with frustration, her drug-clouded mind still unable to fully grasp the situation around her. The stranger grabbed her, and threw her to another. "Keep this one," she remembered hearing. "We'll have some fun later."

Timbrel screamed again, thrashing against her unknown assailant.

A bellowing roar came from the edge of the forest. She ceased her struggles. The clouds parted to reveal Eric charging forward in the moonlight like a bull, every muscle quivering with tension. His clothes had been lost at some point, and Timbrel could see dozens of old scars, new bruises, and fresh scratches on his magnificent body. The young warrior snagged an overturned bench by one leg and swung it up, wielding it like a club against the swarming strangers. The rapid pops of shattered ribs, the sharp crack of a broken thigh, the hollow-melon sound of a shattered skull, all of these sounds Timbrel's drug-clouded mind muted. All she saw was the magnificence of her chosen man.

Magnificence that suddenly sprouted a flower of blood, followed by a second and a third. The whistling hiss of arrows worked its way through her ears, the thud of the hits, the grinding noises from Eric's teeth as he continued to charge forward, directly into the hail of arrows. Eric fell like a slaughtered bull, his outstretched fingers almost touching Timbrel's own. He shuddered once and lay still. The moonlight vanished as the clouds closed in.

Shock took over. Timbrel's mind shut down as the invaders passed her from one to the next, her body traitorously reacting to them from the drug's effects. Her hearing left slowly, the attackers' grunts and groans as they violated her burning into her consciousness. She passed into merciful blackness as she heard the last. "Six of us and she's still going strong. This one's a keeper."

Grey clouds rolled overhead and thunder rumbled in the distance when Timbrel woke the morning after her wedding. Her head throbbed, her belly and legs ached, and her hands were tied behind her back with a fiber rope. A rope looped around her ankle as well, tied to a stake in the floor. Her mind worked slowly, as if filtered through piles of milkweed fiber. Try as she might, her memories of the night before escaped her.

The blonde stranger, one of many visiting for Summerfest, walked into what Timbrel now knew for a striped tent. He looked directly at her.

"Ah, I see my newest pleasure slave is awake. With a little training , you'll sell for a handful of gold gryphons. More, if I take you to Nerryon."

Anger bubbled up from deep in her belly."I'm no slave. Captive, but not a slave."

The stranger lashed out a hand and Timbrel's head rocked from the stinging slap on her face. "Do not speak unless spoken to." When the girl did not reply, her captor continued. "I hold your life in my hands. You live only so long as it pleases me to keep you alive. You will be fed only when I am pleased with your performance. You are one of the lucky ones to be chosen."

Timbrel narrowed her eyes. Her captor jerked her across the tent floor by her ankle rope, then dropped his trousers.

Pain pulsed through the girl, surprising her into a cry. Encouraged, her captor pounded into her. Timbrel clamped her jaws shut against threatening nausea and wondered how badly she was injured. She never felt this kind of pain with Eric. Eric. Memory suddenly flooded back.

Eric exchanging vows with her. Eric sharing the wedding cup with her. Eric waiting just as impatiently for moonrise. Moonlit Eric with arrows sprouting from his chest, blood-flowers blooming. Eric falling in front of her. Laughter from the strangers.

128

Laughter from *this* stranger. Thunder rolled, echoing Timbrel's growing fury.

As the stranger gave a long groan and rolled away from her, Timbrel swore to get revenge for Eric's death. Her eyes swept the tent for weapons, but found nothing. She could play along. She could wait for the right opportunity.

Later, dragged from the tent, Timbrel nearly lost her resolve. Bodies lay everywhere in the mud, flies already swarming around the mouths and eyes. The half-elven girl saw her father's body among the others. His short sword lay to one side, strong hand still attached. The blade was crusted with dark blood and flecks of grayish flesh. Two bodies lay near him, neither of which Timbrel recognized. On the other side, her father's body and arm bore defensive marks, as though he tried to shield himself even after the blow that disarmed him.

Her captor dragged her along to the end of the lane, tied her ankle rope to a tree, and pushed her down to the ground. Five other women including Katrina were tied in similar fashion. Timbrel saw bruises on the others and blood crusted one woman's legs. Her anger rose again, barely contained. A moment later she heard the sobbing.

Two more of the strangers herded a dozen dirty children into the lane. Timbrel recognized them all.

One little girl clutched at the leg of the closest captor, crying for her mother. The man looked down with a sneer and beat the child away. At her second attempt to cling, the stranger swung his fist into the side of the child's head. Timbrel heard a loud *crack* and the child fell away, her head lolling at an unnatural angle. The other children screamed in terror.

Timbrel and Katrina screamed out in unison. "Run!" Two of the children broke away from the group and disappeared behind the nearby houses. Their captors gathered the other children and roped them together by their necks. The blonde man slapped Timbrel again, bringing blood to her mouth when her teeth cut her lip. Katrina's mouth was bloody as well.

Katrina stood, smoothly rising to her feet from her back in a difficult dance move. As though she heard slow drumbeats, she rolled her hips and walked up to the stranger who hit her. The dark-haired dancer leaned into the man, whispering in his ear. Timbrel watched the stranger's body language change, becoming less wary. The dancer nudged against him.

"You whore!" One of the other women managed to prop herself on one side. "Your man isn't even dead a full day yet and you're welcoming his murderer into your bed."

"If he wasn't strong enough to protect me, then I'll stay with one who is," Katrina purred. Timbrel noticed that the comment was directed more toward the man Katrina rubbed against, who relaxed into the dancer.

Katrina turned her back on the man, pressing against him and dropping to her knees at the same time. The man's knife suddenly dropped to the ground by his feet as Katrina fumbled and lost her grip on it. Timbrel's captor started to turn.

Timbrel pulled her knees beneath her and flexed, the bruised muscles in her abdomen and thighs protesting. She rose to her feet in the same way as Katrina, if a little less smoothly. The movement loosened the last few pieces of the half-elf's wedding dress. All three of the strangers stared as the shreds of Timbrel's tattered dress slithered to the ground like reluctant snakes, leaving the girl completely nude. She stood proudly, posing with her torso half-turned, as though she were ready to run on a moment's notice. The eyes of the two men she could see widened with pleasure. Neither paid attention to Katrina. Timbrel gave a little kick with her free foot that scattered the shreds of her dress, as well as allowing her to transition to a second dance pose.

"Whore and the get of a whore," muttered the same woman as before. Timbrel ignored the comment and glanced over her shoulder, catching the eyes of the last of the strangers. She gave a little smile. The man smiled back and stepped forward, only to be stopped by Timbrel's original captor.

"This one's mine. Pick another." The other man stood uncertainly for a moment, then backed down. "Have some quick fun with them now, we're moving out by sunset."

Katrina gave a long sigh and stepped away from her captor. Timbrel could see the weight of the blade as it pulled down the dark-haired dancer's wide skirt hem, but Katrina continued to roll her hips while walking. Timbrel did the same, in part to distract the men from focusing too closely on Katrina. The other women shunned both dancers when their captors herded them together down the street, leashed by their ankles.

They locked the women into separate rooms of the inn, the men visiting them in turns. Katrina had a bit more freedom, bringing a meal in to Timbrel's captor. As he began to eat, Katrina slipped a kitchen knife under the edge of the floor mat. "The others already have theirs," she whispered. Timbrel could hear the shrieks of the other women, and the sounds of the following beatings. When Timbrel's turn came, her original captor was rougher with her than before. She tried to remember the tricks that Katrina had taught her, tricks to bring a man to the height of his pleasure. Unfortunately, the half-elven girl had never tried them before, intending to save them for her wedding night. Her captor forgave her, however, praising her for her attempts to learn and feeding her generously from his heaping plate.

The girl burned with anger, but restrained the impulse to spit the food back at him. Twice she readied herself to try for the knife, but each time he turned his head and would have seen her. A sudden shout and scuffle in the next room sent her captor running out the door.

Timbrel scooped up the knife, cut her hands free, and strapped the blade to her calf with a strip of rug. Timbrel saw Katrina down the hallway, her hands also free. The woman in the next room lay dead, her throat slashed open and a bloody kitchen knife nearby. Two of the strangers immediately grabbed Timbrel and Katrina before the third man opened the next door. This woman, the one calling the dancers whores, lay unmoving with a knife in her heart. The third and fourth women sliced open their bellies.

Katrina looked as sick as Timbrel felt. Why hadn't the women attacked their captors? Why did they turn the knives on themselves? Even Soliari would never have killed herself after a rape. Timbrel was the living proof of that.

When the captors searched Katrina and found her knife, the dark-haired dancer grabbed the hilt and attacked her captor. They struggled for a moment, Katrina on top of the man. They rolled, and Katrina sagged. The man rolled aside, leaving the dark-haired dancer gasping. The knife had turned sideways in their struggle, the sharp blade slicing across the dancer's abdomen and spilling her insides through the gap.

Timbrel's nausea rose again, her recent meal spilling across the ground in waves as she knelt on the floor to conceal her knife. Helpless to stop them, the girl hung limply between her captors as they found and removed the knife she had secreted. Her captor dragged her back into the room, and the half-elven girl looked up to see her captor dangling manacles. Submissive, the girl turned and let him restrain her hands behind her.

The manacles seemed to excite him, and over the next several hours Timbrel endured her captor and his friends. When the last of them fell asleep and began to snore, Timbrel slowly extricated herself from beneath his arm. A moment later the manacles lay loose on the floor.

Timbrel rubbed her wrists as she looked around the room. The knives removed from Katrina and herself shone on the side board. Timbrel crept up to the knives, choosing the better blade and silently returning to the men. She knelt over the first, leaning in to kiss him deeply as his eyes bulged open and she sliced his throat. He died silently, the blood spraying across her still-naked breasts. The second died the same way, waking to a deep kiss and the kiss of the blade. He flailed about as he died, kicking the third man.

As Timbrel turned, the third captor rose to his feet. His eyes widened as he saw the blade, and he backed away from the girl. She slashed wildly as he turned and fumbled with the locked door. Blood soaked his clothing in two places as the man ran down the hallway. Timbrel smiled. Time to look for the children.

She found the children locked up together in the kitchen storeroom. They cringed back as Timbrel opened the door. She sent them back to their homes to gather food, clothing, and water skins, and made them promise to return to the inn. Looking down at herself, Timbrel could understand their reaction. Blood dripped from her naked breasts and streaked her abdomen. Her hair was a sodden mess. The girl drew a bucket of water from the inn's well, scrubbing at her skin until all traces of the blood were gone. Carefully she slipped upstairs to her room to choose new clothing. Using the blanket on the bed as an impromptu pack, the half-elven girl gathered travel clothing, two dance outfits, her cosmetics and some food. As she passed through the common room downstairs, she snagged two water skins from the possessions of dead visitors, then gathered four more to share with the children. The next human village lay a three-day walk to the north, more likely four days at the speed she expected the children to keep. Once she safely brought them there, she would return to her mother's home. Soliari was in for a surprise. Her invisible daughter had bloomed like a rare flower, and would not be hidden away again.

### 

*The ocean between Sweetwater and Rockhold*

Nayev flew through some of the most difficult winds he had ever encountered. The storm just would not let up. Beneath him, ancient ships lay beneath the waters, some battered pieces riding the waves to the shoreline.

Nayev couldn't believe how many wrecked ships lay on the bottom of the sea as he neared Rockhold. Most showed signs of life: seaweed and schools of fish. The newer ones did not appear damaged enough to have sunk in this storm.

The storm died down as he neared the *Lady Elizabeth*. He banked to the left and landed near a promontory, then changed and walked to the end of it, hailing the ship.

"Have you seen a north-bound ship with an elf girl aboard?"

A man with a thick beard shouted back. "Who's asking?"

"Nayev of the Mountains. I'm trying to find her."

"Ahh, *you're* Nayev. She spoke of you. I left her at Rockhold just before the passes closed. I'm sure she'll stay for the festival in a few days. Do you need passage?"

"No, thank you. I have my own transportation." He waved as the *Lady Elizabeth* moved on. Once the ship passed out of sight, Nayev flew on towards Rockhold.

### 

*Rockhold*

The storm continued for a week, leaving an inch-thick glaze of crystalline ice across the entire city of Rockhold. Exiting the Inn became a lesson in ice-climbing, and even Krys carried the short metal ice axe so popular among the locals. Krys stalked along the flattest streets of the city, unwilling to risk his dignity on the icy slopes. His plans to travel westward were thwarted by the weather. No guide would take them from the city under the icy conditions, and the passes remained closed from the blizzard, probably for the season.

The humans hurried by, their features hidden by thick woolen cloaks with fur collars. Unimportant unless one of them could guide the group westward, Krys ignored them. If only the dragon left Sarin's horse alone! The saddlebags contained some of the historian's oldest maps. Krys tried to remember the last time he examined one. He could almost picture it. A trick of memory suddenly brought the map to mind, flashing behind his eyes for just a heartbeat before fading. He tried to grasp a last detail. An old Hinjin site lay near here, just to the west. Situated near one of the many warm springs in the area, the building's ruins should be within a few miles.

The Hinjin built their structures to last. Even when the surface buildings took damage, Krys often found extensive underground sections that partially survived. Krys found this most often in areas of intense magic. Trapped in the area until springtime, he might as well do some research.

Jherik jumped at the chance to explore. The Henin elf chafed almost as much as Krys from the inactivity. Sarin turned down the invitation, content to huddle by the fire at the Crystal Inn. The old elf visibly aged during the journey, a sure sign that his life neared its end. In spite of the signs, Sarin still woke gasping in the night from dreams that he would not speak of. Perhaps fear aged his teacher, thought Krys.

Timbrel could not be found. The innkeeper had seen her leave with the young captain, but poor weather canceled weapons practice. Krys could only imagine what sort of pleasant exercises she put her young lover through. The wizard couldn't blame her, though. Back in Ravali he would have found himself a companion for the winter as well. Humans, however, were not to his taste. He would rather remain celibate.

After packing enough food for an overnight trip, the two elves climbed the western wall of the caldera that surrounded Rockhold. Moving from icy field to icy field along the terraces was less difficult than transversing the final pastures. They found the trail almost immediately after climbing the final icy wall beyond the highest pasture. Carefully following it, the two elves stopped at a wide shelf of rock.

The land dropped away to the west, the upper reaches steeper than the human-worked walls within the caldera. Thick snow blanketed the entire area except for a few white plumes of steam marking the hot springs that bubbled up everywhere in this territory. The land rolled away below, forests of conifers erupting from the snow like geysers dotting the lower slopes.

Krys tried to bring the map to mind again, without much success. He was left with a vague impression of the location he wanted, an impression that coincided with the slight mound in the snow. He pointed their destination out to Jherik.

The Henin warrior nodded, then suggested a path through the landscape that might be passable. The two set out, ice axes in hand and woven snowshoes ready for the lower reaches. Jherik led, his grin reflecting his enjoyment of breaking a new trail. Krys followed in his footsteps, glad that they were of a similar height and stride. They secured their ropes and descended the steepest part. They left their ropes dangling behind them.

Barely three hours passed, most of it spent running over the deep snow. The snowfall actually helped them, Krys realized, smoothing out the irregularities in the landscape and giving them an even surface to develop some speed. As they neared the mound, a rough tumble of rock poked up on the far side. When they reached it, the two found shelter almost immediately. The tumbled rock turned out to be partial walls with a section of collapsed roof. They had to clear frozen rocks from a door, but once inside the temperature quickly rose.

Krys cheered as the sudden glow of lights and wafts of warm air filled the room. Jherik looked around warily, his sword held loosely in his right hand. A further door promised rooms with more than the empty countertops and wheeled metal table in the corner of the first.

The door led to a long corridor. Small dark boxes attached beneath the doorknobs of many of the doors opening onto this corridor. Jherik poked at one with his sword. The tip dislodged a layer of caked dust, sending clumps to the floor and raising a thick cloud. As the cloud thinned, slowly dispersing in the corridor lights, Krys could see the edge of the door offset a fingers width from the door frame. A sharp pull on the handle opened the door, its lock broken long before.

The room within had been rifled. Cabinets hung open, some splintered around their locks. A pile of drawers balanced in a corner, the remaining contents long turned to dust. Krys picked up an ancient book nearby, only to have the yellowed and curling pages crumble to dust at his touch. Even the ink on the cover puffed away like a multicolored cloud of spores.

"There's nothing usable here," Krys called out to Jherik.

"Here, either. There's just one door still locked." Only the farthest door remained intact, though someone had made efforts to break through its thick metal. The lock-box under the knob differed from the others, having a fist-sized round hole in the front instead of a thin slot. As Krys joined Jherik and knelt to examine it, he landed on something sharp. A small piece of round mesh, slightly bent from being pried off of the door's lock-box. Krys put his hand on the wall, peering inside. He saw a few scratches, but as far as Krys could tell, nothing had been damaged inside the lock-box.

"Aw-tory... Shen-co." Krys scrambled back from the door. The voice came out of the lock-box itself. Jherik sheathed his sword, knelt by the door, and looked inside the box. No reaction. Frowning, the Henin warrior braced himself on the wall as he rose.

"Aw-tory...Shen-co." the box spoke again. Jherik slid sideways, his right-hand remaining flat against the wall while his left hand drew a dagger. "Aw-tory...Shen-co." the warrior slid further to the side, his fingers trailing across the stone of the wall.

Krys suddenly laughed, his deep voice echoing through the halls. He pointed to the wall, where their handprints smeared the dust across the smooth square of grey embedded in the wall, similar in color to the dust and slightly larger than a man's hand. Krys bent over and laid a finger on the square.

"Aw-tory...Shen-co," the box responded. The wizard poked at the Hinjin artifact again, activating the predictable words.

"I wonder what it means?" Jherik asked. Krys had been wondering the same. Why couldn't Sarin have come with them? No, he thought, that was asking more than the old historian could give. Perhaps in the springtime. If the old elf lived that long.

"I'm not sure. It's no language that I ever learned. Sarin might know." Krys took out a piece of parchment and a small stick of charcoal, carefully copying the words. He also drew a sketch of the box and square. He added four Hinjin numbers that he discovered engraved on the side of the box.

Stumped by the door, the two elves searched the rest of the open rooms. Little remained except dust, scattered trash, occasional furniture in various states of disrepair, and some faded writing scrawled on the wall. Krys copied the wall words as well, then stowed his parchment away. They made a comfortable camp in one of the middle rooms, barring the door and eating some of their rations with water melted from the snow. Jherik discovered that the snow melted faster in front of the metal grating that seemed to be the source of the warm breezes in each room.

Jherik woke Krys twice on the first watch, and the two listened to noises in the night. The deep rumblings seemed to come from far beneath the floor, and were shortly followed by the scurry of mice.

When Krys' turn came, Jherik shook the wizard's foot. "You have to keep moving, Krys."

"They're just mice." *I hope.* Krys worried more about what else might come through the grating. He sat nearby, listening to the various noises carried by the tubing that Jherik discovered behind it. The wizard startled when the light suddenly dimmed to blackness. He jumped up in surprise, only to have the lights flicker and glow again. By the end of his watch, Krys had learned the exact timing of the Hinjin lights, waving his hand in the air just before they turned themselves off.

When they ventured out in the morning, the sun glowed in the eastern sky, turning the clouds blood red.

"We have to leave now. It's a bad omen." Jherik headed for the door. "Come on, Krys. We don't have any time to waste."

"All right, let's go. This door isn't going to open today in any case."

They ran off across the snow, a warm breeze at their backs. The snow grew mushier as they traveled, eventually slowing them to a waddling walk as the snowshoes sunk in ankle-deep slush. When they reached the steepest part of the slope, the two elves stopped dead.

The ropes lay an inch deep inside the ice the coated the upper slope. It took almost the entire morning to climb the two hundred-foot slope without it. Meltwater streamed across the slick ice, running past the men's gloves and up their arms. Footholds that Jherik laboriously chopped out of the ice slickened with water by the time Krys stepped in them. The wizard lost his ice axe the third time that he tried to re-chop a foothold.

It started to snow by the time they reached the top of the caldera wall. Large white flakes swirled down from grey clouds that completely obscured the sun. Krys felt a little disoriented, barely able to follow Jherik's lead. With a *whoop*, the Henin elf suddenly disappeared.

Krys stood on the lip of the caldera, unable to see the city below through the thick, swirling flakes of snow. A gust of wind propelled him forward across the ice and he stepped out over empty air. The wizard landed badly, bruising his hip. Krys could feel himself sliding, but there were no handholds. Nothing but wet ice. He found himself airborne again, landing with a *thud* in one of the upper pastures. He slid while climbing to his feet, skidding towards and over the next terraced wall before stopping. Jherik flew past, landing on his rear.

By the time Krys regained his feet, Jherik was on hands and knees close to the lower edge of the pasture. Together the two elves navigated their way back to the city, then carefully slid along the snow-filled streets to the Crystal Inn.

### 

After a week of mingled fear and excitement, Rockhold's priests finally rang the bells that called everyone together shortly after sunrise. "We have lured the sun back," they announced. "The days will become longer. Tonight we honor the Sun's Rebirth!" Cheers erupted in the streets. In spite of the thick ice, people scrambled about making festival preparations. The market cave was rearranged, the cloth separating the booths removed and the tables shifted to one end to make room for dancing. Local musicians and snow-trapped minstrels spent the morning practicing their songs. Timbrel found herself caught up in the preparations.

As late afternoon approached, merchants appeared at the Inn with racks of fine clothing. The girls from the kitchen came out giggling.

One tugged at Timbrel's sleeve. "You must dress properly for the Festival, so the sun will continue to come back. He likes bright colors like flowers. The merchants allow us to wear the pretty clothes for free tonight. Come, choose a dress."

The half-elven girl allowed herself to be led to the racks of dresses. Bright reds and yellows competed with blues and greens to draw the attention of the milling women. Timbrel chose a blue dress that both complemented her hair nicely and nearly matched one of her dance outfits. Long enough to reach past her knees, though not entirely to the floor, the tall dancer saw that the neck and sleeves of the dress could be adjusted with their drawstrings to fit her properly. To lengthen the dress, she planned to wear her dance skirt beneath it. She bought a matching pair of blue velvet slippers on a whim, far more comfortable than bare feet for dancing on a rock floor. From the number of slippers disappearing from the merchants stock, she would not be the only one so shod.

The excitement in the Inn heightened as Timbrel dressed and applied a few cosmetics. She pulled her hair back from her face, exposing her ears, and decided at the last minute to wear some of her dancing jewelry. Large hoops dangled from her small earlobes and she put her ankle bells into a small pouch. She would wear her cloak and boots across the ice, but change into the new slippers and strap on her bells when she got to the Market cave.

Krys and Jherik had taken another of their secret exploring trips. Timbrel would have liked to see them dressed formally again. Instead, she spent an hour convincing Sarin that he must attend the festival, and that he should wear a bright new robe. They finally settled on a bright red sash that the elderly historian would use to belt his current robe. So attired, they set off for the market turned Festival cave.

Lanterns hung from the walls, lending a softly glowing light to the room. Timbrel and Sarin chose a table in the middle where they could watch everything around them. The tables soon filled, and servers from the different inns took turns bearing trays. The inns seemed to be competing with each other for the best food served.

The nobility involved itself as well, each family supplying drink to the tables. Fruit juices, ale, and wine were available everywhere, and tiny tumblers of liqueur accompanied the desserts. When the servers cleared the last course, the dancing began.

The men of Rockhold milled about the tables, each choosing a woman by the hand and asking her to dance. The floor filled quickly with couples. Timbrel sat at her table, watching as men would slow nearby and contemplate asking her, then move on to another table. She wished Captain Harnek was here, but earlier he chose to remain on duty and allow his men the freedom of the Festival.

"I can dance with you any night I please," he said. "Let my men enjoy their special night."

After watching the others dance for an hour, Timbrel grew bored. A few people reclaimed their cloaks and left. Sarin, looking exhausted, suggested they do the same. Tempted, but not certain of the proper etiquette, Timbrel remained. Sarin walked away from the table.

"Dance with me, Lady Timbrel?" The tenor voice surprised her. It sounded just like the so-called wizard Nayev. She turned so quickly that her chair nearly tipped.

The golden-haired wizard caught the chair easily, holding it steady with one hand while offering the other hand to the amazed half-elf. "Dance with me?" He repeated.

Timbrel stood with his assistance. "Nayev, what are you doing here?"

"Dancing with a beautiful woman, I hope." He led Timbrel out onto the floor. The music changed to an ancient song of new beginnings. They moved around the floor in an elven court dance, holding each other the prescribed handsbreadth apart.

"Why haven't I seen you here? Where are you staying?" Timbrel was full of questions.

"I have my ways of getting around." Nayev suddenly changed the pattern of his dance. Timbrel concentrated on her feet, soon learning the new pattern, which felt familiar. She looked into his eyes and smiled, then added variations of her own. Nayev moved with her, adapting as perfectly to her changes as if he were reading her mind.

One song blended into another, the two lost in their own private world of dance. The other couples stepped aside to give them room, turning to watch the growing complexity of the dance. Nayev lifted his arm as Timbrel began spinning, her hair brushing his sleeve. He caught her as she collapsed, whirling her in a large circle before spinning her back to her feet.

Timbrel laughed with glee. She had never danced so well with a partner. Nayev matched her step for step.

When the music stopped, Timbrel caught her breath. The handsbreadth between them shrank to a fingersbreadth. She tilted her head back. The sky blue of Nayev's eyes seemed to expand and fill her vision, blocking out the rest of the room. "Dancing the skies," she thought. "Dancing with Nayev is like dancing the skies." Her lips parted slightly, ready for a kiss.

Screams interrupted the moment. Timbrel and Nayev whirled simultaneously to locate the source. A pale woman ran in from the cloak room, cowering behind her friends. "He's dead! He's murdered!"

People pressed forward. As Nayev guided Timbrel through the crowd, his lips touched her ear. "We'll dance together again sometime," he murmured. They entered the cloak room, once the crowd parted. Sarin lay sprawled on his side in a pile of cloaks, bleeding heavily. A dagger stuck out of his back, quivering in time with the historian's heartbeat. Timbrel broke away from Nayev's arm and ran to the old elf. She knelt at his side.

He took a ragged breath.

"Sarin, I'm here. It's Timbrel."

142

Sarin's pale eyes opened wide, losing color as she watched. "Beware of the dragon," he whispered. The old elf chuckled, then clutched at the mound of cloaks as pain wracked his body. "Murdered by a common thief. I always thought it would be a dragon like my brothers."

###

Nayev rejoined Timbrel at Sarin's side. The old elf lay on a pile of bloody cloaks, the blood spreading slower now. The smell suddenly overwhelmed him. Not the smell of blood, but the musk of dragon. More specifically, Sarin smelled like family.

Was Sarin one of his? He could no longer reject the idea that he left offspring behind.

Why didn't he check? Why didn't he go back to see her?

Now he had to track down the rest. Was Krys one of Sarin's offspring? Or Timbrel? He needed to learn more.

And yet... He didn't want either of them to be his offspring. He liked Krys, and Timbrel... He felt something much stronger for her. Far stronger than he felt for Sarin's mother a thousand years before. He cared for her. If only she was a dragon.

But first, he would hunt down and kill the one who killed his offspring. Who killed his *son*.

Nayev sniffed again near the dagger: the faint hint of something–silver and licorice and rust--tickled his nose.

Timbrel still knelt at his son's side, tears streaming down her face.

Nayev backed away, then headed for the swept stone in the middle of the city. He changed and flew, following the scent of the killer towards the pass along the southern road.

###

Sarin's funeral over, Timbrel wanted nothing more than to curl up in Nayev's arms, but her love left shortly after the killing and did not return.

No one she met knew anything about the man who danced with her. None of the innkeepers recognized his description. Their last dance together–oh so familiar at the time–she finally recognized as the *Akeni*, an ancient elven courtship dance, back when marriage was for life. Jherik and Krys returned in time to try and find the killer, but neither had seen Nayev. There was no evidence the man had been there at all.

"I think I dreamt him," she whispered into the wind. Captain Harnek came by every evening to ask her to dinner, and then brought food when she turned his invitations down.

"You have to eat. You cannot waste away because the old man died. Was he your grandfather?"

She mourned for Sarin as a grandfather, yes, though they were not related. He listened, and counseled her, and might even have given his blessing about Nayev; but that could never be now.

Timbrel sobbed anew, finally admitting to herself that the biggest hole in her heart was Nayev's absence. The only time she could remember feeling this bad was after Eric's death. The two could not be more different. One tall and the other of medium height, one dark-haired and the other golden, one as strong as a bull and the other as wily as a fox.

She wondered if she would ever see him again. Twice now he had rescued her: the first from the man when she bought cheese and the second so recently. Nayev's presence that night prevented her from leaving with Sarin. If she had, she too would be dead. Perhaps someday she could rescue him in turn, though she could not imagine how that could ever happen. She was just a dancer and a healer, while he was... She stopped. Just what was he?

### 

*Lucifron*

Kadeesh heard the harsh scream of the hawk before he saw it. The brown bird plummeted toward the ground, spreading its wings and tail at the last moment to display the startling reddish markings. It settled gently on Kadeesh's left arm, gripping the padded leather bracer. A tiny case swung from its leg. The kidnapper retrieved the message, frowning at what he read. He pulled out a sheet of parchment and carefully wrote, thinking a moment before drawing a sketch near the top. He turned to his men. "Ready the two women for travel. We are pursued."

One man nodded and left. Another looked directly at Kadeesh. "How much of the camp do ye want broke down?"

"Leave everything but the slaves and your personal packs. I'll get my own in a few minutes."

"Where're ye going?"

"To the wall. I have a posting to make." Kadeesh left, latching the compound fence behind him.

### 

*Rockhold, springtime*

Timbrel stood with Captain Harnek on the heights above the city. Tiny plants pushed their way through the snow and bloomed with white flowers barely distinguishable except for circles of pale green. Spring warmed the air and the passes were finally open.

"I will miss you." The young captain clenched a fist on the hilt of his sword, his eyes bright with unshed tears.

"We must move on. Perhaps our paths will cross again?" she suggested. Actually, she wanted to travel. Some of her herbs were in short supply, particularly those used in the bitter tea. If she remained, she might have to stay for a lifetime. Better to be on the road than to bear a brood of children at such a young age. Unless the right man came along and she changed her mind.

Harnek touched her on the arm, interrupting her unbidden thoughts of Nayev. They returned to the city hand in hand. In this city she would always be Harnek's woman, even if her thoughts strayed elsewhere.

They strayed more and more often these days. The golden-haired Nayev, so close in coloring to her own, fascinated Timbrel.

145

She dreamt of him often. More and more she hoped that they would cross paths again. She hoped that he would ask her to spend the night with him.

Timbrel flushed with embarrassment. She had always been the aggressor, asking the captain and other men to share her bed in the past. Sometimes the asking came without words. Why did it matter so much to her that Nayev be the one to ask? Why couldn't she get the golden-haired wizard with a secret out of her mind?

The Crystal Inn, so quiet during the harsh winter, overflowed with boisterous men when they arrived. The Captain left her at the door, hurrying to his duty. Timbrel walked inside, scanning the group for new faces. With two groups of new travelers, one arriving from each of the now open passes, the crowd within had tripled. Timbrel spun in place several times as hands grabbed her on her way across the room. She hurried up the stairs, fleeing to the safety of the shared room.

Krys and Jherik packed their bags. Krys looked at the girl through narrowed eyes. "Be ready to leave in the morning. First light. Say goodbye to that captain of yours tonight."

"He's on duty tonight, a double shift. I already said my goodbyes." She turned on her heel and bent over her pack, twitching her rear at Krys. Jherik stood to one side, watching her. Aware of the scrutiny, Timbrel suddenly straightened. "I'm going to dance tonight."

Jherik looked alarmed. "Are you certain that is wise? The newest patrons..."

Timbrel interrupted him. "They're just men who haven't seen a woman in days. No worse than the sailors who brought us here."

"But..."

"I'm dancing." She stopped and looked at Jherik's worried face, then grew angry at his possessiveness. "It's not like you've had a woman, either. So don't criticize them."

The Henin elf turned away, muttering under his breath. Krys looked at Timbrel, then glanced toward the door. Taking the hint, the girl led the way down the stairs.

146

The noise was worse than ever, a ship having arrived in the interim. Sea and land travelers clumped together at their tables, insulting each other in loud voices. The barmaids ran quickly between tables, barely avoiding the grabbing hands of the men. A group of hunters arrived, buying their stay in the overcrowded inn with the lean carcass of a fresh-killed deer. Their cloaks smelled of pine needles and blood.

Krys moved around the room, trying to hire a guide through the mountains. Jherik stayed with him. Timbrel gained permission to dance from the innkeeper, but could not find a minstrel. With the previous minstrels already gone once the passes opened, and no new arrivals, Timbrel would have to depend on the crowd for her music. With a rough group like this, that could be a problem.

She caught up to Jherik first.

"Can you act as a bodyguard for me tonight? There are no minstrels and the crowd might get a little wild."

"You shouldn't dance. I won't fight to save you if you insist on being stupid."

"You won't have to fight. Just stand and look fierce. You're good at that." She turned away, unaware of the surprised look on Jherik's face. "Maybe a minstrel will come in," she muttered.

Jherik touched her shoulder, startling her. She whirled to face him. "What's the difference between having a minstrel or not? Everyone will just clap."

Timbrel rolled her eyes. "Of course they will. And that will be the only rhythm for me to dance to. There will be no control."

"Control?" Jherik looked confused.

"Over the speed of the dance. I give the minstrels signals to slow down and speed up the music, like this." The half-elf demonstrated with her hand. Jherik could see how those watching would easily miss the signals.

Jherik looked at the floor and shuffled his feet for a moment. "I can play the pipes."

Timbrel stared at the warrior elf. "What did you say?"

147

"I can play the pipes. I'll play *The Greensward* for you, if you think that will help calm the crowd." He looked embarrassed by the admission.

"Why didn't you say so? We could have had more gold built up if you'd only told me before."

"We already have far more than we need."

Timbrel looked the tall elf in the eye. "You still don't understand the human world, do you?" When he did not reply, she sniffed. The smell of roasting venison permeated the air, joining the all-pervasive smell of vegetable stew. "I'll be dancing immediately after the evening meal. When I go upstairs to change, you follow and get your pipes." She put up a hand to stop Jherik's sputtering protests. "I want you to precede me into the room and begin to play. If you can, get that large table cleared for me to dance on." She indicated a long wide table with thick legs. Six long benches surrounded it.

"By the time you come downstairs, it will be clear," Krys interrupted. "I hope you're ready for the consequences of your dance. The tension is so thick right now that I'm afraid someone will be murdered."

Timbrel thought about the wizard's words. She worried that someone might be murdered before the night was over if she didn't dance. If she did, however, she thought that they would seek out women instead, or perhaps brawl a little. "I don't think I can distract them from fighting entirely, but I don't think it will be so bad."

Krys nodded and took Jherik aside. Timbrel could hear him complaining about the lack of available guides. Ignoring the elves, she worked her way around the room, chatting with the men. Timbrel learned the names of six different guides before the venison was served, though she had only identified one. She shared her information with Krys as they sat together for the meal.

###

When Timbrel rose from her meal, the crowd had turned restless. Insults volleyed across the room between tables of hunters, sailors, and various merchants. Jherik followed her up the stairs and stood in the hallway while she changed. A moment after she opened the door he retrieved his pipes.

She heard an outcry below, followed by a crash. Timbrel winced, imagining Krys clearing the table. She stayed on the stairs, out of sight from most of the crowd, until she heard the first strains of the music. Jherik was an adequate piper, though not as skilled as a true minstrel. It would do.

Leaping from the stairs and madly spinning across the room, Timbrel leapt to her makeshift stage. She used the beginning of her dance to sidestep, measuring the exact area she could use. After visiting all four corners of the long table, she spun back to the center and began dancing in earnest.

While she danced, she remained sensitive to the crowd. She glanced at the group of hunters, the sailors, a merchant group, and various others in turn; all eyes were focused on her.

Enjoying the attention, Timbrel danced her excitement and joy at the thought of being free again. She could sense the crowd's empathy with her, having been confined by harsh weather and closed passes themselves. The few visible weapons in the room lowered, and most were resheathed. When the room felt safer, she signaled Jherik.

As his piping slowed and steadied, someone began a slow drumming on a table. The beat slowed further, double thumping like a heartbeat. Annoyingly, Jherik slowed his piping further to match the anonymous drummer. Timbrel slowed her dance, matching the heartbeat and adding a sensuous quality to her movements. Eyes half-lidded to emphasize her exotic qualities, the half-elf met eyes with a man in the back. She danced as if mesmerized by him, then turned to the next man bold enough to meet her glance, as though choosing a companion.

One of the hunters rose and Timbrel signaled Jherik to play faster. The Henin elf ignored her hand motion. The hunter pushed through the crowd. She signaled again, only to be ignored a second time. The hunter closed on her makeshift stage. She signaled a third time, working the movement into her dance and making it obvious. The music picked up speed just as the hunter reached the table.

Timbrel spun across the stage, keeping away from the hunter. The drunken man suddenly climbed up on the table, lurching at the girl. She continued to spin as the man grabbed at her, dodging from his path and pushing him slightly off-balance as he neared the table edge. He swayed and fell off into the crowd.

A second man tried the same, leaping to the tabletop. Timbrel dodged him as well, though it took her several tries before she assisted him from the stage with her foot.

The first hunter returned, focused on his quarry. In spite of the girl's best efforts, he grabbed her lower arm. She spun and twisted, expecting his grip to loosen.

*Crack!* The sound rose above the noise of the crowd.

The music stopped as the man staggered backward, clutching his arm and moaning. White shards of bone spiked through his skin, tinged with red.

Timbrel backed to the far side of the table as blood fountained from the hunter's arm, pooling beneath his feet and running across the table.

At the sight of blood, the suppressed violence in the room erupted. Timbrel tried to stay on the table as long as she could defend herself. A hand grabbed her ankle and yanked her into the general melee. She kicked and wiggled, trying to get her feet beneath her and stand. Her stomach clenched and the floor gave way.

Falling into a pit of dust, Timbrel held her breath as long as she could. Coughing and choking noises surrounded her. Her lungs began to burn.

A large hand grabbed her by the waist and pulled her upward, out of the dust.

Blinded by the dust, her eyes streaming tears, Timbrel fought against the arm that cradled her. She heard words she could not understand, followed by Krys' distinctive laughter. A moment later she was dumped unceremoniously on the stone floor.

Timbrel wiped furiously at her eyes. Krys stared down at her from his full height. She turned her eyes to her rescuer. She focused on... a belt buckle? Her eyes traveled upwards, far past Krys' height. A giant, nearly twice Timbrel's height, stood with his head bent between the rafters of the inn's common room.

His long, slender face seemed stretched lengthwise. His shoulders appeared slender in proportion to his body, yet she realized they were wider than Eric's had been. Looking downward, Timbrel saw that the dust on his pants stopped halfway up his thighs, about chest height on the girl.

The giant bent over, fished around in the dust with his arms, brought up another coughing man, and then a chair that he added to a pile of furniture.

She scrambled to her feet, the stone feeling solid beneath them, and wiped her eyes again. Only a portion of the floor was turned to dust, a square about ten feet on a side.

At a word from Krys, the giant searched around one last time, bringing up two stools, then climbed out of the hole.

Timbrel's belly clenched as Krys spoke one of his *words*. The dust shifted, settled, and became solid stone again. *He cast this before. I thought it was the shock of falling.*

At least she wasn't sick this time. She wrinkled her nose rudely at Krys, letting him know what she thought of his display of magic. Timbrel knew she would have gotten free of the crowd before very long, and most of her bruises would heal by midmorning tomorrow.

Krys continued to speak with the guide in the other language, though Timbrel recognized a few words similar to old elvish. The giant pronounced them differently, his language tending more towards the long vowels. The girl practiced silently. As she grew accustomed to his accent, she began to understand a few words. Not enough to understand the entire conversation, though she caught the words for "guide" and "gold" in the midst of it. The giant named himself Halar.

151

###

# Chapter Six

*The Western Pass from Rockhold*

Halar watched the girl bravely keeping up with the rest. He guided them slowly, making things easy for her. Girls should never travel the mountains on foot, he decided. Especially pretty ones like Teembara. Fishing her out of the dust pit was one of his better ideas. Too often his impulses resulted in problems, like the time he killed the giant spider standing over an unconscious warrior. He did not know that it belonged to the warrior as a pet. The spider stood as tall as Halar, and their battle raged across the ground. In the end, the warrior woke, took a single look at what happened, and warned Halar to stay in the mountains.

"You are marked by the spider," the warrior said in the human tongue. "If you come to the plains, or even the forests beneath the mountain, you will attract them. They will kill you if they get the chance."

Personally, Halar thought the warrior worried that he might kill another pet. But then, the first time he tried to follow the road to Nerryon he did see several giant spiders waiting in the shadows. The mountains suddenly looked good.

Karas signaled a halt. Halar liked the elf. Both Karas and Zharak were not as short as most of their kind, and Karas actually took the time to speak in the Tallfolk tongue. Of course, Halar could understand most of the human tongue, even if he chose not to speak it. The language that the group used between them puzzled him. He thought it an elf tongue, but a few of the words seemed almost like words of Tallfolk.

Teembara's birdlike voice rose over the sound of the mountain birds. Halar chuckled silently, his long chin bobbing with glee. The third stop of the day and the tiny elf-girl chastised the warrior-elf again. Whatever he had done, or perhaps *not* done, she showed no sign of forgiving him.

Karas quieted them with a comment, though Halar could see that the argument would start again soon. Zharak acted as protective as a lover, though it seemed to bother Teembara when he did. Perhaps Zharak asked her to bed?

Yes, fishing her from the dust pit was worthwhile. A pretty girl to look at during the journey, a guide job paying more than double his standard fee, and the chance of playing with the girl. If Karas held true to their bargain, that is. Halar congratulated himself on his shrewd bargaining, holding firm to double his normal price. He had finally agreed to discount the fee, but only if Karas arranged for Teembara to spend the night with him. Then and only then would he return the excess gold to the elf. Karas thought it a bargain, but Halar knew better. The Tallman would keep his full fee no matter what.

Karas signaled to continue. Halar took them to a side trail, stopping to remove a small boulder that appeared to block the path. When they passed through, he replaced the boulder and loped back to the front. The Tallman preferred to keep his private shortcut to himself.

After a few twists and turns, the pathway evened out. Teembara rode nearby, asking questions in a curious mix of human tongue, gestures, and some words that sounded close to Tallfolk speech. Halar smiled and did his best to answer her questions, even using a few of the human words. Surprisingly they did not bring up the usual memories of Nerryon's cages and whips, but instead associated themselves with the pretty elf-girl.

As they camped for the evening, Halar saw the longing look on Zharak's face whenever the elf looked at Teembara. The Tallman sighed, taking his roll of sleeping furs around the corner of the trail so that he didn't have to watch the two together. Teembara's voice rose, chastising the warrior yet again. This time she slipped into the human tongue. Halar listened secretly.

"You were supposed to watch for my signal and play faster. Didn't you see my signal?"

154

"I noticed all three times. I wanted to watch you dance slowly just a little longer."

"So did they. That's what caused all the trouble. You waited too long."

"Timbrel..."

"Don't even ask. You belong to Kareni."

"We are not married *yet*. I don't actually belong..."

The girl chose that moment to storm away from the elf. Halar could hear her soft-booted feet slapping on the flat surface of the stone. Finally, she climbed on a boulder near the camp. The wind whispered past, dropping the temperature by the minute. He heard Karas say something to her in the elf tongue, and her soft reply in the same.

Halar huddled miserably in his furs. Unlike the elf travelers, he felt the cold. He also felt the loneliness of being different than the others. None of them could know how it felt to be shunned.

Halar sensed a difference in the wind. He looked up to see Teembara, her thin blanket draped over one arm. A moment later she slid into his furs, a tiny spot of warmth that soon made his entire body glow.

### 

*Lucifron*

When they reached the outskirts of Lucifron a week later, Krys spoke a few parting words to their guide.

The giant held out of pouch. "You kept your end of the bargain," the huge man grumbled. "You sent the girl to me. Here is the second half of your fee returned."

Krys looked at the money, then over his shoulder at Timbrel and Jherik. While the group still had plenty of money from Timbrel's dancing, a little more would not hurt, particularly in the human lands. He started to reach for the pouch, hesitated, and pulled his hand back.

"Keep it. I never told her about the bargain we made. She went to you of her own free choice."

The giant stood motionless in front of Krys, his mouth slack. Nearly two minutes later, he spoke. "Her own choice? You didn't tell her?" The guide seemed suddenly embarrassed, unable to look Krys in the eye.

Timbrel ran up. She launched herself into Halar's arms and kissed him as her legs dangled in the air. Krys turned away from their short goodbye. Timbrel returned to the horses with a perfect white flower tucked into her hair. The Tallman guide had already vanished back along the trail.

They could see the city of Lucifron long before they got there. Built on a rise like an inverted bowl, the palace stood in the center of the city, fortified with crenellated stone walls. Down the slope, large mansions with extensive grounds stood just inside a high stone wall surrounding the area, pierced by two gates. Further down the slope, two and three-story wooden houses clustered together into squares with shared walls and an inner gated courtyard. Several signs hung outside the houses, but Krys could not make out the shop names at this distance.

Small shops and inns lined the main road into Lucifron. Krys led the others past, through the main gates of the city. A second stone wall surrounded this area, with four guarded gates. The lowest portion of the slope, revealed after they passed through the gate, held rundown buildings. Three-story complexes were used as houses and shops. Many of the courtyards had no gates, and left the impression that the inner doors facing the courtyard might be the only entrances to some of the dwellings. Open marketplaces filled with tented stalls sprang up between the buildings. Near one such open market, Krys found an inn.

Timbrel squealed, delighted with the name. A whitewashed building with a small enclosed yard, the Lovely Dancer Inn included a stable and pasture downwind. Several horses stood in front, and a young man in the Inn's colors untied one and brought it to the stables. Krys noted with approval that two of the other horses had white-wrapped saddles, a sure sign that official messengers stayed here.

Once inside, the girl's excited squeal quickly died away.

An actual stage, raised above the tables and out of reach of the patrons, stood at one end. Krys understood the girl's silence when he spotted the two brass rings set in the floor of the stage, shiny with continual use. Krys looked around the room, unsettled by the bright enameled collars on the serving wenches. They wore matching silver bracelets enameled with stylized designs, and also adorned with a small welded ring suitable for running a chain through. No matter what Timbrel said, she was *not* dancing here. Not that the girl showed any signs of wanting to.

The messengers sat at a far table, their white cloaks as easy to spot against the room full of darker cloaks as bleached bones against dark soil. Krys put up his hood and moved to a table in the corner. Jherik joined him, also hooded. The two stood silently while the table's occupants started to twitch uncomfortably. After a minute or two the seated people gather their equipment and moved. Krys and Jherik sat down.

Timbrel moved across the room with great difficulty. Her hood down, she attracted far more attention than Krys liked. In spite of the catcalls, however, she made steady progress and finally sank into her seat with a sigh.

Jherik made the room arrangements while Krys ordered their meal. Timbrel spent her time sitting quietly in contemplation until the bowls of thick gruel arrived

"Thinking of your favorite guide?" Krys asked. The half-elven girl jumped guiltily.

"No." Her cheeks colored slightly. "Someone else."

"Jherik?" Krys suggested. He dodged as Timbrel slapped at him.

"Of course not. I don't look at married men."

"Who, then?" Krys looked to the left as he thought. "Not your Captain back in Rockhold? I thought you got over him before we were outside the caldera."

"I did. Just someone else who is not who he appears to be. I don't want to talk about him."

Krys shrugged in assent, realizing belatedly that he used the human gesture the wrong way. These humans and their body language. So difficult to understand, like trying to understand Timbrel when she rode near their guide. The two spoke no language in common, yet the girl managed to converse with him for hours using a stew of gestures, words, sounds, and he didn't know what else. After watching them for the first hour, Krys became convinced that the girl somehow threw meaning into everything she did, from the tilt of her head to the point of her toe. If only he could interpret some of it.

He didn't understand her ideas about sex, either. Somehow she chose from a large group of willing males, but Krys couldn't understand how she made her choice. She seemed to favor warrior-types. But then, that could just be because they heavily weighted the available pool of choices. He discerned no real pattern.

After the meal, Krys thought about the last month of winter. He and Jherik explored the Hinjin building west of Rockhold only one other time, during the Festival. They climbed down the slope and went straight to the mysterious door.

Krys placed his hand under the lock-box. "Aw-tory...shen-co." Krys touched four numbers on the panel, the same four numbers that had been scratched into the side of the box. The door opened with a hiss. Jherik followed him as he pushed through the door. The air was stale and unmoving. Another door led to a set of stairs, which Krys sprinted down.

A second door with a lockbox greeted him. "Authorization code" squawked from the box. The door unlocked with the same numbers.

As he pushed the door wide, Krys could see a dozen glass tubes, most with red lights overhead. Each held a preserved corpse: goblin, elf, human, a bipedal lizard, a blue-skinned humanoid with bat wings... A tiny part of Krys' mind thought that Sarin would have enjoyed seeing the variety of humanoid creatures. The final corpse stood inside the tube, strapped to a metal board. Other straps held small tubes against the corpse, their purpose unknown. The hairless corpse, a short white shroud wrapped around the loins, was pale with shriveled, leathery looking skin. The face was a death's mask, skin tight against the bone with closed eyes. The ears had once been pointed, but instead resembled mere flaps of hanging skin. Krys' heart raced and he could not catch his breath. The light over the tube glowed amber.

"Skin over bones. So that's what it looks like." Jherik's strange chuckle underlined his discomfort. The warrior touched his fingers to the tube, and then drew them back with a sharp hiss. "It's cold."

Krys looked around. Panels of lights blinked, some of which corresponded with the colored lights above the tubes.

Jherik walked up and ran his hand across a panel. Lights changed color several times and started blinking, then turned back to amber.

"Stop touching things. You don't know what you might accidentally start." Krys turned back to the tubes. A few had labels beneath them, inscribed in a variety of alphabets. The only one he could read was under the near-skeleton in the last tube. "Damnech."

"There's nothing here for us." Krys turned toward the door.

"Goodbye Mr. Skull." Jherik thumped on the top of the tube before he followed Krys out of the room and slammed the door.

Neither heard the soft humming that began as the light over the twelfth corpse turned green.

### 

*Lucifron*

Timbrel and Jherik talked after breakfast about their route before Krys staggered down the stairs.

"Over here." Timbrel waved. "We saved some sausage and bread for you."

Krys seemed to have trouble focusing on them, so she waved again. She turned to Jherik. "What is up with him lately? He mutters in his sleep..."

"So do you," Jherik said. "You twitch and cry out and mutter about a child called Fafar and someone named Eric. Is that your secret boyfriend's name?"

"No. Fafar was my human father's village. I'm more worried about Krys. He's been acting strange ever since you found those tubes." Timbrel's back cramped. She started to stretch before remembering where she sat.

Last night, shortly after the evening gruel was served, the proprietor chained a slave girl by the wrists to the two rings, giving her less than a ten-foot circle to dance in. Chained like that, it was impossible for the girl to spin. Timbrel felt immense pity for her. The crowd turned ugly early, and the slave's master pacified them by taking bids for an evening's entertainment. It was only after he unlocked the chains from the rings and tossed them to the winner that Timbrel understood what they won. She left the room in disgust, shadowed by Jherik.

Krys reached their table and waved the food away. "There are records I must find in the city hall." He turned for the door.

Timbrel looked at Jherik in surprise.

"Did he say anything to you about this? I thought we were looking for a guide to the west." Jherik's words echoed Timbrel's thoughts. Uncertain, the two followed their friend, Timbrel stopping only long enough to wrap up the last of the food and stuff it in her pack.

The city hall, an imposing stone building with an entrance on one end, stood three stories tall. A seemingly endless flow of bureaucrats in the colors of various factions made it difficult to enter. Timbrel finally stepped between two men wearing green and red and moved inside with them, her hood drawn up to cover her sun-bright hair.

Once inside, the entrance opened into a long hallway lined with doors. The bureaucrats crowded the hallway. Pages ran at breakneck speed between the doors and up and down a set of

160

stairs. Timbrel's eyes ached at the flurry of activity. She started down the hallway, peering inside the few open doors to catch sight of Krys. Jherik struggled to enter behind her.

At the end of the hallway, a single door stood open. Timbrel noticed a figure cloaked in light brown walk boldly inside. She continued looking for Krys unsuccessfully. When she reached the end of the hallway, she stepped inside and looked about curiously.

Scraps of parchment, bark, and leather lined all four walls, each covered in writing.

"Wanted: Alandar the warrior for murdering my brother. 300 gold gryphons for his head. Body don't need to be attached." Contact information followed, naming one of the many inns in the city.

Startled, Timbrel looked at the next posting. The half-elf continued reading along the wall. Some of the postings named the wanted people, while others merely described them. Some wanted them alive, while others didn't specify. Most of the posted rewards offered gold. The girl continued reading, fascinated.

"Wanted: Kryslandir the elf. Last seen in Rockhold. Accompanied by two others. Beware of the swords of Jherik and the wiles of Timbrel. 10,000 gold chains for Kryslandir, 5,000 each for the others. Contact Aless in Nerryon." A description of each followed, fairly accurate in the details.

Timbrel looked in horror at the posting, then carefully ripped the parchment and slipped it off the nail. She rolled it up tightly and tucked it beneath her cloak. Krys needed to see this.

The girl continued down the wall, reading the other postings. No others named her group, as far as she could see. A sudden bump startled her as the brown cloaked figure suddenly backed away and bowed.

"I'm sorry, I wasn't watching closely." The young man stood, his hood falling back to reveal hair the color of his cloak, gold-flecked green eyes exactly level with her own, and pointed ears peeking up through his hair.

Timbrel blinked in surprise. From her mother's tales, Timbrel was the only half-elf born in thousands of years. The girl never expected to see another one in her lifetime. She looked again, studying him closely.

Timbrel's pointed chin, like her mother's, gave her a heart-shaped face. The young man's chin squared off like a human. His cheekbones were less prominent, though his ears stood almost as tall as a full-blooded elf. When his ears were covered, only his eyes could betray his mixed blood. Timbrel stared deep into his eyes for a moment, watching the ovoid pupil dilate and contract. She suddenly remembered her manners.

"No harm done.," She acknowledged, pushing back her hood to reveal golden hair. The stranger's pupils dilated sharply, and Timbrel smiled at the evidence of his surprise and attraction.

"I am Gareth. Are you elf?"

Timbrel giggled. "Half. I am Timbrel."

Gareth cocked his head, a very human gesture. "My father is elf. Except for him, I've never seen an elf before. I've always wanted to."

Timbrel giggled. "I know two true-blood elves in this city. Perhaps you can meet them."

They chatted amiably, two young half-elves standing close together. After a while, Gareth's questions grew more pointed.

"Is it true that your friend Krys can do magic? You said he lit the fire with it, can he do anything else?"

"Oh, he can do a lot more," assured Timbrel. "He practices new things almost every day. He even made enough wind to blow our ship all the way to Rockhold before the storms could get there."

Gareth looked momentarily unsettled.

Timbrel patted his arm. "Oh, don't worry. I don't belong to Krys or Jherik."

"Jherik. He's the one with the sword, you said? What's he like?"

Timbrel babbled about Jherik's great single-handed victory over the entire city militia in Rockhold, neglecting to mention the

162

size of her captain's army as well as the general state of unpreparedness there. Gareth's face fell.

The sound of footsteps echoed from the hallway. Gareth twitched his own hood up, then reached over and pulled Timbrel's into place. "We're not supposed to be in here unless our hoods are up," he whispered. A black-cloaked figure strode into the room, boots clicking on the stone.

The girl suppressed a giggle. She'd already broken rules and made a friend, all without even trying.

Gareth leaned over to whisper directly in her ear, the soft fabric of his hood brushing against her cheek. "I'll see you later. Did you say you were staying at the Lovely Dancer?"

The girl nodded and looked at the wall again for a few minutes while the other half-elf padded out of the room. After his quiet footsteps faded down the hall, she turned and left as well.

### 

Jherik finally gave up trying to enter the building. *Too many little humans to get past.* He relaxed outside, leaning against a tree. A few minutes later, the crowd parted and spat out a disgruntled Kryslandir.

"There's no record of any elves brought into the city. I suppose they don't keep records of slaves."

Krys looked to one side, his eyes almost as unfocused as Timbrel's after she met the wizard Nayev.

At least they hadn't stayed at *that* tavern. Between the cheese, the local hatred of elves, and the wizard Nayev, Shassilar was nothing but trouble. He could only imagine what Nayev might've done to Timbrel, casting a love spell on her or something. Perhaps he had. For days afterward, the girl rode with a dreamy expression on her face, one that still recurred at odd moments.

Nayev glowed with power, too, more power than Jherik had ever seen before even in an elf. While they parted as friends, Jherik felt trepidation about the prospect of becoming close to someone with that level of sheer energy. Lately Krys seemed to be developing more power as well, almost as if something unlocked it. A frightening thought.

Timbrel's giggle rose above the general hubbub of the bureaucrats. The churning mass of color split apart to reveal the girl, cloaked and hooded but obviously in a good mood. She rejoined them in a rush.

"Did you see where he went? He'll meet with us tonight." The half-elven girl looked back and forth, searching for someone.

Jherik groaned silently. Another man already. "Who is he?"

"Gareth. The half-elf. He's another half-elf!" Timbrel jumped around.

Jherik groaned aloud this time. The noise roused Krys from his quiescence.

"You're back. It's about time. We have places to go, travel to arrange..." Krys strode off towards the Lovely Dancer Inn, leaving Jherik and Timbrel blinking in confusion.

Timbrel looked at Jherik. "What's wrong with Krys?" She asked.

"I don't know," replied the warrior. "He acts like a different person."

The two returned to the Inn, their thoughts centered on Krys. High above, directly in line with the sun, a presence hung in the air and watched their slow progress. With a snap of golden wings, the watcher flew over to the mountain to perch and contemplate what it had seen. The warrior-elf and the dancer were not the only ones concerned with the odd behavior of their friend. Krys was beginning to walk like an old enemy, the watcher thought. One that had been destroyed... Or had he?

### 

Timbrel thrashed in her sleep, broken bits of memory strung together like beads on a string, the whole a multicolored nightmare. Memory beads glittering like gems cut by Eric's father from a larger stone. Eric's leave-taking. Eric's triumphant return. Their vows. The faint licorice smell of the wedding cup. The

164

inability to think straight. The suddenness of the attack. Eric's fall. The horror of the rape. Her dry, burning eyes as she pieced her broken memories together. The grief that she could not express aloud. Her cold, empty heart when she used her body to distract her captors. The warmth of their blood as it sprayed across her breasts. The running steps of the one that got away.

Timbrel sat bolt upright, staring around the room. Jherik slept against the door, his breath catching slightly. A faint murmur came from Krys' bed. The smell of licorice hung in the air, left over from and bringing back memories of her dream. She waved at the air to banish the dream and the memories.

*Likshas* is a mild narcotic, she thought, especially to elves. Timbrel once experienced the herb as an aphrodisiac as part of her wedding ceremony, but that may have been the influence of her human blood. Humans only knew that use.

The elves knew better, and banned *likshas* centuries before. After her return to Ravali, Timbrel learned about the ban from the healer Allowei during her apprenticeship. The drug made the Genjin creations more suggestible, reacting somehow with the potions the Genjin used to shape the elves. An elf under the influence of *likshas* could have his thoughts changed and molded into a new shape as legends said some of the ancient priests did. The high crime of the ancient priests, creating new people from old. That angered the gods and they left, their very towers floating toward the skies. The wonderful gardens of the gods were left blackened and burnt to bare stone.

They marched down the stairs. Krys flung open the door of the Inn, startling the sleepy door guard. Timbrel saw movement outside. "Wait!" She cried.

Gareth stood, crossbow pointed at Krys' head.

"No!" Timbrel cried, trying to pull Krys down. The bolt left the crossbow and sped upwards. A muffled noise was followed by a groan as a cloaked figure fell from above the door and crumpled on the paving stones.

Gareth pushed Krys aside as he ran to the fallen figure. Prodding it cautiously with a stick, he bent forward. Timbrel gasped as a goblin's fanged leer was revealed. Gareth pulled out a piece of parchment and compared the sketch with the face of the goblin. He lifted the goblin's lip, revealing a broken fang on the upper right side. Smiling, the half-elf hauled the goblin's body across his shoulders.

"I'd like to stay and meet your friends, Timbrel, but business suddenly rears its ugly head. His ugly head, actually." The young man disappeared into the darkness.

So had Krys, the girl realized. She and Jherik hurried to catch up to the elf.

###

*The Spider Forest*

The golden-haired elf princess stumbled as the small group hurried along. The soft *whisk* of an arrow passing overhead frightened her enough to regain her feet. A small cry from one of the slavers convinced her to run even faster. The forest thinned rapidly, the giant trees weighted down with immense spiderwebs falling behind as she ran. Only three of the slavers remained. The others had gone down under the nearly silent arrows, twitching and frothing at the mouth.

The tree line broke. Lostaria ran across the stubble of a long abandoned field, weeds growing waist high in the warm spring weather. The arrows stopped as their hidden pursuers ended the chase at the edge of the forest. Lostaria continued running until she fell, too exhausted to rise.

Kadeesh cuffed her across the face. "We don't rest until we reach the road."

Her disappointment was palpable. If only Kadeesh could have fallen. Perhaps she could still escape, though. She looked at the dark forest behind her and shuddered. That way invited death.

The Urramach Princess raised her head and looked across the fields.

The land sloped gently downward, and then flattened. Green squares and rectangles dotted with a few sticks stretched out before her. She blinked and her perceptions changed. The sticks were trees, she realized, immediately overwhelmed with the vast expanse of land. Huge square fields of crops stretched for miles. A dark blot sat in the far distance like a head of log-fungus, gray threads wiggling their way across the green of the fields. A gray haze hung in the air over the blot.

Her perceptions readjusted again. The fungus-blot must be the city of Nerryon, and the threads were roads. The city was immense. A cold knot settled into the pit of her stomach.

### 

*Lucifron*

Timbrel went looking for Gareth in the posting room. Though the half-elf was not there, a second notice about Krys hung on the wall. Timbrel removed it.

The girl turned too quickly in her hurry to leave the room, bumping into a black-cloaked figure and falling to her knees. She looked up to see a dark-skinned man with elven features and golden eyes. She scrambled backwards, her hood falling back.

The girl quickly twitched the hood back into position and stood up. The black-cloaked man put out a hand to stop her.

"Wait. Where you from?" He halted between words, as though the human tongue sounded strange to him.

"East and a sea journey." Timbrel neglected to mention that the journey was around the continent.

"You travel west? Do I. We travel together? Safety?"

"I have to ask the others," Timbrel replied. She tilted her head to look more closely at the man.

An inch taller than Timbrel, but not as tall as a Henin or Ravali elf, he walked with the gliding swagger that the half-elf had come to associate with warriors. His knee-length cloak belled out slightly in two places, probably marking a sword on each side.

"Others?" He asked.

"Yes, warrior, the others I travel with." The dark-skinned elf seemed slightly taken aback at her words. "Can you meet us for the evening meal at the Lovely Dancer?"

"I can."

Timbrel turned to go, and then turned back. "What is your name, warrior?"

"I called Ankh Shess."

The girl hurried back to the inn, stopping only twice to inquire about Gareth. The half-elven guide led a group off to Nerryon earlier that morning. He left no message. Timbrel motioned for Jherik to join her and they climbed the inn's stairs to join Krys. She spoke of the dark-skinned elven stranger.

Jherik stood so fast that his chair flipped over backward. "A Melani!"

Krys looked at her strangely. "What did he look like?"

She described Ankh Shess in detail. When she spoke of his golden eyes, Krys stopped her.

"The golden eyes are a sign of the Terformin, Genjin creations designed for the stars. The Melani were one of the first, but they failed. The long life of elves eludes them. I thought the last few were destroyed during the Mage Wars."

"They torture their own people," Jherik added. "And eat their dead."

Timbrel looked between the two elves in horror. "I invited him to meet with us at the evening meal tonight." The girl squirmed in her chair.

Krys frowned slightly. "Meet with him we shall, then."

###

168

*Beneath the Western slopes of Rockhold*

The green lights winked off as the centrifuge stopped spinning. Damnech opened it, moving almost three-dozen test tubes into individual trays. He carefully transferred the fluid from the top of each test tube to a dozen individual jars, already filled with culture media made from the bodies of the dead lab specimens. By the end of next week he would have over three thousand embryos growing. In a few months, if he could synthesize enough hormones to accelerate their growth, he would be ready to move east. Ready for war. There would be no betrayals this time. Let the paltry trash left behind from the Glorious Starlift try to stop him.

The Terformin rubbed his itching chin. A fault in the cryo chamber left him hairless and almost without body fat, and the nerves of his face had not yet adapted to the feeling of bone so close beneath the surface. He stared at the polished surface of a cabinet, studying his reflection. The cartilage in his nose and ears degenerated along with the body fat, leaving behind the skull-like appearance. The skin of his nose flapped outward when he exhaled, and he had quickly learned to inhale through his mouth to avoid suffocating. His eyes sunk in their sockets, no longer supported by a thick layer of fat. The skin of his cheeks lay directly over the bone. At least his teeth were intact, though his gums receded and bled. He turned back to his task, chin still itchy.

His ill temper increased by the inconvenience, Damnech continued moving about the lab. Well protected from the sunlight, deep beneath the ground, the Terformin continued his plan. He would have his revenge. Elves, humans, their allies: every group would fall to him until he found the secret to call back the ship and return to the stars. He had not failed in his mission. The ship failed, and a faulty lifeboat trapped him here.

Scratching at his chin again, Damnech moved to the recording equipment. He thought for a moment, deciding what to include for the first learning tape. As the clones grew, he would supply new tapes and reuse the old with later batches.

### 

*Lucifron*

The evening meal was short. Ankh Shess arrived early, and Krys questioned him thoroughly.

"I travel west and meet with seller. If package is right I pay him and go home. I say this before." Shess leaned forward. "Why you ask again?"

"What item are you buying? Where is home?" Krys looked at Timbrel. "I don't think he understands what I am asking."

Timbrel thought that the Melani was better at the human tongue then he admitted. The gaps between his words gave him plenty of time to think about his answers.

"So what do you think? Can he travel with us?"

"Yes, Timbrel, I think he is safe enough. But can he track as well as he claims?"

"I excellent tracker. You see. When leave?"

"We leave in the morning."

The dark-skinned elf melted away into the night, leaving the three to themselves.

Jherik stomped over to the bar and spoke with a waitress. He returned to the table. "I don't think he should travel with us. I don't trust him."

"Why not? Can you give me a reason?"

"Well, I think he's nice." Timbrel was interrupted as the waitress brought two mugs and set them in front of Jherik.

Jherik grabbed a mug in each hand and drained them one after the other. The waitress immediately brought two more mugs. Jherik picked them up.

Timbrel just shook her head. Why did Jherik act like this? She was never going to figure the elf out.

After Jherik drained the fourth mug, he kept repeating himself to Krys. As he waved his arms around to make a point, he jostled the waitress' tray. There was a muffled *thunk*.

"Oh!" the waitress squealed. "You're wearing armor."

170

Jherik looked embarrassed, flipping the front of his cloak aside to reveal gleaming plate beneath.

"Sorry, Laurel."

Timbrel groaned inwardly. Krys just rolled his eyes.

Laurel bent over Jherik's shoulder. "What army do you serve with?"

"Elven Royal guard." Jherik kept his voice low.

Laurel suddenly straightened, her eyes wide. "You're a *noble*? Here?" As if remembering her place, Laurel suddenly ran off to the kitchens. Jherik looked bemused.

"Are you going to tell her you're engaged?" Krys asked.

"Of course he is," supplied Timbrel. "Or I will."

Krys pushed her toward the kitchen. "Why don't you get us some food? I don't think *we* have a waitress yet."

Timbrel reluctantly left, Krys murmuring to Jherik behind her. Laurel returned with two more mugs. The Henin elf started on the seventh mug, his left hand curled around the eighth.

The half-elven girl returned just as Jherik wobbled to his feet. "I do not feel very well," he announced. "I am going outside." Timbrel and Krys watched him crash his way against tables and stagger out the door.

Krys frowned again. "He didn't drink enough for that to happen. Let me see those." The elf indicated the last two mugs Jherik drained.

As Timbrel passed them to Krys, she wrinkled her nose. A faint licorice odor wafted from the dregs. "*Likshas*," she spat. She set the mug in front of Krys.

He sniffed it once, and turned pale. Without another word he swept the mug to the floor along with half the contents of the table. Timbrel turned toward the door, alarmed at Jherik's danger. She saw Laurel slipping out the door, loosening the laces on her shirt.

Laurel's earlier comment about nobles suddenly made sense. Laurel was a hearth-girl, forced to work at the Inn for a few scraps of food and a greasy spot on the kitchen hearth at night. A relationship with a noble, particularly one that resulted in children, could bring her into a better state of affairs. Nobles were expected to support their bastards in both the human and elven worlds, and many brought the child and its mother into their residence to receive even better care.

Timbrel ran for the door. It took only a few minutes to locate Jherik and Laurel. Jherik's armor lay scattered on the ground, and the elf fumbled with the laces of his trousers as Laurel, already stripped to the waist, kissed him.

"Jherik!" As Timbrel called out his name, the elf raised his head and looked in her direction. His head wavered, eyes already unfocused. Timbrel could smell the licorice fumes on his breath. Laurel's eyes were unfocused as well, and the waitress rubbed herself on the warrior. Jherik looked slowly down at his pants, concentrating on the laces.

Timbrel sighed and then spoke sharply. "Get away from him!"

Laurel pulled back and then leaned forward again. "He wants me," the waitress whispered. Her voice slurred.

Timbrel shook her head, wondering why she bothered to try and save the warrior from his urges. *Because they are not truly his urges.* As a last resort, the half-elf stripped to her loincloth. She began to whistle *The Greensward.* Both Jherik and Laurel turned at the sound.

The half-elven dancer leapt forward, dancing to her own whistled tune. She made the dance as seductive as she could, meeting and keeping Jherik's eyes. The Henin warrior brushed aside Laurel's fingers, frantically plucking at his clothes. His body swayed to match Timbrel as she danced closer.

"No!" Laurel's plaintive wail cut through the whistling. The girl fell to her knees in front of Jherik, unleashing his pants and pulling them to the ground. The Henin elf shook his legs free of the fabric, his eyes never leaving Timbrel. His wrapped undergarment barely contained what lay beneath, and the fabric launched across the clearing when Laurel unwound it far enough. The waitress rubbed herself on the elf, vying for his attention.

Jherik's eyes started to waver. Timbrel leapt closer, trailing her hands across his shoulders in the lightest of touches. Jherik pushed the human girl aside.

Timbrel spared a glance for the cowering waitress. "He's mine, little girl," she whispered. She leaned forward to brush her lips lightly against the warrior's. Jherik's hand reached out to grasp the half-elven girl by the waist.

Laurel burst into tears and ran down the street. Timbrel could hear her sobs fading in the distance. Meanwhile, Timbrel had problems of her own.

Jherik's grip on her waist was far stronger than the girl expected. She pulled his fingers back, one by one, careful not to hurt him. He maneuvered her towards the wall, and the dancer realized that she would not be able to fend him off effectively. Ducking and twisting, she finally leaned forward and bit his lip, distracting him enough to break free.

He caught the corner of her loincloth as she retreated. Drawing her in, the warrior found himself holding a limp piece of cloth. The girl danced away from his grip, her pale body glowing softly in the moonlight. He pursued her, lurching along the empty street.

Timbrel lured him into the pasture by the stables. Jherik continued to stagger after her, his long arms reaching out to catch her. The warrior suddenly tripped and fell, body unmoving in the grass. Alarmed, Timbrel crept up near him, ready to avoid his reaching hands. Another time she might have accepted his drugged advances, but Jherik still belonged to Kareni, and Timbrel was completely out of the ingredients for the bitter tea. As a half-elf, she should not be any more fertile than a mule. But Soliari had lied to her before. She had no wish to test her fertility with anyone, particularly Jherik.

The warrior remained still. Timbrel bent closer, finally tracing her fingertips along the side of his head. Startled at the touch of moisture, she drew back her fingers to see blood. She lifted his head to find a small rock, its one sharp edge bloody. Timbrel checked the wound. Jherik would wake without difficulty

173

in the morning. The drug in his system would keep him sleeping until then.

Running as quickly as she could, Timbrel gathered up the scattered bits of clothing she'd left behind, as well as Jherik's pants and loincloth. Krys intercepted her on her way back to the pasture.

The elven Wizard raised an eyebrow. Timbrel stood before him, her arms filled with clothing. Krys' eyes fixed on Jherik's pants. "You move quickly, I see."

"I did nothing." Timbrel defended herself, her head held high. Some of the clothing in her arms overbalanced and fell. Krys' eyes widened.

"Nothing. And what did you do to the girl?"

"I sent her home." Timbrel picked the clothes up again, continued into the pasture, and bent over the motionless warrior.

The *likshas* continued to do its work, leaving a puddle of moisture across the warrior's abdomen and a half-smile on his face. Timbrel wiped him up with a handful of grass as Krys caught up to her.

Timbrel rolled Jherik's clothes into a bundle before turning to her own. Her loincloth was completely soiled, so she set it aside while she donned the rest of her clothing under Krys' watchful eye. When she turned back, Jherik had curled his fingers tightly in the loincloth again.

"Can you help me get him back to the room?"

### 

Jherik woke with the sun slanting across the bed. He stretched catlike, feeling every muscle flex. The throbbing ache in his loins was gone for the first time in weeks. He rolled to one side, his eyes lighting on his armor, his shirt, his pants, and his loincloth. Puzzled, he reached for the last garment. He never slept without it. A stain on the fabric brought back the first fragment of memory.

The warrior sat bolt upright. Timbrel standing before him, whispering "He's mine." The touch of the dancer's fingertips across his shoulders. A warm weight pressing against his hips. The half-

174

elven girl's loincloth dangling from his fingers as she stood naked before him in the moonlight.

Alarmed, Jherik looked down at the floor. Timbrel's loincloth, soiled with mud and straw, lay by the bedside on top of his armor. What had he done?

A light knock on the door startled him. He pulled the sheet up around him as the latch rattled. The door was bolted. After another knock, a slip of thin white bark slid under the door.

Jherik waited until the footsteps retreated before he picked up the bark. Dark lettering decorated one side. Jherik swore softly as his fingers rubbed off some of the charcoal left from a burnt piece of wood. He wiped them on his leg, and then wiped them again. At last he looked at the message. Written in the human tongue, the letters poorly shaped, it read:

"You were wonderful last night
-Laurel"

Laurel? Who was Laurel? Jherik could only remember Timbrel, the half-elf dancing as he held... oh. Another memory opened. The waitress. Jherik looked at the note and flushed red. Apparently he'd been with both women. Kareni would kill him.

Timbrel's distinctive tap sounded at the door. Jherik scrambled back to the bed, pulling the sheet over his lap as he sat down squarely in a wet spot. He sprang up as if bitten and flattened himself against the far wall of the room.

"Jherik? Are you well?" Timbrel's voice held a note of concern.

"Go away." A quick glance at the door reassured Jherik that the bolt remained in place. For just a second he wondered about that.

Timbrel's voice interrupted the thought "Jherik, come on. We're supposed to leave this morning. The sun has been up for hours."

The Henin warrior clung to the wall. Whirling bits of memory threatened to suck him in like a tornado pulling at trees.

Laurel stripped to the waist. Timbrel standing completely nude. His own pants discarded in the mud.

"Go away." His voice strangled in his throat. He wanted Timbrel to come in and continue whatever they had done. Telling her to leave was the hardest thing he ever did. He tried to think of Kareni, but remembered only his fiancée's sharp tongue. "Go away," he repeated.

"As you wish." Timbrel's soft footfalls patted down the hallway.

Jherik breathed a sigh of relief and slumped to the floor. He still lay there an hour later when Krys called at the door.

"Go away."

"I'm trying to, but my pack is in the room with you. Open the door or I'll do it myself."

Jherik stayed by the wall, pulling the sheet over his lap as the bolt slid to one side. Krys opened the door.

The wizard glanced around the room. "I see you had a good time last night." He walked across the room and grabbed his pack. "We're leaving from the stables in twenty minutes. I suggest you get dressed for the journey."

Jherik arrived in ten.

###

# Chapter Seven

*West of Lucifron*

Ankh Shess rode a little ahead of the others. The trail's vegetation thrived, but Shess found enough traces to follow the last group to pass through. The day-old trail frustrated him. Even with his tracking skills, they were not catching up. The rumors must be true. The guide Gareth knew the trail better than any other.

The fields and plains of Lucifron gave way to fast-growing stands of trees. The trees thickened quickly, darkening the forest floor. Shess held back a little, waiting for the others. They did not see as well in the darkness as he did, though the men managed well enough. The girl's eyes were faulty, giving her great difficulty seeing far enough to comfortably move through the darkness.

A shame, really. Except for her weak eyes, she was exactly what he was sent for. Elven, female, skin the color of moonlit water, hair the color of sunlight, and eyes as blue as the sky. A perfect gift for the dark gods that sheltered his people from harm. And of course, with such a perfect gift the sun god might allow the Melani free access to the surface world again.

The others led their horses, following his lead. He smiled. Yes, this girl would do, but another sun-haired elf woman waited for him in Nerryon. He had sent gifts of gold to reserve her purchase. Perhaps he could arrange for this one to accompany him as well. Surely the gods would be pleased to have two bits of sunlight in their dark kingdom. They might well take away the wasting sickness that affected so many of his people.

Shess was one of three warrior-priests that began the ritual journey this year. The first of the companions crumpled to the ground just outside the jagged break that led to their home cavern system. The Melani's skin swelled and opened in the red sores of Death's Kiss even as Shess and the other ran past. They swam through two streams, trying to hide their scent from Death. Shess removed his shoes each time, swimming with them overhead in spite of his companion's warnings. When they ran through a field of multicolored flowers, the looping stems had tripped the other. Covered in dirt and dust, they continued to run.

Death waited within the colors, however. The other started to limp, his shoes not yet dry. His pace slowed, he struggled and fell as Shess outdistanced him. Far past the field, Shess climbed a rise of rock and looked back. The other lay still, collapsed over a bush as if climbing to his feet, his skin already breaking out in Death's Kisses.

Shess left him behind, running for the protection of the rock's shadow. The sun glared menacingly down at him, seeking out his hiding places in a slow march. Shess darted from shadow to shadow, trying to stay ahead of the sun's direct gaze. His skin burned like a spray of cinders from a bonfire.

By tradition, Shess could only return home with an elf companion. The very few survivors of the journey above, their skins wrinkling quickly as they aged prematurely, always brought an elf. Many others tried to complete the ritual with little success. Shess ran past their bones.

He stopped in his tracks with sudden understanding. The gods did not look for a golden elf sacrifice, but for a Melani one. Those who made the journey sacrificed themselves if they did not find success. Even those who returned sacrificed themselves slowly. The priests said that an elf could last for generations on the life force it sucked from the Melani. If only that drain could be reversed.

A horse snorted, bringing the Melani elf back to the present. The trail split into two parts, half of the group going each way. Shess chose to follow the faint traces of the guide. The road turned darker.

Great white spiderwebs festooned the tops of the giant trees. The forest floor, carpeted in leaves, was empty save for a few patches of moss. Shess bent and picked up a fallen leaf longer than his arm and wider than the distance between his elbow and his fingertips.

Forcing himself to look up, unnatural though that felt, Shess thought he saw movement within the cavern-long webs. Shredded bits hung limply down at the edges like the bloated fingers of those drowned in underground rivers, bleaching from the water's action until the small blind fish nibbled them away. The breeze blew through, undulating the entire web like the surface of the sea.

The sea. Shess did not look forward to that part of the return journey. A week on the constantly moving ocean, hiding from the relentless sun beneath the decks... it nearly killed him. He crawled onto the land, still heaving, unable to eat for almost two days. When he finally regained his appetite, he was ravenous. It took three days of stuffing himself to make up for nine days without food. Not the first time he fasted, it was the first time illness added to his burden. His shame increased when the sailor helping him from the ship mentioned the calm journey.

A sudden cry from the girl caused him to turn. She stood in front of some fungus and scraped it into a clean pouch. Shess stared at the ground in consternation. The fungus was edible in a pinch, but rubbery to chew and with an unpleasant aftertaste. Why did she want to gather that? The small group carried plenty of food.

More movement from above caught the Melani's eye. He motioned to Krys, pale leader of the group. Krys looked up, and then drew a short dagger. The other elf followed suit, drawing an arm-long blade. The web suddenly opened, immense spiders dropping to surround the group.

### 

*The Spider Forest*

Timbrel stepped back and closed her pouch, now full of the glowing striped fungus. Though she only needed a little of the poison antidote for her medicine pouch, she knew that she could trade the rest for other herbs.

The forest suddenly came alive. Spiders taller than the giant Halar dropped from the trees and menaced her on every side. A glance showed her that Krys and Jherik were surrounded as well. She could not see their guide in the darkness beneath the trees.

The girl clutched her short dagger, smears of fungus still decorating the blade. Her cloak fell back from her shoulders, giving her more freedom of movement. She looked up at the closest spider. Unable to imagine where it might be vulnerable beneath the thick black hair, she waved the dagger back and forth. Clicking voices jabbered around her in the darkness. The spiders spoke! Timbrel did not understand the words.

Krys and Jherik moved closer to Timbrel. The single spider between them reared its front pair of legs. Timbrel saw her chance. With a sudden burst of speed, she darted between the spider's back legs, ducking under the creature and rejoining Krys and Jherik. The three stood in a circle facing outward. Another flash of movement and their guide joined them. The four stood together as equals, each brandishing a blade of some sort.

The spiders made no move to attack. They backed away slightly, giving the group more room. One spider crouched down. Timbrel pointed her dagger at the giant creature, expecting an attack.

A nut-brown man scrambled off of the spider's back. He stood slightly shorter than the half-elven girl, his ears both pointed and fully lobed. For just a moment the girl thought he might be some strange breed of half-elf. As her eyes adjusted, she saw the colorful tattoos that hid the rest of his features. His eyes were much lighter brown than his skin, almost amber. He faced the girl, ducking his head between his shoulders rhythmically. His mount did the same, bobbing on its long legs. The movement spread among the other spiders and their riders.

Timbrel looked back at the man and copied the movement. Bobbing her head, she said the only thing she could think of. "Hello, I'm Timbrel."

180

The voices from the darkness sprang up again, clicking away at high speed. The nut-brown elf listened and bobbed his head faster. He straightened himself to his full height, looked at Timbrel, and said very clearly, "Greetings, Timbrel. I am the Stinger."

The tension immediately eased, and the spiders disappeared into the darkness. Stinger remained, flanked by two other riders. Timbrel could barely see Stinger's spider at the limits of her vision. "These are my friends, Krys, Jherik, and Shess." She indicated the elves as she spoke.

Shess seemed paralyzed, moving forward with great difficulty when she introduced him. His eyes widened with fear, Timbrel saw. She patted his hand to comfort him.

Stinger indicated the two riders who stood by his side. "These are riders under my command."

The rider on his left, a woman with serpentine tattoos, smiled at Timbrel. Her teeth were sharpened to points.

Each of the riders held a long serrated sword that appeared white in the dim light. Dressed in loosely laced leather vests over cloth shirts and trousers with leather chaps, leather straps crisscrossed their tunics, each attached to a different weapon's sheath. They wore circular white discs suspended from short leather cords around their necks.

"You are free to walk where you will, Timbrel." Stingers voice had an odd inflection at the end. The girl thought it might be a question.

"We would like passage through your forest."

Stinger bobbed his head very slowly, just once. "I ask of you. You are free to walk?"

Timbrel cocked her head to one side, looking at the Spider Rider. "Am I free to go? To walk wherever I want without my friends' permission? Of course."

"Walk with me."

Shrugging at her friends, Timbrel walked a short distance away with Stinger.

When they were out of sight of the others, the nut-brown man stopped and looked at her. "You are a warrior?" He finally asked.

"A warrior? No, I have no training."

"A wife, then? You have children?"

Timbrel looked closely at Stinger. In the darkness his eyes shone dark amber. Might they be golden in the sunlight? Golden like Shess? "I am no wife, and have no children yet. Why do you ask?"

Stinger suddenly dropped to one knee. "Marry me. Let me have the honor to be your first husband. Let me father your first children."

Timbrel took a step back. "I am not ready to get married yet."

Stinger rose to his feet, his face and voice completely expressionless. "We shall return to the others, and you will spend the night in our camp."

He asked no question this time, Timbrel thought. This was an order.

### 

Krys was impressed with the rider's camp. High boughs lashed together with spider silk, sheets of webbing served as walls and floors, and silken rope bridges connected the treetops. The spiders sometimes came within, but usually they stayed in the trees not far from the webbed camp. Most of the riders were male.

The sunset turned the webbing blood red. One of the riders brought out a woven scroll. Picking at it carefully, the rider pulled a thread of dark silk through the rest, weaving in and out and carefully shaping letters. Krys stepped across a short bridge to get a better view, reaching out to the wall to steady himself as he'd seen the riders do.

His hand stuck to the wall. Krys pulled gently, careful to keep his balance. He pulled again, a little harder. The scroll weaver saw his plight and came to assist him.

The scroll weaver ran his hand down the wall toward Krys' hand. When they contacted, Krys felt a momentary oiliness on his skin and then release. The wizard-elf quickly withdrew his hand.

"You should remain in the visitor's room," the weaver suggested.

Krys agreed. "Can you come with me? I'd like to watch what you are doing."

The weaver seemed delighted. He eagerly began explaining the technique of weaving silk into letters, using a mix of human and Rider words.

When the explanation slowed, Krys ventured a question. "What are you writing about?"

"I keep a record of our journey and the life-forms we encounter. You are different, each enhanced and yet of different types. The dark one seems much like us, but has no memories."

"No memories?" Krys was alarmed. "Is Shess ill?"

"He is well. But he lacks the ancestral renna memories."

"Renna? Is that what your people are called?"

The Weaver looked at Krys, an unreadable expression flickering across his face. After a moment, Krys realized it was amusement.

"We are the Taa, the spider people. A symbiosis. Once we were many, but we lost much renna in the last great war. My scroll will join the others in our city archives."

"Archives? How long have you been weaving scrolls?"

"Not long. Five hundred years." The Weaver stretched his neck up, then bobbed his head twice and scrambled away.

Tempted to follow him, Krys decided against getting stuck a second time.

### 

*The Taa Forest Camp*

Timbrel sat on the platform, watching the Taa woman oil her blade and its leather sheath with the same care a mother lavished on her newborn infant. The wickedly serrated sword was made entirely of fused bone.

"Why did you not honor the Stinger?" The woman's soft voice startled Timbrel. Such a fiercely tattooed warrior should have a fiercer voice.

"Honor him?" The half-elf was confused. Honor the rider for what?

"Accept him as your husband. He seldom asks." She rubbed a drop of glistening oil into the hilt, using her hand to polish the spot.

Timbrel looked at the warrior-woman closely. "Do you have a husband?"

The woman smiled, her filed teeth gleaming in the faint light. "I have honored four. The Great Mother has honored me in return with twenty-three children."

Timbrel gasped. "Twenty-three? But you cannot be so old. How could you survive so many births?" The Taa rider looked like a teen, not old enough to bear a child.

"The Great Mother sent them three and four at a time." She pointed to the tattoos on her left cheek. Around the snake etched there, twenty-three dots were scattered in clusters of three and four.

The half-elf was curious. "Why did you bear so many?"

"Why would I not? Children are the greatest gift, valued almost as much as freedom." The tattooed warrior sheathed her sword. "Six have already died, and the others may not live to honor another. They will fall as warriors. It is the way."

Timbrel watched the Taa rider in confusion. The woman showed no regrets, no sadness over her lost children. The half-elf knew that in similar circumstances she would have been crushed.

"Why do you fight? Can you not just move to the lowlands?"

The rider stood absolutely still. She swiveled her head to look at Timbrel. "We cannot live without war. In such a place we would breed too fast and eventually fight the land for its bounty. Better to fight ourselves than the land. When the weak die, the Taa grow stronger. Once we were weak, hiding in the shadow of the forest from the eyes of the killing sun. Now we simply choose to remain in the forest's shadows. The sun is no longer our enemy."

"Even the weak can be wise."

"And the strong are sometimes killed. We use their renna. This way we do not lose their knowledge."

Timbrel did not ask more about the Renna. She understood that it was a sacred ceremony. Stinger had mentioned it once and grown stiff with insult when she asked again.

### 

On the morning of the third day, the Taa gently let the group down to the forest floor. Krys was relieved. The trees stood thinner here and a wan sunlight reached pale fingers to the trail. The horses waited, still saddled, and protected from whatever creatures lurked in the nighttime forest by a makeshift stall of spider silk. One horse was missing, its pack frame set on the ground. Jherik's armor lay piled to one side.

Stinger waved at the trail. "You are free to pass through the forest as free people should." He stepped forward, four white discs dangling from his fingers on leather cords. The Taa offered a disk to each of the group in turn. Krys bowed his head, allowing the rider to place the disk around his neck. Jherik and Timbrel followed suit. Shess backed slightly away, his hands in a warding gesture.

"I cannot accept such a thing. It is against the beliefs of my home."

Stinger bobbed his head in acceptance. He turned to Krys. "Beware who you travel with. The free may be mistaken for the unfree. Beware the white tower." As Stinger waved his hand in farewell, a dozen male Taa dropped from the trees with their spiders. Dismounting, they surrounded the group.

Three of the boldest dropped to their knees in front of Timbrel.

"Take me as your fourth husband."

"I would gladly be your fifth husband."

185

"Will you take six?"

Timbrel looked around wildly. "No. No. No. I do not choose any of you for a husband."

Krys chuckled as the remaining riders slumped their shoulders and returned to their spiders. A moment later, the riders left on their spiders, leaving the group alone.

"Fourth husband?" Jherik asked. "You have three others?"

Krys laughed loudly. He pointed to Jherik, Shess, and himself in turn. "Which number are *you*, Jherik?"

The Henin elf flushed bright red, spurring his horse ahead. The animal protested, already bowed beneath the weight of its rider and his largest pieces of armor.

"I would not mind," offered Shess. "Do I receive the gifts?"

Krys laughed again. Timbrel snorted, wrinkled her nose, and rode ahead to catch up to Jherik. A few minutes later, Shess rode past and took up his normal position in front.

The trail followed the contours of the land, occasionally curving to avoid large clumps of bushes. The trees thinned into an open meadow. Timbrel carefully steered her horse past several short stumps at the forest's edge, slender enough to be dangerous if the horses stepped on them.

A small cluster of houses stood in the distance. The group followed the trail, the thin path soon joining the larger road. Children ran from the houses to watch them as they approached. A dozen dirty waifs, big-eyed with respect, stood at the side of the road.

A woman with streaks of grey in her dark hair walked out into their path, signaling them to stop. Her unlined face and slim figure probably made her a great beauty among the humans. Krys pulled his horse up next to her.

"Greetings. I am Kryslandir."

"I am Lashana, once in service to the great tower. How may I help you?"

"A night's lodging and some hot food would be appreciated."

"Done. Welcome to Insara." Lashana led them to a large building of stone and wood. They tied their horses to a convenient post set outside near a patch of grass and millet. The horses whickered softly as the elves followed Lashana through the door.

Krys looked around the front room, immediately suspicious. This was no inn, but a residence. Lashana lived in luxury. Padded benches covered in fur lined the walls of her common room, each large enough to easily allow two people to sleep. More furs carpeted the floor. Bowls of sweet-smelling flowers hung suspended from the ceiling. A small fountain bubbled in the corner, copper pipes leading away to other parts of the house.

"Marzh," Lashana called. "We have guests. Bring food."

Krys noticed Lashana eyeing him the same way that the waitress Laurel eyed Jherik back in Lucifron. A servant woman, probably Marzh, brought out hot food in minutes. Even the biscuits tasted fresh. Bread took hours to cook in the best hearthside ovens, and overnight when cooked in the embers of a campfire. Where had the food come from so quickly?

Lashana seated herself on the bench next to him. Krys stood, feeling uncomfortable. He turned at Jherik's laughter. Lashana lay sprawled across the bench behind him.

"You poor thing. Come, let me rub your shoulders."

Krys avoided Lashana a second time and seated himself across the room. *Why is this human pursuing me?* He felt no attraction whatsoever to her.

Shess sat quietly, his golden eyes drinking in the sight. Jherik squirmed and snickered. Timbrel lay on a bench, her eyes closed, and rubbed her temples.

A loud knock on the door rescued Krys just as Lashana cornered him again. The door opened and half a dozen men entered, pushing Lashana aside and bombarding the newcomers with questions.

"My daughter was right. Elves!"

"Which way are you traveling?"

"Did you see the spiders in the forest?"

"Of course they did. They got the bone passes."

"Will you visit the Seer in the white tower?"

"That madman? Why would they want to?"

It took Lashana several minutes to restore order to the room. Timbrel sat up to make room for some of the locals to sit.

One of the local men eyed Timbrel. "Aye, Lashana, you've got competition here, I see." A chuckle rose around the room. Lashana's cheeks turned red.

"I'll send her off with my son if I have to." Lashana glared at Timbrel.

"Oh no, you won't," cautioned one man. "She wears the disk of the spiders. You try sending her off like that and we won't survive."

Lashana's face darkened. "My son has done more to keep the spiders away then you'll do in your life. He stopped their encroachment on our farmlands."

"It's not the spiders that I'm worried about. It's the spreading death from the tower side."

"Don't break another pact, Lashana. We need to keep some fields fertile."

### 

*Insara*

Timbrel was in her element. She questioned her seatmate, and then traveled around the room speaking with the other local men. Within a few minutes she received several offers for the evening, earned Lashana's undying hatred, and learned quite a bit about the tower pact.

The white tower appeared in the forest after an earthquake more than twenty generations ago. A bargain was made by the Seer within to hire an assistant from the village. In return for constant companionship and general duties, the Seer would grant great knowledge and keep the villagers healthy.

188

Over the generations, Lashana's family offered the most assistants. They became prominent in the community. Every fifteen years a young man reported to the tower, learning during his service. When a younger relative replaced him, he became free to raise a family of his own and spent time teaching the tower's secrets to the next generation.

During Lashana's childhood, war raked the land. Elves and humans battled over the forests. Twenty-five years before, when Lashana turned thirteen, the time came to send a new assistant. The only survivor near the proper age, Lashana was sent to assist the Seer.

The Seer accepted the arrangement, and Lashana turned her natural talent for flirtation toward him. She teased him with the promise of marriage if he should ever become normal. Of course, this wasn't likely since the Seer locked himself away for three days of each month, usually around the full moon. The locals told stories of a giant black demon-wolf that terrorized the village long ago. Some thought the Seer became the wolf, others that he kept the wolf as a pet.

The last sighting of the demon-wolf came a month before Lashana came home to the village in her sixth year of service. Her clothing disheveled, her story hysterical and punctuated with tears, Lashana told of the Seer's sudden illness and resulting madness. She refused to return to finish serving her term. As her body began swelling with a child, the villagers relented and sent an older relative. The Seer turned the man away at the tower door. The pact was broken, and the Seer had not left the tower since.

A year later, the trees closest to the tower began to wilt and die. Each year the path of death crept a little farther from the tower. This past year the creeping death reached the edges of the village's fields. What little grew in the affected fields seemed cursed. Fruits grew small and hard, grain supplied little nutrition, and neither could be successfully fermented into the sour beer that the villagers made. If not for the records of knowledge stored within the white tower, the villagers would have burnt it down long before. Rumors said that some had tried, with little success.

189

Several men told Timbrel that Lashana had been free with her favors since the birth of her son. The creeping death must have affected her womb, though, since she never conceived another child. Some said she came back with a little of the Seer's madness.

Timbrel thought the story was sad, and she understood the woman's pursuit of Krys. Lashana must be awfully lonely for a second child, especially if her son left home to wage a boundary war against the Taa. After the locals left with their news, Timbrel watched as Lashana repaired to another room in the house, shoulders drooping. In spite of the distance, Krys slept poorly. The sound of his tossing and turning kept Timbrel awake.

By late afternoon the next day, the sun gleamed off of the domed peak of the white tower. Escaping Insara's endless welcoming ceremonies and Lashana's attentions, Krys led them off to the tower.

### 

*The White Tower*

They reached the end of the green fields after a few hours' ride. The next field was sparse, the few plants streaked with yellow and brown. Beyond, Timbrel could see dead plants stretching to the edge of a leafless forest. In the far distance, deep within the forest, a white tower stretched like an accusing finger into the darkening sky.

Timbrel found herself staring at the tower over and over again as they set up camp at the edge of the forest. She glanced around guiltily and immediately felt better when she realized that the others stared as well. The very top of the tower glittered and gleamed like a jewel in the last rays of the setting sun.

Timbrel settled down to sleep. The ground was lumpy and hard, and no amount of tossing and turning softened it. Timbrel felt unwelcome. She shook her head, trying to dislodge the idea. It came from Lashana, she knew. *She is so bitter*, the dancer thought.

190

Could it be her guilt at breaking the pact between the Seer and the village? Or was there more to it?

In spite of the hard ground, Timbrel fell into a half-sleep and began to dream. A mist seemed to rise from the ground, obscuring everything. When it dissipated, the air smelled fresh and green. The crops grew much larger than Timbrel had ever seen before. The forest bristled with leaves and rustled with life.

The sweet scent of fruit drifted on the warm, moist breeze. Animals scurried through the fields and forest. Insects flitted and birds sang, the colorful flash of their bodies clearly visible against the dark green foliage. Lighter green dotted the treetops, much taller against the tower. The tower still gleamed white, but seemed friendlier. Timbrel's dream self trod the well-worn pathway, the scent of leaf mold tickling her nose into a sneeze.

As she neared the tower, a huge black wolf burst from the thick brush. Timbrel looked at the animal without fear. Its eyes were large, golden, and seemed very human. So human, in fact, that the dancer found her own eyes brimming with tears at the sorrow so plainly expressed by those silent eyes.

She woke crying, tears spilling down her cheeks. Shess crouched near her feet, about to prod her awake for her watch. He looked at her strangely.

Timbrel pulled her foot away before he could touch it. She turned her back and wiped her eyes, afraid that the tears would keep coming. An aching sadness suffused her.

The half-elf found it difficult to move quickly. Her bones and muscles ached from the hard ground. She imagined herself an ancient human, tottering along. Every injury she had ever taken, every sprain, even the soreness from her rape so many years before, all were magnified and simultaneous in their pain. She felt awful.

During her watch, Timbrel took the time to work some of the stiffness out of her muscles. The worst of the pain eased. Uncomfortable and tired, she no longer looked forward to the trek to the tower.

When it came time to wake the others, only Krys still seemed motivated. Timbrel heard him muttering about the archives as he went through his morning routine. Jherik was difficult to rouse, however, and moved stiffly when he did. Shess sprang up at the first nudge of his foot, grabbing for his weapons. The Melani seemed on edge. Had he also dreamed?

The group rode straight toward the tower. The deeper they got into the forest the more the horses balked. They forced the horses to follow the path between the dead white trees with great difficulty.

Timbrel understood their reluctance. The forest would have been bleak in any case. Compared to her dream, it was almost too much to bear. The dead trees stuck out of the ground like gnarled hands, their leafless fingers stretched toward the overcast sky. No leaves hung to whisper against the wind, and no breeze blew to freshen the stale air. The tiny sounds of insects were missing entirely. No birds flew between the branches, no animals scurried in the underbrush. The only sounds were the creak of the saddles and the dull plodding of the horses' hooves, rustling as the dead leaves grew deeper.

The drifts of leaves became several feet deep. Shess rode his horse through the drifts, powdering the leaves that his horse stepped on. The trees rose around them, stark branches laced overhead. Timbrel looked in vain for anything alive. No moss grew on the trunks, nor fungus, nor even a scent of leaf mold.

The dead forest opened up into a brushy area near the base of the tower. A series of white domes stacked one upon the other like bubbles, several scorch marks marred its smooth white sides. Timbrel searched for some sign of the black wolf in her dream. Nothing moved.

Krys found the tower's door without a problem. It had the now familiar lock-box and side panel. Krys placed his hand on the panel.

A different voice issued from the door's lock-box. Much deeper, it spoke the human tongue with a trace of an accent Timbrel could not identify.

"Door won't open. Go away."

Krys looked at Timbrel. She leaned over and spoke into the lock-box. "We'd like to come in, Sir. There are four of us, and we've traveled quite some way to see you."

The voice turned gruff. "I see no one, Lashana. You know this."

Timbrel stood straight and put a hand on her hip. I am *not* Lashana. I'm Timbrel."

"What's going on?" Jherik asked in the elf tongue. "What is the door saying?"

"Calm yourself, Jherik," Timbrel replied in the same tongue. "He thinks I'm someone else."

The lock-box suddenly squawked in elvish. "Elves? Enter please." The door hummed and clicked once. Krys pulled it open. Timbrel stopped long enough to tie the horses to a dead tree and scatter some feed on the ground for them before following.

The room that they entered was almost triangular, its long side following the curve of the outer wall. The short sides each sported a single door, and a third door graced the inside corner.

She looked up as the ceiling emitted another hum. The voice filled the room. "Cross the room and enter the stairwell. I will meet you on the ninth level."

The corner door revealed the promised stairwell, and the elves climbed slowly up its spiral. Timbrel took the time to notice the carvings in the white walls of the stairwell. The artist had been crude but competent, each scene of the story told in a separate box that slowly wound its way up the stairs. The first carving depicted a great light in the sky, closing on the village and its surrounding forest. In the third panel, the sky-light dropped a glowing seed and streaked away through the night sky. When the sun rose, the seed had grown into a tall white tower of stacked bubbles. The tower's inhabitant was an elf, the pointed ears meticulously drawn.

Timbrel realized the others had left her behind. She hurried to catch up with them, ignoring the rest of the carvings.

When Timbrel reached the ninth level, Krys, Jherik, and Shess stood in a loose semi-circle around an elf nearly as tall as

Krys. His dark hair, tawny brown skin, and sorrow-filled golden eyes matched the wolf in her dream. The same golden eyes, she realized, that Shess and the Taa shared.

Timbrel scurried to stand behind them. The elf's eyes flickered in her direction. He suddenly knelt, bowing his head.

"Lady Timbrel, greetings."

Timbrel returned a curtsey, her traveling skirts flaring nicely. "You have the advantage, Lord..."

"Gowell."

Timbrel smiled. It was nice to find someone courteous after all their traveling. "I greet you in return, Lord Gowell." The formalities finished, Timbrel stood from her curtsey. Krys and Shess watched her silently. Jherik's mouth sagged slightly open.

Gowell suddenly swept his arm through the air. "You are welcome to a short stay, and I give you permission to visit my archives should you wish." Without waiting for an answer, the tanned elf turned on his heel and entered the stairwell. Timbrel could hear his pounding footsteps as he ran up the stairs.

Jherik looked at Krys. "What does a short stay mean?"

Timbrel answered. "We have ten days. By rights, our host should provide food and a room for us. Since he did not specify otherwise, I believe we should consider this room as our home until we leave. Do we know where the archives are?"

Krys tilted his hand in assent. "I believe so. What did you do to him, by the way?"

Timbrel tilted her head and frowned. "What are you talking about?"

Jherik piped up, interrupting Krys before he began. "Lord Gowell. A strange one. He just stared at us when we first walked in, even when Krys introduced us. Then he muttered to himself as if we weren't there at all. He didn't even talk to us until you came in."

Timbrel could not reconcile the polite and courteous elf she had just met with Jherik's description. She looked from one to the other of the elves, each gesturing assent.

194

"Some of his muttering described the archives," Krys mused aloud. "Histories on ten, taxonomies on eleven."

"What is a taxonomy, Krys?" Jherik frowned over the strange word.

"I'm not certain. We have ten days to find out. We should get started." Krys led the way to the stairwell.

### 

Shess felt ill. The longer he stayed among the surface elves, the weaker he felt. The effect seemed to heighten with the age of the elf. He supposed that the older elves needed to draw more life energy.

It wasn't too bad near the girl Timbrel. Her usual cheeriness seemed to give him more energy. He felt stronger and healthier near her. Twice the Melani elf restrained himself from showing off his great speed. He wasn't sure what strange urge prompted him to publicly display his capabilities; it went against every lesson he had learned.

Jherik affected him much more. Shess felt a strange weakness when he neared the warrior. Though the Melani elf remained certain that he was stronger than the other, the weakness disturbed him.

Krys bothered him the worst. Obviously the eldest of the group, Krys made Shess feel weak and sick just by standing next to him. Several times Shess found spreading bruises after Krys touched him lightly to gain his attention. They took days to heal. Did Krys concentrate the sunlight in his touch?

This new elf, Gowell, was older still than Krys. Shess felt not only weakness, but also his very life draining out of him when they first stood near their host. The same draining appeared to affect the others as well. No wonder that he didn't see any elder elves. They were either drained of their life by younger and stronger elves, or they drained life so powerfully that no other elves could go near them. Perhaps the younger elves killed the elder at some point.

After only six days, Shess was weakened to the point of panic. By the tenth day he might not be able to lift his sword. He looked across the room at the girl.

Timbrel paced. Her steps started out regularly, but now took on an odd rhythm. At each step she hopped slightly, the balance of her hips shifting. At the end of each series, she spun on her heel into a complicated foot pattern before starting off again.

Shess watched her carefully. Some of her patterns looked like the ritual dancing of the priestesses to his own dark gods. Was the girl a priestess in her own right? That would more than counterbalance her faulty eyesight. The Melani elf grew excited. If only he could find a way to bring both golden elves back with him. He *had* to.

Krys swept by, his green robes nearly brushing Shess. The dark-skinned elf recoiled, pressing backward as far as the shelves of scrolls would allow.

The green-robed elf took charge after Timbrel explained their privileges. Checking every door from the stairwell, Krys discovered that the archives filled every floor from the second to the fifteenth, with the ninth floor excepted. Each morning and evening a selection of hot food lay on the table. Timbrel wrapped some of the breakfast to carry with her for midday. The others followed suit. The fare was adequate to keep them alive, but not particularly tasty. The fruit wrinkled as they watched, and the bread quickly turned stale. The meats seemed old and tough to chew. In spite of the quality, Timbrel thanked their host aloud every day.

Timbrel finished one final spin. "It's time to feed the horses." She slipped out the door. Shess frowned. Their host provided plenty of fodder for the beasts, but expected their group to do the actual feeding. Timbrel spent far too much time at such a menial task. Shess had followed her the second day, watching her rub and pamper the beasts. It did no good, the horses did not thrive on the food any more than the elves did.

196

A faint giggle echoed through the room. The Melani elf clenched his teeth in frustration. The voice started again. Of course. The girl was outside where she could not hear it.

"Ships and storms, ships and storms." The deep voice took on a child-like singsong quality. Shess put his hands over his ears in an effort to block out the voice. It did not work. It never worked. The voice continued. "Visitors, all the same, all different. Spirals twist, spirals turn, all the same. Stretch and spin, wolf and wizard, shift and cast, all the same, all different."

The nonsense words continued, punctuated by the occasional giggle, until Shess was ready to scream at the walls again. Krys continued to read, unperturbed by the noise. Jherik looked uncomfortable, but made no move.

At last Krys looked up at the ceiling. Shess winced as the silver-haired elf spoke. "So light is a side effect of vibration?"

The singsong voice answered. "Light and heat, en-er-gy. Planck and Newton and conservation."

"Light and heat? Hmm. Thank you." Krys bent back to the book.

Shess snarled and stomped across the room. Krys was as bad as the Seer, asking questions into the air and pretending to make sense of the answering gibberish. They would all go mad if the singsong voice did not stop soon.

As suddenly as it began, the odd words ended. A few minutes later Shess could hear Timbrel's step on the staircase. He met her at the stairwell door.

"Did you hear him *this* time?"

Timbrel looked at the Melani, confused. "Hear what? I heard nothing. What do you have against Lord Gowell? He is a perfect gentleman, just a little lonely."

It was true, Gowell's voice sharpened up when Timbrel spoke to him, and he always answered the girl courteously and clearly, even if he did not give her all of the information that she asked for. The girl steadfastly refused to believe that their host acted anything less than kind and courteous.

Shess tried to be kind and courteous as well in his dealings with Timbrel. He had already noticed her sense of loyalty to her friends, willing to stand by them no matter what threatened. If he could share in that loyalty, it would be much easier to bring her to his home caverns. The Melani elf walked slowly among the unintelligible stacks of paper, considering his options regarding Timbrel.

### 

On the evening of the ninth day, shortly before the evening meal, Timbrel climbed the stairs to their highest point. Krys and Jherik busily read documents both ancient and recent, and Shess walked thoughtfully among the stacks on another floor. They would not miss her until after the meal.

Twice before, Timbrel had made the long climb to the top of the stairs. The other two times she knocked at the locked door, waiting for Gowell to answer. Though she could hear some movement inside the room, he never spoke or opened the door. This time she stood silently before the door, listening.

A great sigh could be heard through the door. Timbrel held her breath, listening for any of the muttering which the others insisted they heard constantly. The girl heard nothing of the sort.

Using the bits of wire that she secreted in the hem of her cloak, Timbrel worked at the lock. A moment later she turned the doorknob and softly entered the room.

Gowell sat in a large chair facing the opposite wall. She could barely see the back of his head peeking above the tallest part of the chairback in the room's darkness. She quickly closed the door and let her eyes adjust.

She padded softly to one side. Gowell dressed in black, blending with the darkness. His breathing was soft and regular. He sighed again, turning his head to one side as he slept in his great chair. The chair faced a window filled with stars.

Timbrel frowned. The sun shone brightly outside, yet Gowell's window showed a night sky filled with unfamiliar stars.

A moon came into view, moving much faster than Timbrel expected. A second moon followed the first.

The light from the two moons allowed Timbrel to see more clearly. A square panel of switches and dim lights surrounded the window. A small table stood to one side, the gleam of its metal in the strange moonlight allowing Timbrel to see its outlines. A small painting stood on the table.

Timbrel gasped. The painting showed a rocky promontory above a strange-looking blue forest. A black wolf sat on the rocks, its head tilted back as it howled at the two moons above. The girl glanced between the painting and the window. The moons were approaching the moment captured in the painting. The stars aligned as well.

When the window and the painting matched, a soft chiming began and the lights brightened slightly. Gowell opened his eyes and immediately looked at Timbrel.

"The opposite of war," he whispered.

Timbrel tilted her head. "Is peace," she supplied.

"No! The opposite of war is never peace, never peace." He looked closely at the girl. "You are not afraid."

"Should I be?" Her outward confidence did not waver, though she felt the weak clenching in her stomach that she associated with small magics. "What spell are you casting?"

Gowell paused, his eyes widening and his mouth forming an Oh of surprise. "You are Krys' apprentice?"

"Me?" Timbrel paused. "I do not use magic. What spell are you casting?"

Gowell cocked his head, matching Timbrel and looking directly into her eyes. "How do you know I am casting a spell?"

"I feel it here." She touched her belly for a moment. "What does it do?"

"It moves the trays of food from one place to another."

"Thank you. For everything. The food, the place to stay, making Krys so happy. He studies magic, you know."

Gowell smiled. "Spellcasters may shift, but shifters may not cast. The old truth is wrong."

199

Timbrel had no idea what her host spoke about. "Shifters?"

"A different way of purifying. Like magic, but less controlled."

"Purifying what?"

Gowell tilted his head the opposite direction, still looking at Timbrels eyes. "The hidden poisons, left over from the engin... You wouldn't know of them, would you?"

"The Hinjin?" Timbrel put a slightly different accent to Gowell's word. "The great makers of magic who fought with the Genjin."

Gowell frowned. "The Genjin?"

Timbrel smiled. "The Genjin. The creators. They made the elf, the dragon, and many other creatures. They gave us long life, resistance to disease, and sometimes other gifts. They made the Terformin, too."

Gowell nodded. "The Genjin. Yes, they did make us. Do you know of the ships?"

Timbrel frowned. "No. But the Genjin banished the Terformin to the stars, right before the great war with the Hinjin. The stories say they sucked the land dry before they were sent away."

Gowell smiled sadly. "Yes, the ships took us to the stars. As for sucking the land dry, how do you feel?"

"A little tired. It will pass, I'm certain of it."

Gowell looked more closely at the girl.

Timbrel felt a sudden wave of weariness.

"You are weakened. The stories are true. I *do* suck the land dry."

"You are a Terformin? But you are nice." Timbrel chewed on her lip. "The villagers told me that until twenty years ago you did nothing but help the humans." She looked down and added, almost as an afterthought, "I wish you could help me find my cousin."

Gowell's face clouded. He turned away from Timbrel and stared at the strange window. The moons rose again. He reached out to the panel beneath, his fingers rippling across the lights like

200

grass rippling in the wind. The window changed, flashing one scene after another like a series of paintings: a boat battling a stormy sea, hundreds of skeleton-like men practicing weapons on the sand, a golden dragon gliding through the sky. It finally settled on a marketplace of sorts. The window appeared to move, showing a street lined with cages. Some of the cages held people in various states of undress. Muscular men, possibly warriors, stood testing the bars of their cages. Two human girls fought each other in another cage, scratching and biting at each other like animals. There was a flash of gold in the farthest cage. A golden-haired elf stood at the bars, lecturing the two girls silently. The girls stopped their fight, both throwing bits of dirty straw at the elf-woman. It took Timbrel a moment to recognize her cousin-kin Lostaria.

"The opposite of war," Gowell repeated. "You should leave. It is dangerous for you to be so close to me."

Timbrel wavered on her feet. She darted forward, fighting the lethargy that threatened to overcome her, and kissed Gowell on the cheek before darting to the door. "I will keep your secret, Lord Gowell."

The dancer made her way down the stairs, thinking about their Terformin host. Lord Gowell had been perfectly polite, if a little mysterious. He commanded the Hinjin artifacts in his room, particularly the magic window. His warning about the opposite of war bothered her. Peace should follow war, shouldn't it? Why did his window show what appeared to be a market for selling people? And why did it show Lostaria in a cage?

It took Timbrel far longer to descend the stairs then to ascend them. By the time she reached the ninth level, she dragged her feet with exhaustion. She nearly fell through the door.

Krys leapt to his feet. "Timbrel! What happened to you?" He slid an arm underneath her own, supporting her.

"Just tired," she whispered. Her lips felt strange. She rubbed a finger on them. Her finger came away spotted with blood.

###

*The Dead Forest*

Krys forced them to leave as soon as the sun rose. Exhaustion ruled. The horses seemed tired and reluctant to move as well. Shess seemed eager to go, but completely without energy.

Twice Krys resorted to his spells, creating hotspots under the horses' tails. The beasts picked up their pace, crushing dead leaves to powder as they shuffled through the drifts. They pushed on through midday, Krys handing out stale biscuits saved from the morning meal. He continued pushing the group to ride, refusing to stop until they reached the green line that separated this land of death from that of life.

The farther they got from the tower, the faster the horses moved. By the time they crossed into a green meadow, the horses recovered enough to move almost half as fast as their normal walking speed. The thin crescent of the moon hung over the grass. Krys pushed on for another ten minutes and called a stop for the night.

Timbrel nearly fell out of her saddle. Only a quick dash and catch by Shess stopped her from crashing into the ground. Jherik staggered over to the horses, staking them close by camp. The Henin elf returned and sat by the others. "I'll watch for a while. Get some sleep."

Krys was relieved to see the green glow of an earth elemental adjusting the ground beneath Timbrel. The sounds of insects and night birds competed with the soft sound of wind in the grass. The noises soon lulled the Ravali elf into sleep.

Krys woke to absolute silence. No insects, no rustle of mice, not even the wind. The moon had set. Jherik stood at attention, looking out into the darkness. Shess turned his head and looked at Krys. Krys lifted his head just enough to see Timbrel. The exhausted half-elf slept heavily, her breathing barely audible in the stillness.

Krys considered for a moment, then gathered his power and set a minor silence spell near Timbrel. The vibrations faded from the air by the girl, muting her sounds. Krys listened carefully to the night.

Jherik suddenly gave a yell and charged off into the darkness. Krys scrambled to his feet, as did Shess. Shess drew a long, thin-bladed sword, its edge wickedly serrated. The Melani elf leaned over and began breathing deeply, eyes fixed on his sword. Roaring sounds mixed with Jherik's yells, followed by a grunting. The noises faded. Jherik did not return. Without thinking, Krys sketched a symbol in the air with his hand and threw power into a light spell. The meadow lit up in brilliant white glare. A large animal lay a few hundred yards away, its head bent over a man's prone body. Other animals retreated from the light, turning with cat-like grace. Shess ran at the remaining animal, his blade flashing in the glare.

A part of Krys' mind noted that Shess moved far faster than he should, both in running and in his swordwork. Another part wondered why the beast did not move. A third whispered to Krys that his magic worked spectacularly well, particularly for a first casting.

Shess stood back, bent over and breathing heavily again. After a moment he knelt by the beast and pushed. The creature rolled to one side, a sword hilt protruding from its belly. The Melani pulled on Jherik's arms, sliding the Henin elf's body from beneath the creature. Shess continued to drag the Henin elf several body lengths away from the beast.

Jherik groaned and rolled to one side. He coughed twice and emptied his dinner on the grass. Shess handed the warrior a waterskin.

A thrashing noise in the grass behind Krys caused him to whirl. Timbrel was on her feet, silently screaming at Krys. The wizard winced. The silence extended far enough to mute all but the sounds of Timbrel's feet stomping through the grass. Krys gathered his power and sketched at the air, releasing the silence.

Timbrel's voice suddenly echoed through the darkness. "...kind of a spell did you use, you tree-boring beetle! How dare you use your magic..." Timbrel trailed off, suddenly aware that her voice could be heard.

Krys glanced at the other two. Both stared at Timbrel, open-mouthed. Shess gestured at Krys suddenly. Jherik's mouth work soundlessly.

Krys turned just in time to meet Timbrel's hand. The sound of her slap cracked through the darkness. His face stung as the wizard-elf grabbed the girl's wrists and held them together. He had not seen her so angry since Von's death.

Her voice lowered, pitched just for Krys. "You worm-eaten root of a bale-tree. You keep your magic away from me." She twisted, freeing an arm. A second later it reappeared, a slim dagger held firmly in her hand. "Don't practice your spells on me."

The bright light suddenly faded, leaving the meadow in darkness. Timbrel jerked her other hand free and stalked away.

Krys let her go. She'd be over her fit of temper soon enough. He felt lucky she hadn't used the dagger. He looked out into the darkness toward the girl. Where did the dagger come from, anyway?

### 

*The plains northwest of Insara*

Jherik was horribly embarrassed. He fell asleep on watch, and woke to an absence of noise. A rustling in the grass alerted him to danger. With no time to don his armor, the Henin warrior cast one of his few spells, strengthening his clothing to the toughness of weak armor. It took him two tries for the spell to work this time, a little better than usual, but slower than conditions warranted. When the rustling stopped, he charged the faint shadow he noticed against the starlight.

Yelling his war-cry, he stumbled his way across the meadow in the dim light, almost turning his ankle in a small animal's burrow. A large beast met his attack, nearly bowling him over. He kept his feet, wrestling with something. Its enormously long teeth faintly flashing in the starlight as it snapped at his face made him think of a large cat. His armored clothing repelled the first two attacks, the claws shredding his clothes to tatters but leaving the skin beneath unscathed. When it reared for the third time, the Henin warrior ducked under the beast's forelegs and stabbed it through the belly. He jerked the blade up as the animal sank down.

The stench made him gag. He turned his head aside involuntarily, slowing his reaction time. The beast convulsed once, spraying him with the contents of its intestines, and then collapsed on him. Jherik went down under its weight. A sharp pain lanced through his head as he hit the ground. Stunned and unable to move, the beast's weight pressed down on him, forcing the breath from his lungs. The center of his vision burned white and the edges of his vision turned dark.

He regained consciousness coughing and puking. His lungs burned as he drew a deep cool breath. The animal lay a few feet away. Jherik looked around himself, wondering how he had gotten free. The Melani elf stood to one side, sneering down at him.

Jherik's hatred flared. From his earliest years, the Henin elf heard about the Melani hiding underground like wounded animals. They attacked at night from their hidden lairs, raiding villages and eating their victims. Some said that they even ate their own dead.

Traveling with Shess hadn't changed the warrior's mind. The secretive dark-skinned elf seldom spoke to the others. He tracked well, but Jherik expected that from a raider. He caught the Melani sneering at him regularly.

The Henin elf could stand the personal insult well enough, but he worried about Timbrel. The Melani spent far too much time watching the girl. Jherik tried to speak to Krys, but the Ravali elf simply cautioned Jherik about his jealousy. Jealous? Of what? Timbrel would never spend time with the Melani, not like she'd spent time with him...

Embarrassment flared again. Jherik wished he could remember the details of his night with Timbrel and Laurel. When he asked Krys about it, the wizard's answer had been less than helpful.

"You left, they followed. No one saw any of you for hours afterward."

A shrill voice cut through the darkness. With a start of surprise, Jherik recognized it as Timbrel's. He stared in astonishment as the half-elven dancer screamed at Krys. Jherik had never seen the girl so angry.

"Sunlight in the darkness, isn't she," commented Shess as he stood nearby. The dark-skinned elf's eyes never left the girl, an openly admiring look on his face.

*Wonderful. He's seen my shame.* Jherik's throat constricted into a great lump of muscle. He glanced up again to see Timbrel advancing on Krys from behind. He tried to warn Krys, but the words would not pass the lump. Next to him, Shess waved his arms, distracting Krys from the dancer.

*Crack*! The sound of Timbrel's slap echoed through the night like a whip. Krys struggled with her for a moment, but she got a hand free. Light flared along the blade of a short dagger that appeared in her hand. A moment later the world grew dark.

Listening to himself breathe, Jherik reassured himself that he remained conscious. His head only hurt in one place, throbbing where he landed on the only stone in the meadow. Shess hadn't hit him with anything, then. *Only because the Melani didn't think of it yet.* He stood, letting his eyes readjust to the starlit darkness. What caused the light? Why hadn't he noticed it?

He returned to the others, clutching the shreds of his filthy clothes in front of him. The armor spell ended when he lost consciousness, and his clothing fell apart. He rummaged in his pack for clean clothes, and then moved off into the darkness to change. The filth on his body would have to wait until he found a clean stream. In the meantime, the warrior intended to rest.

When the sun rose, everyone seemed to be feeling better. Shess still kept watch. Timbrel rolled to one side, stretching like a cat as she woke. She frowned and went to speak to Shess, no doubt berating him for not waking her. The Melani elf listened for a moment and laughed out loud. *What an ugly laugh*, thought Jherik, *forced out like a death rattle*. Shess spoke into Timbrel's ear, and then left her standing alone as he mounted his horse.

Jherik could feel the hatred burning in his belly as he watched the Melani. The warrior followed reluctantly when Krys signaled. It was going to be another bad day.

They traveled overland at Krys' direction, searching for the main road to Nerryon. Twice Jherik saw the wizard-elf looking at the tiny Hinjin direction device from the ruins. A few days later they entered a spur of the forest and found the road. Jherik wore his white disk proudly, as did Krys and Timbrel, and no one troubled them.

###

# Chapter Eight

*Nerryon*

The forest thinned to reveal fields drenched in the afternoon sun. The city of Nerryon squatted in the distance like a dark toad. Timbrel shivered. The elves rode their horses hard, eager to spend the night inside the walls.

The gate guards let them through, cautioning them against drawing their weapons within the city walls. Jherik slipped a bright red ribbon across the hilt of his sword, tucking the loose end into his scabbard. He looked up to see Timbrel's curious face. "They'll think the sword is tied in. If trouble starts it can slide out just as quickly."

The girl nodded and tried not to stare as they rode toward the inn. Nerryon was the largest city she had ever seen, easy to get lost in. As they passed several different markets, Timbrel found herself looking for a street of cages. She had confidence in the Seer's window and the visions it showed her. Confidence enough to look for landmarks, she thought, but not enough to tell Krys and the others.

Timbrel turned her head to search the other side of the street. A flash of golden hair caught her attention, but the crowd surged and she lost sight of it. No, the girl told herself, Lostaria is not walking free in this place. My mother's cousin is caged somewhere.

"Spices from across the city."

"Fresh barley, ready to grind."

"Carrots, tomatoes, and zucchini."

The bright tents of the next market offered plants and herbs. Timbrel marked its location in her mind. She needed to replenish her herbs for the bitter tea. She might meet someone interesting during her stay. She smiled to herself when Krys chose an inn only a short block away from the herb market.

As they dismounted from their horses, a human girl stopped in her tracks and stared openly at them. She hurried away suddenly, joining a well-dressed group of giggling teenage girls.

The Traveler's Welcome Inn stood three stories high. Fresh rushes spread on the floor gave a sweet scent in the common room, and a dozen waitresses ran back and forth between the kitchens and the tables. Krys arranged a large room for them. Shess spoke with the innkeeper separately.

Timbrel shared her experience with Lord Gowell and his window. Krys focused on Timbrel's description of the walking skeletons practicing with weapons.

"An undead army," he mused.

Jherik fingered his sword hilt. "How would you fight something like that?"

"Beheading seems to work well for almost anything, I believe."

Jherik frowned at Krys' suggestion, and then tapped his fingers in assent.

As the men continued to talk of war, Timbrel looked around the room. The few scattered women sat silently among groups of men, seldom speaking even when asked a direct question. Timbrel cocked her head to the side as one group left. She heard the distinctive tinkling of metal on metal as the cloaked woman in their midst rose. The dancer's eyes narrowed.

The woman stumbled on her way across the room. One of the men angrily jerked at a tether of some sort, pulling the woman completely off of her feet. Her cloak opened as she sprawled on the floor. Timbrel saw chains around the woman's wrists and ankles. A thin loincloth of bright red wrapped around the fallen woman's hips, and her breasts were painted with blue symbols around rouged nipples. Timbrel realized with horror that the symbols--crude human letters--spelled out prices for different sexual acts like a merchant's signboard.

The angry man hauled the slave to her feet. She quickly wrapped herself in the cloak and scuttled after her master.

Still shaken from what she witnessed, Timbrel was startled when their food arrived. With little appetite, she forced herself to eat spiced bread and beef. Krys and Jherik continued to discuss battle tactics between bites. Their voices ceased as Shess rejoined them, the noble girl from the street following in his wake.

Up close, the girl was older than Timbrel originally thought. Perhaps twenty in human years, the cut of her clothing disguised the womanly body of the girl and made her seem younger. The girl stared directly at Timbrel, a look of distaste on her face.

The dancer ignored the human girl, looking instead at the elves.

Shess bowed to Krys. "My path parts from yours. You have made travel both interesting and safe. May we always meet in well-lit caves." His eyes never left those of Krys.

The Melani elf turned to Timbrel. "Have a farewell drink with me, Lady." The dark-skinned elf proffered his freshly filled cup. A thick golden liquid swirled within. "Nerryon is famous for this honey wine."

Timbrel took the cup and tentatively took a sip. The drink tasted overly sweet. Bolder, she took a drink, draining nearly a third of the cup. ""You're right, it is very good. But do not let me drink it all." The dancer handed the cup back to him.

Shess took a drink and set the cup aside. Timbrel could see that only a third of the cup remained. Before she could finish the cup, the dark-haired girl grabbed it and drained it.

The Melani turned to the girl, suddenly furious. "Anne! This is private. Leave us."

Anne turned her dark brown eyes toward Timbrel. "Can't I come along?"

Timbrel looked at the girl. The brown eyes seemed to be going glassy even as the dancer watched. She looked back at Shess and saw the beginnings of the same reaction. The sweetness suddenly left her mouth, leaving a licorice aftertaste that burned along Timbrel's nerves.

The dark elf suddenly leaned forward, meeting Timbrel's eyes with his own gold. "You are mine," he told her.

"For tonight," she replied without thinking. Her groin and breasts on fire, she stood and took his hand. Shess led the dancer up the stairs, young Anne trailing behind. By the time they reached his room, Timbrel's need filled her. Anne followed them inside, alternately pressing herself to Shess and Timbrel.

Vaguely aware that Shess bolted the door behind them, Timbrel peeled her clothes off and left them in an untidy heap on the floor. She helped Anne as well, the younger girl unable to manipulate the fastenings on her clothes. The two girls turned to Shess, already free of his clothing.

Shess grabbed Timbrel and pulled her close. "You are mine," he repeated as he looked deeply into her eyes.

"For tonight," she murmured and then kissed him deeply. A moment later the three of them sprawled on the bed.

Timbel's senses blurred. She kissed and was kissed, licked and was licked, touched and was touched. Moans, groans, and grunts blended together as the three found pleasure and relief in each other's bodies. Timbrel's skills brought Shess to the brink of pleasure, Anne mounting him to finish. Anne touched Timbrel intimately, bringing her to the crest of a wave that Shess carried her over. Shess and Timbrel worked together until Anne screamed and writhed with pleasure. Touching and kissing blended together into one endless night of pleasure between the three.

Timbrel heard Shess begin to speak a dozen times, the words immediately muffled by kissing lips or other parts of Anne's anatomy thrust in the way. She returned the favor when he tried to speak to Anne, finding more pleasurable uses for his tongue. The longing mounted as the night wore on, unbearable even with constant pleasure. Timbrel gave a contented sigh as she slipped into darkness long after the other two had lost consciousness.

###

When she woke, Timbrel felt wonderfully satisfied. She arched like a cat, allowing each muscle to stretch and fill with blood. The sensation filled her with pleasure. She rolled toward the warmth of the bed, running her fingertips lightly down Shess' side as he lay sleeping. The dancer sighed with contentment, rubbing her breasts against the darkness of his skin.

Her head started to throb as she lay there. Bits of memory floated back. The taste of Shess' mouth. The feel of him holding her while she kissed... Anne? Timbrel sat up and looked around. The human girl was nowhere to be seen. The door was closed but unbolted.

Shess stirred beside her. The Melani elf rolled over, laying his head in her lap. Timbrel touched his face tenderly. She tried to think back, savor the best moments with the Melani as she had with lovers before.

And drew a blank. Her memory refused to replay the pleasure that she should have felt. She felt sated, but the memories were absent. A few scraps floated by, and she remembered the taste of Anne's lips, Shess licking her, someone's fingers. No coherence to the few scraps, no framework to remember anything. Dissatisfaction filled the girl. She would never take *likshas* willingly again.

Willingly? Another scrap of memory opened. The flavor and smell of the *likshas* had been disguised in the honey wine that Shess insisted she try. But Shess drank the wine as well. He didn't know. Perhaps the drink recipe required it.

The memory of bursting pleasure suddenly opened. Caught up in the moment, her body reacted. Timbrel arched her back with a muffled scream, the orgasm catching her completely by surprise. She lay panting afterward, aware of a warm tongue.

Shess had woken during her memory-induced orgasm. He lifted his head and licked at her, golden eyes glowing. "You are still awake. You will be wonderful." He gave her a final lick, then stood up and walked across the room. Timbrel watched his progress, admiring the smooth muscles of his legs. He washed in

212

the basin, using the damp cloth that Anne must have left there before. Timbrel stood and followed him.

It felt good to be clean. Her legs and groin ached, as did the bite marks on her breasts and shoulders. She cupped her breasts for a moment, feeling for other bites beneath them.

"Still feeling pleasure? Very good. You may get dressed now. We will be going down to breakfast."

The word breakfast awoke a different sort of hunger in Timbrel. She dressed quickly, amused at Shess' new way of speaking to her. She tolerated the way he placed his hand on her rear as they descended the stairs, acting like he owned her. Timbrel looked around for Krys and Jherik. Neither were in sight.

Shess guided her to a table along the back wall. He draped a hand across her shoulders as he ordered breakfast.

Timbrel was amazed. No lover had ever acted so boldly in public. When the meal came, the waitress set it near Shess. Timbrel thought she saw a look of pity of the woman's eyes.

Timbrel managed to keep her temper during the meal, in spite of Shess insistence on hand-feeding her like a favorite pet. She bit her tongue when the Melani elf nipped at her sore shoulder before staring into her eyes.

"I have business to attend to. You should wait for me until I return." His voice sounded calm and commanding.

The dancer nodded and muttered under her breath. She watched the dark-skinned elf saunter out of the room, jealous glares from other men following him. After the door closed behind him, she narrowed her eyes and repeated herself.

"I think not." She stalked across the room, going upstairs to the room Krys and Jherik shared. She knocked and entered the room.

"You certainly took long enough," Jherik said.

### 

Krys worried about Timbrel. After she went upstairs with Shess and the girl Anne, Krys smelled traces of licorice beneath the cloying sweetness of honey. Memories of Jherik's problems with *likshas* worried him. Uncomfortably aware that the Melani elf repeated himself twice, telling Timbrel that she was his before taking her upstairs, Krys wished that he could tell the girl about the drug without upsetting her. If she simply chose the dark-skinned elf as a lover, the half-elf would not appreciate paranoid ramblings and might react violently. But it could be too late if Shess bent her mind through the *likshas*, and she would definitely react violently. They could not afford such an outburst until they rescued Lostaria.

Anne stumbled down the stairs at first light while Krys and Jherik shared breakfast. "She is with him," Anne replied to Krys's inquiry about Timbrel, visibly growing upset. "But I am his."

Krys was more concerned about the state of Timbrel's mind than Anne's apparent enslavement. When Timbrel entered their room, Krys relaxed. At least the dancer returned to them.

Jherik stood. "You certainly took long enough."

"He told me to wait for him while he does his business elsewhere." The girl sounded upset. "I'm going out to the market."

She avoided Jherik's reach and left as quickly as she had come in. The two elves looked at each other.

"She's acting strangely, Krys." Jherik stood, strapping on his sword belt and re-tucking the ribbons. "I'm going out after her." The warrior left before Krys could answer, leaving the wizard alone.

Krys opened his pack and pulled out a book filled with his own crabbed handwriting. He started searching through the notes he'd taken during their stay at Lord Gowell's tower. He flipped through three pages, muttering to himself. "Fire spells and the principles behind them, lightning type spells, mass and energy, force walls, mind spells. Here we are."

The wizard flipped to a later page in the book. He glanced through his notes, focusing on the phrase "repetition and brain-washing." Unfortunately, Gowell did not have as much research about spells affecting the mind as he did on other topics. Krys learned a lot just reading Gowell's notes on the principles behind the spells. The light spell in the meadow was the result of some of those principles, thought Krys. Knowing that light could come from vibrating bits, Krys vibrated the air into bright light. The brightness surprised him as did the odd smell of the air afterward, but he controlled it. He would do better the next time.

Krys glanced at the page again. He listed a few guidelines for mind spells. Krys studied the diagram he had copied, designating which portions of the brain connected with different types of thought. One part seem to control movement, another the power of speech. Krys preferred stopping the air from vibrating when he caused silence. He wasn't sure if he could reverse changes he made to the brain itself. A section near the spine controlled the passions. He chuckled. *Timbrel's brain must be very developed in that area.*

Gowell's research had concluded that memories were scattered across the entire brain in small pieces. And drugs like *likshas* no doubt scattered them further, Krys thought. He worried again about Timbrel.

He looked at his notes again. One section of the brain seemed to control voluntary thought. If someone disconnected it, the target would become pliable and unable to make decisions.

Krys snapped the book shut, placing a locking spell on it that created a force band. He found it interesting to compare the few spells he knew previously with the principles behind them and see which parts were really necessary. He no longer spoke with many of his spells, finding subvocalization to work as well when focusing his energy.

Timbrel and Jherik returned shortly, the girl carrying a cup of hot water. She quickly mixed up her noxious smelling tea from some of her new supplies. The dancer made a disgusted face while she drank.

"I thought you gave that up," commented Krys. "I haven't seen you drink any since Lucifron."

"I ran out."

"I see." Krys looked askance at her. The portion she mixed seemed larger than he remembered.

Jherik leaned over and sniffed at the cup. "Can I try some?"

215

Timbrel looked at him, disbelief plain on her face. "You want to try the bitter tea?"

"Why not? You drink it all the time."

Timbrel shrugged and handed him a cup. The warrior sniffed at it, making a face. "Does it taste as bad as it smells?"

"Worse," she assured him.

"What does it do?" The Henin elf held the cup before his lips.

"Oh, it just makes me sexier. It'll make you sexy, too." Timbrel stopped and thought a minute as the warrior brought the cup to his lips. "Oh, wait," she continued in a disappointed voice. "It makes you *girl*-sexy. It might ruin your best part."

Krys laughed silently as Jherik's eyes widened and he stopped in mid-tilt. The liquid lapped at the rim of the cup, a hairsbreadth from the Henin elf's mouth. The warrior slowly lowered the cup and returned it to Timbrel. She turned away to drink the rest of her tea. Krys laughed harder as he caught Jherik checking himself, hand on his groin. The warrior looked momentarily relieved, then snatched his hand away and turned red.

Timbrel set the cup to one side. "He'll be returning soon." Krys knew that the girl referred to Shess. "I'd best meet him downstairs."

Krys tried to use reason to reach the girl. "You don't need to go, Timbrel."

"You could stay with me," suggested Jherik. Timbrel wrinkled her nose, spun on her heel, and marched out the door.

Krys stood and looked at the warrior. "I was trying to keep her here, Jherik, not drive her off." Still concerned, the wizard followed the girl down the stairs.

Timbrel was halfway across the common room when Shess entered the inn. The dancer ran into the Melani's arms, kissing him and pressing her body against him. Krys frowned as Shess slipped his arms around the girl's waist and pulled her closer.

Timbrel took the dark elf by the hand and tugged him toward the stairs, drawing stares from half the Inn's patrons. Krys' heart fell. The girl seemed to be completely in Shess' thrall.

216

The Melani seemed preoccupied. "Upstairs," he mumbled. "Yes. Come along, Anne." The young human girl stepped up to Shess' side from her position a few steps behind. Timbrel backed up a few steps, a shocked look on her face.

"You're taking Anne?" The dancer's disbelief colored her voice.

Shess murmured something to Timbrel, sliding an arm around her waist. Krys watched the dancer stiffen in outrage.

"I...do...not...share." She tossed her head in a human gesture, waist-length golden hair floating across her shoulders like clouds across the sky.

"You'll get your turn later. Now go sit down like a good girl." Krys ducked out of the way as Shess and Anne approached the stairs. He bumped into Jherik, standing immediately behind him.

With a sigh, Krys led the way down the last flight of stairs, passing Shess and Anne three steps from the floor. Timbrel walked a few steps behind them.

Krys readied himself to restrain her, when she stopped in front of the stairs.

"Well," she said brightly. "Shall we go find Lostaria?"

### 

*Celiar's house, Ravali*

Arlis stood uncertainly in Celiar's courtyard, wondering why the Yarite Master had summoned him. Several other young elves slipped through the gates one by one and joined him. He recognized most. *Not one of us is past his first century*, Arlis thought.

Von should have been here, too. The cocky young noble, exiled the previous summer, was as skilled with his weapons as he was full of his own sense of superiority. If only Von mastered signaling and stealth. Even Master Celiar found no trace of Von and his fellow exiles.

Arlis spotted Celiar before the rest did, and pushed his way near the small balcony overlooking one side of the courtyard. The Ravali Regent followed the Master onto the balcony.

Celiar's voice echoed across the courtyard. "Warriors, you have been summoned for a special mission." Two dozen elves snapped to attention, looking upward. "Soliari Regent Urramach, I present to you the best that Ravali can give: skilled warriors also versed in stealth."

The Regent stepped forward, long golden tresses escaping her hood. Her voice flowed like golden honey, far different than the gossips described it.

"My brave young warriors, I greet you." Soliari looked over the group. "I need your help. Ravali needs your help. My cousin, Lostaria Heir Urramach, was kidnapped many months ago. The kidnappers never sent a ransom request, and the rescue party we sent vanished entirely. My scouts have traced my cousin's abduction to the city of Port Kerran. The humans that rule that city may be involved."

Soliari fell to her knees, tears splashing down her face. "I need your help," she begged. "We must force the issue. I need you to capture the human prince and force him to tell us where my cousin is held. She covered her face and broke down into wrenching sobs, her golden hair falling into disarray.

Arlis felt a stirring in his loins. From the distracted expressions on the faces of those nearest him, he was not the only one so affected.

Master Celiar touched Soliari gently on the shoulder and assisted the Regent to a bench before he turned back to the assembled elves.

"Arlis, you are named Captain of this group. Dismiss the others until sunrise and come inside for a full briefing."

Shocked, Arlis sent the others to pack and hurried inside. The Regent lounged on the couch, perfectly composed and sipping a glass of wine. She waved the young captain to his seat.

"I think we can speak frankly here." She glanced at Celiar, who twitched his fingers in assent. "There is a price on Lostaria's head. Her worth has become known to the humans. This will increase the difficulty of your task." She turned to look at Arlis, her blue eyes burning into his soul. "If the human prince refuses to cooperate, kill him."

### 

*Nerryon*

Timbrel seethed inwardly as the three elves entered a rundown section of the city. How dare Shess turn her down in favor of a little girl and embarrass her in front of Jherik and Krys. She saw the two elves lurking in the stairwell before she threw herself into the Melani elf's arms.

Jherik's constant innuendos and offers ever since their trip to Lucifron bothered her. Did he forget his engagement to Kareni? Men. Timbrel was half-ready to give up the lot of them, maybe go with Anne.

The half-elf skidded to a halt. Anne? What was she thinking? Timbrel had never been attracted to women before. When she thought about Anne, however, she felt a warmth like kinship. The dancer shook her head violently, trying to toss her errant thoughts out to the street. They refused to go.

Another side effect of the *likshas*, she thought. Walking slowly forward, she tried to examine her memories. Anne had been under the influence of the *likshas* as much as Shess and herself. Timbrel forgave herself for the unprecedented threesome. The first time she tasted *likshas*, on the morning of her wedding day, she felt attracted to everyone nearby. That part was the drug. The feelings afterward, though, were something new. The dancer frowned. She could not remember such a heavy licorice aftertaste from the dilute dose that she and Eric discussed with the village's healer. The honey sweet cup Shess shared with her, sweet enough to disguise the taste for several minutes afterward, still left a heavy licorice aftertaste.

"You are mine." Another flash of memory. The Melani elf's calm voice as he looked deep into her eyes. He claimed her for the night as so many others had. Was he looking to see if the drug had done its work and made her suggestible?

Timbrel stopped again, so suddenly that Jherik bumped into her. If Shess used the drug on purpose, Timbrel was extremely lucky that Anne added herself to the group. She clearly remembered several times that the dark-skinned elf started to say something, only to be distracted by Anne's lips or her own.

Timbrel suddenly giggled. Poor Shess. The Melani elf tried to bend her mind with his words, and never got a word in edgewise. His weird behavior at breakfast... Another idea struck the girl like a blow, making her stagger. Shess thought that he succeeded.

Jherik's arms dropped on her shoulders, steadying her before he let go. On a whim, Timbrel whirled to face him. Stretching to the tips of her toes, she brushed her lips against the Henin warrior's mouth, and then whirled and set off down the street. Jherik's rude words to her provoked precisely the behavior that Shess would expect from a mind-bent slave. No wonder the waitress pitied her.

The dancer stopped and looked around. Something about the curving street she walked along seemed familiar. "Come on," she whispered and ran around the bend. A tall tower appeared in the distance, its broken carvings hanging down like a wet mustache. The street of cages was just ahead.

### 

*The Street of Cages, Nerryon*

Lostaria struggled as her captors clicked the fourth manacle around her right wrist. Kadeesh paraded her up the street like a prized animal on a leash, her arms and legs chained separately now. The whip at the fat man's side was no idle threat. Lostaria felt its bite her first night in this accursed town. The elven princess bided her time. She would get her chance to escape from the mysterious buyer, if not from Kadeesh.

A few heads turned as they moved up the street. Kadeesh did not seem pleased. "Strip her," he suddenly ordered. "Soliari never said to clothe her."

The few rags she wore were cut from her body and left in the street. *Soliari? My cousin arranged this?* Blinking back tears, the golden-haired elf held her head high.

"Very good," praised Kadeesh. "The buyer likes spirit in his women."

The elven princess ignored him as she stepped carefully through the litter in the street. Twice he jerked on the chains and caused her to fall, but she clambered to her feet and continued. Many more people watched her now.

The slaver brought her to a small building of dark stone. Once inside, they descended down a long spiral staircase. Lostaria could feel the dampness in the fast-chilling air. Her skin prickled and rose into gooseflesh.

The stairwell ended on a rock floor, clumsily shaped from the natural stone of a cavern. Mortared stone walls and doors separated the cave formation into usable rooms. After an endless series of twists and turns that left Lostaria completely disoriented, the slaver ordered her into a large room. A fire crackled along one wall, the smoke drawn upward through a natural chimney formation in the stones. Velvet-covered armchairs and padded benches were arranged in a loose semicircle facing the opposite side of the room.

Kadeesh dragged her to a thick carpet and forced her from her feet. "You should rest, little one. We have hours before the buyer arrives."

Lostaria lay on the carpet, shivering with fear. A thick metal post with manacles welded on its upper end poked up from the discolored stone. Dark brown stains marred the mottled gray of the cavern floor. Many dark brown stains.

Lifting her head, Lostaria saw three doors. The door that she came through was thick oak, an iron bar leaning on the wall nearby to secure it. A thinner door stood ajar near the chairs on one side of the fire, the smell of cooking food wafting through. The last door, metal with a small barred window, had an iron lock set into the door, fastening it to the stone. The door's surface slightly bowed into the room. Lostaria could not imagine what creature would be strong enough to bend it.

She shuddered as the fat slaver's hand dropped to her head. "Your turn comes soon, little elf. Lucky for you that the buyer wants you untouched." The slaver leaned forward and ran a finger across the elven woman's shoulders, circling her birthmark. "This is what kept you alive before I found a buyer."

Lostaria gasped. If her birthmark kept her alive, then her capture *was* part of the plot against the Ravali throne. Could her cousin be so bold? Soliari lacked the birthmark of rule. The only way she could take the throne would be as Regent. Lostaria's heart skipped a beat. How many of the forty-two heirs before her survived?

Soliari must be insane. Without the alliance that Lostaria was sent to forge, the humans might even now be marching on the elves, determined to wipe the slow-breeding race from the world forever. It would be the end of everything. She must find a way to escape before the buyer arrived. The Ravali princess took a deep breath, and then gagged as the slaver forced a cup to her lips. She could not help but swallow the sweet stuff, not if she wanted to breathe again.

### 

*The Street of Cages*
*20 minutes later*

Jherik stood in front of the empty cage. Barely two strides wide in any direction, it had already been swept clean of the dirty straw that cushioned the occupants of nearby cages. Krys stood to one side, arguing prices with the man who seemed to be in charge of the slaves. Timbrel held her cloak closed with a fist and used

Krys and Jherik as a shield, tipping her hood back to reveal her face and speaking softly with the remaining slaves whenever the seller could not see her. She sidled behind Jherik just as the man screamed at Krys and pushed them aside. Timbrel fumbled beneath her cloak. Jherik tried to remain and block the man from the dancer, but the slaver pulled a dagger and pointed it at the girl's hood.

"Remove the cloak. Let me see what mischief we have here."

Timbrel's cloak dropped to the ground. The traveling clothes that the warrior-elf expected were gone. A ribbon of red cloth wound around the dancer's hips, the ends dangling between her legs. Bright blue letters marked her breasts, the nipples bright blue as well. The dancer turned her hip slightly, accentuating her slim figure.

Jherik stared at the girl, remembering the last time he had seen her nearly naked. His trousers grew uncomfortably tight. The warrior thought Krys said something but his blood pounded in his ears.

Timbrel reached out and brushed a finger across the seller's lips. Jherik's eyes followed every motion as she walked slowly toward Krys, rolling her hips with each step. Looking back over her shoulder where Jherik and the seller stood together, the girl kissed at the air before turning to Krys.

"Master," she whined. "Has he paid yet? Can he afford me?"

Krys's voice cut through the girl's spell. "He's worth nothing. Don't waste your time on him." Jherik came back to himself, tearing his eyes from Timbrel and drawing his sword. The peace-tie flapped uselessly in the breeze, nearly as wide as the ribbon Timbrel wore.

The slaver lunged. Jherik's training took over as he blocked and thrust, dispatching the man in a single stroke.

"Stupid, stupid, stupid." Krys pressed his hands to his temples as though he had a severe headache. "He might have known where they took her."

"I know." A small voice called from one of the cages. A young man, voice still breaking, stood at the bars of the cage.

The three elves clustered around him. Jherik and Timbrel stepped back to let Krys have more room.

"Where have they taken her? The one who looked like this." He indicated Timbrel, now wrapped in her cloak again. She pulled her hood slightly back, allowing a lock of golden hair to escape.

"I know, but I have a price."

"Your freedom?" Krys asked. Jherik looked at the lock of the cage. He wasn't sure he could break it.

"Her." The boy thrust his arm through the bars and pointed at Timbrel.

Timbrel stepped forward. "What price will you ask? To look at me?" The girl dropped her cloak again. The boy stared at her. Jherik felt like joining him.

"Does it really cost...do you really cost...so much?" The boy could barely get the words out.

Timbrel smiled. "Ten thousand gold chains? No, I cost more than that. No one can pay my price."

Price? Jherik was confused. Timbrel was no slave.

The boy looked disappointed. Timbrel leaned forward. "Let me tell you a secret." She whispered in his ear for a moment. The boy whispered back.

The boy's arms suddenly snaked through the bars and pulled Timbrel close. The girl tilted her head and kissed him, pressing so close that Jherik expected her to melt through the bars any second. The warrior's trousers tightened again and he turned away.

Timbrel stepped back, quickly closing her cloak. Jherik glimpsed smeared blue. He turned. Blue markings smeared the bars and the young man's chest. The young man smiled dreamily, absently scrubbing at the blue markings with a handful of dirty straw.

Krys turned to go, Timbrel following. The girl sighed. "Well, that won't work twice. I didn't realize it would smear so badly."

Krys chuckled. "Well, it worked once and we got our information. We *did* get the information, didn't we?"

Timbrel giggled. "Of course. He's a little young, don't you think? He's learning the right moves, though." She sighed again.

Krys suddenly seemed uncomfortable. "Um, Timbrel. About the right moves. . ."

The dancer faced the wizard. "You can stop worrying, Krys. I know what Shess tried, and I've been pretending. Besides, I barely remember what happened last night with him. It's all broken into little bits of memory. Very unsatisfying."

Jherik thought about his earlier stay in Lucifron. His memories were just as broken. Could Timbrel have told him the truth? A tiny bit of hope began to grow inside the warrior.

Krys handed Timbrel a rag. "What would you have done if he accepted your invitation?"

"Gone with him." She wiped at a blue smear. "It might be interesting to find out what he's really like without a drugged drink clouding my mind."

"Gone with him!" Jherik sputtered. "Why go with him and not with me?"

Timbrel tilted her head and looked at the warrior. "I won't go with you because you belong to Kareni. I've told you that."

"You seemed happy enough for a threesome *that* night. And last night, too." Krys mocked her.

"I told you already, Krys, nothing at all happened with Jherik that night. I chased the other girl off before she did any damage, and spent the rest of the time avoiding his hands." Timbrel sounded irritated, as though she told the story many times before.

"We didn't do anything? Why do I remember seeing you naked?"

"I distracted you from the waitress. She wanted to have your child and make you responsible for her."

225

"But your loincloth was by my bedside when I woke up."

"Where you dropped it in your sleep."

Krys cut in. "How did he get his hands on it in the first place?"

Timbrel stared at the sky. "I didn't sidestep fast enough."

"You're trying to tell us that you got away from Jherik's grip." Krys' mocking tone emphasized his disbelief.

Jherik didn't know what to believe anymore. Perhaps he had done nothing wrong. Maybe Kareni would not kill him after all. He could hope.

### 

An hour later, Krys had a plan. Kadeesh had taken Lostaria to his townhouse, where he sold his better slaves from a room in the basement. A maimed beggar gave them directions to the adjoining cave. Wounded by a plains cat while building walls and doors into chambers inside the cave, the former mason had been overlooked when the previous owner's men killed the workers to ensure their silence. The wounded man crawled through the caverns for hours, finally finding a hidden exit. Timbrel played her part well, rewarding the information with a kiss.

Too well, perhaps. Krys thought he heard her promise the beggar a night together if they met again. It must be her human side, he thought. Soliari would never have spread her favors so thinly. For Timbrel's mother, the promise of attention was enough coin to buy a man's cooperation. Now, of course, Soliari brokered political favors.

She probably owns a third of the Council by now, Krys thought. Poor Soliari, neither eligible to rule nor to play politics at the level that she would prefer. The Genjin who designed the birthmarks knew well what they did.

The entrance to the cave was overgrown and easy to miss. Jherik knelt to take a close look at the ground nearby. The Henin elf stood quickly, hand near his sword. "Plains cat spoor. Fresh. I need my armor."

Krys was frustrated. The longer they took, the more time for the buyer to reach Lostaria. She could already have been moved again. He glanced at Timbrel.

Timbrel seemed relieved. The blue make-up she wore was smeared beyond recognition. The red ribbon loincloth hung slightly out of place. Krys flicked his eyes away from the girl. Jherik was right. They were not dressed for a successful rescue in the caves.

They returned to the Inn, quickly changing. Jherik fastened his cloak across his armor, hiding the bright metal from prying eyes. Timbrel spent extra minutes scrubbing every trace of blue from her body, and scrubbing at her cloak as well. Krys paced and worried as the time sped by. It would soon be dark.

They descended the stairs quickly. When they reached the common room, Timbrel's face suddenly lit up with joy and she dashed across the room to throw herself into Shess' arms. Krys groaned. Jherik waited outside.

By the time Krys reached her, Timbrel rubbed herself against Shess in embarrassing ways. The Melani elf attempted to fend her off, unsuccessfully. Krys could see the growing effect of Timbrel's attentions. Shess protested with his words, but his arms slid around the girl's waist and he held her tightly.

"I have an appointment...at sunset...to pick up...my purchase..." Shess' words came out between kisses.

"There is no purchase more important than spending time with me," Timbrel purred. "It will wait." The girl dropped to her knees and hugged the dark-skinned elf's legs.

Krys's mind worked furiously. Timbrel showed every sign of delaying and spending the evening with Shess. Lostaria was in danger. Her buyer would arrive at sunset. Timbrel's delay...delayed Shess, Krys realized with a start. Shess must be the buyer.

Heaving a great sigh of disgust, Krys turned on his heel and joined Jherik in the street.

"Where's Timbrel?"

"She's delaying Shess. We may not have much time. Let's go."

227

Jherik grumbled as they ran through the streets. Krys didn't have time to explain. Every minute counted.

"Krys, wait." Timbrel's voice called from the street behind him. She ran up as the silver-haired elf hesitated.

The girl panted. "He's delayed...at least an hour...with Anne...counted on him asking...threesome...I walked out...when he took her upstairs again." Timbrel put her hands on her knees and drew in a great breath.

Krys gestured assent, although he understood only half of what the girl tried to say. "We have little time." He set off down the street at a run.

They found the cave entrance again with little difficulty, though Jherik's armor caught twice in the twisting passageway. The dust on the cave floor showed several very clear footprints, over a handsbreadth wide and clawed. Jherik took the lead.

Timbrel clutched her stomach as Krys whispered a *word*. A pale glow surrounded his hand, enabling the elves to see in the darkness. They twisted through the cave, finally joining a larger cave by a tree-shaped boulder. Timbrel smeared a dab of blue makeup close to the floor on the far side of the rock. "So we can find the exit," she whispered when Krys gave her a questioning glance.

A growl was the group's only warning as a huge cat hurtled at them from the darkness. It knocked Jherik to the ground, slashing sideways with the long teeth that protruded from its mouth. The fangs sliced through the warrior's cloak and scored the metal beneath. Timbrel winced at the noise of screeching metal. Krys quickly deadened the vibration from the air ahead of them.

The close quarters of the cave restricted Jherik's movements. Timbrel threw a rock at the beast's face. The cat sprang across the cave, the girl ducking and whirling as it leapt past her. The beast turned in mid-air and landed in a crouch. Timbrel darted past Jherik, now on his feet and breathing deeply. Krys flattened against the wall.

Jherik's sword flashed in the glow as he hit the beast three times in succession. The cat fell, its spine severed. Jherik dispatched the creature quickly.

"The smell of blood will bring more. Hurry." Krys led them on through the darkness.

Timbrel ran next to Jherik, full of questions. "How did you move so fast? Why did you breathe so hard before you even attacked? Are you injured?"

Krys hissed at them to be quiet.

Jherik leaned close to Timbrel's ear and lowered his voice. "It is a fighting technique. Basically, if you breathe deeply and get more air inside, you can move faster for a few minutes." Jherik's low tones cut through the darkness, slightly breathless and punctuated by the sound of his running feet.

"Save your breath," Krys reminded the warrior. "There may be more fighting ahead." He removed the silence spell along the tunnel.

The cavern twisted abruptly at a thick metal door, snaking around and continuing. A small barred window in the door showed flickering light from the other side. Krys doused his glow spell and looked through the window. Laughter floated into the cavern.

A dozen men lay sprawled on couches near a fire. Two serving girls ran about, receiving blows for their slowness that sparked further laughter, though the attention of the onlookers focused across the room. Krys moved his head, trying to see what they were looking at.

Timbrel pushed him aside, sliding her dagger carefully between the bars of the window. When she turned the polished blade, Krys could see the reflection of a figure against a pole. Lostaria!

Krys tried the door latch, slowly exerting pressure. It refused to turn. A complicated lock was set into the door just above the latch. The wizard-elf looked at Jherik. The warrior signaled negation. With no room to maneuver, the Henin elf could not smash the door open.

Timbrel dropped to her knees. Krys was about to comfort her when he heard the faint click of the lock through the laughter inside. Testing the handle again, Krys found it moved freely.

Timbrel remained on her knees, breathing deeply. She sprang to her feet, pushed at Krys and suddenly wrenched the handle from his hand. Pushing the door open, she sprinted along the left side of the room toward Lostaria.

Krys had seen Timbrel run before, and knew that she could sprint for short distances. He had never seen her run this fast.

"My technique," whispered Jherik.

Those inside started turning–all to the right–toward the open door. Timbrel reached Lostaria and disappeared behind her.

The *snick-snick* sound of the opening manacles came so quickly that Krys could barely think. Timbrel bent, hoisted her cousin over one shoulder, and ran for the door, visibly panting. Krys readied a spell, remembering Gowell's notes about heat transfer. As Jherik held the door open, Krys gathered the heat from the cavern's fire.

Timbrel staggered through the door. Jherik pulled it shut and caught the two girls as they collapsed. The lock flared white with heat. Timbrel pushed Lostaria toward Jherik. "Carry her."

The group ran back the way they came, sliding on a thin layer of frost that coated the floor and walls of the cave. A scream sounded behind them, followed by pounding noises. The door appeared to be holding.

Timbrel fell behind. Krys pulled her along by the arm, noting the girl's exhaustion. Jherik loomed ahead, Lostaria draped over his shoulder. Krys kept a glow spell on his hand, enough to allow them to see their path.

Shouts accompanied a screech of metal behind them. Krys pulled Timbrel forward and around a sharp turn, following Jherik. Timbrel pulled back.

"That way. There." Timbrel gestured toward the side cavern.

Krys called to Jherik. "We almost missed it. Hopefully they will as well. Come on." Krys took the lead. Jherik moved more carefully, carrying Lostaria cradled in his arms. When they reached the exit, Timbrel crawled up first, and then assisted Krys with Lostaria. Jherik's armor wedged again, finally scraping past the edge of the entrance.

### 

*Nerryon*

An hour later and completely unsatisfied, Shess went to his rendezvous. Anne had been insufficient, Timbrel had vanished, and he stalked to Kadeesh's compound in a foul mood. The outer guards let him within the complex without a word. The Melani elf reached the room of trades only to find it empty. The pole where his sacrifice had been held stood empty, manacles discarded in the dust. Splintered furniture lay scattered near the metal door, itself dented and hanging from the hinges. Shess followed the cavern, the dust disturbed by a dozen footprints. He found a dead plains cat, sliced in a style he recognized. Jherik.

Shess could not picture the elf as a slaver, therefore the elf must have been part of the rescue. And with Jherik, Krys and probably Timbrel. Timbrel.

Shess stalked through the streets, his swords striking like a snake to slice off the head of a drunk peeing into a corner. The lifeless body fell, still spraying urine as the Melani elf continued on, silently raging. His purchase, his prize, his sacrifice to the dark gods, vanished. His other prize, the golden-haired Timbrel, had broken her conditioning. Two elves in his grasp, both taken by the twists of fate. His anger mounting, the Melani cut through a thin pole on the roadside. A cloth awning fluttered down to the street behind him.

Stupid humans lost his sacrifice. Manacled to a post. Somehow she split in two, opened her own restraints, and fled through a magically opened door. "Not likely," the Melani scoffed aloud. The slavers had been drinking and enjoying themselves.

231

Twelve men and none of them saw a thing, nor would they again. He left only one alive.

The Melani gnashed his teeth. He had heard the Seer tell Timbrel to look and see where *she* was. His sacrifice to the dark gods, no doubt, though the Melani had not thought so at the time. His little Timbrel, so easily influenced by the slave drug. So pliable, practically leaping into bed with him when he expected far more trouble convincing her. So enthusiastic...

He struck out a rat, chopping the filthy animal in two. Timbrel's enthusiasm in his bed made him forget himself and bite her. The sweet taste of her blood carried with it the slave drug in a form that his antidote did not counteract. Now his patchy memory troubled him, though he was certain he proclaimed ownership of both women.

Timbrel seemed so vulnerable to the drug, his suggestion of their sexual play still in action when he woke up. She acted so taken with him. Acted. Why didn't he see it? Now he was trapped with Anne and no way out.

Shess slammed open the door of the Inn, waking many of those sleeping in the common room. He knew before he arrived that Krys's room would be empty. The group was long gone. Gone with his sacrifice. The Melani elf encountered Kadeesh's men as they returned from searching through the cave. Their story sounded like so much nonsense. The captive could not possibly split in two and release herself. The second must have been Timbrel.

He questioned the others to the point of death, but none saw Timbrel enter the room. She appeared next to the captive, the two as alike as forbidden twins. She ran from the room through the open door, which shut itself and heated the lock. Krys's work there.

Shess left his own work behind. He allowed Kadeesh to live, though the slaver would bear scars enough to chase off even a drunken woman. He gave the slaver a year to capture a golden elf for him. If Timbrel was found, he would return part of the fee he had taken back. At the end of the year, the Melani elf would hunt Kadeesh down personally. The fat man could not run far enough to escape his grasp.

In the meantime, he planned to pay a visit to the Seer's Tower. He would enjoy hunting the tower's master. A dozen cuts ought to punish Gowell for helping the others to rescue his sacrifice. If he could also force the Seer to give him magic, he could rule his people, guiding them into the light for conquest.

### 

Timbrel tried to treat Lostaria with her remaining herbs. Even the glow-fungus from the Spider Forest did not neutralize whatever the slavers had forced her to drink.

The princess nearly bit through her lips with her efforts to shake the poison. Her breathing caught in gasps, and her heartbeat sounded ragged to Timbrel. Jherik was sent to retrieve their packs and horses, but Timbrel had brought her smaller medicine pouch along.

The half-elf sponged her cousin's body while they waited. Lostaria tossed and turned, lost in feverish sleep, unable to speak coherently.

"You'll be all right," Timbrel promised her. "Sleep and get well." Surprisingly, Lostaria's struggles subsided and she fell into a calmer state. Her heartbeat seemed stronger as well. Timbrel bent to wipe the sweat from her cousin's face.

A whiff of licorice escaped Lostaria's mouth. Timbrel gasped. Wild-eyed, the dancer looked at Krys. "*Likshas*," she whispered.

Krys looked concerned. Before he could speak, Timbrel gestured for silence.

The wizard nodded and twitched his fingers over the elven princess. "We can talk now," he announced. "She will hear nothing for hours."

Timbrel looked at the wizard with horror. "You used a spell on her?"

"It is for her protection. How is she doing?"

233

Timbrel shook her head. "Not well. The *likshas* is toxic to her." Timbrel met Krys's eye. "I left the bloodroots in Lucifron's stable."

"When Jherik returns we can ride..." Krys began.

"You and Jherik should take her. There is something I must do before I leave this place. I will meet you in Lucifron. If I am delayed further, you must make a tea of the bloodroot, one nodule for a small kettle of water, and give it to her three times a day. Then take her to Rockhold and bring her home by ship. Right now she's the most important person in the land."

"To prevent war?"

Timbrel thought back to the Seer's window, and the images of the walking skeletons. "To forge an alliance before we are all attacked by something else."

The sound of hoofbeats approached. Jherik rode up and dismounted. "Where do we go next?"

Timbrel took her pack. "Put Lostaria on my horse," she instructed. She ducked underneath, using the red ribbon-loincloth from her pack to gently tie the Princess's legs and waist to the saddle. "I will join you later. Now ride."

Krys and Jherik rode away, leading Timbrel's horse with Lostaria tied into the saddle. Timbrel hefted her pack and turned back to Nerryon. She had to find Shess and stop him, or every Ravali elf would be in danger. Heading back toward the slave markets, the half-elf watched for the Melani.

She searched only a few streets when a whisper caught her attention. "Timbrel, is that you? Come here."

She glanced down the dark alley where the strange voice came from. A dark shape leaned against the wall. She walked closer. "Who is it?"

"Timbrel?" The voice asked again. It was not Shess. She turned away.

"It's her. Get her." Four short figures rose up around her. She struggled as they grabbed her, hearing the bones of the first man's arm snap as she twisted free. There were too many hands to avoid them all. One swung a small leather sack. Blinding pain exploded on the side of Timbrel's head.

###

# Chapter Nine

*Nerryon*

Timbrel woke slowly, her sense of touch the first to recover. The rough cool stone of a floor beneath her body. The prickling scratches of rope on her wrists, tied behind her back. The open weave of homespun fabric wound tightly across her breasts and loins.

Her nose wrinkled with the mixed smell of dung and mold. Footsteps and whispering voices faded into her consciousness. The half-elf opened her eyes slowly. Dim light filtered across the room. She could see metal bars.

"She's awake." The same voice that called her in the night whispered from behind her.

Timbrel rolled over to face her captor. More bars separated her from a group of young humans, all with the gangly look of teens in the midst of their final growth. One held his arm in a sling. Taken by a group of teen boys. The dancer berated herself silently for her stupidity. She should never have turned her back on the first stranger, and never returned inside the city when she was too exhausted to think straight.

"You really are the Timbrel, aren't you?" Their leader stepped forward. His face glowed as he knelt outside of the bars.

"I am Timbrel, yes." There was no use in denying the truth. "Why have you tied my hands?"

"Because Kadeesh says you're dangerous. You're some kind of sorceress."

"A what?" Timbrel looked at the boys in disbelief. "Who is Kadeesh?"

"He's a slaver," piped up another boy. "He's gonna pay us lots of money for you."

The leader of the group glared. "Shut up, Len. Don't tell her anything."

"You shut up, Ban," Len muttered as he shuffled away.

Timbrel watched the exchange with interest. The other boys pushed Len out of the room. She looked at Ban. "So Kadeesh told you to insult me."

Ban looked confused. "Insult you? How?"

"Magic is a great crime among my people. To call me a sorceress is to insult me."

Ban pulled out a scrap of parchment. The boy opened it, moving his lips as he read.

"This says you're an elf, and you have golden hair and blue eyes. It also says to beware of your feminine wiles and magics, and cautions any who catch you to restrain your hands." Ban's dark eyes looked directly into hers. "It also says you killed a man."

"I have."

"How did you kill him?"

Timbrel noticed that Ban stayed further away from the bars than before. "I slit his throat with a dagger."

Ban visibly relaxed and leaned closer to the bars. "We took that away from you already." His eyes flicked to the side of the room. Timbrel followed his glance. Her clothing and the contents of her pack lay in an untidy heap against the wall. The blue and gold of her dance skirts peeked out from the pile.

"The rope is very uncomfortable. If you untie my wrists and give me my blue skirt, I'll dance for you."

"You're a dancer?"

"You've already been through my things. You know that I am."

The boys put their heads together and whispered. Ban finally turned back to her. "You can dance for us. We'll see if you're any good. Now turn around backwards and stick your hands through the bars."

Timbrel followed his instructions. A hand reached in to cup her breast. A moment later it disappeared, followed by the touch of fingers untying the rope. Timbrel pulled her hands back inside the cage, then stood and stretched. The boys held their breath as one.

237

The blue skirt waited on the straw inside the bars. Timbrel turned her back on the boys and removed the homespun strip they had provided before stepping into the skirt. The silk swirled around her ankles.

"May I have the top? It is the same color."

Several boys scrambled to her pack at once. Fists flew as they argued over the privilege. The triumphant winner, his eye already swelling, handed her the blue silk shirt.

Timbrel turned again, shrugging off the homespun and sliding into her top. The shirt felt cool against her skin as she gathered the lower portion and tied it beneath her breasts. She stretched again with her arms in the air, her chilled nipples erect and pressing against the silk. The boys knelt to watch her.

Beating time with her foot, Timbrel moved around the inside of her cell. Before long she was spinning and swaying in time with a country song popular in Fafar. Though she kept the dance simple, the boys swayed with her. After a final spin, the half-elf sank to the floor in front of Ban.

Ban's face flushed red and his breathing came in ragged gasps. He met Timbrel's eyes and did not look away. As his breathing started to calm, he shook himself like a wet animal.

"You say you have no magic?" he whispered, then turned and shouted orders to the others. They scampered away, leaving Ban alone with Timbrel. "They will bring food and water to you. Perhaps we will not sell you to Kadeesh. Perhaps we will keep you. Others will pay well to see such a dance." Ban stood shakily, holding the bars of the cell for support.

Timbrel touched his hand. "You could let me go."

Ban stared into the dancer's eyes. "I will sell you when I don't want you anymore." The leader of the boys tossed Timbrel her ankle bells and walked out of the room, his gait far less smooth than before.

###

The search went on for Timbrel. Kadeesh hired new men to search the plains south of the city. The trackers were unskilled and found no sign of the girl.

Krys and Jherik worried quietly about the dancer, but kept their attention focused on healing Lostaria. Her condition improved slowly.

Shess searched for the white tower, his mind filled with thoughts of magic and his missing prizes. The tower eluded him, and the Melani elf did not recognize the subtle pressure of magic against his thoughts.

Gareth tore down fifteen notices in Lucifron, all mentioning Timbrel. He had met Kadeesh before, and set out for Nerryon to instruct the slaver to forget the girl.

Soliari anxiously awaited word from Celiar's special unit. Only two deaths had come to her attention: Von and Sarin.

Nayev was called before his elders.

Timbrel danced for her captors and their select audience, waiting her chance to escape.

### 

*Dragon Valley*

Nayev approached the Council ledge. The elders perched around the edges, disapproval clear in their expressions.

"Have you completed your task yet? Have you removed your elven offspring?" The Council spokesdragon leaned over to look closely at him.

"Yes, the last of my offspring is dead. There are no more. I don't know what you were so worried about." Nayev thought about Sarin's death by assassination. A horrible way to go. And yet, the old elf's last words still haunted him. *I always thought it would be by dragon, like my brothers died.* Nayev frowned. *Who were the dragons that killed my other offspring?*

239

"We have another task for you. Anyana. Her mate has left her after the injury of her surviving daughter. We have chosen you to be her new mate."

"I have no interest in mating with Anyana. That may have been her former mate's excuse, but the reality is that no one wants to be with her. She is mean-spirited and does not fulfill her obligations."

"Regardless, you will mate with her and be responsible for her injured child." The spokesdragon nudged Nayev with his nose.

Nayev pushed the dragon's nose away with both arms. "I will make arrangements for the care of the child–who is almost an adult–but I will not mate with Anyana."

Grumbling and shouts mixed as the members of the Council shuffled about.

"What can you expect from a pervert?"

"No respect for authority."

"Doesn't he understand our birthrate is falling?"

Nayev brushed some invisible dust off his shoulder. "I'm done with this. I'm going back to the human lands."

"That should be safe enough for now, but you *will* return to mate within Anyana. Keep our laws in mind: you may not mate with an elf. It is forbidden. It will dilute your bloodlines, and they are very valuable."

The wizard left the ledge, squeezing through a narrow crack before the dragons or anyone else could follow.

### 

*Nerryon*

Gareth arrived in Nerryon still picking bone arrowheads from his armor. The Spider Riders were bolder now, determined to reclaim the entire land as forest. Gareth tangled with them before, and respected the warriors for their single-minded pursuit and quick adaptation to his tactics when he seldom left any raiding parties alive. It was almost as if the Riders' dead spoke to them. Maybe he should remove the bodies from the forest the next time.

No, he decided. Let them have their funeral rites. As warriors, they deserved a proper resting place. Gareth smiled. More than once he traveled around their underground city, lengthening his journey by several hours. The half-elven warrior suspected that the Riders knew he observed their children. He also noticed that the Spider Riders never pushed toward his home village as they expanded their forests. More than one Insara child came screaming to Lashana about the spiders chasing them in the forest, but no children disappeared since before Gareth's birth. It was a game of sorts.

A deadly game, he reminded himself as he carefully withdrew an arrowhead from the leather collar that protected his neck. Only the thinnest layer of leather remained between the bone point's poison and his skin. He would have to be more careful the next time. Time. There was no time. With Kadeesh's sights set on Timbrel, Gareth grew angry. The slaver had no right to target those of elven blood. Let the fat man be satisfied with taking humans.

Gareth thought about Timbrel's open and trusting nature, bringing him to meet her elven friends. When he met her in Lucifron's posting room, she had innocently broken the rules of the assassin's assignment room and convinced Gareth to do the same. Did she not understand how he made his living? Gareth frowned. Did she truly think him just a guide between Lucifron and Nerryon? He'd saved her life once already. Of course, the bounty on the goblin that attacked her made the effort more than worthwhile. Perhaps he should just find her and use her as bait. The contract that Kadeesh posted should bring the lesser bounty hunters and marginal criminals out in droves.

Gareth shifted form, his long loping run eating up the miles. It took less than a day for him to reach the outskirts of Nerryon. He waited for the cover of darkness before shifting again and entered the city. The gates closed behind him, warding off the marauding cats.

His few wounds healed, Gareth stretched to his full height. He double-checked his weapons, always amazed that they survived the transition in one piece. He prowled toward the slave markets, remembering Timbrel's scent. Twice he smelled the scent faintly, but each time it merely clung to the clothing of those who might have passed her by. He needed a fresher trail to follow.

The bounty hunter continued through the night, his energy unflagging. The girl's scent, reminding him of sun and flowers, could not be found. He rounded a corner and drew back, curling his upper lip against his teeth. The sharp tang that he associated with Kadeesh was very strong. He turned to track the fat slaver.

Gareth caught up with Kadeesh just outside the former mercenary's compound. The slaver looked pleased to see the half-elven bounty hunter and invited him within. Gareth went cautiously, cataloguing possible exits through windows and other doorways as he moved. His scar itched with tension. It took an effort of will not to scratch the right side of his face.

"Lone Wolf! Just the hunter I wished to see." Kadeesh overflowed with good cheer.

Gareth's scar itched madly. "Kadeesh," he acknowledged, tipping his head forward without looking away from the slaver's eyes.

"You are my best tracker, my best hunter. I need your services."

"I am not yours, Kadeesh. I work alone."

"I employ you at times. Now is such a time. I have lost a slave."

"A slave." Gareth let disdain color his words. "I do not track missing slaves."

"This one is special. The slave and her...her sister are traveling together. I will pay for the two. More than you can imagine."

"I have a good imagination."

Kadeesh named a sum that shocked Gareth. With money like that, he could live a life of luxury. At least until the next time he shifted.

"You are willing to pay so much for two women. What would you pay for your own life?"

Kadeesh paled visibly. The young bounty hunter suddenly understood the high price. The recovery of the women somehow tied in to the fat slaver's own survival. "Who placed a price on your life? When do they collect?"

The fat slaver trembled. "I have less than a year to locate the women and notify my buyer. Otherwise I become the prey."

"Who is this mysterious buyer?" Gareth was curious to know who could terrify Kadeesh more than he could.

"A Melani," whispered the slaver, looking around as though he might have been overheard. "An evil thing from the far east. They warned me against making a deal with such a demon, but I ignored the warnings. I sent the message in the ancient ways."

Gareth stood and looked at the slaver. "Boil in your own stew. I have better prey to hunt." Gareth turned and left, wishing that he could force the shift and simply kill the slaver. He had nearly a month before that would be possible again. A terrible shame.

Gareth continued to prowl the streets. Kadeesh, having broken the most ancient traditions of his profession and dealt with the Melani, was useless to him; Kadeesh was a ruined man, though he was unlikely to live long enough to realize it.

### 

Timbrel turned at a scuffling noise down the alley from her cage. When it did not repeat, she continued working at the cage's lock with two stout broomstraws. An open manacle attached to a chain lay on the floor behind her.

The dancer stopped to listen again. Ban had checked on her less than fifteen minutes before, but he could return at any minute. She smiled to herself as the first pin in the lock lifted. Only two more to go.

The boys left her overnight in her dancing cage while they tried to clean the remains of a pulped date she stuck in the lock of

243

her normal cell. The half-elf begged the treat the evening before, then chewed the fruit to a sticky pulp hidden in her mouth. She lay on the cell floor until Ban and his group arrived to untie her hands and move her to the other cage. Using a dance move, she bent her knees beneath herself as she lay on the floor, then smoothly arched her back and rose to her feet. Having shown the boys that her tied hands did not restrict her movements, she sauntered to the cell bars for her daily untying. Attaching a manacle to her leg, they leashed her with a short chain for the walk to her dancing cage. Timbrel pretended to stumble over the chain, her hand darting to her mouth and transferring the sticky pulp to the inside of the open lock. She made certain to move slowly enough for the boys to observe her 'escape efforts'.

As she hoped, the boys decided to chain her in the dancing cage overnight, wearing naught but the homespun bands. A few straws lay on the floor, left over from the daily sweeping. Timbrel knew that she could pick the lock. The manacle on her ankle was the work of seconds to remove.

The last tumbler clicked open just as soft footsteps rounded the corner. The dancer darted across the cage and snapped the manacle around her ankle again. She sat in the back corner of the cage, waiting for the footsteps to pass.

The footsteps slowed as they approached. Timbrel risked a glance up, found herself looking at the face in the shadows. The moonlight played on the scar that ran down the right side of his face, highlighting his half-elven features. She knew that his eyes were green.

"Gareth," she whispered.

"Timbrel," replied Gareth.

The girl looked up and down the street, quickly unlocked her ankle and slipped out the cage door. As Gareth watched, she opened the door of a small shed and pulled her pack out. In the distance, she heard Ban's voice approaching. "She's worth every silver bit you paid."

"They'll be hunting me," Timbrel whispered as she tugged Gareth into the alley.

244

"They already are." The two moved down the alleyway, sliding in and out of shadows cast by the mounded garbage.

Gareth blended into the shadows even better than Timbrel did, impressing her. They darted across the road. Timbrel started toward the south gate of the city. Gareth laid a hand on her wrist. "This way."

Gareth led her through a twisting path, then down through a basement and into a large sewer pipe. The pipe was broken a few strides away, giving access to a cave. He dropped to the ground first, his head cocked as he listened. He took a deep whiff of the air before reaching up to help Timbrel down.

"What are you listening for?" The girl heard nothing but the slow drip of water from the broken pipe behind her.

"Cats." After a moment he started down the cave. Timbrel was grateful that Gareth seemed to know his way through the caves that honeycombed the region. She wondered if this cave connected to the other in Kadeesh's basement. After two hours, she could finally smell the night air. Timbrel could see the faint outlines of Nerryon behind them. The forest loomed close.

Timbrel stopped and dug in her pack. "Wait, I have to change clothes." Gareth turned his back to her, watching for danger. Dressing quickly in her traveling clothes, Timbrel tucked the homespun bands into her pack, next to her dance skirt. Her blue dance shirt was gone, though she found and strapped on her daggers.

Gareth seemed to approve. They moved out across the plains, heading for the forest.

### 

*Near Lucifron, to the north*

Krys and Jherik gave Lostaria the red bloodroot soup for two full weeks before she recovered enough to travel. A single bloodroot lay in the bottom of the pouch. There was still no sign of Timbrel.

"She said to go on without her, that she'd meet us in Lucifron or even Rockhold." Krys repeated himself yet again to Jherik.

Lostaria asked as well after she woke. The Princess remembered a sweet drink just before their arrival. She remembered Timbrel unlocking her wrists, but little beyond that. Krys noticed that Lostaria rubbed her birthmark shoulder while they rode, as if the stain in her skin would help her remember.

They traveled just outside of Lucifron, trekking through the edges of the desert that bordered the city to the north. The horses adapted well to the shifting sand, and they carried full water skins. The Spider Forest lay far to their south. Only one thing disturbed the wizard-elf: footprints. Hundreds of footprints.

As near as Krys could tell, the human sized footprints were traveling between Lucifron and the mountains near Rockhold.

Lostaria moved into his vision, with the same sunlit shade of golden hair as her cousin Timbrel, and as slender a body. The resemblance ended there. Lostaria's sharp features included high cheekbones and a pointed chin, which gave her a triangular face. Her taller ears came to points far more prominent than her half-elf kin. With smaller breasts than Timbrel, the princess was still a beautiful elf.

"Kryslandir? When is my cousin rejoining us?" Lostaria's eyes flashed storm-grey, darker than Krys's own.

"I am not certain. She may have gone to the Seer again. He helped us to find you."

Jherik, riding back to report, looked horrified as he overheard. "She went back to Gowell? Didn't you see how sick she became after she spoke with him?" The Henin elf wheeled his horse to the south, ready to ride for the white tower.

Krys restrained him with a hand. "Young as she is, Timbrel is an adult. Her choices are her own. For the most part, she chooses well. Trust her on this."

Jherik scoffed. "Her choices? She chose to sleep with Shess instead of rescuing her cousin."

Lostaria's eyebrows rose. "Tell me of this," she demanded.

246

Krys sighed. "Shess, the Melani who contracted to buy you, tricked Timbrel into drinking wine laced with *likshas*. Her reactions to the drug are... different." Krys searched for words to explain. "Her human side moderates the effect into a... a..."

"Into sex," supplied Jherik.

Krys glared at the Henin elf. "She spent a night with him. And with another woman. Together." Krys looked uncomfortable. "Shess tried to bend Timbrel's mind, but it was not as successful as he thought. Timbrel discovered Shess' purpose. She sent me ahead to rescue you while she offered herself to him for sex. To delay him..." Krys trailed off, unable to continue.

Lostaria frowned. "Timbrel freed my wrists, did she not?"

"The Melani chose to spend time with the other woman. Timbrel awakened a need in him, but he felt secure in his control over her. Instead, he sought to control the other. That one delayed him, though not in the way your cousin intended. Timbrel reached us before the rescue attempt."

"I think it was well that she did." Lostaria rubbed her wrists, no longer chafed from the manacles. "I look forward to speaking with her. She seems resourceful."

"Resourceful," Jherik spluttered. He turned his head away.

"Are you betrothed to her? Do you not agree with her choices?" Lostaria's voice chilled Krys.

Jherik froze. "No, I am not betrothed to her. I am to marry another." Jherik's voice was sullen.

"Perhaps you should think again about your betrothal. You seem not properly enamored of your own." Lostaria reprimanded the Henin warrior. Jherik looked at the ground, chastened.

### 

*The edge of the Spider Forest*

Gareth woke with Timbrel in his arms. The tiny cabin that sheltered them showed sunlight through the crack under the door. He stretched as she dressed.

"They're still hunting you, I think." *Too bad. He would've liked to hold her longer.*

Timbrel looked at the ground. "I do not mean to put you in danger. I can travel on alone to Lucifron."

"Alone? You'd never get through that forest on your own." Gareth looked at the girl. She seemed determined.

Timbrel lifted her chin. "Don't feel that you have to stay. We're only together so long as our paths cross. There is nothing permanent between us."

Gareth stared at the girl. While tempted to admit that he liked her, better that she not know that. She could never accept his shifting. He must remain alone. Safer for everyone. The thrill of danger energized him, almost as much as a nearing shift.

"I..." The girl began again, the words difficult for her this time. "I would not be upset if our paths crossed again. You are unskilled, but I can teach you..."

Timbrel trailed off as Gareth glowered. Of course she knew immediately that it was his first time with a woman. He growled to himself.

Her warm hand touched his arm. "I have no complaints. It was fun." She giggled, poking at him.

He shook off her hand, opening the door slowly. The scent of men hung in the freshening breeze. "They are closer than I thought. We must go." They headed out into the forest together.

The trap sprung. A dozen men burst from cover, firing arrows at the two. Timbrel winced as one sliced past her, scoring her arm. She glanced at the arrow, now lodged in the tree next to her.

"The arrows are silver." She ducked again, twisting away from another shaft.

"Silver?" Gareth let out a curse. "These hunters seek me." Silver would not harm him more than any other metal, but the superstition remained. It meant the hunters knew he shifted. He whirled and melted into the forest, pulling his dagger as he circled the hunters from behind. Three days ago, he thought, he could have forced the shift. So soon afterward, however, he did not have

248

enough power. The last hunter in the attacking group, now hiding clumsily ahead of him, went down with a slit throat. Gareth wiped his blade on the man's shirt, waiting for his next opportunity.

A cry rose up ahead. "We have the woman!"

Timbrel's voice cut through the hunters' exaltation. "What are you doing? Let me go!"

The sounds of a struggle were followed by a soft *oof* that climbed the scales.

Gareth's blade found another hunter, the man's attention riveted on the girl. The next two hunters dropped silently. *Only eight to go.* He glanced through the underbrush.

One of the hunters dragged Timbrel to one side by the hair, and threw her roughly against a tree. He held his sword to her throat. "Tell me where he is."

"Where who is?" Timbrel's voice sounded so innocent.

"The filthy thing you travel with." Venom practically dripped from the man's words.

Gareth didn't recognize the man's voice or his face. Familiar hate in the tone, though.

"Thing?" Timbrel's tone of disbelief warned Gareth that she was about to act. "What do you mean, thing?" The girl sounded insulted. Gareth brought down another guard, the last who was not in the immediate sight of the others.

"It isn't a man, it just looks like one."

Gareth pulled his sword just as Timbrel lifted her chin. Her voice was frosty. "What have elves ever done to you?" She slapped away the hunter's sword and rose to her feet.

Chaos reigned as Gareth charged the hunters. His sword took down two more of them before the others could react. Someone blew a hunting horn. The sound choked off in the middle. Crashing noises through the brush warned of the arrival of more hunters.

Gareth grabbed Timbrel by the shoulder. She spun and sliced at him with a slender dagger, pulling back as she recognized him. His tunic flapped around the slice revealing a shallow scratch reddening on his belly. An apologetic look flickered across her face.

"Run. There are more of them coming. Run and I'll find you after it's over." Gareth pointed. Timbrel sprinted ahead, dagger in hand.

Gareth turned back to the other hunters. His sword clashed against another before spinning into the trees from his numbed hand. Timbrel shrieked in the distance.

Anger surged inside Lashana's son. Without thinking, he triggered the shift. Gareth screamed as the pain lanced through him. Bones and muscles melted, reshaping themselves in new configurations. The scar on his face burned as the skin rolled back, revealing a longer snout filled with much larger teeth.

Dropping to all fours, the wolf that was Gareth spun about, snapping his jaws at the hunters who surrounded him. Bones broke as he caught arms and wrenched them from their sockets. His thick brown fur warded off most of their weapons, the sword blades sliding to the side rather than cutting flesh. A searing arrow strike across his right flank provoked a yelp of pain.

The brush parted and Timbrel threw herself bodily on Gareth's opponent from behind, overbalancing the hunter. As they tumbled to the ground, Gareth made short work of the others.

### 

Timbrel sprinted. Pursuers filled the woods, far more than Gareth warned her about. She'd been grabbed and left a man writhing in the dust with blood between his legs. She had to warn Gareth.

The hunters attacking Gareth faced another foe, though Timbrel did not realize it until she jumped on the back of the closest hunter. She tumbled to the ground, shifting her weight to keep the man pinned in place. She'd pinned men before during love-play. Only now did she realize how potent her skills could be. The longer she kept the man pinned and distracted, the better the chance for Gareth to escape.

A growl sounded. Timbrel's breath caught as she saw a huge brown wolf with a black patch on its chest. The wolf lunged for the fallen hunter's throat as Timbrel scrambled backward and pushed herself to her knees. Their gazes locked. Warm green eyes flecked with gold looked out at her from thick brown fur. Familiar eyes.

"Gareth?" Her voice filled with wonder. She stood, all fear of the brown wolf gone. She touched the trembling animal's shoulder, ran her hand along his fur until she found the wound on his flank. "You're hurt."

The wolf gently took her hand in his mouth and pulled.

Timbrel smiled. Yes, it was time to go. She spotted a discarded sword in the brush, brought it out and carried it with her. She and the wolf slipped through the forest, avoiding hunters when they could.

Timbrel tripped and fell. Something tightened on her ankle and dragged her across the clearing. Gareth whirled and attacked a hunter. In a moment he was surrounded. They surrounded Timbrel as well, the men dragging her through the darkening forest by a rope. She struggled and bit at them. The high branches clicked in the breeze, reminding her of another clicking. One of the hunters pulled her ankle loop tighter.

"No!" Timbrel shouted. "I do not choose to go with you!"

The forest came alive. One hunter struggled to breathe through a sticky white blob that dropped on his face. The mandibles of a spider cut another in half. The rest fled into the forest. A Spider-Rider dropped to the ground, his bone sword flashing in the sunlight of the clearing. The ankle rope parted. Timbrel looked up to see a familiar face.

"Stinger."

"You are well, Timbrel?" The Rider gave her an appraising look.

"Well enough. I thank you for your assistance." She noticed that the Riders collected the dead bodies and carried them into the forest.

251

"We will discuss payment when the intruders are gone." Stinger's voice was matter-of-fact.

Timbrel suddenly remembered the missing horse from her first visit. "I need to return to my friend."

Stinger nodded. The spiders surrounding the clearing disappeared into the forest. "I will accompany you."

The two followed Timbrel's trail backwards, the brush crushed and broken by her struggles. The wolf lay panting on the ground, bleeding from more wounds than Timbrel could count. Two Spider-Rriders leaned over him, pulling an arrow from the animal's shoulder.

"Leave him alone." Timbrel darted forward to stand next to the wolf. The animal let out a breath and collapsed.

"His meat is our price," Stinger said. Timbrel whirled and glared at the Rider.

"No, I will not let you take him." Timbrel pulled her dagger from its sheath. "You must kill me before you can have him."

Stinger stepped forward, a look of regret on his face. "Our arrows are poisoned. It is dead. You have not bred children yet."

"You may not have him." She looked around at the dead and dying hunters nearby. "You may take his entire kill, but you may not have him."

"Those bodies belong to the wolf and to you, Timbrel. We would not take your kill."

"Then trade with me. Take my kill in exchange for his body."

Stinger looked perturbed. "It has never been done before."

"Be the first." Timbrel swayed slightly, exhaustion setting in.

The Rider looked to the sky. The other Riders and their spiders vanished. "It shall be as you ask." Stinger melted into the forest as Timbrel fell to her knees and cradled the wolf's head. She traced the white line of the scar that marred his muzzle. Tears dripped down her cheeks. She felt very alone.

###

Timbrel knelt, weeping silently by the inert body of the wolf. Tears streamed down her face, dripping across the wolf's neck and dampening the brown fur. The shadow of a cloud darkened the forest path for a moment, reflecting her mood. With a sudden burst of energy, the girl scooped a depression in the soft loam by the side of the path. She dragged the wolf into the shallow grave, bending to hug the furry neck one last time. She scraped leaves into the hole, concealing the body from sight, then scattered loam on the leaves. As a final tribute, Timbrel gathered branches and wove a protective cage, staking it firmly into the loam to deter animals from disturbing the grave.

*They are coming. You are pursued.* The voice whispered in her mind, barely audible against the noise of the breeze in the brush. The girl looked around but saw no one.

"Who speaks?" Her voice swept away on the breeze.

*They are nearly upon you.* The whisper in her mind was urgent, as urgent as the freshening breeze. *Run down the path to the clearing. I will meet you there.* In the distance, Timbrel heard a loud *crack* followed by a muffled curse.

She fled down the path, stretching her stride to its fullest. The brush flew past her, the path beneath an oak tree suddenly opening into a small meadow. Sunlight reflected golden off the grass and a large rock formation. She carefully edged out into the clearing.

*Quickly!* The voice in her mind spoke louder. She cast about, looking for the source. The rocks moved.

Timbrel shrank back to the oak tree as the rock formation unfolded to reveal a large wedge-shaped head. Two lines of tusks stretched from the tip of the nose to the eyes. Thin spines rose from the top of the head. The sky-blue eyes focused on the half-elf as the dragon's head swiveled toward her.

*Climb in front of my wings. Now, Timbrel.* The dragon uncoiled itself, stretching across most of the meadow's end. It crouched to the ground, wings folded back and one foreleg extended to assist her in mounting. The sun glittered across its golden scales. From the wings back, spikes rose along the spine.

The girl stood frozen in place.

The dragon whispered in her mind again. *Hurry.* A branch swished along the pathway behind her, striking against something solid. Another muffled curse, very close.

Timbrel bolted like a startled rabbit, running straight at the dragon. She scampered up its side, seating herself on a large plate-like scale that covered the spine in front of the wings. She leaned forward, held onto the front edge, and screamed in her thoughts to the dragon. *Let's go!*

The dragon pulled in its foreleg, bunching its muscles. It sprang into the air with powerful hind legs, barely clearing the treetops. The wings snapped out to the sides, joints locking in place as they began to beat. The dragon slowly rose, its body lurching with each wing stroke.

Timbrel clenched her hands around the edge of the scale. The scale-plate that she sat on was ridged along the spine, though not as sharply as the other scale-plates along the neck. Her pubic bone grated uncomfortably against the ridge. When the dragon rose high enough, the wings tilted slightly. The girl could feel warm air rising around them. The dragon circled until it reached a height that let Timbrel see for miles. Behind them, tiny as ants, the hunters swarmed in the meadow. The dragon glided toward the eastern mountains, barely visible as a smudge on the horizon. The wings turned again, beating parallel to the ground in a slow rhythm. Timbrel found herself rocking in time with the pulsing pressure of the ridge.

"Where are we going?" She shouted against the breeze.

The dragon's voice whispered in her mind. *Where do you need to go? I can take you wherever you wish.*

Timbrel tensed. Why would a dragon offer her such a service?

*We have a mutual friend,* whispered the dragon. *He thought you should rejoin your companions.*

Timbrel silently tried to imagine who she knew that would speak to dragons. As her mind focused on the Seer, she felt the dragon's anger.

"There is a returned Terformin? Where?"

"Why do you want to know?" Timbrel perversely thought of flowering meadows with trickling streams and colorful butterflies.

The dragon gave her no answer. Timbrel frowned, wondering what went through its mind. The creature was as secretive as Nayev.

Nayev. Now that the girl thought of the young wizard, she realized that he might speak with dragons. She considered the possibility, remembering the young man's sky-blue eyes. Blue like the dragon's eyes, she thought.

Her recent experience with Gareth came to mind. Gareth shifted into a wolf before he died. Could Nayev shift form as well?

*Lucifron ahead.* The dragon's voice intruded on her thoughts. Timbrel looked at the northern side of the forest near Lucifron. She saw no sign of Krys. Perhaps he was in Rockhold already? She had spent several weeks dancing in Ban's cage.

Before she could say a word, the dragon curved off to the north. The desert spread out below them. The late afternoon sun warmed the air and the dragon spiraled upward again. They glided toward the mountains between Lucifron and Rockhold. Timbrel looked down at the sand and gasped. A wide trail of footprints wound through the sand. The dragon adjusted his flight, following the trail. The disturbed sand narrowed and became a single well-worn track through the wastes. The trail ended by the myriad caves scattered throughout the foothills.

"What caused that?" she asked. The dragon said nothing, but the girl could feel his concern. They flew through a high pass, the dragon beating his wings to gain the last bit of height necessary for the passage. As they curved back toward the trail through the mountains, Timbrel spotted Krys, Jherik, and Lostaria. They traveled with Halar, the giant who guided Timbrel through the pass before.

The dragon flew down to a bare spot of ground an hour's travel past the group. He flapped his wings heavily, settling carefully to the ground. Timbrel remained seated on his back, her eyes half shut and mouth slightly open.

*It is safe. They will reach you soon.* At the dragon's words, the girl carefully climbed down from its back. She concentrated carefully to keep her legs steady. After a moment she circled to the dragon's head.

"Who sent you?" She asked.

The dragon twitched its mouth into a grin. *A mutual friend.*

"So secretive."

*Who wants to tell all their secrets?*

Timbrel smiled. The dragon's attitude was so much like the young wizard's. "Thank you for the ride."

*Perhaps we will fly together again sometime?*

Timbrel tilted her head and looked carefully at the dragon's expression, trying to interpret it. The dragon reminded her so much of Nayev with his smug amusement. He must be the dragon's friend. "Do you have a name that I may thank you properly with? Or should I just call you Nayev?"

The dragon jerked his head back and peered closely at the girl. She heard the faintest whisper against her thoughts. *Who told you?* The dragon craned its head around. *They are almost here*, he announced, bunching his muscles for a leap.

Timbrel blew a kiss as Nayev the dragon leapt into the sky and hurried away.

###

# Chapter Ten

*The foothills west of Rockhold*

Damnech screamed in fury. The sound echoed back from the mountainside where the clones stood staring at him, their mouths stupidly hanging open. The four clones he armed with static rods seemed fascinated by the shiny brightness of the metal. Only one closed his hand properly over the curve of the weapon, and he was holding it upside down.

*I should have hired traitors.* The clones were loyal, but almost too stupid to train. Worse yet, they each carried the traits of degenerate facial cartilage and the absence of body fat. Damnech had not understood how much that would affect their intelligence and eyesight, among other problems. He kicked the nearby stone, mentally cursing the cryo chamber and incubators. He refused to admit that the fault might lie in his own genetics.

The clone holding the weapon shuffled forward, holding it towards the target. The clone squeezed its hand. Lightning flashed out and down, searing the hapless clone's foot to the bone. The smell of burnt flesh mingled with the sharpness of ozone. The clone wobbled, its damaged foot throwing it off balance. It still held the static rod upside down.

"Give me those." The four clones obeyed immediately. Three marched up to the Terformin and dropped the weapons in his hands. The fourth overbalanced and crashed to the ground. It crawled forward, handed the weapon to Damnech, and collapsed at his feet.

*Useless, they are all useless.* Damnech surveyed the group. Skeletal faces, the skin stretched tight across noseless skulls, stared back. Many of them blinked their golden eyes against the afternoon sunlight. Like the others, this group could barely wield swords. The sealed cache of thirty static rods he had found was useless to him. Only six of the three thousand clones he tested so far had been able to use the rods properly, and he lost more than three dozen during the testing. Like this one. Without a word, Damnech fired the static rod at the clone by his feet. Lightning flashed, ozone stung his throat, and the clone lay still.

The Terformin looked up at the sun, gauging the time. He would test another group in the morning.

### 

*The Pass to Rockhold*

Teembara was waiting when Halar led Karas and the others along the path to Rockhold. Halar swept her up in an enthusiastic hug. The half-elven girl grinned, immediately sliding into the strange language she and the guide developed on the trip westward.

The resemblance between Teembara and her cousin amazed Halar. Seeing them together, the giant could pick out the differences in their faces. Teembara's face was like a halved nut, what the humans called heart-shaped. Hostaree's face was more triangular, like the sides of Tallfolk gambling dice.

Halar had fond memories of games played against his brothers. The Tallfolk guide might have been smaller than his siblings, but he was smarter. He figured out how to flick his wrist when he threw the dice so they flipped entirely over twice, and landed with the same side up. Even now his brothers did not realize the trick.

Teembara enthusiastically told of her adventures, switching between the elven speech that he could vaguely understand and their personal language. Halar smiled gently at the tiny girl. It would be nice to camp just to spend another night with her. Unfortunately, they would reach the gates of Rockhold before the sun's rest. A momentary frown crossed the giant's face. Karas had instructed them to hurry. The little elf-man thought speed was important.

The girl spoke of seeing footsteps in the desert. Halar paid more attention. He too had seen footsteps, tracking them between small caves. The creature that he caught looked more dead than alive, a living skeleton with a fine layer of stretched skin holding it together.

"The skeleton men?" He asked, looking for clarification. Teembara stopped her tale and looked straight at the giant.

"Did you see them? How many are there?" The girl always asked questions. The other three elves looked blankly in her direction. She stopped to translate.

Halar bent over and picked a wildflower's seed pod growing along the side of the trail. The giant cracked the pod open, sending hundreds of tiny seeds into the wind. "More than this," he explained. "They are like ants on a piece of rotting fruit."

Karas spoke sharply to the others. Halar caught something about being sure of the form.

Teembara grew angry. "I have seen them," she said in the elf tongue, "in the Seer's window." Halar understood only half of what the girl said, but it was enough.

"They are the walking dead. The dead that walk. They will cover the entire land like insects on the march." Halar watched Teembara pale as she translated his words for the others. "The Tallfolk legends call them Tarafora. They were born in times past, and the golden light of burning suns shines through their eyes. They live far past their dying time. The golden watchers, the Daraga, will return to fight them. The warriors will tear the land to pieces, killing everything. The great wars of the Daraga and the Tarafora were the true cause of the land's dying. The Genaji made both, but the Tarafora followed the Hinaji. When the Daraga attacked, the Tarafora grew angry and tried to kill the entire world. When they return, the battle will happen again, but this time the Tarafora will win."

Karas frowned as Teembara translated. The elf motioned Halar aside. "Tell me the tale again, please." Karas spoke the Tallfolk tongue as he had before, slowly and haltingly. Halar repeated the childhood story to the silver-haired elf. Karas nodded slowly. "I think I understand."

### 

Krys turned back to the others. "Timbrel translated the giant's tale very accurately. It seems we must find the Daraga."

Lostaria, silent since her cousin's return an hour before, finally spoke. "An alliance with humans will help as well. When we reach the docks, I will take ship to Port Kerran. I can still try to forge that alliance." She looked directly at Timbrel for the first time. "You seem to have a knack for making friends. Find the Daraga and convince them to help us. If we have to stop the walking dead from overrunning our land, then so be it. Do whatever you have to. I understand you are... resourceful." Lostaria continued to watch her cousin as if waiting for a reply.

"I will do what I can." The half-elf looked thoughtful.

Krys noticed that Lostaria had not given him any orders. She barely spoke to him on the journey, and ignored Jherik completely after chastising him. The Henin elf, for that matter, uncharacteristically remained silent while traveling with the princess. It had been an uncomfortable journey.

It was a relief to pass through the city gates. Rockhold bustled with activity. Three cargo ships arrived, and the town turned out in force to unload and store the various crates, bags, and baskets. Krys arranged two rooms at the Crystal Inn, one for the women to share. Timbrel took Lostaria upstairs to familiarize the Princess with the inn's facilities.

Krys and Jherik remained in the common room. They took an empty table in the far corner. It wobbled when Jherik leaned an elbow on it.

The Henin warrior flexed his hands. "I'll be glad when she's gone," he muttered. The brown-haired elf flexed his hands again. "She scares me."

"The Princess? Yes, it's been difficult." Krys waved for a waitress. After a moment a red-haired girl came by. Krys ordered bowls of stew and some bread and cheese. The redhead hurried off.

Jherik looked uncomfortable. "She doesn't like me, does she."

260

"Lostaria? She doesn't know you. You act like a lower caste elf much of the time, you know."

"Not her," Jherik corrected. "Timbrel."

"Timbrel likes you as well as the next man. Well, maybe not *that* well." Krys chuckled. He stopped as Jherik frowned.

"When she is with us, I feel like I am stronger and faster than before." The Henin elf looked acutely embarrassed. "I do not doubt myself so much," he admitted.

Krys considered the warrior's words. He too felt Timbrel's presence keenly. His magic worked more smoothly when she was nearby, the spells having a measurably greater effect. He thought back to the ever-present elementals that dogged their journey. Did she somehow attract them?

"Your magic is related to fighting, is it not?" Krys teased out an idea about Timbrel.

"Minor enhancements of my strength and speed, a few armoring spells, and a blade-strengthener. Why?"

"You used an armoring spell on your clothing when you fought the plains cat?"

Jherik slashed assent with his fingertips, his embarrassment showing plainly on his face. "My tunic fell off in shreds when the spell wore off."

"How badly were you injured? Compared to fighting without the spell."

A puzzled expression twisted Jherik's features. "Not badly at all. Another time they might have clawed me to ribbons," he admitted. "Instead, I got myself squashed under a dying beast." He slumped his shoulders and looked at the table. "I didn't think it would weigh so much."

"Does your armoring spell usually work so well?"

Jherik didn't answer, which told Krys what he needed to know. Timbrel somehow enhanced the magic around her. No wonder that people felt more comfortable when she was nearby. Whatever traces of magic they had–Krys admitted that even humans seemed to have a little–Timbrel enhanced, creating a sense of well-being. Even Lostaria relaxed somewhat since Timbrel rejoined them.

It was unlikely that Timbrel understood her own power. With her beliefs about magic... "So prejudiced," he muttered under his breath.

The redhead arrived with steaming bowls of fish-laden stew. The savory smell of herbs tickled his nose and his mouth watered. Krys and Jherik dug in with relish.

### 

Lostaria was actively frightened. She spent the last twenty minutes listening to Timbrel talk about the rescue group's exile. From what the half-elf said–Lostaria envied her cousin's memory–the group had been summoned during the morning. The messengers arrived just before the exile was pronounced. That the group conveniently followed the strictures of the ancient traditions while being essentially useless worried her. The Councilman's odd subterfuge in slipping the group necessary information and directions unsettled her as well. Too many coincidences. Lostaria sensed an underlying plan.

The two women washed themselves in the room. Lostaria was startled to see the Urramachi royal birthmark on Timbrel's ankle.

"May I see that mark?" Lostaria slid into the polite behavior expected between equals.

Timbrel looked embarrassed, but extended her leg. "I am sorry," the half-elf apologized. "I meant to keep this hidden. My dance bells will cover it." As soon as Lostaria looked up, Timbrel buckled on the leather strap of bells. The leather extended just far enough to completely cover the looping flower.

"You are the youngest daughter of my kinswoman Soliari, are you not?"

Timbrel looked up, nodding in the human style. "I am."

"I have heard about you, about the efforts your mother took to conceal your existence."

262

"I am a great embarrassment to her, I know." Timbrel pulled her skirt into position and knotted the drawstrings.

Lostaria continued her probing. "Soliari is not aware of your birthmark?"

Timbrel spun to face the princess. "Of course not," she protested, her voice tinged in horror. "My first nurse encouraged me to hide the mark from her. I was told Soliari would find it infuriating."

Lostaria could understand why. She slipped her own borrowed dress down over one shoulder. The identical birthmark showed itself against the palest expanse of skin. Timbrel gasped.

"It is the royal mark of the Urramachi." Lostaria resettled her dress. "Infuriating would not begin to describe Soliari's reaction. Your nurse saved your life."

"It means nothing, anyway. I am a half-blood, and ineligible for anything." Timbrel's tone said the matter was closed. "We should go down and eat."

Lostaria looked at her cousin in dismay. Timbrel was dressed as a human dancer, her legs exposed for all to see. "Your clothing..."

"Is just perfect," finished Timbrel.

They descended the stairs and Timbrel went to the far end of the room. Several uniformed guards stood nearby as the princess sat with Krys. Krys waved in the air, and a human with flame red hair brought a bowl of fish stew to Lostaria. The elven princess stared.

Music started, far different from the stately rhythms of the elves. At first it seemed discordant, but Lostaria soon appreciated the emerging patterns. *The musicians are quite skilled*, she thought with a start. The basic pattern stayed the same even as each musician played a variation. The result was an ever-changing series of chords that wove in and out of the whole, giving it a richer depth.

She glanced at the end of the room, only to make a shocking discovery. Timbrel was *dancing*, weaving her body through the music's rhythms. Jherik sat among the musicians, playing a simple set of carved pipes.

Lostaria glanced around. The crowd thought her cousin quite skilled. The princess' respect for her cousin grew further. Timbrel had taken one shame, her half-human blood, and had combined it with another, the dancing of humans. The combination somehow transcended the shame and became something glorious. The elven woman realized that she had seriously underestimated her cousin's capabilities, simply because of the girl's mixed blood. A serious character flaw in herself, she thought. She must remember to look past the surface, especially with humans. Lostaria considered the point, slowly realizing that her prejudices might have kept her from understanding the true nature of those around her.

The room erupted in applause. The clinking of coins startled Lostaria. She watched a small child run up and gather the coins while Timbrel bowed low to one of the guards. He assisted her to a standing position, and escorted her to the table. The child followed behind, shirt pulled up to create a basket for the coins.

Krys welcomed them to the table. "Greetings, Captain. Please, have a seat. Lady Lostaria, this is Captain Harnak. Captain, this is Lady Timbrel's cousin, Lady Lostaria." The Captain sketched an elegant bow in the tight space between tables. He seated himself between the two women. The child gravely presented the coins to Timbrel. She returned two to the child, and then pushed the remaining pile across the table to Krys. The historian added them to a thin pouch.

"I trust you are ready for war?" Krys's comment hung in the air over the table, the words not matching the light tone the elf had used. Lostaria was able to translate the human's speech well enough, much better than their giant guide's abominable attempts.

"War? We are not at war. My scouts in the hills have reported nothing, as always. Besides, we have three times as many soldiers since your last stay with us."

"You will need many more. There is a great army approaching. We crossed their tracks and followed them as far as some caves on the other side of the mountain. I would be concerned for your city."

Lostaria watched the two men discuss the city's readiness. Jherik joined the group a few minutes later. They quickly reached an agreement for Jherik to give the city guards additional training, though the captain would not authorize the same for the city at large. Lostaria remembered the tracks in the sand. There were hundreds. According to the giant, they numbered in the thousands.

She looked around the room. The giant was not visible, and Lostaria had a vague memory of an animated conversation between the guide and her cousin just outside the city gates. The only word that Lostaria remembered clearly sounded like "gather." Gather what? Gather warriors, gather evidence... It seemed both would be needed here. The city felt secure. A false security, Lostaria could see. The human alliance would be needed quickly.

She waited for a lull in the conversation. "Krys, I need to arrange passage. Tonight would be best."

The tall, silver-haired elf swiveled his head and stared at the Princess. "Let me find out who is trustworthy."

Timbrel giggled. "I think I see someone." The half-elf pointed to an overflowing table. A dozen sailors crowded around it, pushing and shoving each other for seats on the few benches. Voices rose in volume, and the group hovered on the verge of a brawl. The dancer ran to the table, her ankle bells tinkling. "Captain Overton," she called.

Lostaria stared as a rough-looking human stood up. Scarred and reddened by the elements, the bushy-bearded sailor looked like a character from a childhood story about human pirates. The fierce-looking human suddenly smiled with broken teeth and welcomed Timbrel in a crushing hug. The dancer whispered in his ear for a moment, and the two broke away from the rowdy group.

The pirate swaggered over to Krys. "I be leaving on a south run in the mornin. If the wind is with us, it'll take two weeks to run the coastline. How many are travelin, and how far do ye need to get?"

Lostaria stood up. "Port Kerran, and I'll be traveling alone." The pirate named a price, and Krys counted out a small portion of Timbrel's dancing coins.

It unnerved Lostaria a little when the pirate peered into her face, squinting. He dropped his voice to a near whisper. "Do ye have a birthmark on your back? Looks like this?" The pirate dipped a finger in Jherik's ale and drew a crude flower. It resembled the Urramachi birthmark.

Lostaria looked at her cousin. Timbrel nodded almost imperceptibly. It took a moment for Lostaria to remember that it was a gesture of assent. "I do," she admitted.

The pirate pushed the coins back to Krys. Lostaria was crestfallen, convinced that he turned down her passage. The pirate leaned forward. "I'll take ye fer free. Anyone that has that large a price on their head, and instructions to keep them as far from the Port as possible, must be doing something important. Besides, yer traveling with *her*." The pirate gestured at Timbrel. He shrugged a shoulder. "She's the only one been nice to my cabin boy. The poor thing is part goblin, you see, and a little slow." The pirate tapped his temple. "He has his uses, though."

The pirate captain suddenly stood. "Nice to chat with ye," he announced. "I'll see ye at first light." He returned to his table just in time to separate two sailors as they tried to punctuate their conversation with fists.

Lostaria leaned over and whispered to her cousin. "What did he mean about the cabin boy?"

Timbrel rolled her eyes, the gesture so exaggerated that Lostaria stifled a laugh. "He's a big goblin-man, but like a child. He kept sneaking up at night and sleeping behind me. I don't see how he could stand to, I got so sick the entire trip. I just woke up every morning with him curled near my back. He's harmless."

Lostaria dropped her chin, then nodded. She had seen a man like that on her first trip away from Ravali. The human stood large, but had the mind of the sleepy five-year-old child. He couldn't have harmed anything on purpose. Reassured, the princess ate heartily.

266

###

Timbrel and Krys saw Lostaria off to the *Lady Elizabeth* the next morning. Jherik was busy conducting his famous drills. It took only three times before the soldiers of the militia stopped him from running the length of the practice field. A large crowd gathered to watch them practice.

After the drills, the elven warrior became alarmed to learn that the silent scouts were not reporting "no activity." They simply did not report. It took less than half an hour to identify the missing scouts. All five were assigned to the western side of the mountain.

"Can you send a larger group? Send messengers back each hour?" Jherik paced. Captain Harnek was far too calm for the situation.

"Why should we concentrate them like that? They'll learn more if they're spread across the entire mountainside."

"It does no good if they vanish before they tell us anything. A larger group is more likely to survive an ambush, and if they send a runner back every hour then we'll have a good idea of where the enemy is. Especially if they suddenly vanish."

"And if the enemy is more than twelve hours away?"

Jherik clenched his fist. Were all humans this complacent? "Then we will know we have at least that much time to prepare."

Captain Harnek frowned. "We cannot upset the populace like that. Trade would come to a complete halt. This is our best time of year, the time we catch up from the winter storms. If we tell them to prepare for war, the gem cutters will leave. The merchants will close their stalls and take ship to the south. And all for what?" The Rockhold man finally got upset. His voice rose in volume. "This city will never fall. The rocks themselves will prevent it. We have guards on all four gates, and watchers along the sea cliffs."

"They could just come straight over the walls," suggested Jherik. His rear twitched with the memory of sliding down the icy terraces. "Krys and I used that method for several trips outside during our last stay."

"Certainly not," scoffed Harnek. "You were here during the winter."

"And we climbed. Your cliffs won't stop a determined foe, especially on the way in. If we have a large, well-organized force to deal with, we must be ready for anything."

The captain leaned his head back and looked along the length of his nose at the elf. "You say we. Why?"

Jherik drew a deep breath before answering. "I'm staying until it's over," he declared.

The elven warrior could not interpret the odd look on the captain's face. The captain laid a hand on the Henin elf's arm. "You really believe what you're saying, don't you." Harnek patted the warrior's arm. "I'll send out a group of twelve scouts at first light tomorrow with instructions to send a runner back every hour. And when the last one comes back safely, you're going to buy dinner for all fourteen of us."

"Agreed. And when they bring back news of the enemy, you'll call the town council together for a war meeting." The captain readily agreed, chuckling a little. The two warriors shook hands, a human custom that sealed the bargain. The wind changed, floating the scent of hot sausage past the two. In silent agreement, they went to the Crystal Inn for breakfast.

Krys and Timbrel sat at their usual table in the back. The girl's hands fluttered in constant motion as she spoke. Her weight shifted as she leaned forward, providing an ever-changing illustration of her words. Her head tilted to one side as she listened to Krys speak. Captain Harnek slid into a chair next to the girl. She flashed the Rockholder a brilliant smile.

Jherik felt a pang of jealousy as he sat by Krys. Why couldn't she smile at *him* that way? He was easily twice as skilled a warrior as the captain. Why couldn't she see it? Sometimes she could be so blind. Like with Shess. The Henin elf frowned at the thought of the Melani elf. The Melani tried to enslave Timbrel. If Shess hadn't gotten her angry by spending time with another girl, the dancer might have been lost. It didn't help that Krys thought Shess was a slaver, only away from home long enough to buy the captive Lostaria. He wondered where the Melani elf had gone.

### 

*The White Tower*

Shess stood in front of the Seer, his swords drawn. Melani stared at Terformin, golden eyes meeting the same shade. "Teach me the secret of magic, old man. Transform me into a creature of long life."

"I cannot do so," Lord Gowell replied. "I will not." He stood next to his chair, a painting showing a strange night sky behind him.

"You can. I heard you say it. That you changed the type of magic you have. Tell me your secret." He advanced on the Terformin, his swords loosely held in a relaxed guard position.

Gowell reached behind his chair. Shess heard the scrape of metal on stone. The Terformin stepped to one side, both hands wrapped around the hilt of the sword almost as long as Gowell was tall. The blade glittered in the faint light of the room.

Shess inhaled. Once, twice, three times he drew the air deep inside his body. He could feel his muscles tingling.

"I have no secrets. Genjin secrets. Blood secrets. Genjin wor-orked we-ell." The Seer's voice took on a sing-song tone.

"No!" Shess yelled, the word both a denial and a battle cry as he attacked the taller Terformin.

Swords slashed, glittering in the faint light, slicing at Gowell's robes. One caught in the fabric, the other sliced clean. The robe fluttered as the fabric parted. The sound of metal on metal screeched through the room.

Shess stepped back, his extra speed fading with the extra air. Gowell's robe gaped wide, showing blue-black armor beneath. The armor fit Gowell like the shell of an insect, and the Terformin's sword swung through the air much faster than Shess expected. The Melani ducked, twisted, and parried. He struck with his other sword. Another rent appeared in Gowell's robe.

Shess dropped back again, completely in shock. His parry sword, the one on the right, had been cut in half. Not broken, cut. Gowell's sword swished past, dangerously close. Ducking forward, Shess closed with the Terformin. The great sword is useless at such close range, he thought. The Melani aimed for a joint in the armor, driving his sword into Gowell's shoulder. Metal screeched in resistance and blood poured from the wound, splattering Shess.

Gowell stepped back quicker than Shess thought he could and brought the over-long sword down from overhead. The blow connected, Shess' arm numbing from the shock of contact. Blood coated the room, some from Shess and some from Gowell, the two mixing into one puddle. Their eyes gleamed, gold reflected in gold.

Shess struck again, the shorn sword widening the earlier gap. His other sword breached the armor again. Shess felt weak, convinced that the Seer used his magic. The Melani erupted in fury, lashing out at the Terformin for his secrets and for what he was. The dark-bound and the sky-free battled on.

The end came suddenly. Gowell went down under a flurry of blows, one last rush from Shess' pain-filled muscles. Shess relaxed. The great sword suddenly connected, the Terformin so well-trained that he completed the swing even as he fell. Pain tore across Shess' chest and he fell into the sea of blood that washed across the floor.

The Melani crawled away, fearful of chase, tumbling down the stairs. Bruised, bloody, and disoriented, he felt his life energy fading far faster than it should. He crawled, limped, and finally ran to the edge of the circle of death; saw the green line of the forest spotted with yellow as he approached it. Darkness took him.

He woke in the field, skin stinging from the sun's light. The skin on his arm shone as white as the tree trunks, dead and curling away from the gleaming new black skin beneath. The sun had burned him again, like in his first days on the surface. Shess rose to his knees. The wound across his chest was shallow, already closed with a thick scab. It would scar well. How long had he lain here?

The grass beneath him was dead and brown. Four days, then. Surprised that he had any skin left at all, Shess rechecked his skin. The sun's light did little more than an hour's worth of damage. He resettled his clothing, protecting the damaged skin from further sunlight. He was tired, more exhausted than he could ever remember. The last attack used up all his energy.

Shess rose, seeking shelter from the plains cats. The Melani elf stumbled through the brush, hearing the welcome trickle of a tiny stream. He fell to his knees next to the water, its coolness a perfect complement to his fevered brow.

### 

*On board the Lady Elizabeth*

Lostaria cradled the half-goblin's head in her lap. She had realized quickly during the southern journey that Captain Overton's cabin boy possessed wind-magic. They slipped around storms and ran at the highest speeds possible before the wind. Because of the captain's efforts, she reached the port in a remarkably short time.

She disembarked from the Lady Elizabeth and thanked the captain. "This should not take very long. Please wait for me to return."

"I'll send a dozen sailors with ye, to protect ye and keep everyone else honest." Captain Overton stroked his beard. "In fact, I think I'll come along." He signaled and some of his men came on to the dock. "We be a protection detail today. Let's make sure there be no funny stuff."

The captain swept Lostaria down the dock and brought her straight to the palace. Two of his men stayed behind with the palace guards while the captain escorted her into the throne room.

Prince Ragnar arrived almost immediately with just a pair of guards. He embraced the captain. "Salty, I didn't expect to see you again so soon, my friend. There isn't trouble, is there?"

"Trouble and trouble again, Sir. This here be Lady Lostaria of the elves, who just been rescued from kidnapping. She wants..."

"I want to formally sign the alliance between us. There isn't much time, though. Rockhold is about to be attacked by some kind of skeleton men, if they haven't already gotten there. We need to bring them help right away."

"What tale is this? 'Skeleton men'? And Lostaria has been missing for nearly half a year. Regent Soliari is in charge now, and she does *not* want the alliance."

"Soliari oversteps herself and breaks our laws. I am Lady Lostaria of the Urramachi, and I have a letter from Captain Harnek... Oh." Lostaria flushed pink. "I left the letter on the ship."

"We'll be right back." Captain Overton caught up to Lostaria, sailors trailing behind. "You could've just shown him the flower mark."

"I want it all as properly legal as we can manage in less than a day. I saw the footprints in the sand, Captain. There were hundreds of them."

They reached the docks as another large ship tied up. As they watched, twenty elves came down the gangplank and formed up on the dock. All wore matching armor.

As the last elf came forward, the others raised their swords. "For the Princess!"

Lostaria smiled and inclined her head. "Why, thank you. I wasn't expecting a reception."

The leader of the group turned. He was very young for such a position. "Who do you think you are? You're interrupting our drill."

"I am Princess Lostaria Urramach, and you will mind your tone with me."

The leader snapped to attention with a saucy salute. "Yes ma'am, Your Highness, ma'am. Right away, ma'am." He turned back to his men. "Fall out. Use your time for a meal and we'll reassemble in an hour, without..." He looked Lostaria up and down. "...spectators. Dismissed."

The elves broke rank and disappeared into the town in groups of three and four.

Lostaria clenched her fist. "I have *never* been ignored like that before."

Captain Overton touched her sleeve. "They probably didn't recognize you, Princess. Yer not exactly dressed for high court, are ye?"

She looked down at her borrowed dress. Light brown and barely beneath her knees in length, the human dress was salt spotted and stained with hard travel. After what she went through, carrying an extra change of clothing had been the last thing on Lostaria's mind in her rush to leave.

"Captain, can you recommend a decent inn so I can freshen up? After I retrieve Harnek's introduction from the ship, that is."

The captain motioned to one of the honor guard. "Warren, me boyo, take the men and escort the princess to the ship, then over to the Oldham Honors. She is to have a suite of rooms with a private bedroom and enough room in the outer room for you all to bunk in as bodyguards. Let her have a small meal and then order a hot bath with soap and a shampoo, and I'll be by in a bit with what she needs."

Lostaria left with her guards and let them settle her into the rooming house. It wasn't until she scrubbed the last of the dirt off, rinsed her hair four times, and relaxed in the hot water that she realized how much she had missed this.

When she left the tub, she put on a thick robe, and followed the house servants back to her rooms.

A magnificent full-length crimson dress, designed to be worn off the shoulder, lay across the bed. A piece of black velvet lay on the nearby press, cushioning a tiara set with rubies, ruby earrings, and an assortment of matching necklets, bracelets, and rings. Harnek's letter of introduction lay beside them, rolled and tied with a crimson ribbon. A hairbrush, comb, and small pots of cosmetics were a welcome addition. A small mirror lay on the press as well.

She put the brush down, her hair now in loose waves. It surprised her how difficult it turned out to be to twist the brush just so without tangling her hair. A knock on the door startled her. She picked up the tiara and set it in her hair before answering the door.

The knock sounded again just before she opened it.

"Captain Overton, come in."

The captain bent over in a sweeping bow. "Your beauty be astounding, me Lady." He stood again. "I have difficult news. Several of my men, spending their wages on a relaxing drink or two, were listening to the elves from the other ship." The captain coughed slightly. "It seems some of the lads understand a bit of the elf tongue." He coughed again.

Lostaria suppressed her surprise and shock. "Continue."

"It seems the lads overheard a plot to kill Prince Ragnar here. They blame him for your death, Lady. I think it best you meet with the Prince tonight to sign those papers, and head off the assassins at the door."

"Do you think they'll recognize me?"

"You look like a princess now, and your birthmark shows nicely."

"Are you positive they're going to wait for nightfall?"

"No, Princess, I am not."

"Well then, Captain. Will you escort me to his Majesty immediately? I would like to get the paperwork out of the way before I save his life." She graciously took the captain's elbow and they walked out into the hall.

When they reached the palace, they were admitted immediately. Prince Ragnar apologized as soon as he saw Lostaria, even before she handed him the letter of introduction.

"I did not recognize you. I understand that you had some difficulties before you came here."

"If by difficulties you mean I was kidnapped, then yes. However, I do believe that the creatures marching on Rockhold will overwhelm the city, and then will move on across the entire country. So let us sign this treaty, and then together send warriors north to assist." She hesitated and frowned. "Did I say send? I meant to say take. I will go with them and assist as well."

The Prince looked puzzled. "Shouldn't you be retaking your own throne first?"

"My throne will be at risk from these invaders if they are not stopped. Stopping them is the most important thing in the world right now. Well, stopping them and stopping a group of elven warriors from assassinating you."

"You seek to threaten me into signing the alliance with you?" Ragnar motioned to his guards.

"I did not send those warriors here. The so-called Regent sent them. If we win at Rockhold, Soliari will be Regent no longer, no matter what she thinks."

The two sat down and went over the treaty together, making a few small changes here and there. When they were both satisfied, they called in a half-dozen witnesses and signed it.

The Prince called for a scribe. "Make a dozen copies and bring them back here for signing." He sent the man off with the signed treaty.

They shared a light meal and small talk while waiting for the copies to arrive.

Instead, the door burst open and the elven group came in, weapons drawn.

The Prince's guards surrounded him, but the Princess calmly walked forward. "What is the meaning of this?"

The leader of the elven soldiers stepped forward to meet her. When he got close enough to see her birthmark, he visibly paled and fell to his knees.

"Now *that* is more like it." She looked down at the soldier. "Whom do I have the pleasure of addressing?"

"Cap... Cap... Captain Arlis."

Lostaria cleared her throat. "Captain Arlis, I am puzzled. What purpose did the Council have in sending you here?"

"It wasn't the Council, Your Highness." Arlis' voice squeaked.

"Regent Soliari sent us. She told us you were dead." The voice came from someone in the ranks.

The Princess threw back her shoulders and stood as tall as she could. "As you can see, I am not dead. As I am not dead, there can be no Regent. If there is no Regent, her orders do not stand. My orders, on the other hand, must be obeyed." She turned her head slowly, scanning the room, then looked back at Captain Arlis. "Captain Arlis, I order you to bring your group of warriors north by ship to assist in the defense of Rockhold against the Terformin. When you arrive, you will meet up with Kryslandir, Jherik, and my cousin-kin Timbrel. If the battle is already joined, then you will assist as you can until you can meet up with those I mentioned."

Arlis snapped to attention, saluting crisply. "We are to travel north, assist in Rockhold's defense, and meet up with Kryslandir, Timbrel, and Jherik. We leave immediately."

"I shall send a company of soldiers as well." The Prince sent a runner to muster his troops. "We shall leave in an hour."

Captain Overton leaned over and whispered in Lostaria's ear. "They're not going anywhere until the tide is right in another six hours. Best they pack, have a good meal, and we three ships travel together back to the North."

"Prince Ragnar, Arlis, Captain Overton has pointed out that the tide will determine when the ships can leave. The three ships should travel together. I will travel with Captain Overton and a contingent of soldiers from the Prince. A second ship, if such can be located, will carry the Prince's additional troops. Captain Arlis, your group will travel on the same ship that you arrived on." She turned. "Captain Overton, I leave the finding of the second ship for the humans to you. I wish you to lead the three ships to the north as quickly as possible. You have a reputation for weather luck. I certainly hope that reputation is well-founded. Are there any questions?"

Some of the prince's guards whispered among themselves before one stepped forward. "Did you say the Terformin, Highness? As in, the yellow-eyed demons that tried before to take over the world? There are stories of ancient warriors trapped and killed, and that the demons can kill with a touch."

"Many of those stories are true. My grandfather's grandfather fought against the Terformin. We must stop them before they gain a foothold."

An elven soldier standing behind Arlis dropped to one knee. The others dropped one by one until the entire company knelt, save Arlis. They spoke together. "We swear fealty to you, Princess Lostaria Urramach, heir to the Matriarch's throne. We will follow you to the land of the dead if necessary."

They found a second ship quickly, and all boarded the fully provisioned ships before the designated hour.

Lostaria faced another problem. The only way to ensure a quick journey was to depend on the goblin's magic. Though the thought of it made her skin crawl, and it would no doubt disturb her elven warriors as well, she knocked on the Captain's door.

"Captain Overton? I must have a word with you." Lostaria slipped into the captain's cabin, smiling at the goblin-man crouching in the corner.

"And that word is?" The captain seemed in a hurry. Looking out the window, the elven princess could understand why. Dark storm clouds massed on the horizon. If Lostaria remembered her weather-lore correctly, a terrible storm approached.

"It is imperative that we reach Rockhold as quickly as possible. Can your cabin boy's wind-magic cover all three ships?"

The Captain looked startled and clapped a callused hand over her mouth. "Don't be speaking of that, Lady. Even the boy doesn't fully understand what he's doing. He thinks it's fun and games."

Lostaria thought fast, pulling Overton's hand away. "Can our team of three ships break the record for the fastest race?"

Overton smiled, his broken teeth reminding Lostaria that he was a pirate. "Break the record? That we can, Lady. That we can." He glanced at the cabin boy, who grinned back at him.

The captain gave a small nod. "Storms are always tiring, and the poor boy gets nightmares from them, but the ships will sail through just fine."

"Perhaps I could soothe him while he sleeps? Maybe I can chase the nightmares away."

The half-goblin grinned and ran to hug Lostaria. "Pretty," he crooned. She tried not to shudder.

###

# Chapter Eleven

*Rockhold, ten days later.*

Jherik waited impatiently on the outside of the Western rim. The scouts reported the enemy less than an hour's march away and closing. The past two weeks had been an endless grind of drills, trying to train the newest members of Rockhold's militia in basic teamwork. Jherik tried placing the established members with the new recruits, with mixed success. Many of the established soldiers considered the newcomers to be intruders. Even with actual reports of the enemy's approach, the soldiers still seemed resistant to the idea the Rockhold would ever be attacked, much less fall.

Jherik looked with surprise at the soldiers; almost a third of the new recruits were women. Some came to stand beside their husbands, the children under the care of relatives. Others had never been married. The established soldiers squawked, but Jherik found the women to be the hardest workers of all. They trained ceaselessly, and quickly developed skill at breaking through the lines during drills. Smiths of all types laid aside their jewelry and other metal work to forge light blades for the women. The lighter swords could not damage the enemy as much with a single blow, but the women worked in smoothly coordinated teams. The elven warrior just hoped the teams would remain intact.

Captain Harnek decided to follow Jherik's drilling strategy for the battle. Jherik was assigned to lead a group of twenty who would attempt to break through the enemy lines, regrouping to harry the enemy from behind. The rest would work in teams to slow the enemy's progress. He cautioned them to remember that the teams immediately behind them would finish off a wounded enemy, but if they turned to give chase, they gave the enemy a free shot at their backs.

The enemy. The scouts returned with little information beyond distant sightings and approximate numbers. The enemy soldiers were grey men of some sort, men that marched for hours at a time without breaking their ranks. They sheltered in the caves that honeycombed the western slopes outside the caldera. Some carried swords; others held short spears and sometimes wore bits of armor.

Jherik looked down the slope, convinced he'd seen movement at the edge of the tree line. He gathered his group together, laying an armor strengthening spell on himself and six of the others. He might have armored twice as many, but needed every bit of strength for the coming battle.

A cry went up from the watchers. The enemy came running, darkening the upper slopes as far as the eye could see. His spine crawled at their silent progress, save for the occasional *tink* of a stone clicking against another. Jherik motioned for a runner to take the news to Harnek.

The Henin elf tensed, looking for a less defended spot in the approaching wave. He heard a clanging rise from behind him, signal bells he thought, and charged forward. He glimpsed two of the closest members of his team and then greyness swallowed everything.

Jherik twisted, turned, ducked, and slashed as he ran. Limbs dropped off the enemy in a spray of blood. A few of the bodies dropped to the ground behind him, sending the orderly lines into disarray as he charged ahead, fighting against the flow. He felt the pressure of the enemy's blows, but no accompanying sting. *My armor spell is working*, he thought, slashing sideways at the nearest enemy and ducking beneath the overhead swing of the next.

He lost his footing on a steep part of the slope, skidding uncontrollably downward. The enemy fell and skidded along with him, their bodies creating a small avalanche of grey that piled up at the tree line. The elf slashed at some of the arms and legs waving from the pile, disabling as many as he could without pausing in his objective. Just how many of them *were* there, anyway?

Arms and legs aching, his sword running with dark red blood, Jherik finally broke through the back of the line. He continued forward for a moment, expecting to find another wave in the depths of the thickening forest. He took a deep breath before turning, afraid to see how many of the enemy survived. His neck burned where the leather thong rubbed it raw. He repositioned it, glancing at the white bone disk it supported.

A second warrior broke through the lines. Jherik slipped past the trees to join him. To join *her*, as it turned out. Jherik recognized Becca, one of the youngest women in his unit. They rested for a moment while two others joined them. No more broke through.

*Four isn't enough. We can only make one team.* Fear flooded through his veins and cold sweat rolled down his back. The raw spot on his neck burned furiously. They needed more warriors.

The fear crashed against him like a wave and broke, receding. "Becca," he shouted, grabbing the woman's shoulder and turning her to face him. She wiped vomit from her mouth with a sleeve. "Have you ever had a child?"

Becca stepped back. "Not yet. I won't birth this one for another six months."

Jherik was dumbfounded. "You're pregnant? Why aren't you in the caves?"

"If we don't win this, everyone in the caves is going to die. The enemy won't stop with the soldiers. You saw the remains of the merchant group that the scouts found. The grey men killed every man, woman, and child."

"Can you still run?"

"I'm not running away. I can fight." Becca looked ready to draw her sword on Jherik.

The elf backed a step away. "That's not what I meant." The elven warrior pulled the bone disk out into the light, and then snapped the leather thong with a quick jerk. He handed it to the woman. "Take this and run to the west until you see the spiderwebs in the treetops. When you reach the webs, or see the spiders, hold the disk out and yell out the word 'Stinger'. Tell them that I sent you. Then tell them what you just told me."

Becca reached for the disk, then re-knotted the thong and slipped it around her wrist. "I run until I see spiders and give them your message. How will I know which spiders to tell? There must be hundreds in the forest."

"They are large spiders," he said. "Believe me, you'll know."

The girl turned to go. "Wait," he called. She turned to face him "Take off your helmet and let your hair fly free. It will keep you safe."

Becca ran lightly off into the forest, hair flying behind her.

Jherik turned to the others. "Now it's our turn. We have to do as much damage as we can until help arrives."

### 

*Rockhold*

Panic ruled the city. Timbrel dodged to one side, narrowly avoiding a young man running in circles. Another block and she found the makeshift hospital. The apprentice healers hung sheets of cloth against the inevitable dust and grit. The most experienced healers worked in the center of the hospital with jars of herbs and piles of equipment available. Apprentice healers and helpers were stationed around the edges, ready to evaluate the wounded and pass them within, or simply treat the lesser injuries themselves. Rockhold's chief healer directed Timbrel to stay with the apprentices.

The half-elf's arrival calmed the others. Her air of confidence in her ability to treat shallow cuts, scrapes, bruises, and simple fractures encouraged the other apprentice healers to band into complementary groups. Each group of three or four apprentices could handle all four categories. Two young girls, both extremely new to the craft, stayed with Timbrel. She quickly evaluated their skills, and demonstrated a few basic concepts. While they would never be ready for the battle, they were as prepared as possible in this short time.

The waiting was difficult. Her helpers spent time practicing their stitching on a rag, struggling with the knots. After a while, Timbrel sent one of them around to check for needed supplies. Soon several apprentices ran about collecting basins and bowls for the healers' use, as well as slicing cloth from a merchant's booth into extra bandages. Arguments broke out between healers as the tension mounted. Captain Harnek sent runners to Timbrel informing her of the situation; she sent them on to the chief healer. The scouts reported regularly. The enemy approached, less than two hours away.

Pennon flags unrolled on the western rim of the caldera as the units passed information. Red over yellow. Timbrel could read a little of the code: Attack imminent. A few soldiers moved over the western rim, dropping from sight. Light flashed and thunder rumbled as if lightning came from a clear sky.

The clash of swords echoed from the nearby hills. Timbrel huddled with the other healers, waiting for their part in the conflict. The sound of gravel dropping from the east was almost obscured. Almost. The half-elf's superior hearing caught a *tink*. She turned to look for the source, her eyes widening in fear. Hundreds of enemy soldiers poured over the nearly unprotected eastern rim of the caldera, overwhelming the few soldiers posted there.

"No!" She cried, pointing. The enemy soldiers swarmed on the topmost tier of the terraced fields and pastures. Some ran along the terrace, trying to circle behind Rockhold's soldiers. Others continue to descend, their objective apparently the city itself. Timbrel looked wildly around. A few apprentices ran to the west. The majority milled in fear. One backed up, shock already in her gaze. The young girl tripped over a brass basin with a *clang*.

The sound broke Timbrel from her fear. Grabbing a smaller brass bowl, she banged the side of the basin. Mimicking her idea, a loud cacophony of *clangs* soon rose from the hospital.

It was enough. Many Rockhold soldiers on the western rim turned and saw the danger approaching from behind. Small units of soldiers rounded the terrace to meet the foe. The battle was truly joined.

Someone fell from the western rim, the body tumbling down the terraces until it lay on the floor of the caldera. Two apprentice healers ran out with a makeshift stretcher to retrieve it. Their shrieks drew Timbrel to assist.

A skeletal figure, skin stretched tightly across its bones, lay crumpled on the ground. Broken bones stuck through the skin of both legs, and three ribs protruded as well. There was little blood. Timbrel bent forward to drag the body out of the way. As she reached for its arm, the skeletal hand closed around her wrist.

The grip surprised her with its strength. She jerked back, unable to loosen the hand. The skeleton opened its eyes and grinned. It grunted half-formed sounds as the girl dragged it along the ground. Its other hand closed around a gatepost. In spite of her best efforts, it dragged Timbrel backward. The skeletal warrior snapped its teeth at her.

"Let her go!" A three-legged stool arched down to smash into the skeleton's arm. Wood splintered and a bone snapped as Timbrel jerked away. Skin tore and she tumbled backward. The skeletal hand still locked around her wrist twitched twice and stilled. The horrified half-elf pulled her dagger, prying the fingers loose enough to remove it.

The sound of drumming wood caught Timbrel's attention. The two apprentice healers used the broken legs of the stool to beat the skeletal warrior into a bloody pulp. It bled less than Timbrel expected, but at least it didn't move anymore. She ushered the younger girls back to the hospital, each clutching a weapon. Timbrel also brought the enemy warrior's weapon harness with her.

The harness felt stiff and flexible like well-oiled leather but was slick to the touch. It exuded an odd, almost overpowering smell and resisted Timbrel's efforts to nick it with her dagger. The harness provided space to sheathe three weapons, as well as providing a number of empty pouches for small items.

Timbrel laid it aside. *Krys would be interested in this.* In the meantime, she had soldiers to treat.

The wounded retreated over the caldera's edge, helping each other descend the terraces. Once begun, the trickle swiftly grew to a rushing torrent. Stretcher bearers ran up with the worst. Men groaned, bleeding and bruised. Soldiers wearing slings pushed past in the opposite direction, grimly determined to return to the battle in spite of new-set broken bones. Horrible burns showed bone through blackened flesh. Missing limbs strapped with belts to stop the bleeding. A throat bitten open, intact red and blue veins pulsing and slowly oozing blood with each breath.

The healers were overwhelmed. The wounded lay on the road nearby, the apprentices treating them where they lay. More and more often the anguished cries of the healers rose up, unable to defy death.

A brass banging on the other side of the hospital alerted Timbrel and the rest. Living skeletons moved among them, slashing with swords and gnashing with too-large teeth. A healer screamed, the sound shifting to a bubbling hiss. A skeleton menaced one of Timbrel's assistants. The half-elf grabbed a basin full of bloody rags and bashed it over the head. Its skull cracked in pieces, as did the basin, the sharp ceramic shards providing new weapons for the beleaguered healers.

Timbrel turned at a muffled groan. Several walking skeletons methodically killed the wounded laying in the street. Timbrel ran out, followed by an apprentice from the next group. The apprentice threw rocks, driving most of the skeletons away. The last skeleton, its body encased in a hard shell of armor, ignored the rocks. Timbrel grabbed a sword from the belt of a dazed warrior with a bleeding lump on his forehead.

The sword was heavier than she expected. She gripped it with both hands and tried to hold it at an angle from her body. She wove back and forth, flicking the tip of the sword toward the skeleton. The creature hesitated, backing away slightly.

Timbrel struggled to keep up the pretense while the apprentices pulled the wounded soldiers closer to the hospital. Jherik made it look so easy when he instructed the soldiers. The half-elf's arms burned and faltered. The tip of the sword sank closer to the ground. Pain seared across her side.

She staggered back, ribs burning from the skeleton's slash. Arms reached around her from behind, easily taking the sword from her fast-numbing fingers.

The soldier whose life she had saved pushed her aside as he curled his hand around the hilt. A moment later the skeleton fell, its head rolling along the street. The soldier continued on as Timbrel's helpers pulled her back. The half-elf bit her lip as the girls inexpertly stitched her side shut, still having trouble with their knots.

### 

Krys stood with Captain Harnek on the western rim. From his vantage point, he could see both inside and outside the caldera that held the city of Rockhold. Jherik's group of runners huddled close together. Timbrel was inside the city, somewhere near the cluster of multicolored cloth that surrounded the hospital. Strong men, unable to fight efficiently because of crippling leg injuries, waited with cloth slings to lower injured warriors down the terraced fields of the upper caldera.

Pennons unrolled on their poles. Krys looked at the treeline hiding the enemy and was startled by their silent advance. Jherik's group gave a cry and split apart, running straight into the enemy lines. Krys could trace their paths by the disruption in the endless wave of enemy warriors.

The first wave of Rockhold warriors stepped forward to meet the enemy. Within the caldera, an alarm bell rang, soon joined by others in a great cacophony of sound. The captain swore and turned around. Krys glanced inside the caldera. Ant-sized healers milled around the hospital, many gesturing at the far side of the city. Krys's eyes traveled upwards.

Black water pored over the eastern rim of the caldera. On each terrace the stream split, some running around the terrace and the rest continuing to pour downward in a slow waterfall of black.

A very slow waterfall, Krys realized. He looked again. The waterfall was made up of enemy soldiers.

"They circled behind us. The city is in danger."

Krys's words fell on empty air. The captain ran to his flagman. Colored pennons unfurled, prompting an immediate response. Groups of soldiers ran for the terraces, traveling their length to meet the enemy. Others descended to the bottom of the caldera, rappelling down ropes held by the sling men.

In spite of their rapid movement, Krys could see that the soldiers would not reach the hospital before the enemy did. The enemy continued to pour over the heights like water.

Water. Rain. Krys tried to judge the distance between his own position and the opposite rim. He had never tried to cast a spell at such a distance before, but he could see the enemy clearly. The elven wizard gathered his power, surprised at how quickly he felt the tingle run through his body. This place must have power to spare, he thought.

The tingle built to physical pain, burning along his bones. When he could hold no more, he released it to gather clouds over the enemy. The elven wizard evaporated water from the hot springs that edged the south side of the city, as well as taking water from the stream in the center. When the water vapor began to condense he added the final ingredients. He drew impurities from the air, imaging burning yellow dragonstone and its deadly fumes. It was surprisingly easy this time, much easier than his attempt to draw the acid rain to the assassin Von. Krys drew as much dragonstone into the cloud as he could, and then sent the last of his energy into sparking the reaction that turned the water to acid and dropped it as rain on the enemy below. The elf sagged to the ground as he released the power.

His back against a rock, Krys watched the cloud condense and drop its entire load of acid. The rain fell in the city, not distant enough to reach the enemy on the rim. Krys looked down, exhausted and angry with himself.

The enemy on the third tier down suddenly reacted. They milled about in confusion, and then threw themselves to the ground. Some fell over the edge of the terrace, coming to a halt on the next.

The next wave of enemy descended, walking across the bodies of their brethren. Halfway across the terrace, they also fell to the ground. It was working! Wave upon wave of the enemy continued to descend to the terrace, finding it a death trap. They seemed incapable of changing their actions.

The torrent slowed, and Krys fought to turn his head. Still weak as a newborn, the wizard managed to stand and look at the outer west side.

The enemy was stalled. The outnumbered Rockhold soldiers managed to hold their lines. The trails of disarray left by Jherik's group wound down through the massed enemy, too many trails ending far too short of the enemy's rear. The enemy's rear. Krys snorted. The enemy's rear could not be seen. They still boiled out of the tree line like angry ants, marching inexorably upward.

He looked down. The hospital was its own hive of activity. The slingers lowered the injured soldiers, stretcher-bearers meeting them at the base of the terraced cliffs. The stream of wounded carried to the hospital became so thick that bodies were laid in the street. Krys could see pockets of fighting in the streets nearby.

Recovering, the elven wizard gathered his power again, finding the process more difficult. Flashes of light from the fighting outside of the caldera threatened to distract him. He formed a second cloud, smaller but more potent, and sent it out to rain on the enemy's western troops.

Exhausted again, Krys slid back to the ground to watch the effects. Enemy soldiers milled about, falling to the ground and getting trampled by those that came behind.

"They really are like ants," he muttered as the march across the acid continued. He marveled at their mindlessness.

As the sun sank toward the horizon, a scuffle to his left, too close, startled Krys. He fought to turn his head, saw the grey clothing of an enemy soldier, looked up, fastened on its grinning skull-like face. Recognition flooded through the elf. The face of Damnech's corpse. Krys froze, unable to act against the Terformin.

The gold eyes stared dully. Damnech raised the sword. Numbers and lights flashed through Krys's mind. The sword hovered overhead. The memory of Damnech in the glass tube, the light amber.

Harnek's sword sliced cleanly through Damnech's neck. The grinning skull rolled over and came to rest next to Krys's foot. The elf sat unable to move, petrified at the control the Terformin had over him.

A second enemy soldier loomed up, its face identical to the first. Krys' eyes widened. Damnech was dead. The light was not green. He was dead and now his corpse walked a hundred times, a thousand times. Harnek dispatched the second as quickly as the first.

"Damnech," Krys whispered. "How can the dead walk?"

The sun slipped below the horizon. Krys waited for the next attack. It did not come. He wobbled to his feet and looked down. The enemy had inexplicably withdrawn.

### 

Desolation. Timbrel wandered the ruins of Rockhold by moonlight, the utter desolation of the cityscape cushioned by a thick blanket of shock.

The endless wave of skeletal warriors stopped as the sun dipped toward the horizon. It was not that the wave ended, but rather that the skeletons fell back and retreated. Like a wave by the seashore, Timbrel thought. They pull back only to crash again on the shore, bringing even more destruction.

The healers, already overwhelmed by the wounded during the battle, fought to keep their hospital safe for their patients. Shards of broken bowls, their sharp ceramic edges useful weapons to defend against the marauding skeletons, littered the streets that surrounded the makeshift hospital. The bowls could have been used in the hours after the sun set. Few warriors escaped the battle without at least a minor wound, and many of the most seriously wounded had been unable to reach the hospital earlier. The moans of the wounded at midnight kept time with the throbbing of her ribs. Together they were too much for the half-elf, driving her to the relatively quiet heights above the city.

A sentry staggered past, the soldier managing a wave for Timbrel in spite of his exhaustion. She waved back, trying to encourage him. Sentries stalked the heights on all sides of the city now. A hard lesson had been learned about leaving any part of the caldera unprotected. The sentries periodically called out to each other and to those below, reporting the quiet state of the night and keeping each other awake.

The streets ran thick with congealed blood, nearly two inches deep in the street by the hospital, fouling streams within feet of their sources. A constant flow of apprentices with buckets brought clean water back to the hospital. Timbrel imagined that a similar bucket line existed on the far side of the caldera, near the market cave where the women, children, and elderly sheltered.

Even the heights were not immune to the bloodbath. To reach her perch, Timbrel stepped around blood-soaked terraces, the bodies of the skeletal warriors so thick that she could have used them as a bridge and never touched the ground at all. She feared that the bodies would rise up yet again. The skeletons were so difficult to kill. They ignored wounds that would leave the strongest warrior writhing on the ground. One skeleton tried to walk on a leg so badly broken that the shattered bones twisted and ground on the rocks. The creature slumped to the ground, looking puzzled, a victim of blood loss.

Rockhold could not withstand another such attack. Half of the soldiers and several of the healers lay dead. While Jherik's training had been instrumental in keeping the soldiers alive, the sheer numbers of the enemy overwhelmed the Rockhold militia. Even if Lostaria managed to complete her mission of alliance between humans and elves, she would return to find Rockhold an empty city. Or worse yet, a city of living skeletons.

The breeze freshened, bringing Timbrel the scent of salt air and the mournful sound of piping. Curious, the half-elf followed the sound up towards the steepest edge of the caldera. She climbed carefully, using her fingertips to catch at the edges of sharp cracks. She slipped once, the resulting pressure against the rocks neatly slicing her finger open before she found a ledge to stand on. The girl delayed long enough to bind the wound, and then continued her careful journey.

As she settled on another narrow ledge, a glimmer of white in the darkness resolved itself into a pale young man, still in his teens. Timbrel listened as he piped, tears spilling from her eyes and splashing on the rock beneath her. She knelt, feeling the sadness of the music drop around her shoulders and weigh her down.

After an eternity, the piper stood and threw his pipes over the side of the cliff.

"No." Timbrel reached out to him.

The piper startled and teetered on the edge of the cliff.

Timbrel grabbed his sleeve and pulled him back to safety.

"Why did you scare me like that?" The young man accused the girl. "I could have fallen off."

"I wanted to hear the music. You play beautifully."

"I'll never play it again. It was my friend's song, my friend that died today. Never be played again. Not his song, not his pipes." The young man's voice caught in a ragged sob and he hurried away, wobbling dangerously on the ledge. Timbrel let him go, the sad weight of his music still echoing in her memory and holding her back.

The girl sat on the ledge, looking down over the city. The moonlight's stark shadows made the ruined stone buildings seem a pattern of light and dark stones. Captain Harnek's house lay in ruins. She looked up at the cloudless sky. The stars mocked her, refusing to explain how lightning rained down from the heights and blasted buildings apart with no storms. At least the sheltered people survived in the market cave. Whatever gods sent the lightning to aid the enemy had been fooled if they sought to destroy the children.

The sky began to lighten in the east. Timbrel started the long descent back to the city streets. If their luck held, the soldiers would have time to eat something before the final battle. Timbrel sighed. Today the healers would carry knives to defend themselves. A trio of soldiers grumbled about their assignments to guard apprentices carrying water. Few soldiers thought that they would survive the day. Instead, she heard them taking bets on how many enemies they would kill before they died. The boasts were quite impressive, but Timbrel thought the numbers were just not enough.

###

*Along the Eastern Mountains*

Nayev flew toward Rockhold, urgency lending him the strength to lead the four other dragons that agreed to accompany him. The dragons flew in a wide vee, the others drafting slightly behind Nayev's wingtips. They made a dark smudge against the nearly full moon, though the dragons following could easily see the golden scales of their leader.

Nayev's tail whipped in frustration, momentarily slowing his flight. Dozens of dragons remained on his home mountain, most as complacent as the Rockhold humans. Even when the communicator chattered to life for the first time in centuries, the dragons refused to believe that the Terformin returned. The message had been short, too short to trace its location. "Extinct volcano on the northeast corner of the continent looks like a good place to land. Seems populated. That can be corrected. Over and out." It felt like a warning directed at the watchers. Instead, the dragons argued among themselves. The majority claimed that without an answering voice, the radio signal echoed from the past. The sky-watchers reported no trace against the stars.

A few of the dragons accused Nayev of simply wanting to involve himself with the affairs of humans again. True, he heard Timbrel in his mind as clearly as he heard the other dragons. That happened only once before, ten centuries ago when Nayev first discovered that he could shift to a human form if he stored enough energy. The skill was a throwback to the old days when the Genjin first created the dragons to detoxify the land and sea, each dragon type created to fill a specific niche. Their secondary mission, a mission exclusive to the golden dragons, involved watching the skies for returning Terformin and eliminating them to end the plagues. To accomplish this, the golden dragons were created with a much higher intelligence than the other dragons, and the ability to shift to human form. Each shift somehow detoxified the ruins of the cities. Before the second generation of dragons even reached maturity, the land was clean enough for the humans to emerge from the sheltering caverns and repopulate. The ability was lost to disuse, and by Nayev's generation it was merely the stuff of legends.

His rediscovery of the ability made the young dragon vulnerable in ways he never imagined. He liked the feel of the human form, wearing it for so long that some of the oldest dragons told him tales that they learned at an early age–that some dragons reverted to human form and remained that way for their lives. Nayev focused on the word 'reverted,' wondering if somehow the Genjin created the golden dragons from humans in the first place.

A young elf maiden caught Nayev's eye, and then caught his heart as the hormones of his young human body surged and took over. He stayed with the girl for a year, never worried about the consequences. He hadn't thought about her for close to a thousand years.

She had birthed four, he recently learned, one of them monstrous and sickly that died soon after birth. The other three fought for life, males all. Two of them were caught by dragons in the first blush of their youth as they rode out of their protected valley. Their mixed scents probably drew the other dragons close, and the two elves did not survive the contact. The third retreated into the valley, protected beneath its repellent sonic fields, never to leave again.

At least until recently. Sarin finally left the valley less than a year ago. A newly mated dragon told Nayev's brother Novich of the strange scent trail, prompting his journey that ended in

Rockhold. Nayev had been curious about his supposed offspring, but did not meet Sarin before an assassin stole the elf's life.

His eyes burned. He remembered the assassin's surprise at facing a dragon, right before Nayev's rage took over. He did not leave many pieces.

Pain lanced through Nayev's forefoot, quickly fading to an echo of a memory. Timbrel must be hurt again. At least this injury felt minor, unlike the breath-stopping pain across his side earlier in the day. He felt much closer to the half-elven girl than he had to the other elf-woman, but they shared so many things. Their courage. Their inner strength. Their dragon-colored looks. The dragon could easily imagine himself staying with Timbrel for a substantial number of years. He would be more careful about offspring this time. Then again, he'd spent so long in dragon form that the young dancer would practically have to fly a mating flight with him to make him fertile.

###

*The caves west of Rockhold*

Damnech screamed his frustration to the skies. If only the sun stayed up an additional hour. If only he hadn't trained the clones to return to him at the first sign of fading daylight. If only the damned things weren't so damaged.

He hated this planet. A second-generation terraformer, he remembered his parents' tales of the uprisings against their kind. They were lucky, escaping to the glorious stars to explore and begin a new life on a far world. Their efforts did much to change an inhospitable place into a lush new world ready for an expanding population.

When the ship returned and clamped onto the original habitat, only Damnech remained inside. He'd done his best to break free, but had only succeeded in destroying the bubble. When the ship landed on the western slopes of the mountain, he'd escaped from its clutches only to discover that it had brought him back to the home world, where there was a price on his head just for existing.

His first series of attacks, using men he gathered from the local cities by promising them treasure, netted him the information that the volcano sheltered the item he sought: the speaker to the stars. If he could just reach that communicator, he could call the ship back and return home.

The locals got in his way. He thought of them as the left-behinds, those not good enough to explore the galaxy. They refused to acknowledge his superiority, forcing him to slaughter great numbers of the inferior beings. It was like swatting bugs. He put his plan into action when they closed in on him. He sent his few remaining followers out with information to find his cryo-stasis chamber and how to release him.

The plan worked, but not soon enough. Too many centuries passed before he awakened. Unwilling to make the same mistake twice, he cloned himself and put the resulting embryos through an accelerated growth phase, maturing them in a matter of months. The cryo-chamber failure that left him without body fat carried through to the clones, leaving them with poorly functioning brains and with severe night-blindness.

He screamed again. A dozen of his better clones walked off the face of a cliff in the gathering darkness the night before, dashing themselves to pieces on the rocks below. He'd been unable to round up all the returning soldiers, though the rest would find him when the sun rose. One last batch of clones had matured during the day, providing him with replacements for some of the fallen. He'd lost almost a third of his army in a single day. This time, they would completely crush the humans who stood in his way, leaving Damnech free to find the communicator. If the rest of the clones died achieving his aims, so be it. They were faulty in any case.

Damnech busied himself replacing the power units in the static guns. They damaged much of the town yesterday, as well as destroying dozens of human soldiers. At least a few clones were intelligent enough to tell friend from foe and aim a weapon. The next attack would be a simple sweep directly over the enemy. If he could find the women and children, that would demoralize the rest. Yes, Damnech thought. The women and children would be targeted for special destruction.

### 

*The Spider Forest*

Becca ran through the forest. The nearly full moon hung low in the sky and its light barely filtered to the forest floor. It illuminated the roots and branches after Becca stumbled over them. She glanced wildly around for spiders, and then continued her run. The city might be destroyed by the time she reached Jherik's mysterious allies.

She reached for the white disk, and then whirled madly about when she realized it was missing. A shaft of moonlight slipped through the trees, illuminating the disk near the last root she'd fallen on. As she stood, she leaned against a tree to catch her breath. She turned, peering at the tree in their darkness. The dark and shaggy bark hung on the straight trunk like clusters of black bristles. There were no branches at ground-level. Becca looked up, trying to follow the trunk in the weak light. At twice her height, it suddenly bent at an angle. An angle that started to move.

Becca's eyes widened as she backed hurriedly away from the spider's leg. Her mouth working soundlessly, she waved the white disk before her like a flag of truce. A high chittering noise echoed around her, completely encircling her.

"Jherik said ask for Stinger. I need to speak to Stinger." Becca squeaked the words out, her voice half-strangled with fear.

"Stinger." "Stinger." "Stinger." The word replaced the chittering. A dark skinned elf suddenly dropped to the forest floor. He signed for Becca to approach and examined the white disk. He gave a chittering cry, grabbed Becca by the arm and pulled her up in front of him as he mounted his kneeling spider.

The spider leapt to its feet, continued into the trees, and hurried along at a dizzying pace. Trees flashed past Becca's face. The spider suddenly dropped to the ground, scurrying along the rocks and entering a large cave.

Becca's eyes took long minutes to adjust. Gradually she became aware of pale green lights set along the walls, providing her just enough light to see her companion. His face resembled Jherik's with its high cheekbones and pointed chin, and she saw pointed ears as well. The resemblance ended there. Her companion was short, shorter than Becca's own five and a half feet of height, and his skin was nut-brown in the light. Turquoise and red tattoos curled along his cheeks and forehead.

The glow became stronger, or perhaps her eyes adjusted to the darkness. They rode down a wide street, huge stone buildings clustered on each side. Like a mystical city beneath the ground, composed of glowing palaces and peopled with nut-brown elves wearing all manner of clothing. Elves that clustered closely around the spider she rode.

Becca suddenly fell through the air, dropping toward the crowd. The elves caught her gently, and then carried her forward to one of the palaces. In a matter of minutes, they sat her on a cushioned bench. A Spider-Rider sat facing her, still in uniform.

"I am the Stinger," he said, bowing deeply. Becca noticed that his teeth were filed into triangular points. She shuddered and took a deep breath.

"I am Becca, sent by Jherik. My city is being attacked. The attackers, who look like the dead walking, are killing women and children. Even though I am pregnant, I have picked up a sword to help defend my city."

She could not read Stinger's expression. His voice remained perfectly even as he asked, "Does your city require breeding females to become soldiers?" The spider-rider seemed to have trouble with the last word, drawing out the nuances of the final syllable.

"Oh, no. They want me to hide in the caves with the other women and children. But if I don't fight, there won't be any city

297

left. And the enemy kills everyone. I saw a small boy carrying water to the goats ripped apart by their lead forces."

Stinger touched her hand, his gentleness startling from such a savage-looking exterior. "Come, you must rest. Your child inside may be damaged if you exert yourself further."

Becca jerked her hand away. "No! I have to get back to Rockhold. If you won't help us, then I'll just return by myself."

"Your city means so much to you."

"My family is there. My sister, her children. My own child will be born there, too, or die with me while defending our way of life." She looked wildly around, finally focusing her eyes on the exit. "I have to go."

Stinger was behind her, helping her up, before she even saw him move. He looked up and chittered toward the ceiling. Hundreds of answering chitters startled Becca. She had thought herself alone with the Rider. Instead, she had been heard by a large number.

Spiders began dropping into the room, many with riders. One knelt nearby.

"It is time to help your city. You may stay here, or ride back with us. We will set you down before we fight. Our ways will not permit otherwise."

"A ride sounds good. I just hope we are in time."

The spiders leapt upward and over the walls of the open-ceilinged room. Within minutes they returned to the forest, an ever-growing number of spiders joining them in a leaping race to save Rockhold.

### 

*On board the Lady Elizabeth*

The trip had been hellish. The freak wind carried all three ships, sails straining to the point of destruction. The winds died down long enough to replace a shredded sail on one of the other ships, then sprang back to fill the sails and drive the ships onward.

The storms grew near and attacked with an insane fury. Sailors and soldiers both muttered in fear as the storm winds calmed and allowed the ships clear passage, though the sea rolled and chopped beneath them and the rains washed freely over the decks.

One particularly strong wave left a huge shark behind, snapping as it rolled across the deck and toward the elves' horses. The elven commander kept his head, calling out commands for the war-trained horses to strike out when the shark came within reach. The twenty-foot fish skidded across the deck, propelled by the simultaneous kicks from three horses. The next wave carried it overboard, along with an elf who was quickly rescued. Lostaria noticed that her warriors remained near the center of the cargo deck after seeing the shark on the other ship. She didn't blame them.

At night the cabin boy slept with his head pillowed in her lap, moaning and thrashing in his sleep. Her touch seemed to soothe him, allowing him the rest he needed to keep up the pace.

The days flew by. Lostaria hoped that they would reach Rockhold in time. The scouts' reports had been patchy at best before she left. Would the city still stand when they arrived?

###

# Chapter Twelve

*Rockhold*

Krys trudged upward with Captain Harnek, his mind in turmoil. Yesterday the enemy had been faceless. Today the wizard knew that the enemy carried Damnech's face, each and every one of them. His dreams reminded him over and over again of Damnech's corpse. Despair welled up. How much use could he be during the battle when he couldn't strike at the enemy?

Captain Harnek swiveled and stiffened. Krys looked up as a scout tied two pennons to a staff. Red over yellow, Krys thought. The enemy is on the move.

The signal repeated in other places, alerting the troops below. Armored units moved forward and worked their way over the crest of the caldera. They would protect the heights with their lives. Jherik's armor gleamed among them, the only fully matched set. There would be no hit and run tactics today. Only three had returned from Jherik's original twenty, and one of them might never leave the hospital alive.

Even Krys could see the slumping postures of the dispirited soldiers. No one expected to survive the day.

The closest soldiers hugged against the wall, armor clattering on the stone. Whirling, Krys saw the green pennon flapping in the breeze. The elf pressed against the wall and searched the skies.

The green dragon seemed to float lazily overhead, then folded its wings and dove with surprising speed at the western side of the caldera. It passed close enough to Krys that the acrid scent of the dragon stung his nose. The dragon's dive carried it past the heights and down the outer edge of the ridge. The dragon's growls and the clatter of weapons and armor mixed with loud shrieks from the enemy.

300

"By the gods, it's helping us." Harnek's words carried on the freshening breeze to the soldiers, who repeated it. They stood taller, weapons at the ready.

Lightning flashed into the clear blue sky from the enemy's ranks. A moment later, the dragon came hurtling upward. It crested the ridge and headed straight out to sea carrying two struggling bodies. The madly beating wings and rudder-like tail were marked with black streaks.

The initial bolt of lightning acted as a signal. Lightning flashed all around the caldera's rim as the enemy began a concerted attack. Krys watched in horror as rows of armored men fell. The breeze carried the scent of burning flesh to the heights. The elf's stomach lurched. He glanced back at the city within.

A line of children scurried madly back to the caves from the spring. Krys silently wished them luck in regaining safety. He turned back to watch the battle, the line swiftly approaching his position from the outer slopes. The elven wizard tried to gather his power, but the image of Damnech's face kept intruding on his thoughts.

Captain Harnek sent runners to the signal post, and the pennons quickly changed. Krys lost track of the messages as his mind filled with colored lights, red lights and amber. *Had he somehow woken Damnech and caused this?*

The elf lost his breath in a *Whoosh* as he hit the ground on his back. Harnek stood before him, battling an enemy that slipped through. As the creature's head rolled away from its body, Krys felt the sting of a fine scratch across his skin as it oozed a thin line of blood under his slashed clothes. He shook his head fiercely, driving away the images of Damnech and his lights.

Lightning flashed past, blinding Krys momentarily. A tearing noise followed by a thunderous crash grabbed the attention of every Rockhold defender. Krys swiveled his head. Below was a scene from his worst nightmares.

The blast had loosened the inside of the eastern ridge, shattered rock tumbling and falling. A slowly thinning haze of dust and dirt hung over the city. Krys heard the combat behind him as he stood and stared down. The weight of the moving rock tore off the side of the mountain and dropped it in front of the sheltering caves. A wide scar in the rock cut through the many terraces that lined the walls of the caldera. It was impossible to tell how deep the scarring went, or if the caves survived. Even if they held, the women and children trapped inside had little food and water, and a finite supply of air.

The elf ran to the edge of the ridge and dropped to the first terrace. He sprinted around the caldera, dropping twice more to find a terrace that connected with the scarred area. He skidded to a halt at the edge.

The gouge ran deeper than it looked from the opposite side of the city. Mentally trying to calculate the amount of rock that already slid past, Krys shuddered and gave up the effort. The mound of rubble shifted, settling slightly. The rock he stood on transmitted groaning vibrations to Krys' feet. The caves could collapse at any moment. Taking a deep breath, the elven wizard jumped into the gouged area and slid down the face of the mountain.

Rock and dust tumbled around him. He slid faster than he expected, and Krys had a sudden vision of plunging into solid rock at the base. He threw his weight diagonally, trying to slow his descent by moving across the cut as well as down. Slowing slightly, Krys focused on zigzagging down the gouge.

The rubble mound loomed, and Krys found himself knee-deep in a tangle of branches. Climbing free, the elf carefully scrambled down the mound. A few cuts from the tree branches stung, but Krys ignored them. He faced the mound of earth and stones, summoning his power.

A plume of dust blew out from the base of the rubble. Stones and earth began to shift. Krys hurriedly cast a second spell, fusing the edges of the rock dust back to stone. The ceiling of the short tunnel dipped lower than he hoped, but he could get through. Walking inside, he used his tunnel to shelter him from shifting rubble as he powdered another section, again lining the walls with fused stone.

He gathered his power again, surprised when it flowed quickly through his bones. A faint glow at the edge of his vision dimmed, noticeable only by its lack. He cast the spells again, quickly shoring up each section as he created it. The rock dust, thicker now, settled into his firm tunnel in great drifts.

Krys waded forward through the dust. He tried another spell, creating a wind to blow the dust out of the tunnel. The air whirled madly around, stirring the dust into a choking cloud too thick to see through. Krys pulled his tunic across his mouth and bent double coughing. He wouldn't try that again.

The dust took a long time to settle, taunting the elf. He sighed, and then went into a paroxysm of choking coughs that stirred up even more dust. Pulling his tunic up to cover his mouth again, Krys gathered his power. The power came more slowly now, and the elf felt the weight of exhaustion settling in.

"No," he told himself. "I have to keep going."

The elf continued to tunnel forward, the rock dust now chest deep. He staggered and nearly fell, then gathered power again. Deep inside, a small voice reminded him that he had far exceeded his capacity for spells. Another voice silenced the first, reminding him of the women and children counting on him. He cast the spell again, sinking to his knees in the dust as he barely cast the stabilizing spell. The dust settled over his head as the elf sunk to the ground.

Coughing and choking sounds roused him from his momentary lapse. Krys joined them, lifting his head free of the dust as he crouched on the floor. The elf coughed and spat, then realized that the dust level was still dropping. He had broken through!

A dozen people helped him stand. Small children darted up, reaching out to touch his arm before running back to hide behind their mothers' skirts. A fine layer of dust was now settling over everything in the cave. The mountain groaned again, sending vibrations through the floor.

"Wrap your faces," Krys commanded. "The tunnel is filled with dust, sometimes higher than your heads. Let the tallest go first to make a path through the dust for the shorter. The roof of the tunnel is lowest right before you reach the outside. Leave everything behind but your children. Now go!"

An ominous groan squelched further protests. The side wall of the market cave bulged inward. Krys sent the tallest people through the tunnel as quickly as possible. When the worst of the choking sounds ceased, he sent the children through as well. A faint cheer echoed through the tunnel.

Krys was about to go through the tunnel when he heard sobbing. Whirling, he hunted for the source of the sound. Three small children hid behind a pile of cloaks, clutching each other in fear. Two of them tottered when he stood them on their feet.

The elf gathered them up, tying makeshift scarfs around their faces and setting them on a leather cloak. "Hang on tightly," he cautioned them. He pulled the cloak across the dusty floor. It slid easily.

The children giggled, clutching the edges of the cloak with white knuckled fingers. Krys easily pulled the makeshift sled to the tunnel entrance. The mountain groaned again, the bulge inside the cavern suddenly splintering into deadly shrapnel. Krys dashed into the tunnel, towing the children behind. The market cave crashed down behind him with a roar.

The tunnel itself groaned as the rubble above slid into the gap created by the collapsed cave. The stresses were too much, and the tunnel's end collapsed, starting a chain reaction. Krys sprinted through the deepening dust, praying to the absent gods that the silent children still held tightly to the cloak, and praying that he would win the race to the outside. *If only I had Timbrel's speed.*

A child's shriek brought him to a stop, and the shattering tunnel caught up with them as he retrieved the fallen child. He stood quickly, bumping his head on the low roof. Gathering the last of his power, Krys cast his spell against the rock as the tunnel shattered around them.

###

Timbrel put her hand across her mouth, aghast when the mountain came down across the market caves. For a heartbeat's length the healers all stood to watch the destruction of the mountainside, then set back to their work with grim determination. A few healers sobbed as they worked, their tears washing the wounds they stitched.

Timbrel glanced up the western slope and immediately wished she hadn't. Abandoned signal posts stood throughout the upper third of the slope, their black pennons signaling 'retreat'. To the east, the freshening breeze quickly blew the haze of dust from the mountain's collapse away. The enemy approached, breaking through the defender's lines and racing down the mountainside like streams of angry ants.

Timbrel turned back to her work, stitching wounds and binding bones together with every scrap of cloth she could lay her hands on. They had run out of straight sticks long before. The last three legs she splinted used the scabbards of the soldiers' swords tied on with strips from their tunics.

A cloud crossed overhead, then another. Screams rose at the far side of the hospital. The enemy had broken through.

Dagger in one hand and a ceramic shard in the other, Timbrel ran to protect the hospital and its patients. The wild cries of the healers as they slashed the enemy joined the dull clang of brass bowls and discarded helmets across skeletal faces. As she approached, three of the enemy soldiers turned away from the others and ran towards the half-elf. Timbrel ran from them, luring them away from the hospital. If only she could lure them into the range of the Rockhold soldiers.

The girl glanced upwards, plotting a quick path along the terraces and their connecting stairs. She ran, never quite fast enough to lose her pursuers. The stitches across her ribs ached. More footsteps joined the first, heavier. They must be closing! Without a backward glance, Timbrel ran like the wind. The footsteps followed, some closer than others.

She ran up the stairs between terraces, taking the steps two and three at a time. She headed for the clearest section of the ridge, one she felt fairly certain was still held by Rockhold. She glanced over her shoulder for a moment, and skidded to a stop in horror. Small plumes of dust puffed out from the base of the rubble against the sheltering caves, whipped away almost immediately by the steadily growing wind. *The caves are collapsing!*

The red and yellow flicker of flames ran across the uppermost terraces on the eastern slope. Timbrel shivered as another cloud shadow passed over her.

The sound of a dislodged stone reminded her of her peril. The enemy closed on her. The girl spun and ran along the terrace, dodging around a skeletal warrior that climbed to cut her off. She fled up the terraces.

The ridge loomed ahead, promising an end to her running. Her side hurt across her ribs. She placed a hand on her side, felt warm wetness. She must have pulled some of the stitches. The blood trickled slowly; it would wait.

She ran along the last terrace below the ridge, aiming for the stone steps that would give her access to the top. A dozen skeletal warriors dropped from above. She was cut off. Timbrel looked wildly around for a path of escape, finally dropping to the terrace below. She landed on a dead body, squealing as its cold flesh rolled beneath her feet. Crawling away, she glanced back at the corpse's face. Captain Harnek.

### 

Halar stood near the healer's place with a dozen of his Tallfolk brothers. They would protect the healers from the dead that walked, from the Terafora. It helped his mood that Teembara was here as well. Halar liked protecting the tiny girl with golden hair.

The Tallfolk had been unobtrusive until now, standing behind nearby buildings and carrying the wounded to the hospital. With their longer strides, they could move much faster than the tiny yoomans.

A scuffle to one side sent the Tallman into action. Halar reached up to his rocks, conveniently piled on a nearby roof. He lobbed them at the dead things, knocking them down. His brothers did the same, but Halar thought he knocked more down than they did. When the tales were retold, he would score more points.

The rumble of the mountainside drew his attention. Halar watched the mountain slide down, covering the children's hole. The Tallman was horrified. Bad enough that the enemy controlled the lightning, but worse to use it against children.

Shadows passed overhead, far too quickly for clouds. Halar looked skyward. Five golden shapes arrowed across the city in perfect formation. The Tallman watched as they rose past the thick rock dust to spit flame at the enemy on the eastern slopes. The Daraga had arrived. Teembara did her job well.

A little cowed at the thought, the Tallman looked across to Teembara's healing place. She was not there! He looked around, spotting the girl as she ran to attack several dead things that were too close.

Signaling his brothers to attack the dead things, Halar ran to pull Teembara out of danger. The girl suddenly veered to one side, a handful of the dead things following her. Halar was impressed. He never knew she could run so fast with her short legs. When she started to climb the stairs, he followed. The dead things might trap the girl on the slopes.

The Tallman ran along, his feet thudding into the ground. Teembara put on a sudden burst of speed. She climbed steps and ran along the terrace to the next set of stairs, suddenly stopping to gaze out across the valley. *Her face is paler than usual, but it is difficult to tell because of the dirt.* He continued to follow her, worried that the others might catch up too soon and injure her.

Halar's brothers approached, climbing straight up the terraces to intercept him. Halar stood only two terraces beneath Teembara when she suddenly backed up. The Tallman could see dead things dropping down, surrounding her. She jumped from the edge, landing and rolling over on the ground. As Halar climbed to join her, he found her frozen in place, looking at the face of a Rockhold yooman.

Halar's brother roared from the next terrace up, waving the sapling he pulled from yesterday's rubble to use as a club. Halar looked up to see a line of giant spiders, their tiny riders waving weapons. One of the spiders lunged forward, neatly snipping the head from a dead thing.

"They're on our side," Halar said to himself, then shouted it. "They're on our side!"

Several of his brothers hesitated, but others were too caught up in the battle fury. Halar leapt to the next terrace, grabbing his brothers by the arms, restraining them. "They are pets! The spiders are pets!"

The rider on the closest spider stood and looked directly at Halar. When their eyes met, the rider saluted him with a pure white weapon. Halar saluted back. The spiders and their riders moved south along the ridge, dropping into the midst of a group of dead things. Halar's brothers enthusiastically followed.

### 

The fight to regain the sea-heights was wearing on Jherik. More than once the elven warrior wished he had left his armor behind because of its weight, but just as often he was pleased with the heavy stuff when it turned yet another blow. It also helped to weight him down in the rushing wind. More than one of the skeletal warriors blew off the ridge that overlooked the sea to the north.

The wind suddenly died to absolute stillness. Jherik took advantage of the lull and charged upward. The skeletons were thick here, and the elven warrior used every combat trick he ever learned just to hold his own. It was not enough. Gradually, step by costly step, the skeletons drove the Henin elf backward into the city.

The mountain rumbled again to the east, sending vibrations throughout the caldera. They feel almost rhythmic, Jherik thought, like marching feet. A quick glance to either side reassured him that the skeletons were not receiving reinforcements.

Jherik fought in the eerie stillness. Weapons and armor clashed, but the creatures made no sound even when wounded. Arms dangling, they attacked with their teeth. Legs dragging behind, they crawled to the attack. The damn things wouldn't stop until they were dead, and some of them seem to try even then.

Damn things. They looked hauntingly familiar. Jherik continued to fight the creatures while his mind trying to match them to a previous experience. "Damn," he muttered. The elf stopped in surprise. "That's it! Damnech. The dead body in the tube. They all look like Damnech." Certain that this information was important, Jherik began to fall back. A cry from above drew his attention.

Elven warriors in full armor came spilling out the sea cave connection, attacking the skeletons from the rear. Behind them, human warriors spilled out and ran around the terraces to assist the beleaguered Rockhold soldiers. Lostaria's voice rose above the noise, directing the units. Relief washed through Jherik, and his knees sagged with sudden weariness.

Finally able to break free of the battle, the Henin elf headed for the few colored pennons left. He needed to tell Krys about Damnech. It was time to regroup and share information.

### 

Halar picked the half-elven girl up from the terrace. She hung limply in his grasp, tears creating streaks on her dirty face. Not sure where to bring her, he carried her with him as he rejoined his brothers and their spider allies. The dead things were nearly gone. A few spiders still pounced, neatly snipping the heads off the enemy. The Daraga swept through the skies, clearing the heights with their flame-balls. New soldiers retook the sea cliff, some still wobbling from their long boat journey. Halar smiled. He remembered his own journey by boat. It took him days to learn to stand on the boat, and days more to learn to stand on land again. They were lucky they could fight at all.

The shadows of the Daraga swept past, and the great golden creatures hung in the air. They drifted nearer the spiders, their huge wings flapping slowly to keep them in position. With a thud the five great beasts set down on the rocks of the ridge.

One of the Daraga seemed to be speaking, its voice growling toward the spider riders. Teembara suddenly twitched and sat up in Halar's grasp. She squirmed her way down to the ground, and then set off running toward the dragons.

Halar stood frozen as the girl ran directly in front of the lead beast. A trick of the rocks and the dying breeze brought her words to him. He translated slowly.

"No!" She waved her finger at the Daraga. The great golden head dropped toward the girl, dwarfing her. "They live here. They were born here. They never left."

The beast's great head jerked back as if surprised. One of the golden beasts drew in a deep breath. Unable to watch Teembara's immolation, Halar turned his head to the side. He closed his eyes tightly, waiting for the sounds of the Daraga spitting fire. After a moment of complete silence his eyes opened. Far across the city, at the base of the landslide, a stream of tiny figures ran through a widening dust cloud. They ran *out* of the cloud, Halar realized. It must be the trapped people, the trapped children. As he watched, more of the mountain caved in. The dust cloud by the exiting people grew larger. The rubble started to sift downward, following a straight line toward the people. A sudden puff of dust obscured everything.

Halar risked a glance back toward Teembara. The Tallman stepped back with surprise, tripping over an unseen stone and landing on his rump. The girl stood between the lead spider and the lead Daraga, her hands on her hips. She defied the Daraga! Even more unbelievable, the creature seemed to be thinking about what she said. What kind of power did this tiny girl have?

They reached an agreement of some sort and the girl and one of the spider riders touched hands to the great golden snout of the Daraga. The five Daraga turned and leapt from the ridge, their wings snapping out like sails in the wind. They spiraled upward, circled several times, and soared over the western ridge.

Halar stood carefully, aware that his hands shook. He suddenly feared the tiny girl. Sadness filled him, for he liked her. It was well that he did not discover her strange powers before the time they spent together.

Teembara beckoned to him, calling him to stand before the spiders and their riders. Halar remembered the warning he had been given, the warning he had ignored to return home and ask his brothers to fight. The Tallman joined her, shuffling his feet.

The lead spider rider beckoned. Halar recognized him by his tattoos as the same rider that told him to stay away from the forest. The Tallman hung his head and approached.

"It has been long since we last spoke." The rider used the human tongue.

Halar nodded, not trusting his voice or his command of the language to answer.

"You may have the freedom of the forest." The rider's voice sounded gentle.

Halar stepped back. "What?" His voice squeaked out past the lump in his throat.

The rider chuckled. "You have the freedom of the forest." The nut-brown rider tilted his head slightly. "Be *careful* next time."

"I will not hurt your pets again, I did not know, I did not understand, I..."

The rider cut Halar off with a gesture. His voice sounded tired. "They are not pets, just... oh... all right. They are pets." The rider gave a weary sigh and mounted his spider. Halar and his brothers slowly waved as the huge spiders leapt down the outside wall of the caldera, heading back to the forest.

### 

Timbrel sat on the terrace wall, staring at the huge scar on the mountainside. Krys had survived the final collapse of the caves, his spell blowing the last bits of rubble to dust even as it fell on him.

He saved three children as well, covering their bodies with his own. The wizard seemed to enjoy being a hero.

Jherik enjoyed good treatment as well. He and the small unit of elves that Lostaria brought were credited with re-taking the seawall. Lostaria added a small title to Jherik's stature, one that granted him the lowest levels of true nobility. If Kareni had thought to break their betrothal over his bloodlines, she would find it much more difficult now.

Lostaria asked for Timbrel to join the celebration as well, but the half-elf declined. Timbrel mourned Captain Harnek. The group funeral seemed too impersonal to the dancer, and she spent her time in seclusion from the others. Seclusion under the sun and the sky.

Timbrel hung her head. She felt guilty on top of everything else. In spite of her sad heart, she still found herself searching the skies for signs of Nayev. How could she mourn and yearn at the same time? It made little sense.

She smiled to herself as she remembered the confused look on the dragon's face when she lectured it. A slight flush touched her cheeks as she relived her embarrassment at discovering that the dragon she lectured was *not* Nayev at all, merely one of his friends. Nayev stepped forward to complete the negotiations with the Spider Riders, a feeling of smug satisfaction touching the mind-echoes she heard of his words. Timbrel suddenly wished Nayev sat with her. She had so many questions for him.

As if in answer to her wish, she heard the scuff of a footstep on the path. An elf, one of Lostaria's warriors, approached her.

"May I sit with you?" His phrasing was educated and polite, but Timbrel did not recognize him. Her elation collapsed.

"You may. I am called Timbrel." The half-elf waved a hand to indicate a stone a respectful distance away.

The elf ignored her suggestion and sat next to her. "I know. I am Arlis. I understand you lost someone close to you."

Timbrel's eyes filled with tears. She turned her head away, unwilling to let Arlis see her cry. She fought to hold them back,

312

but a single teardrop trickled down her cheek and hung from her chin.

"I do not wish to speak of this, nor do I wish to celebrate." Timbrel's voice came out colder than she planned. Arlis disturbed her in some way that she could not pinpoint.

"Again, I understand. Perhaps we can speak about the new Baron of Rockhold, Alexander?"

Timbrel snorted. The self-styled Baron of Rockhold, a distant relative of past lords who had long since given up their claim to the city, stepped forward to take charge. The previous leader died in the first day's battle, and Harnek, long expected to be his successor, died during the second day. Timbrel's eyes welled with tears again.

She stifled them and took careful control of her voice. "He is... pompous." Timbrel could think of no better word for the young man. Before the sun set on the second day, immediately after Lostaria had given her few awards to the elves and to the men under her command, Alexander declared a week of celebrations. It was the fourth day now, and Timbrel was still not ready to celebrate. As far as she could tell, most of the surviving Rockholders were not ready, either.

Captain Overton sailed south, muttering about squeezing in an extra run for foodstuffs this season. For all his gruff and mercenary exterior, Timbrel found the pirate to be softhearted. She could easily imagine a sudden drop in prices for grain, one that Overton would grudgingly pass along to the Rockholders, even if it originated directly from his own pouch. He treated his men fairly, and was one of the very few captains who maintained the same crew from year to year. They seldom missed the tide.

"I can see that I'm boring you," Arlis said bitterly. Timbrel realized that he had been speaking for several minutes while she was lost in her thoughts.

"It is not you, it is Alexander who bores me." Timbrel took a deep breath. "Perhaps my head will clear with a walk." The girl stood first, dismissing the warrior from her presence. To her consternation, he rose as well and took her arm.

"The sea breeze will lighten your mood. Shall we walk down to the docks?"

Timbrel was trapped. She could not politely decline the elf's request, and she was unwilling to lower herself by treating him rudely. With a sigh, they walked to the north road, climbing to the sea cave and then descending the long series of switchbacks.

The exercise lightened her mood, as did the tang of the salt air. She would never admit it to her companion, however. The docks were nearly empty, the two ships that waited for Kerran's men and Lostaria's elves tied at the furthest of the floating docks, and a few smaller boats scattered near the rest. Timbrel remembered watching the ships come in during the Rockhold springtime. Within a week, every space on the floating docks filled, ships tied on to other ships, and still others anchored in the harbor beyond.

Now the harbor lay as desolate as Timbrel's thoughts. She allowed Arlis to lead her down the docks, his voice chattering away with inconsequential things. "He's as brainless as Von pretended to be," she thought.

They jumped between floating docks, Timbrel thinking about Von's apparent brainlessness. Suddenly she did not want to be alone with Arlis.

Timbrel shivered. "Perhaps we should turn back. There is a chill to the breeze."

Arlis put his arm around her, pulling her close to his chest and breaking all sorts of protocols. "I will warm you, Timbrel. Besides, we have only a few docks to go."

The half-elf glanced up. He spoke true. A single small boat bobbed by the next dock, but only four floating docks lay between the one they trod and the two large ships. Almost in calling distance. Timbrel determined that she would have a larger escort back to the city.

Arlis suddenly pulled her closer, wrapping both arms behind her. She struggled, reminding him of the impropriety. She struggled again.

Timbrel heard footsteps running along the dock. Turning her hips, she suddenly leaned into Arlis's groin, crushing him with her pelvic bone. The elf gasped and cursed, but did not let her go. She struggled to reach her dagger, but her arms were pinned at her sides. The footsteps came closer, yielding hands that helped restrain her. An acrid-smelling rag was thrust into her mouth. The taste puckered her throat and the world started to dim around the edges. Timbrel fought against the drug. As her sight dimmed and muscles turned to water, the half-elf slumped to the dock. She felt herself lifted and carried, then handed to another. The lapping of the waves grew louder.

"Stow her below. Do you have her pack?" The voice was familiar, and clearly in command.

A second voice answered. "Here. No one saw me take it. They were all at the celebration."

"We'll be having a celebration of our own, soon. The buyer will be pleased." Timbrel struggled to listen as the voices faded.

"That means a bonus for everyone. Right, Kadeesh?" The rest was lost with the shreds of Timbrel's consciousness.

### 

*Somewhere at sea*

Timbrel's mouth was dry. She tried to swallow, her gummy throat protesting. Hands pushed a bowl of water against her mouth. The half-elf greedily drank half of it before she tasted the acrid tang. The fuzzy world faded.

### 

*Rockhold*

"Krys, have you seen Timbrel this morning?" Jherik paced back and forth. His pack lay ready on the bed.

"I have not seen her since yesterday, when she went walking on the heights again. No doubt she is cuddled up with some man or other." Krys wasn't worried. Timbrel would check in by late morning as she usually did.

"Are you certain she is not avoiding us?" The Henin elf looked worried.

Jherik had a point, Krys thought. Timbrel had ducked out of the beginning of the award ceremony several days before, and had made herself scarce since then. She spent most of her time on the heights, as far as Krys could tell. She skipped the ongoing celebrations, including last night's dancing. That wasn't like Timbrel at all.

"You may be right. Look on the heights if you need to find her. She may just want time alone."

"I'll be back in an hour." Jherik practically ran out the door. Krys rolled his eyes. The warrior elf could not disguise his feelings for the girl. Except for the one night, she had not encouraged him at all. Krys still didn't credit her denial of all wrongdoing that evening. After all, they *were* both naked when Krys found her kneeling over the unconscious warrior, and he *was* clutching her loincloth in his fist. Life might get very interesting if they passed through the Vale of Henin again.

Krys took his time dressing, and then descended to the common room of the inn. The smell of sausages hung in the air. Four soldiers saw him coming, jumped to their feet and cleared the table for them. Tempted to ignore them and take a different table, he thanked them and sat. The last few days of hero worship began to wear thin.

The waitress rushed over with a plate of bread, cheese, and sausages. "Here you go, sir. Fresh from the oven." The bread steamed, and Krys waited a moment for it to cool off. He thanked her and set to his meal.

A shadow fell across the table. Krys looked up to see the wizard Nayev standing there. The elf gestured at a chair and the man sat. Almost as soon as he pulled the chair in, the waitress arrived with a plate for Nayev. The young man tried to wave her away, then picked at the food on his plate. He seemed preoccupied.

Krys watched the young wizard, waiting for him to speak. Eventually Nayev looked up and met the elf's eyes.

"I understand that you rescued the women and children from a collapsed mountainside." Nayev's voice was carefully neutral.

Krys had a sudden sinking feeling. "I did." Krys sighed, weary of the conversation before it began. He did not want any more congratulations.

Nayev lifted a golden-yellow eyebrow. "You used a rock spell to accomplish this." He kept the same neutral tone with absolutely no inflection.

Krys lifted a silver-white eyebrow in return. "I did," he carefully answered.

Nayev leaned forward. "Where did you learn it? Did Sarin teach it to you?"

Krys was surprised to hear the name of his mentor. "Sarin? Sarin cast no spells."

"Then where?" Nayev asked eagerly.

Krys frowned for a moment. Where had he first learned it? He had a vague memory of seeing a clod of dirt fly apart into dust, then trying to mimic the effect. At some point he adapted the spell to work with rock. The reverse of the spell, forming dust into rock, was a natural outgrowth.

"It just came naturally to me," Krys admitted. "I've fine-tuned it over the years."

Nayev sat back, a troubled look flitting over his face before it settled back into the neutral expression. "Are you related to Sarin?"

Krys bit his lip. "Of course not. He was my teacher, not my father."

"Your teacher?"

"My teacher in history. He inspired me to become a historian."

"History. Not magic?"

"History. I discovered the magic myself when I explored old ruins." Krys frowned. "Why are you so interested in this? You are much more powerful than I." Krys could not help but be aware of the green glow of Nayev's power hovering at the edges of his vision.

"I am considering you as an apprentice."

"Me?" The elf asked. "Why would you select me?"

"The dragons are masters of rock magic. It is..." Nayev paused for a moment, searching for the right word. "...an unusual ability to find in a wizard." Nayev studied Krys' face. "Only the strongest can manage to work with stone."

Krys looked Nayev directly in the eye. "Can *you* work with stone?"

Nayev sat back, his laughter pealing across the room. When he recovered himself, he leaned forward conspiratorially. "Of course. I can shift forms as well. That is what I would teach you. Will you learn?"

Krys considered for a moment and then answered formally. "What you offer is tempting." He made a sudden decision. "Absolutely."

Nayev looked satisfied. A mischievous and worried look danced across his face. "I have one further question for you."

"Ask away." Krys had a question as well, but it would wait.

"Have you seen Timbrel? I have not been able to find her."

###

# Chapter Thirteen

*Somewhere at sea*

The boat tossed back and forth, the storm-driven waves thudding against its hull. Timbrel opened bleary eyes, slowly remembering. Her hands and feet were tied with strong cord. Her muscles felt like water. She was weak as a fish gasping on the shore. She started to sink into sleep again, but the boat's movement kept her awake. She drew herself to her knees, every muscle protesting. When did her legs and arms get so flabby? How long was she drugged?

A small cask of water was roped a few feet away to the side of the boat. Beneath it lay the bowl that Timbrel vaguely remembered drinking from. A flask stood to one side, in easy reach.

She opened the flask and cautiously sniffed at the contents. Acrid fumes made her head whirl dangerously. She quickly recapped the flask and replaced it. The plug on the water cask gave her a struggle. Stale water sluiced down across her face. The half-elf drank greedily, relishing the flat taste as if it were the purest spring. Her head cleared, leaving a dull throb that the girl could ignore well enough.

She replaced the plug with difficulty, using her fist to pound it back into the hole. A search among the other containers sharing the small cargo space revealed slightly moldy way-crackers and withered limes. After scraping the mold off the crackers and peeling the limes, the substandard food filled her empty belly.

*I'm too weak to escape*, she thought wearily. *I have to build up my strength*. Carefully lying down in her original place, Timbrel stretched and flexed her legs and arms. The muscles protested, but gradually loosened.

###

*A Melani Island*

Kadeesh returned to the docks, his belly bouncing with his steps as he whistled in the faint starlight. Three elves as dark of skin as his buyer followed him, ready to take the purchase into their complex. He stepped down into the boat, frowning. The girl still lay in the cargo hold, but something was different. He shrugged it off as his imagination.

Two of the dark elves lifted the girl easily from the hold. The third, the only one that spoke an understandable tongue, turned to the slaver. "She has clothing?"

"Clothing?" Kadeesh nodded. Usually the buyers wanted to strip their purchases immediately. It tended to make them accept their new situation a bit faster than otherwise. He gestured at the girl's pack, suddenly happy that he had not thrown it overboard during the storm. The dark elf lifted the pack with care. The buyer paid well, so Kadeesh chose not to ask questions. Besides, his life was his own again. Why would he question that?

The slaver looked back toward the small settlement. At night, lights sprinkled the buildings. When he docked in mid-afternoon, the few buildings in the village were deserted. Not until an hour after sunset did he see any elves. It disconcerted him that he had not heard their approach.

"I'll leave in the morning," Kadeesh thought. By then his two associates would stumble back from the bar. What could go wrong?

###

*Rockhold*

Krys panted heavily. The power sang along his bones, burning them from the inside out. Small bruises appeared on his arm like dark freckles. He could not absorb any more power.

320

"Let the power flow through you, down to your tiniest bit." Nayev's voice gave Krys something to focus on. "There is another shape within you. Let the power set it free."

The burning pain in his bones magnified, ripping along his limbs and doubling back on itself. Krys tried to hold his concentration as the pain spread. Muscles shredded and healed near instantly. His bones crumbled, and then reassembled themselves into longer and longer structures. *I am rocks and dust*, thought Krys, lost in a madness of pain..

The elf lost his balance, falling forward and barely catching himself with strangely elongated arms. Vertigo washed through him, spinning so quickly that his stomach lurched. He shut his eyes tightly and opened them just as quickly when it amplified the vertigo. His arms were a mass of darkness, bruised pinpoints merging into one solid skin-sized bruise, only his skin wasn't his skin anymore.

Pressure built within the elf, pressure that threatened to explode and rip the struggling elf into a million tiny bits. Krys resisted long enough for the pressure to follow his new bone structure. *The shift is not finished*. He gave himself over to the pain. The pressure exploded, and Krys felt himself fly apart.

The world slowly stabilized. The elf felt a profound sense of relief. He glanced at his arm, expecting to see the blue-black of bruises. Instead, glossy scales the color of a storm-swept midnight overlapped his arm, which no longer jointed the same as before. Or rather it did, but the proportions of wrist and forearm had changed drastically. His eyes traveled outward. The scales grew finer as they approached and covered his hand. Krys inspected the clawed paw at the end of his arm. His thumb had migrated to the back of the hand (or was it a paw? A foot?), giving him more stability. Three toes splayed out forwards. Krys flexed his forefoot, surprised to find his thumb still opposable, allowing him to manipulate fine objects. He wiggled the missing fifth finger and felt a twitch. The finger, shortened and migrated upward along the elongated wrist, created a slightly movable dew claw.

His fingernails lengthened and hardened into claws, and Krys could sense their rocklike nature. Feeling the urge to stretch, Krys felt a double movement as though he had disjointed his shoulders. He twisted his head easily and looked directly down his back. Two large wings sprouted from his second pair of shoulder blades. He flapped them experimentally. Dust and tiny pebbles scattered.

*It will take you some time to adjust to the new body.* Nayev's voice sounded within Krys's head, as well as along the ground to his left. Krys twisted his head the other way to look at the human wizard. Nayev sat perched on a pebble, his body shrunken smaller than Krys's paw.

*No, not shrunken*, Krys thought. *I am larger.* A puddle of water pooled in a shallow depression in the rocks. Krys vaguely remembered passing a small pond on their way to the open space where Nayev coached him. The former elf lumbered over to the puddle, then stared at his reflection. A dragon's face looked back at him. The bruises faded as he watched, leaving a silver cast to his scales. Steel-gray eyes reflected back into his own.

Krys turned to Nayev, a question forming in his mind. The human wizard hopped down from his pebble and leaned forward against the rock. Krys watched the tiny wizard suddenly expand in size, bones lengthening and wings finally erupting from his back. The pebble shrank and vanished as the process continued, as did a significant portion of the rock beyond. Nayev's dragon form also started blue-black and finished half again Krys's size, with golden scales that matched Nayev's hair.

*Not so young as you thought.* Nayev rumbled and shook his wings, then turned his great head to look at Krys. *There are exercises that you should do to strengthen your muscles and wings. Climbing rocks is one of them. Shall we investigate the caves on the west wall to see if Timbrel lies within?*

### 

322

*Nerryon*

Shess stalked the streets of Nerryon. Rats skittered away from his path, sensing the death that hung in the air around the Melani elf. Slaves crawled to the opposite side of their cages when he stormed by. Shess enjoyed the smell of fear in the air.

His agents still searched for the golden girl that caused him so much trouble. Shess frowned. With agents scattered throughout the continent, he had hoped to hear something positive in their regular reports. Even Kadeesh reported in, perhaps not realizing that the Melani elf planned to have him killed regardless of his success or lack thereof. Shess had already set those plans in motion.

If Kadeesh did not succeed, he would die before the first day of the planting season passed. If successful, his instructions were to bring the girl to a Melani outpost on an island to the northeast.

The inhabitants had special instructions to hold the girl for Shess, and to kill any who accompanied her. The dark-skinned elf could picture Kadeesh's expression when he realized that the tavern served him poisoned wine. A wine that would paralyze him for a full two days, leaving him conscious to enjoy his dismemberment.

Shess twitched his hood up out of habit, no longer needing to shield himself from the sun. His battle with the Seer, that horribly wrong battle that left the dark elf bleeding and unconscious, gave him some of the Seer's powers. Though Shess could not yet cast magical spells, the sun no longer injured him. The days of blistered and peeling skin were over.

He paid a price, of course. Things died when he walked past. Shess noticed it first when he woke up in the forest a few miles from the Seer's tower. The bushes and trees wilted around him, and the moss beneath him was brown and crumbled into dust when he moved. He found it easy enough to follow the trail of wilted vegetation back. The knowledge inside the Seer's tower would have given him the spells he craved, as it had given the silver-haired elf Krys the knowledge he needed, but the white tower was sealed up tight.

He gave up after two days, recognizing that the Seer refused to leave the tower and knew of his presence besides. Instead, he returned to Nerryon, sending out messages and putting the rest of his plans into motion.

Hunger struck the Melani elf like a physical pain. He shook for a moment, grasping the wall nearby, and then hurried to a special section of town. It took Shess only a few minutes to find a willing woman, this one brown-haired like Anne. They rented a shabby room at a small inn nearby, one of many couples to stay for just a few hours time.

The slight movement of the bedbugs within the horse hair-stuffed mattress slowed as he ate his fill of fast-withering fruit. He smiled, knowing they would die before biting. The nameless girl smiled as she lifted her skirts.

The dark-skinned elf threw her down on the bed, and then removed her chemise in one motion. The long shirt cleared the girl's head, but left her arms entangled. Shess lay next to her, licking her exposed shoulder. The girl's skin blistered and shredded, leaving raw flesh beneath.

The sight of blood excited the Melani. He savagely bit the girl's shoulder and breasts, before moving up to her neck. He bit carefully, enough to make her bleed heavily but not enough to kill her. He felt like leaving this one alive to die slowly over the next few days.

His bloodlust sated, Shess pushed aside her skirts and took care of another need. The girl moaned and twitched. With each stroke, his anger grew. Timbrel stole his purchase, his perfect elven sacrifice. Anne had been the half-elf's dupe, keeping him engaged in sex while the golden-haired girl stole away his prize. When he realized his loss, he returned to the Inn to find Anne gone as well.

He no longer worried about Anne. His new powers from the Seer would heal him of any damage the young assassin could do. She would die slowly, just from being near him. The Melani elf frowned and thrust harder at the hapless girl beneath him, thinking about his ridiculous fear of the child-like woman when he first recognized the symbols on her pendant. His fear drove him to bed Anne far more often than the desirable Timbrel. He had been afraid to say no.

Of course, he counted on Timbrel being controlled by the slave-drug. The golden-haired bitch somehow slipped those bonds. Anne had something to do with it. Perhaps the young assassin gave the dancer an antidote to the drug afterward, though that never changed the outcome before. When he next saw Anne, he would kill her slowly.

Shess fantasized the different ways he could kill Anne, getting more elaborate with each stroke. When he thought of the perfect death, his body released in a paroxysm of pain and pleasure. The nameless girl beneath him screamed in pain, and then lapsed into unconsciousness. He withdrew from her, blood spatters adding to the collection of stains on the mattress. The skin of her chest blistered where he had touched her. He felt energized and ready for anything. Leaving a copper chit on the small table in the room, he left without a word.

A message waited for him when he returned to the Inn. He glanced at the signature: Kadeesh. The message was longer than he expected, but made him smile. Timbrel had been found and captured, on her way now to the outpost island.

Shess twisted his lips in a sneer. His plans set in motion, the girl waiting for him. He wrote a quick message to his agent at the outpost, outlining the training he expected the girl to be given. Given the hard way, he thought, since she resisted the drug. She should be encouraged to dance. He nodded to himself, completing his instructions. Within the hour, a fast hawk winged its way to the outpost. With any luck, it would arrive before Kadeesh. Shess felt lucky indeed.

###

## The Melani Island

Timbrel's new captors carried her into a large stone building. She lost track of the twists and turns, only keeping a general sense of moving downward. The last door opened into a subterranean plaza, barely lit with green glowing moss growing on the stone pillars that supported the roof of the chamber. Warriors moved about restlessly, challenging the priests who carried her. When the warriors moved aside, the priests carried the girl down along a wide flight of stone stairs into a lower chamber.

The glow was dimmer here, the moss unable to grow on the lower, metal-clad portions of the pillars. A series of cages stood along the floor, widely separated from each other. They threw Timbrel roughly into the fourth cage, her arm scraping on the floor, then tossed her pack into a cabinet about twenty feet away. The girl froze in horror. She thought the faint light glittered along dozens of metal instruments when the cabinet opened. Sharp and pointed metal instruments.

Two of the Melani elves returned to the staircase, vanishing in the darkness above. The third locked the cage with a large key. He stood staring at Timbrel for almost ten minutes. Timbrel remained still for as long as she could, then glanced around her cage and up at the lock. As soon as she did, the dark-skinned elf stepped back, chanted, and waved his arms about in a complicated pattern. More complicated than anything Timbrel had seen Krys use. With a satisfied look, he turned and vanished up the stairs.

Timbrel was worried. The Melani had cast some sort of a spell. Her belly cramped, but was it from magic or severe hunger? Warily, the half-elf sat in the center of her cage and squinted hard. A faint greenish glow clung along the bars and lock of her cage. Opening her eyes wider, the girl tried to convince herself that the faint green might just be a reflection of the glowing moss. But what if she was wrong? Could it harm her?

Remaining at the center of her cage, her eyes slowly adjusted. A human warrior in the next cage periodically shook the bars. The man wore no armor, just torn quilted padding on his chest and back. He paced back and forth like a caged bear, his hair and beard as black as the beast's fur.

The cage beyond held two elves of a sort Timbrel had not seen before. Short as humans, the two elves had a stocky build and exaggerated elven features with longer than average ears that came to a much sharper point than usual. One of them stared in the girl's direction. His eyes shone golden in the dim light.

Timbrel hurriedly looked away. The other cages appeared empty of life, though some held heaps of rags and other trash. Bored with her captivity, Timbrel stretched and twisted her body. Already she moved more flexibly than her first attempts on the boat, but she was not satisfied.

Her stretching led to some simple dance moves, repeated over and over. The girl could feel her muscles protesting, but continued until the haze of discomfort receded into a near meditation. In her mind the cage disappeared and she danced on the sand of a wonderfully quiet lakeshore. She smoothly moved across the shore, avoiding the lapping water.

A cold splash soaked her to the skin, bringing Timbrel back to reality. A Melani elf stood to one side, an empty bucket dangling from his hand. "Bath," he croaked out in poorly pronounced elven, then hunched over in racking spasms. It took Timbrel a moment to realize that he laughed at her. She stomped her foot in anger.

"Let me out of this cage," she demanded. The Melani laughed again. "You have no right to keep me captive."

The Melani looked up, grinning. "You not captive."

"Then let me out of here."

The hunching laughter began again. When the dark elf regained control, his grin widened. "You not captive, you *slave*."

Timbrel stood tall, her face tilted slightly upward. She did not realize how much she resembled her cousin Lostaria at that moment. "I am no slave," she pronounced. "*Only* a captive." She turned her back on the staring elf.

His laughter effectively stilled, the Melani muttered to himself as he moved to the next cage. Timbrel did not recognize the language. She sat down in the middle of her cage, watching the Melani's progress. As he passed the human, he stopped to throw small stones at the man. His diversion quickly ended when the canny warrior caught the stones instead of dodging and pelted him back with a few well-aimed shots. Bleeding from his forehead, the dark-skinned elf ignored the other cages and moved up the stairs.

Timbrel clapped her hands, acknowledging the man's victory. He bowed to her, and then flexed his arms in the air. When he spoke, Timbrel understood enough from his tone of voice to realize he thanked her, even though the words were strange.

"You're welcome," she answered. The man bowed again, and then returned to his pacing.

### 

*Rockhold*

Krys was exploring caves near the base of the western wall when he noticed something strange. The walls of the cave gave way to a regular smoothness, and then ended in a door. Krys could see a tiny lock-box next to it.

*Nayev, I found something.* The elf still found it strange to speak mentally when in dragon form, though he got steadily better with practice. This time he only moved his scaly lips.

Nayev peered into the cavern opening, his head blocking the rest of the sunlight. *Interesting. Are you ready to shift back?*

*I am. What do I do?*

*Build your power carefully, and then let go of yourself. Shifting is easier as you become used to each body.* Nayev withdrew, leaving the wizard-elf space for his spell.

Krys felt the power build within him. When he could barely restrain it, he allowed the shift. The agony began swiftly, but ended almost immediately. At first Krys thought that the shift failed. He wiped the sweat from his face, and then steeled himself to try again. Shaking the sweat from his hand, he drew a deep breath.

328

And let it out. His hands, the fingernails a bit dirty and ragged, were elven. He had returned to his original form. A moment later Nayev walked into the cavern, whistling. The cavern-mouth seemed smaller than Krys expected. A large rock flow nearby blocked the entrance. He didn't remember seeing it before.

"You might want to do your shifting outdoors," suggested Nayev. "The extra mass has to go somewhere."

Krys happily discovered that he could still hear Nayev in his mind, at least when he concentrated. It could be a useful trick to speak between minds in an emergency. The elf looked up to see Nayev inspecting the lock-plate.

"What do you make of this?" Nayev tapped at the keys, but the box remained stubbornly silent.

Krys leaned forward, staring at the box and trying to remember the sequence that worked for the tube room. He punched the symbols carefully. As he hit the last, the box creaked and screeched. After a moment, the lock clicked. "Override complete," squawked the box.

The two wizards pulled the door open. Nayev jammed a small rock into the hinges to keep it from closing. The room inside was small, with a single bench placed before a wall covered with lights, dials, and small squares with symbols. Krys found himself drawn to the wall

"Krys, what are you doing?" Nayev's hand on his shoulder pulled Krys back from the wall. The elf jerked his hands back from turning dials and touching symbols.

"I am not certain. Just trying to see what it does." Krys was mortified. He knew better than to carelessly touch Hinjin artifacts.

The sound of ten thousand bees vibrated in the air, startling both wizards. Krys tried punching buttons, hoping to make the noise stop. It lessened in volume, allowing the two wizards to speak. At the same time, a gray square on the wall turned black. A small green light lit beneath the blackness. Krys pulled his hands away again. What was he doing?

"We need to get out of here." Panic edged the elf's voice.

"I agree," said Nayev, backing toward the door. "This isn't helping us find Timbrel. We'll fly a search pattern to the east. After that, I don't know where we can look."

"Nayev, what if she is in trouble?"

"I don't know, Krys. I just know I have to keep looking."

The black square made a crackling sound and flashed momentarily white. Krys stumbled backward, closing the door as the square started to speak.

"Say again? Over."

The closing door cut off the sound. Nayev and Krys looked at each other for a moment.

"Let's try that search pattern, Nayev."

The human-looking wizard agreed, powdering stone and reforming it to seamlessly cover the doorway before smoothly shifting to dragon form. Krys staggered with exhaustion when he tried to gather power to do the same, finally consenting to climb on Nayev's back. The ridges on the saddle-shaped scale stuck up uncomfortably, but the search was important. Besides, Krys was certain that Nayev recognized the voice from the black square. Unfortunately, the elven wizard did not know if the voice was from a friend or an enemy.

### 

*The White Tower*

The Seer sat at his screen, trying to bring back the momentary contact with no success. Gowell heard the voice of the elf Krys speaking about a search, and the other voice–Nayev–mentioning Timbrel. Was Timbrel missing?

Gowell remembered the girl well. After all his years of loneliness, she seemed able to understand much of what he said. Her very presence helped him to focus his thoughts. She returned a measure of sanity to him after his long solitude.

The Terformin searched for signs of the girl, flipping images through his screen. He scanned images from a few days before, looking for signs of the girl. She had been missing for several days, he realized. Krys and Nayev climbed outside the caldera, searching through caves.

Gowell set his screen to scan, randomly checking the areas outside the caldera. With no sign of Timbrel, the Seer found himself stopping on one image to stare. A huge dragon, the shape of the legendary watchers, flew over the same area.

He leaned back, remembering when news of the watchers had been broadcast to the habitats. A Terformin, homesick for the land of his birth, managed to return in spite of the ban. The watchers attacked, driving him back into space. The man lived long enough to broadcast his warning before dying of his injuries. Many of the Terformin considered the report an elaborate hoax.

Gowell believed the warning. The rich paid well to stock their private lands with exotic creatures. Before volunteering for the retrovirus that made him eligible to explore space, he designed quite a few such creatures himself. If only he hadn't tried to modify himself. His personal retrovirus mutated with unintended side effects.

He reversed the satellite image on the screen. The dragon flew backwards, landing in a reverse leap, and melted into a man. A man? Gowell stared at the image, understanding breaking through. The watcher-dragons were shifters, just as Gowell had been when he first started to explore the nearer portions of space. Where Gowell's shifting ability was designed to make him immune to most types of radiation, the dragon-watchers ability must have been designed to hide them from casual observation. An excellent way to spy.

Gowell concentrated on his screen again, the images randomly flickering. A woman staggering in the streets caught his attention. The image came from Nerryon. The dark-haired woman seemed ill, unable to keep her feet. Her skin was split and running blood from multiple sores.

Ready to write a plague warning for his local village, Gowell remembered that he had no messenger at hand. He also remembered something else. The woman's sores looked like the illness that his own condition brought on others. It had taken only one visitor's death before the Seer refused all helpers. He did not wish to see another die the same way through his own carelessness.

The woman slumped to the ground, her neck lolling to the side. Gowell stared with horror. Someone with his own condition bit the woman. Who else carried his retrovirus? He had been careful not to spill blood near his elven visitors.

Spilled blood. The dark-skinned elf that challenged him spilled blood. Both of them spilled blood. Gowell remembered flashes of the battle, the two of them wrestling after their blades broke. Wrestling in the blood. His thoughts began to take the familiar sing-song pattern, but he fought against it.

Gowell focused on his screen. He needed to locate two now. Timbrel, who might have mated with his son Gareth, and the dark-skinned elf who spread destruction in his wake. He tried to locate earlier images, hoping the system had not yet erased them.

### 

*The Melani Island Outpost*

The half-elf glanced over to the next cage. It remained empty. The human warrior had been taken from his cage two nights before and not returned. Timbrel ate her single meal of the day and slept heavily.

After she woke, Timbrel stared at a dark-skinned elf woman through narrowed eyes. The dancer stood defiantly tall in the center of her cage. The woman outside waited impatiently.

"You learn to speak properly," the woman said haltingly in elvish. "You no eat you no speak." The woman broke into a slow sentence in her own tongue, pointing to objects as she did so. She then translated, again pointing at objects.

The half-elf spat through the bars of her cage, coming dangerously close to their magic. She still refused to touch them, uncertain what spell clung to the bars and lock. "I will not speak your filthy tongue."

332

The Melani woman shrugged, the human gesture seeming natural to her. "You must be prepare. You speak, you eat. *He* say." She pointed to a small sign mounted on the bars of Timbrel's cage.

The dancer had been unable to see any words on the sign when it first appeared the day before. Based on the metallic taste in her mouth, she suspected that they had drugged her food or water before putting the sign up. "What does the sign say? Who is *he*?"

"*He* is you owner, the life that returns. The *Ankh*."

"The Ankh?" Timbrel frowned. She had heard the word before, but could not remember where. A scattering of ripe fruits spilled across her cage floor. The dancer looked up.

"Very good. You speak, you eat." The Melani woman smiled, the expression pulling her face into a grimace. Timbrel understood that the expression was supposed to comfort her. She nibbled at the food, alert for signs of drugging. When she looked up, the woman was gone.

Heaving a sigh of relief, Timbrel began her daily workout. Her muscles limbered up a little more each day. The girl felt healthier. Also hungrier. Perhaps it would not be so bad to learn a little of the language. She could certainly use the food.

A pair of Melani warriors walked past. Timbrel shouted out to them in human and elven tongues, but they ignored her. "What does the sign say?" She pleaded as she sunk to the floor of her cage, exhausted.

After an hour or so, Timbrel dragged herself to her feet and checked for guards. She checked her cage for magic again, as well as the next cage. The faint green glimmer of the closest bars mocked her. The other cage showed no such glow, nor did the other empty cages. She sighed heavily, barely able to move. There seemed no point in trying to escape. The lock was simple enough, but the magic frightened her. Why try to escape, if she melted into a sludge of blood and bone when she touched the bars? She remembered Von's gruesome death.

Timbrel began her stretches, her body resisting as though she were standing in water. It almost seemed pointless to dance. Instead, she forced herself to go through the motions, hoping the dance would transport her mind away from the endless darkness. She shifted her hips, slowly turning and stopping to pose, but the music faded from her head and she slowed to a standstill, unable to gather enough energy to spin.

Suddenly angry with herself, she forced herself through the motions again, spinning and leaping. The half-elf found glaring flaws in her performance, flaws magnified by her dark mood. Still driving herself, the dancer worked on her dragon dance. The battered tunic she wore, still stained with the blood of skeletal warriors, took further damage as she fell heavily in her cage, scraping her side across her now-healed stitches. Determined, she stood on the tips of her toes, trying to emulate the hummingbird-like beating of the dragons' wings. The tunic caught at her shoulders, interrupting her balance and precipitating yet another fall.

As she stood up again, the girl angrily tore the tunic from her shoulders and threw it to the ground. In a brief burst of rage, she stomped on the offending bit of cloth, scraping it along the ground and finally hearing a satisfying *rip* before kicking it towards the corner. The tunic hit the bars and fell, draping partially out of the cage. The girl ignored it and continued working herself through her exhaustion.

Finally calm, Timbrel looked across at the tunic. She retrieved it carefully, and then held it at arm's length to inspect it for damage from the cage's magic. Battered and ripped, the fabric appeared reasonably intact. As she shook it out, Timbrel had an idea. A few minutes later she grimly balanced on her toes, flapping the tunic in place of wings. She found that the flapping cloth helped her maintain her balance, but her toes were scraped and sore afterward.

The scuffle of a footstep caught her attention, and the girl quickly dressed in the battered tunic. A moment later, the Melani woman approached her cage.

"It is time for another lesson."

###

*Rockhold*

Nayev scrambled across the western side of the caldera. Traces of Timbrel still eluded him, but he had sealed seven caves with recently used incubators. Krys, exhausted, recovered in Rockhold while Nayev continued the search.

The wizard shifted to human form and slipped into another cave that smelled of the skeletal Terformin. Flickering light in the depths drew his interest. Nayev approached cautiously.

A flickering torch illumined the inside of a bubble-shaped cavern. A Terformin bent over a rough-hewn plank table, dripping blood from its finger into tiny glass tubes. Tubes similar to those near the now-sealed incubators.

The Terformin whirled, a flash of silver in its palm. Nayev threw himself to one side as lightning crackled past and slammed into the curving side of the tunnel. The tunnel collapsed partway, rubble blocking the exit. The wizard darted forward in the dust cloud and slapped the weapon away.

Nayev tilted his head slightly to look at this particular specimen. Unlike the ones he flamed on the inner rim, this one had a wrinkled face with flaps of skin hanging where the nose and ears might have been. It moved with far more purpose as well. The Terformin lunged.

"Left behind," the golden-eyed creature hissed as it waved a surgical knife. "Kneel before me, you ignorant savage."

Nayev's eyebrows rose in surprise. This one spoke, though with a poor accent. Its attitude was poor as well, much like the attitude of the other returning Terformin. These offspring learned fast. It gave the wizard little choice.

"Terformin, we exiled you and your kind. Leave now, or I will kill you."

"Exiled? No, we left you behind. You will be the one to die."

The Terformin lunged again. Nayev sidestepped again, flinching as the knife scored a deep line along his leg. Pain flared and the dragon almost lost control of his shape. It would do no good to shift in these confined quarters. Instead, he retreated down the blocked corridor. The Terformin pursued him.

The wizard powdered the blockage almost without thinking, limping backwards down the tunnel. He hobbled out into the open air and stood, his hands against the rock. The skeletal Terformin followed, attacking again as it neared. Nayev sidestepped and triggered the shift.

A heartbeat later the Terformin cringed against the rocks, an angry dragon staring down at it. The dragon snapped at the terrified creature, lifting him bodily from the ground. Bones crunched as the dragon chewed and spat the remains out on the rocks.

*I do not have time for this*, thought Nayev. *There are more caves to search for signs of Timbrel.*

### 

*The White Tower*

Lord Gowell continued his increasingly frantic search for Shess. The dark-skinned elf left a trail of dying women behind him, though the Seer still had not found the infected warrior. Gowell sighed and searched instead for Timbrel. He found some surprising images of the girl standing between dragons and giant spiders, followed by a seeming accord. "No fear, no fear," he muttered to himself. "Should have met her first. No change, then. Never tried to change myself."

His thoughts slid into a daydream of the life they could have led, his black wolf protecting her slight form. The black wolf changed to brown, and he saw again the image that truly endeared the girl to him. The image of her defiance when his son fell. The image of her weeping over Gareth's wolf body. The image of her refusal to give his body to the spiders.

He wondered how she would react when she met his son again. She obviously thought Gareth dead. Gowell smiled to

336

himself. The Shifted were difficult to kill, and always returned to their original form upon death. Gareth must have been surprised to awaken in a makeshift grave.

The Seer studied his screen. The girl's golden hair, darkened with dirt and blood, made a tiny spot on the docks. He enlarged the image and studied it. She walked accompanied by someone else–an elf?–near the end of the floating docks of the caldera city. Two dark-haired men crouched on the deck of a small boat tied up nearby. Further along, two large ships appeared to have normal activity.

The next image of the same area occurred twenty minutes later. There was no sign of the girl. Gowell studied the image in detail. He found her companion–definitely an elf–near the base of the docks, obviously returning to the city. The girl was gone. For that matter, so was the boat. Gowell frowned. The boat left during the intervening few minutes. The two docked ships appeared to have the same level of activity.

She must have gotten on the small boat. Gowell returned to the previous image and enlarged it further, getting a good view of the boat and its visible crew. In the larger image, he could see that the crew held short pieces of rope in their hands as they crouched. The girl left unwillingly.

The Seer dashed about his chamber in anger, battering his fists into the walls. He swept the wolf painting from the control board. It crashed to the ground. He gradually focused again, picked up the painting and returned to the screen. He could look for the boat later. He had to find the infected dark-skinned elf before it caused more deaths.

### 

*The Spider City*

The search for Timbrel had been fruitless. Krys flipped through crumbling documents, gnashing his teeth. The young Spider Rider assigned to assist him in his research scuttled forward. "You need another book?"

Krys looked at the child. Only three small tattoos marked her face, a blue one on the bridge of her nose and two red ones along her hairline. As she gained in training and skills she would earn more. The oldest Riders had tattoos covering their faces, torsos, and even hands. Perhaps other places as well. Krys did not ask.

The wizard Nayev returned to the south, seeking help to find Timbrel. Jherik remained in Rockhold, helping to rebuild the city and waiting for any messages from the girl. Krys used his new dragon form to fly over the Spider Forest, searching for her. When he landed in a clearing and shifted back to his elven form, Stinger found him and invited him to search the archives.

It was a hard decision, but Krys managed to find a dual purpose in accepting. The Spider archives included information on ancient ways of seeing at a distance. Krys did not yet understand the underlying principles, but he thought he might find enough information to create a spell that would allow him to find the girl. Unfortunately, all of the ancient methods seem to involve Hinjin artifacts, or placing some sort of eyes into the sky. Krys wasn't sure how the latter would work, or whose eyes should be used. He needed more information.

Time was running out, though the elf couldn't say why he felt convinced of that. Nayev seemed to feel it too, though the human wizard appeared to have some special connection with the girl. Krys wasn't sure if their exact relationship was romantic. If so, he approved. Timbrel drifted from one short-term relationship to another. Perhaps she sought some form of approval. Nayev might give her that. It was certain that the half-elven girl would never receive that from Soliari.

Soliari. Krys looked up from the ancient book and stared across the room, picturing Timbrel's mother in his mind. As beautiful as her daughter, though more classically elven, Soliari was as embroiled in politics as she was selfish at heart.

Krys remembered falling in love with the elf woman, and the way that Soliari led the brilliant young historian to believe that he could earn his way into her heart. He risked his life for her, searching through ancient ruins that still held traces of deadly magic for the information she craved. Information that would have allowed her political ambitions to flower.

Instead, his information barred her from the royal heritage she craved. She would never forgive him for that, Krys realized, though she blamed her sudden dislike on his attempts at magic. Her heart hardened toward him and she sent him away.

Krys flushed with embarrassment, thinking about the centuries he wasted trying to regain her favor. Her favor ended as soon as his usefulness did. The woman used her beauty as a lure. At least Timbrel was more honest about it.

Honesty. A trait that Timbrel must have learned from her father. Krys chuckled to himself. Soliari spent her entire pregnancy complaining about the thieving bit of a human soldier who did the deed. Timbrel's conception was one of the last acts of war before the cease-fire between the humans and the elves. An entire human generation passed since then, and most of them forgot the war and its causes. To the elves it was a mere eyeblink. The elves still considered Timbrel a child of sorts, her thirty-one years far too young to make major decisions.

Soliari, only a year younger than Krys, made her first play to influence the Council by the same age. She was not eligible to sit because of her royal bloodlines, even without the damning information Krys found, but she laid the groundwork early. She and Von's Master Celiar had done their best to influence the Council, though they had not been very subtle at the time. She learned subtlety over the years.

Krys grimaced again. Soliari threaded her fingers through the entire Council. Even the Voice had not been immune to her manipulations, though Marahir obviously did not approve. The councilman's actions convinced Krys of that.

Lostaria's kidnapping showed an entirely new side of Soliari, as did the reports from the elven warriors of her Regency.

Leave it to the woman to find the only way she could satisfy her craving to rule. It would not be much fun for Soliari when Lostaria returned. When Krys eventually returned, Soliari would find life even more difficult. He would have a final answer from her. Lostaria granted him high enough status that Soliari could not use it as an excuse to avoid the wizard. Is she truly magic-shy? Or was she secretly a Yarite?

###

# Chapter Fourteen

*The White Tower*

The Seer paced the length of his chamber, giggling. He thought he found the girl, but where to send her for safety? He giggled again, the madness almost overtaking him. His thoughts took on a high-pitched, singsong quality. Two tasks, two tasks, aw-all one. He found the boat and lost it and found it again. An island in the sea, a small city, everyone a dark-skinned elf but her.

Gowell shook his head, trying to clear his thoughts. They remained singsong in spite of his best efforts. He struggled to keep them coherent.

The girl, the elf, Timbrel. Her captors brought her to an island city. The screen showed it as abandoned, at least during the day. At night it became busy with Melani elves. A single image showed her being carried within the largest building, carried by three of the dark elves. The little boat was tied to the city's docks.

The dark-skinned elf, the infected one, the spreader of death. His trail led to the seaside as well, where he took passage on a larger ship. The disease, the plague, the slow death appeared on board. Bodies fell in the water, bodies heaved by the other sailors. Only a few sailors left, the dark-skinned elf ruling over them somehow. The ship heading for the island.

Two tasks, two tasks, aw-all one. He can reach them both in time if he revealed himself. The Seer paced faster. How could he balance his own life against the others? So far a distance. An easy distance. A few hours travel by shuttle. The shuttle would attract her dragon. If he rescued her, her dragon would be distracted. He might make it back to his tower. She might stop the dragon from killing him. Maybe. Maybe better to go somewhere else and hide.

Gowell struggled with the decision. He wanted to rescue Timbrel. She was nice to him, and to his son. His son wasn't nice to him. Listened to Lashana too often. Worst messenger ever.

Always a distraction. Made him think she wanted to stay. Made him promise to stop the wolf. He stopped the wolf, all right.

The Seer giggled, and staggered across the room in an attempt to control himself. The wolf was better than the hell he created for himself. The Genjin designers knew what they were doing. He only knew a scattering of their easiest techniques. How could he know that the retrovirus would mutate inside him? It never died; he knew that now because he infected the Melani elf. He was lucky that Lashana did not get infected.

For a moment, his mind cleared. Gowell winced at the memory of his first feverish hours, the hours immediately after he injected the new retrovirus. Lashana was supposed to stay away, but she never listened, never understood. All restraint gone, he acted when she teased him, taking what she always promised and then held back from him. He learned of Gareth's birth from the images on his screen. Later, Lashana made the trek to the tower and left him a long letter.

Gowell frowned, his mind clouding again with the shame of his act. At least Gareth was well educated. The Seer left messages to Lashana at the edge of the fields, messages with directions for Gareth's education and the coin to hire the best masters the Seer could learn of. Lashana followed most of the instructions, though she never brought Gareth to the tower. Perhaps she never told him about his father?

"No! Never!" The Seer whispered to himself, giggling his words. With an effort, he forced his mind to focus. He was going to rescue her. Going to rescue the nice girl. Rescue Timbrel.

Must hide from the dragon. Play the game, play hide-and-go-seek. If he went *here* and the dragon went *there*. Gowell thought for a moment. It could work. If the dragon went somewhere else, he wouldn't be seen. Where could he send the dragon? And how to trick it into going there?

The dragon-man, the dragon-man, waiting for the gi-irl. The singsong voice began again, giving Gowell the clues he needed. Tell him Timbrel will be there, make him wait for her. Gowell changed his screen to a map of the continent, and then chose a hook-like beach far to the south. He noted the distinctive rock formations nearby, and carefully composed his message. The communicator brought the dragon to the caldera; it would bring the same dragon to the curving stretch of beach. Far out of the shuttle's path. He could remain unseen.

The Seer sent his message quickly, barely finishing before the singsong voice started again. He stopped in horror. He had forgotten. How could he deliver the girl to the beach without being seen? He needed to find a go-between. Gowell hunched over his screen, flipping through images. The shuttle could leave right after the dragon arrived at the beach. He only had a few hours to find and contact someone the girl would trust.

### 

*The Melani Island*

Timbrel missed the sunlight and open spaces of the world above. Without freedom, she had so little energy it became hard to dance. Only the memory of the dragons dancing in the skies kept her trying. She felt no joy in the dance, only a faint yearning.

She had become adept at understanding the Melani tongue over the endless weeks, a fact she tried to keep hidden from her teacher with purposeful blunders. Twice she woke from dreaming in the new language, sick to her stomach with fear that she would become like the dark-skinned elves around her. In one dream, she ordered the Melani around like Soliari.

Two warriors walked past, discussing the impending arrival of the Life-bringer. One glanced at Timbrel's cage and nudged his friend.

"He doesn't need to bring the sacrifice with him, it is waiting there to be his bride."

"Hush. You know the penalties for talking about it. What if the sacrifice hears us?" He looked directly at Timbrel's cage before looking back at his friend.

Timbrel gave no sign of understanding.

"There's no danger of that. Merana fears punishment because the sacrifice isn't learning the tongue fast enough. It cannot understand the spoken word. Can you imagine how upset the Life-bringer will be if it forces him to address it in another tongue?" The two continued past, their voices fading into the darkness.

Once they left, Timbrel sat up hurriedly. She was being groomed to be a *bride*? She frowned. She would never willingly marry any of these people. She wouldn't marry anyone from any people. Well, maybe Nayev. If he asked her.

At the thought of the young wizard, Timbrel felt a small glow inside. She enjoyed being near him, even his dragon form. If only she knew how he felt about her.

Not that it mattered. She would never see daylight again. She was trapped in this darkness, destined to be in a magic-infused cage the rest of her life. If they ever made the mistake of letting her out, she'd run away. They would have to kill her to keep her. Or leave her caged, but that was already killing her. Timbrel finally admitted it. This captivity affected her like a long illness, sapping her strength and her will to live. It would be better to die quickly than to linger like this.

A scuffling noise on the stone alerted her to the arrival of her teacher. Merana, the warriors called her. The Melani woman approached a cage with a bucket and a bundle of cloth.

"You will wash yourself," she instructed Timbrel in the Melani tongue. Timbrel's eyes narrowed. She disliked the woman's tone of command. Merana placed the bucket between the bars of the cage and pushed it inside.

Timbrel cautiously approached the bucket, wary of the leather lash Merana used to punish her in the last few days. She glanced at the foamy water within, disliking its sharp scent. In perfect Melani, Timbrel replied. "I think not, Merana." The half-elf kicked the bucket over, splattering Merana with the contents.

Merana stood frozen. Timbrel use the words of a superior instructing an underling, a far stronger tone than Merana used.

After a moment, the Melani woman held the bundle of cloth towards Timbrel.

"The... The Life-bringer asks that you wear this to meet with him." Merana used a servile tone. The woman's behavior underwent a shift as well. Merana practically crawled.

Timbrel kicked at the bundle. It unrolled to reveal a dark silk dress, cut to leave the shoulders and much of the bosom bare. Timbrel lifted her head and stared at Marana. "I don't like it."

Merana scuttled backward toward the cabinet. "The Life-bringer insists. I must follow his instructions over yours, Lady." Merana's inflection implied an extremely high rank.

Timbrel wrinkled her nose. "I don't like it," she repeated.

Merana, a panicked look on her face, opened the cabinet and removed Timbrel's pack. Rummaging inside, she pulled out Timbrel's traveling clothes. Turning back to the cabinet, the Melani woman chose a short knife and ran it along the length of the skirt. The knife sliced cleanly through the fabric. Merana continued, never looking up from her task, until the entire outfit lay shredded in fingerwidth strips.

"The Life-bringer insists that you wear the dress he has chosen." Merana did not look up.

The half-elf was furious. "I will not."

Merana flinched with each word Timbrel spoke. She pulled Timbrel's blue dance skirt out of the pack next. Again she shredded the cloth, the silk resisting the knife blade slightly.

Timbrel's eyes widened. There were only two more sets of clothing in her pack, one the blue dress she wore in Rockhold when she danced with Nayev, the other a golden silk dance outfit that she bought immediately before the war in Rockhold. It had never been worn. It was the outfit Timbrel dreamed of for the dragon dance.

Timbrel sighed. The mysterious Life-bringer won this battle. "I will wear his choice of dress. I suppose it is marginally better than this rag." Timbrel waved at her shredded and stained tunic, adding as much boredom to the gesture and her voice as she could summon. Merana looked profoundly grateful.

345

Still refusing to wash, Timbrel slipped into the dress. At one time it would have fit her perfectly. Now she had lost so much weight that it hung on her like a sack. Or would have, if there had been shoulders in the dress. Instead it dropped to the floor, a pile of fabric around her ankles. With no other way to adjust the dress for a better fit, Timbrel finally resorted to asking Merana for one of the blue strips from her shredded dance skirt. The half-elf carefully knotted the center of the strip to the front of the dress, keeping the final knot inward. She tied the two ends of the strip behind her neck to support the dress.

Unable to hide the horrified look from her face, Merana fled into the darkness.

Timbrel smiled with momentary pleasure at the woman's clear fear. Suddenly disgusted, Timbrel mentally berated herself for the moment of pleasure. The half-elven girl could not understand why she was changing into such a horrible person, or how to stop the process.

A sound from above drew the girl's attention. Warriors marched in step, as though in a parade of some sort. The noise grew closer.

Four lines of Melani warriors in full armor descended the stairs, several with flags hanging from their spears. A single warrior in elaborate armor descended at the center of the group. The lines of warriors formed a square around him.

He dismissed them sharply; his words and tone revealing a person of extremely high stature. This must be the Life-bringer, Timbrel thought. Few males had such a high status. The warrior approached her cage.

Merana groveled, ducking so low she left blood on the floor from scraping her knees. The pile of shredded cloth remained by the cabinet. The warrior glanced at it and back it Merana. The woman paled slightly, scuttled to the pile, and gathered scraps.

Timbrel stood at her full height, her head tilted back slightly. She lifted a single eyebrow as the warrior unlocked and entered her cage. He stopped just inside the door, turning his back on Timbrel to close it and then removing his helmet.

"You are dismissed," he called out. The warriors turned and marched back up the stairs, still in formation.

Timbrel stared at the Life-bringer's back, wishing him ill. Merana scuttled away again, leaving the two alone. Timbrel's disapproval was evident on her face. If only her captor would turn around and see it.

As though reading her mind, the warrior turned. Timbrel's face went slack with astonishment. "You."

The warrior gave a sneering smile in return. "Greetings, Timbrel," Ankh Shess said. "You make a lovely bride."

### 

Timbrel woke on the floor of her cage, her left shoulder stinging. The dark silk of her dress rustled as she pushed herself to her knees. The girl thrashed about, feeling claustrophobic in the dress. She shakily stood, untying the blue strip that held the dress up, and allowing it puddle around her ankles. She stepped carefully out with one foot, and then kicked the dress savagely toward the bars with her other foot.

The shreds of her tunic still lay on the floor. The Melani elf had used it to cushion his armor. Several new tears dotted the worn fabric, but the girl put it back on. It was perhaps the only thing she still had control over.

The half-elf gently probed the wound on her shoulder. Shess bit her again, and the skin around the bite blistered and peeled. Some of the skin fell away at her touch, revealing an oozing red sore beneath. She would *kill* Shess for this.

A wave of vertigo hit. Timbrel wobbled and jerked her hands back from the bars. She had nearly touched them to steady herself. The world stabilized again, but not before Timbrel saw Merana.

Or what was left of her. The Melani woman lay crumpled on the ground, one arm still touching the last of the clothing strips. Blisters covered the woman's face and shreds of skin hung from

347

her features. Timbrel turned away, unable to look at the horror. Shess should have killed the woman cleanly.

Her anger sparked again. Timbrel tried to remember the dark-skinned elf's short visit. When Shess first revealed himself, Timbrel stepped back in fear. Her legs felt boneless and she sank to the ground. She lay there, understanding that she was nothing more than a sacrifice to the Melani, expecting to die. Everything seemed so pointless. Why trade one death for another?

"Do what you must," she whispered. She could not say afterwards what language she used. The dark-skinned elf touched her hair gently, brushing it aside from her shoulder. He kissed her left shoulder, a kiss that burned with pain, then bit deeply. Blood welled, and Shess sucked at it greedily.

Even through the pain the girl could not manage the energy to move. She silently accepted death, waiting for its final touch. The Melani moved her hair again, and then froze when he recognized the strip of blue that supported the dress. The warrior screamed Merana's name, striking the woman to the floor with his gloved fist.

"You were supposed to encourage her to dance, not prevent it!" After beating the woman until her blood spilled across the floor, the warrior removed his glove. "You deserve to die slowly." He touched his hand to the damaged face, raising horrible blisters. Timbrel's consciousness faded slowly. Her last thought had been to welcome death.

Timbrel's eyes narrowed. The dark elf should have killed them *both* cleanly. Instead, the damned Melani let her live, feeding off of her like a leech. She tossed her head, small pieces of hair flying up in a cloud. Curious, Timbrel inspected her hair. Some of the cleanest strands were damaged, dried out and broken by the Melani's touch. The dirt coating the rest had taken on an odd hue, crumbling beneath her fingers.

Her mind finally began to work. Timbrel looked again at Merana's body and her own shoulder. Dry and cracked, the edges of the wounds oozed blood. Bleeding like Timbrel's lips after she kissed the Seer.

A sudden surge of concern for Lord Gowell swept through her. The girl had seen the Melani elf fight, and could only imagine the tortures Shess put the Terformin Seer through while wringing his secrets from him. Somehow the Melani had caught the Seer's curse like a disease. Surely Shess did not mean to give it to her as well.

Alarmed, the half-elf tried to plan for the next visit. She would not willingly embrace death, or worse than death, at the hands of the Melani. She would fight for her freedom.

No sooner did Timbrel make the decision to resist than a Melani woman, this one much older than Merana, shuffled out of the darkness. "You are to ready yourself for *him*."

Timbrel looked at the woman in disbelief. "What will you do if I refuse? Die like Merana?" The half-elf gestured at Merana's body.

The woman staggered backward, hands covering her mouth. She turned and fled into the darkness.

Timbrel grinned, finally in control of her situation. The grin faded when she spotted the basket of food near the cabinet. She was suddenly conscious of hunger, the first she felt in weeks. Hunger for food that remained out of reach.

Sounds from above echoed down the stairs, followed by Shess and his marching warriors. The dark-skinned elf dismissed them a second time, moving directly to Timbrel's cage. He wore embroidered silk today, rather than his armor. She stood defiantly in her rags, arms folded across her chest.

"Go away, Shess. I haven't eaten yet." She used the tones of the superior speaking to a slave.

The Melani elf jerked his head back in surprise. He glanced around, finally focusing on the basket. The warrior lifted a large round apple from the pile and carried it to the girl's cage. He proferred it through the bars.

Timbrel looked down at the withered fruit and wrinkled her nose rudely. "That one is unacceptable. Remove it!" Her voice cracked out like a whip, sending Shess into a half-turn.

Abruptly, the Melani turned back to her, hatred gleaming in his eyes. He dropped the apple on the floor and touched the hilt of his sword. "You anger me, Timbrel." His words emphasized their equality.

"You disgust me." The girl tried to goad him further. She'd rather die quickly than be cursed to live without touching. She saw the fruit wither in his hand.

Shess started forward, drawing his blade. He hesitated, and then threw the sword to one side, followed by his other. "You won't get away from me so easily, girl."

Timbrel backed away from the door of her cage, careful not to touch the bars. Shess unlocked it, entering and closing the door behind him. Timbrel noticed that he did not lock it in place. When the warrior reached the center of the cage, the girl ran forward and struck.

Ducking his extended hand, Timbrel spun in a dance move as she passed him, lashing out with one leg. Her foot slammed into his solar plexus, and her leg extended an additional six inches. Shess went down on the cage floor, gasping.

Timbrel grabbed the dark silk dress of the night before and used it to shield her hands as she pushed the cage door open and leapt to the ground. She ran into the darkness, quickly surrounded by more armored warriors.

"Do not injure her. That is *my* privilege." Shess' voice called out from the darkness behind her.

Timbrel struggled against the warriors, but they quickly overwhelmed her. She bit savagely at a restraining arm. A blow struck the side of her head. Pain sparkled and blackness raced across her vision.

### 

*The Spider City archives*

Krys struggled to interpret the ancient tome. The young rider assisting him paced between stacks, unable to help. The text was unreadable, with too many unfamiliar words. What were a 'satellite', a 'photograph', and an 'infra-red image'? A 'spy camera' might be a floating eye, he thought, but what did 'Star Wars' have to do with it? The historian thought the last phrase referred to a battle between the distant stars, but it made no sense in the midst of a tome about locating far objects. The elf closed the tome in disgust.

Another dead-end. Last week his researches had stalled at the Hinjin recommendation of using a 'computer' to find a 'cell phone' and 'trace' the 'signal'. How could a prison-sound assist in locating someone? And Timbrel would not likely set up flags and pennons to be followed. Krys did not believe she left voluntarily.

Frustrated, he prowled between the stacks of the huge archives. The young rider scurried about, sampling books from each stack in an effort to help his researches. She had been very useful in finding books and tomes that pertained to the subject; it was Krys that could not interpret them.

"Krys." The voice called the elf from the distance. He turned to locate its source.

"Krys." The voice seemed clearer, and somewhat familiar. The elf peered around. He did not see anyone in the archives except the Rider girl and himself.

"Krys." The insistent voice filled his thoughts. His thoughts?

The elf leaned against a stack of books and frowned in concentration. *Nayev?*

*Who else? I've received a message with a location for Timbrel.*

*Where?* Krys' head pounded, still not used to communicating by thought.

*If the message is accurate, she will be in Sandy hook within the week. I'm going to investigate the area.* Nayev seemed eager. Too eager, perhaps.

*Who sent the message?* Krys asked, suspicious.

*I believe it is the same one who told me of the trouble in Rockhold. I trust the voice.*

*Be careful. It may be a trap.*

*You sound like an elder dragon. I fly. We will visit you soon.* Nayev's mind voice suddenly silenced.

Krys staggered from the stack. His head pounded. Why did talking with the young dragon exhaust him more than shifting forms did? He waved to his assistant and gave her their signal to end the day's work. The young Spider-Rider scampered to his side, assisting the elf to his assigned quarters.

### 

*The White Tower*

Gowell checked his screens a final time before keying in the final sequence. The shuttle's engines roared into life, sending plumes of dust and smoke into the sky as the tiny ship carefully lifted from its hidden cradle. Once clear of the ground, the mad Seer piloted the tiny ship to the east, flying low to the ground and avoiding populated areas. It would take several hours to arrive at the island, and he hoped to land well after sunrise. The settlement would be deserted. The Terformin had no plan yet as to how to find the girl in what promised to be a large underground complex. Besides, he had to find and stop the infected dark elf before the creature learned how to spread the disease any further.

### 

*The Melani Island*

Timbrel woke again on the floor of her cage, her right shoulder sore and oozing blood. Damn Shess, feeding off of her like any number of parasites. Her foot stung as well. Apparently clothing didn't shield her completely from the blistering effects of his touch.

The basket of food leaned against the side of her cage now. Timbrel carefully put her hand between the bars and tried to reach

352

it. Her fingertips just brushed the topmost apple, sending it rolling down and out of reach. Her shoulder hovered a fingerswidth from the bars. Holding her breath, the half-elf pulled her arm carefully back into the cage.

The room seemed dimmer than usual. Shess' presence had withered some of the glowing moss. The girl stared out into the darkness, barely able to see the next cage. At least her left shoulder started to heal, though the itch maddened her.

A female voice protested in the distance, followed by scuffling noises and male laughter. A few minutes later a Melani girl stumbled towards Timbrel's cage, barely able to keep her feet. This one was much younger than Merana, in her teens. She wore threadbare fiber clothing, almost like worn out homespun. Timbrel felt sorry for her.

The Melani girl pouted and glanced back into the darkness. Laughter floated back. Timbrel grew irritated at the hidden men.

"Silence!" The dancer's voice cracked out like thunder. The Melani girl turned a shade paler and wobbled on her feet. The laughter died immediately, followed by the sound of receding footsteps. Timbrel stared after the sound. More footsteps left.

Glancing back at the servant girl, Timbrel frowned. The Melani girl was on her knees and shaking. The dancer's voice gentled. "What is wrong?"

The girl shook, too terrified to speak.

"Can you give me an apple?" Timbrel held out her hand. The girl plucked one from the basket and held it up by her fingertips. Timbrel took the offered fruit. "Thank you," she said in elven. The half-elf had learned no such phrase in the Melani tongue.

"Do... do you require another apple?" The servant's voice shook, but Timbrel understood the words. The young Melani woman's word endings indicated an extremely low status. Timbrel frowned again. Merana led her to believe that only men could occupy such a low level. Women were generally treated much better. How was Shess somehow an exception to the rule?

"Another apple, yes. And your name."

353

The girl reacted as if struck. She scurried backward, and then slowly crept forward to give Timbrel a second piece of fruit. As the dancer took the apple, the girl turned a pleading glance upwards. "Why do you wish to enspell me, Mistress?"

"Enspell you? I cast no spells."

The girl looked visibly relieved. "I am Vanisi," she whispered. She shivered again.

"Vanisi. It is a serviceable name." Timbrel searched for words for a moment but could not find a gentle way to ask. "Explain your status."

The young girl paled again, then knelt on the floor next to the cage and looked down. "My mother committed a great crime, stripping herself and all her issue of all rank."

"And her crime?" Timbrel left the question hanging, observing the girl's reactions.

Vanisi managed to cringe without moving. "She... she dared to love my father."

How could a culture punish such an act? Were men truly so downtrodden here? How did Shess have such power in a place like this? "Why do you not leave?" Timbrel asked. "Go to the surface world and stay. Take a ship and explore."

"The sun is deadly to us. Only the strongest can travel during the day and survive to return. Only the purest are permitted to try. The few that live return with a sacrifice." The girl stopped, glancing up at Timbrel and paling again.

"Go on. I take no offense at your words."

"The Life-bringers return with a sacrifice, and give up the rest of their lives to care for it. It is because you enspell us and suck the life from us."

"Suck the life from you? What do you mean?"

"You have the sun within you. The Life-bringer will wither before his time, his skin turning to wrinkles. His hair is already losing its color. His life will feed your own, letting you live for many lifetimes. His wife and their children will care for you as well. Only by keeping a piece of the sun in our land can we gain the Sun-god's forgiveness and be allowed back upon the surface."

Timbrel frowned. Why would she want to live many lifetimes? Surely six centuries were enough for any elf. An odd thought struck Timbrel. "Does the cold season come to the surface here?"

"The season of white?" The girl shivered. "Yes, and those of us with low status must check the docks every night in spite of the white burning on the ground."

"How many seasons of white pass in a woman's lifetime?" Timbrel asked specifically about women, Merana having told her that men's lives were brutal and short.

Vanisi thought for a moment. "Thirty seasons of white pass in a woman's lifetime. Forty if she is one of the favored."

The half-elf reeled. Forty years for the oldest? Even the humans lived longer than that. Krys said the Melani elves were failed Terformin. Now she understood why.

Marching noises approached from above. "Not again," Timbrel muttered.

Vanisi looked at her strangely. "You do not want the warriors to change their guard on you?"

"I do not want to speak with Shess again."

The Melani girl looked shocked. "You are truly angry at the Life-bringer?"

Timbrel nodded. "Angry enough to attack him yesterday. The results made no difference. I am still here."

"Then it is true. The Life-bringer is injured."

"Injured?" Timbrel was suddenly interested.

"It is said that he required the lives of four men before he could stand yesternight. I did not believe the rumor. This Light-bringer is different from the others. His touch kills. I did not believe anyone could touch him and survive." Vanisi turned worshipful eyes on Timbrel. "If he can be injured, then he can be killed. There are many who wish this cruel Life-bringer stopped. It is not right that he has learned your cruel sun-magics."

Timbrel thought for a few minutes and extended her hand. "Vanisi, touch my hand with a finger. Just for a heartbeat."

355

The Melani girl looked terrified, but touched Timbrel's hand as though it burned her. After a moment, she looked up and touched the dancer's hand again. Her dark-hued finger lay warm against the half-elf's skin.

"I am not dying," she whispered.

Timbrel smiled. "And you will not die because of me or any of my kind. It is Shess who has been cursed to kill with a touch. He even injured me." Timbrel showed her right shoulder to Vanisi.

"He injured you? That is against our laws, to injure a sacrifice. He is no Life-bringer, but a *Khensu*, a death-bringer. I will tell others."

Vanisi retreated into the darkness. "Wait," Timbrel called after her. The girl reappeared. "Can you open the cabinet? I need to be armed when Shess returns tonight."

"I cannot. He will not return tonight. He goes into a week's seclusion to prepare for his anointing. Only then will he take you below as a sacrifice." Before Timbrel could ask another question, the dark-skinned elf girl disappeared from sight.

### 

The camp on the rocky shoreline seemed abandoned. A small green-painted boat rose and fell with the ocean tide, tied to a tree. Its sail was rolled and tied, ready to be freed at a moment's notice. Bits of dry leaf lay along the sail and filled the cockpit of the boat, blown from the heights of the island.

The camp lay an hour more than a half-day's travel from the nearest settlement. A small shelter of overlapping branches nestled between two large stones, covered in windblown leaves. The fire-pit, scooped in a bit of sand at the base of a protruding rock and lined with stones, remained cold. No footprints marred the infrequent patches of sand.

The camp might have been abandoned for a season, but it had only been created three days before. The assassin waited.

356

### 

*Sandy Hook*

Nayev flew ever-larger circles around the hook-shaped spit of land. The area bustled with fishermen, but few swimmers. Twice the young dragon saw dark shadows beneath the water, shadows of fish large enough to swallow some of the fishing boats. The sailors took it in stride, changing their courses slightly to avoid the great fish.

Other sailors waited near the docks, hoping for a place on the next boat. The red and white of their shirts attracted the dragon's eye as he circled. A few sailors traveled the beach searching for valuable shells. He saw no sign of Timbrel.

The voice had described Sandy Hook and its distinctive rock formations in detail. Timbrel was to arrive here. Nayev searched again.

The dragon shifted to his human form, checking the beach and asking about the girl at the various inns clustered near the docks. The sailors made loud comments at the lost young gentleman's expense. Nayev continued searching. It had only been three days.

### 

*The Melani Island*

Gowell turned about, frustrated. He'd been lost in the depths for days. The settlement did not look very large from above, but the underground complex was more extensive than he expected. Avoiding guards, the Seer gained access to a little-used corridor that brought him several levels down. A door snapped shut behind him and locked him in.

Dozens of guards protected the new area that he explored. Just how deep did the complex go? An angular script that bore no resemblance to anything the Terformin had ever seen clearly marked the walls. Overheard conversations were meaningless, the words completely unfamiliar. He ran a fool's errand, trying to rescue the girl. Soon he would need rescue as well. Twice he killed pairs of guards. Both times he heard no alarms. His luck could not last.

A giggle forced its way up, almost escaping. The madness threatened to overtake him again. Gowell felt like a ghost floating along the hallways. Ghostie, ghostie, can't hear, can't understand. The Terformin buried his face in his hands, comforted by the smell of the black leather gloves. His sword was strapped across his back, the sheath ready to release at the slightest twist. He could find his way out if he ever found the girl.

The sound of guards marching in formation drifted through the corridor. Gowell crouched slightly and grasped his hilt, waiting for the inevitable confrontation. Instead, the sound faded. Curious, he traveled the length of the corridor at a quicker speed, bypassing several doors. The corridor opened out on an underground plaza, complete with descending stairs. The Seer ducked back as the marching soldiers returned.

The soldiers marched up the stairs in formation. An officer barked an order and berated the unit after they stopped. Soldiers reformed their lines and began again, marching around the plaza and descending the stairs. Gowell could hear the echo of their feet in a much larger area. He sighed. Another level to search. Timbrel could be at the center of the world by now.

When the soldiers marched away, Gowell slipped out of the corridor's end and descended the stairs. Another plaza stretched before him, metal-sheathed stone pillars supporting the roof. Access doors lined the nearest wall, and he could see a cage of some sort in the distance. He followed the line of doors, spotting one that he recognized as an elevator just before the metal sheathing of the wall ended. The rest of the wall was rough-hewn stone: limestone. The complex had entered a natural cavern system. How far down could it go?

The sound of the marching grew louder and as the soldiers returned. Gowell sprinted along the wall, climbed the stairs, and ducked back into his previous corridor. He started back, exploring doors as he went. There had to be a connection to the lower access doors, if only he could find it.

### 

Timbrel rubbed the last bit of loose skin from her right shoulder. After almost a week, the bite wounds had finally healed. The blisters on her foot healed as well. Vanisi returned twice a day, feeding the half-elf and whispering the latest rumors about the building rebellion against Shess. No longer Ankh Shess to his people, many now called him Khensu Shess, the Death-bringer. His status fell like a stone into the depths. He ruled now by fear alone.

Vanisi held a bucket of soapy water. "You are to prepare yourself. He comes to claim you tonight." She motioned with her hand, pointing into the darkness.

Timbrel tipped the bucket over with her foot. She heard a faint *clink* as it fell. The water ran along the floor of her cage and dripped over the side. A sharpened piece of rusty iron remained inside the bucket. The still-filthy dancer glanced at Vanisi, who busily counted apples. Timbrel slid the makeshift knife with her foot, hiding it beneath the crumpled dress that still lay on the floor where it fell after her last escape attempt.

"He is mistaken," Timbrel replied. "I will not make any efforts for one so low." A gasp sounded from the watchers in the darkness. Timbrel continued her tirade against Shess. "Why should I bother? His touch will wither me and kill me in a matter of days, if it takes that long. If I am to be a withered corpse, why should I make the effort to look beautiful? No, a sacrifice can be beautiful, but there is no such thing as a beautiful corpse."

A low mutter at the darkness rewarded her efforts.

"He does not even arrange for my proper care. He killed Merana, one of sufficient status to prepare me. The second servant ran off and never returned." Timbrel knew that the second woman also died at Shess' touch, a widely circulated fact that Vanisi shared with her. "Instead, I suffer with the ministrations of a classless child. At least the child has observed her betters. I get minimal care, but not through any agency of his. He should be called the Death-bringer, not the Life-bringer."

More mutters echoed in the darkness. Timbrel thought she could pick out four separate voices.

Vanisi stood quietly next to the cage.

"I am sorry, child." Timbrel whispered in elven. She shifted back to the Melani tongue. "The insult was not directed at you."

"I understand. You say what you must." Vanisi looked at her feet for a moment, then back to Timbrel. "After he is gone, will you name me one of your attendants?"

Sadness overwhelmed the half-elf. The dancer did not intend to remain among the Melani. Once she got past Shess, Timbrel planned to find the surface or die trying. Vanisi, of the lowest rank, could not understand the need for freedom. The Melani girl could only aspire to a slavery less harsh. The Seer had been right, Timbrel realized. The opposite of war was not peace. It was slavery.

The darkness beyond suddenly bustled with the noise of many people passing. A faint hooting and honking of instruments warned Timbrel that Shess's ceremony would soon start.

Timbrel looked at the door to her cage. She had stayed within, afraid to touch the cage and its lock for weeks because of the weak magic she thought she saw along the bars. The half-elven girl squinted and looked at the bars. There was no more glimmer to the metal than the dying moss accounted for. Timbrel narrowed her eyes in disgust. When had she given up her war for freedom? Her cage had no magic. She had remained captive for weeks, a slave to her own fear.

In one smooth motion, the dancer swept the makeshift knife from beneath the crumpled silk dress and leapt to the door. Timbrel grasped the bars of the cage with one hand, using the point of the knife to work the lock. It clicked open at the first touch. The door swung wide, an irresistible invitation for Timbrel to leave.

Vanisi stood to one side, the Melani girl's mouth gaping open in surprise. The girl recovered herself as Timbrel jumped down from the cage. "You lied, Timbrel. You lied to me!" Vanisi's shout echoed above the other noises in the darkness. "You *do* have magic. You *elf*!" The girl spat the last word like a curse.

### 

Gowell stood in the end of his corridor, peering out into the darkness. None of the doors reached anything of significance. All these wasted hours, hours he could have used to move elsewhere. Now he was trapped by the crowd massing in the plaza. Soldiers stood in ranks, some stretching their arms against the confinement of the colorful uniforms that replaced their earlier clothing. A group of musicians hooted and honked their instruments, tuning them. A moment later they fell silent. The crowd stilled with them.

In the sudden silence, a woman's voice shouted from below. "Teyena, Timbrel. Teneyena. Alayika, pa *elf*!"

Gowell's head snapped to the right. Timbrel? Elf? The girl must be right down the stairs, in one of the cages.

The musicians honked their instruments, obeying some cue the seer could not observe. The soldiers began their long march around the plaza. Whatever was happening was beginning now. There was no more time.

"No time, no time, run run run." The voices in his head became less sing-song as he sprinted toward the stairs. A pair of guards loomed out of the darkness, blocking his way.

Gowell drew his sword, dodging the guards' weapons and swinging the blade at them as he ran past without stopping. His two-handed sword sliced deeply through the spine of the closer guard with little trouble, and opened the belly of the second. Gowell reversed his swing as he ran, the hilt of his sword tracing a figure eight as he kept the blade in motion.

A shout behind him was followed by pounding feet. In a moment he found himself surrounded by soldiers. His sword cleared a steady path as he strode backwards towards the stairs, slowly descending them by feel.

Among the soldiers hampered by their dress uniforms, many held back just beyond his sword's reach and blocked their fellows. The Terformin swung his sword from side to side. His loose robes stuck to the sweat running down his chest and arms, destroying the cloth's usefulness for deflecting blades. The long hours of fighting against imaginary foes began to pay off. The dark-skinned elves fell back. Gowell descended another two steps.

### 

Timbrel barely jumped out of her cage when Vanisi started to scream and curse. As the dancer turned to run, the Melani girl tackled her from behind. The makeshift knife skittered across the floor. Vanisi wrapped thin arms around the half-elf's ankles. Timbrel fought to free herself, unwilling to kick the younger girl.

The plaza above came alive with noise. Instruments honked, feet tramped, and shouts were followed by the sound of fighting. Vanisi's revolution against Shess must have begun. Timbrel fought harder to escape from the girl's tenacious grip.

The fighting spilled over onto the stairs. Timbrel looked up to see a flood of Melani warriors following a tight knot of battle. The knot centered on one individual, towering a full head above the others. The attackers suddenly backed away, allowing the lone man to descend a few steps.

Fighting broke out in the midst of the warriors as some tried to push their fellows out of the way. The general chaos only helped the lone man make progress.

"Units two and three, descend and flank." Shess' voice cracked above the noise. The Melani soldiers hurried to follow their orders, streaming down the sides of the plaza-spanning stairs and regrouping beneath the lone man. The other soldiers drew back again.

"Vanisi, run. Run for your life. Regain your clan name. Go, up the stairs, to the boats. Go now!" Timbrel wiggled free of

Vanisi, darting toward the chaos. If she could only slip past the soldiers while they were focused on the lone warrior. The dancer watched for an opening.

The lone warrior turned partway. The faint light allowed Timbrel to see the man's profile. An elf.

"They gather behind you," Timbrel shouted in elvish. "Watch out!"

The warrior turned, his sword already in motion. The soldiers in the front rank fell like wheat at harvest. He hit them with such force that the tumbling pieces of their bodies knocked the next rank of soldiers from the stairs.

Timbrel couldn't take her eyes away. The warrior stood, black robes clinging and flexing with the elf's muscles as he swung again. His smooth movements reminded Timbrel of Gareth fighting against the hunters. He wasted no motion; every move aided the warrior by pushing his enemies backward.

A trick of the light allowed the girl to see the warrior's face. She gasped as she recognized Gowell. Movement up the stairs drew her eye away.

The soldiers at the top of the stairs parted in a vee, drawing back to make two columns. The point of the vee moved steadily downward, closing on the Terformin Seer. Shess pulled his swords, the twin blades flashing in the faint light.

The soldiers below Gowell suddenly fell back. Timbrel found herself scrambling from their path, crouching near the cabinet. She worked at the lock, determined to arm herself.

When she glanced up, the character of the battle had changed. Shess and Gowell stood at the base of the stairs, locked in combat, and evenly matched. Gowell's long sword somehow blocked both of Shess' shorter ones while she watched. The soldiers fought among themselves as well, cries of "Ankh" and "Khensu" erupting spontaneously from the battle. Timbrel looked back at the cabinet, her ragged fingernails trying to catch and press the lock's pins. A shout rose, followed by silence. The lock clicked as the last pin fell into place. The cabinet door opened slightly as Timbrel glanced up.

Lord Gowell stood over the body of the dark-skinned elf. Shess' head lay several feet to one side. Gashes in Gowell's robes showed fast-healing flesh beneath, flesh that knit itself together before her eyes. Shess' body twitched. It seemed to shrink in on itself as the half-elf watched. The soldiers closest to Shess' remains edged back.

"Burn it," Gowell muttered in elvish, loud enough for Timbrel to hear. "Burn the remains."

The girl stood, the open cabinet momentarily forgotten. Adopting the most commanding posture and tone that she knew, Timbrel let her voice crack out across the crowd. "The Khensu Shess has brought his own death. Burn the remains of the Death-bringer, and Death will leave this place."

"Burn the Death-bringer! Burn the Death-bringer!" Soldiers took up the cry. They brought in wood and lit torches as the girl watched.

Gowell moved to the girl's side. "Timbrel?" he asked. The Terformin seemed unsure of her identity.

"Of course," she replied in the elven tongue. "Am I so different?"

Gowell did not answer. Tongues of flame licked up from Shess' body, far faster than Timbrel expected. Someone threw the Melani's head on the makeshift pyre.

"Leave now, leave now." Gowell's words came out in a whisper. The Terformin moved toward the metal wall. Timbrel darted back to the cabinet and grabbed her pack, then followed him.

By the time she reached the wall, Gowell stood by an open doorway. The room inside was tiny. Timbrel could easily touch the opposing walls by extending her arms.

"Can't touch, can't touch." Gowell shook his head vigorously. "I will stay, you go. This will take you above." The Terformin touched the wall of the room, then stepped out and held a hand against the doorway.

Timbrel looked at the Seer and laid a hand on his sleeve. "We go together."

364

"You will get sick so close to me. I do not want you to die." Gowell's voice was strained.

"Better to die at the hands of a friend than in the arms of an enemy." Timbrel reached out and tugged at his arm. After a brief hesitation, Gowell joined her.

The tiny room suddenly vibrated. Startled, Timbrel jumped back. Her shoulders smacked into a metal wall. The open door had vanished. Taking a deep breath, the dancer resumed her hold on the Seer's arm. Her fingers stung slightly, but she ignored the sensation.

After a final lurch, the room stopped moving and the doorway reappeared. Timbrel stared in disbelief. Instead of the darkness of the cage room, the doorway opened on sunlit sand and tumbled stones. Timbrel stepped down out of the room. The sand was uncomfortably warm under her feet. A fresh breeze blew past, carrying the scent of the sea. Her eyes stung from reflected sunlight.

Gowell stood to one side, staring at the girl's blistered hand. He raised his golden eyes. "That way. One waits for you." The Terformin gestured along the sand. He turned the opposite direction.

"Wait." Timbrel ran back to the Seer, touching his sleeve. She stood on tiptoe and gave him a quick kiss on the cheek, then stepped back. "Thank you."

"Thank *you*. For myself. For my son." Gowell backed away, gesturing again across the sand. "One waits for you."

Timbrel staggered slowly across the sand. Too much had happened over the last few days. She rubbed her bleeding lips with her good hand, her mind retreating as she trudged across the sand.

###

# Chapter Fifteen

*The Assassin's Camp, Melani Island*

The assassin looked up at the sound of thunder rumbling. The sky was clear. It was the signal she waited for. She would sail at dawn, with or without Timbrel.

Anne busied herself about the camp, cooking fish while she watched the various approaches. The sun sank low in the sky, tinting the clouds blood-red. "Red sky at night, sailor's delight," the young assassin muttered to herself. The weather would be perfect in the morning. She would make good time.

Another phrase nibbled at the back of her mind. "Bloody day done, red the sun." Assassin lore, drilled into her mind since her third birthday. It made her very effective, that early training. That and her small size. Anne had been blessed as well with a youthful appearance, making it easy for her to slip into the retinue of powerful families while doing her work.

She preferred to freelance, picking off slavers and the occasional Melani elf. When she finished this little side job of transporting Timbrel to the docks at Sandy Hook, Anne intended to hunt down Shess. It had taken Gowell almost two hours to convince her to wait until *after* the rescue.

Anne looked up at a movement against the sand. A figure stumbled and staggered into the edge of her camp, dragging a familiar pack. Anne looked on in shock.

"Timbrel?" She finally asked. The figure stopped and looked up, then fell to its knees in a patch of sand. Anne ran to help the half-elf.

The brown-haired assassin would never have recognized the dancer save for the flash of Timbrel's blue eyes. The half-elf's clothes and skin were crusted with dirt and blood, her hair so greasy and matted that its color could not be discerned. Oozing sores covered her lips and her left hand.

The rags she wore hung from her right shoulder, barely covering the breast on that side. A thin strand of cloth reached to the half-elf's waist on the left side, supporting a few shreds that hung across her groin. The back hung in individual strands that looked ready to part at any second.

A pale oval of new skin was visible on Timbrel's left shoulder, and stripes of new skin grew across her back.

Anne felt her anger rise and harden into a knot in her belly, a knot the young assassin would tap for extra energy when she came back on the hunt.

"Shess," Anne growled, focusing her energy.

"The Death-bringer is dead." Timbrel's whispered words in the Melani tongue startled Anne. How long had the half-elf been captive, to speak their tongue so well?

Anne supported Timbrel as far as the fire, settling her on a log before bathing the half-elf's wounds and giving her some baked fish on a broad leaf. As she watched the battered dancer pick at the food, Anne remembered the three years of language lessons in basic Melani. The language was difficult but immensely expressive, reflecting the status of the speakers, their relationship to each other, and their tasks. Timbrel spoke it like a native. A high-status native.

The night grew darker. Timbrel drew her knees up to her chest and wrapped her arms around them, staring out into the darkness. Her blue eyes were red-rimmed and bloodshot.

"You should sleep. We leave in the morning." In spite of their supposedly rivalry, Anne felt a tenderness when she thought of Timbrel. An aftereffect of their shared night with the *likshas* drug, no doubt. Anne didn't mind. The dark-haired girl had developed great respect for Timbrel.

After Shess pushed Anne away and ran to retrieve his purchase, the young assassin understood that Timbrel risked her own freedom by offering to spend time with Shess while her companions rescued the other elf woman. The young assassin smiled. Shess chose her over Timbrel because she left the pendant of her guild showing, a guild the Melani recognized. Timbrel was just as devious.

Avoiding Shess after his return and convincing the Melani that he lost all three women was easy enough. How he recaptured Timbrel remained a mystery. The last Anne heard, Timbrel had been in Rockhold three months ago assisting the healers.

Timbrel's breathing changed, slipping into a soft sighing. The half-elf finally slept. Anne draped a blanket around the dancer's shoulders, protecting her from the night insects. She had no spare clothing on her boat, nothing that would fit the dancer.

An hour before dawn, Anne bolted upright at the half-elf's terrified screams. Timbrel dreamed, twitching and whimpering in pain. The young assassin watched, her anger at the Melani growing. Shess might not be alive, but now that Anne knew where one of their settlements touched the surface, she looked forward to a hunt to end all hunts.

### 

Timbrel woke as the first light of dawn spread across the eastern sky. It took her a moment to remember where she was.

"Good, you're awake." Anne sailed the small boat by herself, using her bare toes and occasionally her teeth to assist in pulling on the rope attached to the small sail while her other hand steered with what looked like a bent oar to Timbrel.

Anne promised four days of sailing, but Timbrel found it hard to keep track. The sea had been reasonably smooth, rolling itself into giant hills of water that the small boat easily climbed, crested, and descended. Not as smooth as the Lady Elizabeth, but nice. Anne was a skilled sailor. Timbrel tried to remember their destination. She thought hard.

"Why are we going to... Sandy Hook?" There. She remembered. And she remembered to speak in the human tongue, as well. A major victory.

"One waits for you there. I am just the delivery service."

Timbrel's blood turned cold. Anne's words reminded her of Arlis' before he turned her over to Kadeesh, and later when Kadeesh turned her over to the Melani. Shess is dead, she reminded herself, dead and burnt. There were other Melani, though. Many more than Timbrel believed possible.

"Who waits?" Her voice faltered. Timbrel discovered that she could still feel terror. Terror that Anne would mention Kadeesh, or the Melani. Even facing the skeletal warriors had not affected her like this.

"I do not know." The younger girl suddenly changed direction, releasing the rope she held and transferring another to her hand. She pulled the new rope, using her teeth to secure it as she repositioned her hand. The single sail flapped loose, and then pulled around behind the mast. The wind filled it and sent the tiny boat off across the tops of the hill-like waves. Anne continued to tighten the sail, avoiding conversation.

Timbrel sat in silence, her mind dwelling on her fears. The last time she saw Anne, the girl went happily upstairs with Shess. For all Timbrel knew, the girl was allied with the Melani.

No, she told herself. She would not allow her fears to stop her again. Her stupidity about the cage taught her a lesson. She needed to remember it.

The dancer looked at the dark water they traveled over. Shapes moved in the depths, shapes she could not make out clearly. No, she told herself fiercely, I will survive this journey. I will escape again, if I need to. I can always escape.

She looked back at Anne. The younger girl felt like a favored human sister to her. Timbrel was torn between her fears and the desire to trust the girl. Anne did nothing wrong except to stand between Timbrel and Shess, frustrating the dancer. There was nothing wrong with that, Timbrel told herself. I could have used someone to stand between us again.

Timbrel scratched idly at her left hand. The new skin itched. She remembered holding Gowell's sleeve as she said goodbye. Her eyes filled with tears. Lord Gowell, the noblest of the Terformin, forever denied the touch of another. His life was

369

tragic, yet he lived on and helped where he could. Gowell helped her find Lostaria, and saved Timbrel herself. She sighed.

If only she could have seen Nayev again. Her brief meetings with the human wizard flashed through her mind. The tavern where they first met when she bought the cheese. Their interrupted dance in Rockhold. Did he know the significance of the *Akeni*, that ancient betrothal dance? His dragon-form, carrying her back to her friends in time to assist Rockhold. Where was her dragon-man now?

The dragon-man. Timbrel froze. What if he were not a man shifting to a dragon, but a dragon shifting to a man? What about the ancient ban between dragons and elves?

Panic built. The one light in her existence, the one thought she clung to throughout her captivity, could Nayev be forbidden to her? The panic crested with the waves and subsided. The little energy Timbrel recovered during the sea-journey washed out of her bones, leaving her lifeless inside. Truly she had nothing left to live for. She even lacked the energy to throw herself into the sea.

Depression crashed down on the girl. She stretched by rote, the motions barely worthwhile. All thoughts of the journey's end lost their meaning. It was inevitable that she would be captured again. How could she have thought otherwise?

Timbrel lay huddled beneath the blanket, wondering why she bothered to protect herself from the sun anymore. It was not worth it. Even the barely heard shouts of others could not break the half-elf's black mood.

The boat bumped against a dock. Timbrel stood at Anne's urging, and shuffled along the dock with her pack. She ignored her surroundings, sitting on the wood and letting the blanket fall from her shoulders. A gust of wind caught the cloth and pinwheeled it from the dock. The blanket landed in the water, floated for a few minutes, and slowly sank. Timbrel watched it expressionlessly.

A few sailors walked past, shying from the dancer. As the sun approached the horizon, the dock became deserted. Timbrel continued to sit, too exhausted mentally and physically to move.

The clouds turned myriad shades of pink and purple behind the setting sun before Timbrel heard the whistling. There was no particular pattern to the notes and no discernible tune. It came closer for some time before Timbrel raised her head to look at the source.

A lone sailor strolled down the beach, his red and white striped shirt stained pink with the setting sun. The golden-haired sailor stopped near Timbrel and squatted. Blue eyes stared into her own.

Timbrel had trouble focusing on the sailor's face. When she did, the energy leaking away from her limbs seemed to hesitate, stop, and reverse its slow path. The ghost of a whisper sounded in her mind. *Timbrel.*

"Nayev?" Her voice came out a cracked whisper, barely audible. "What are you doing here?"

"Looking for you. Are you ready to go?"

Timbrel didn't have the energy to ask about the destination, nor did she care. She could trust Nayev to take care of her. With an immense effort, the half-elf stood and stretched. She followed Nayev down the beach, ignorant of the worried look on the wizard's face.

Nayev stopped at the water's edge and waited for the girl to catch up. When she did, he took her hand and they waded out into waist-deep water.

She looked around, puzzled. "Where is your boat?" She asked, the words difficult to form.

"I don't have one. Just hop on my back." Timbrel took him literally, overbalancing the two of them into the brine.

It took Timbrel a moment to find her feet. The half-elf looked around. A few shorebirds hopped along the sand, poking their beaks deep and occasionally bringing up the squirming delicacy. A small boat floated near the shore, angling toward the shallow part of the beach. She spotted Nayev, swimming away from the beach.

Nayev waved. "Come on, Timbrel."

Uncertain if she had the strength to swim, the dancer pushed off the bottom and followed the wizard. Nayev dove beneath the surface, his feet sticking up momentarily as he sank into the depths. Timbrel tried to float in place. The cold water sapped what little strength she had. Her pack dragged at her.

A sudden swell of water beneath her startled the girl, and she drew her feet in close. Something large passed by underneath her. The wave created by the swell hurtled toward shore, crashing on the sand and swamping the small boat. Sputtering sounded, followed by a stream of human invective nearly hot enough to turn the offending wave into steam.

Something touched Timbrel's leg, rising beneath her. After a vague feeling of alarm, the girl recognized the touch of Nayev's scales. She found the saddle scale and positioned herself.

The dragon continued to rise beneath her, swimming strongly in the water as he lifted her completely free. A few moments later Nayev spread his wings into the air and stroked downward.

Timbrel was nearly thrown from her seat. She grabbed the edge of the next scale and re-seated herself more comfortably on the ridge.

Nayev's wings beat quickly, trying to find enough lift for the dragon to clear the waves. Timbrel would have giggled on a better day; instead, she clung to the scale for stability. It felt like Nayev tried to run on the surface of the water, beating his wings madly. The splashing faded as he rose into the darkening sky.

The wind chilled the girl and the drying salt water added a layer of stickiness to her hair and the rags she wore. She shivered.

*Cold?* Nayev asked, the familiar voice sounding comfortably in her mind.

"No," she replied, though she lied. A moment later the wind turned warm. The warmth, the comfort of Nayev's voice, and the relative safety of the dragon lulled the girl into sleep.

###

*Near the Spider Forest*

She woke with a start, still clutching the scale on Nayev's back. The sun shone high and the dragon spiraled slowly downward toward a thick forest. The sleep had done wonders for her body, and her mind slowly began to clear.

Nayev settled in a large clearing, his wings sending whorls of dust and dry leaves into the air. Timbrel watched the slowly turning spirals, remembering the dragons' sky dance. She carefully kept her thoughts shielded. It would be embarrassing if Nayev heard them, particularly if he was forbidden to her. No sense in teasing him, or causing him pain. She felt pain enough for both of them.

*She is a mess, Krys. Perhaps the sight of another elf will shake her mind free?* Nayev's voice whispered so quietly in her mind that she could barely hear him. Krys?

Kryslandir strode across the clearing, accompanied by several of the Spider Riders. He waved them back and leaned on a rock near the center of the clearing. Timbrel watched in horror as the elf's skin turned black, then stretched far beyond its normal boundaries. The flesh beneath seemed to bubble. The girl felt a scream rising, when there was an audible pop and Krys expanded in size, finally settling into the form of a smallish black dragon. The color drained from the dragon's limbs, leaving them the same silver color as Krys' hair. The wings fanned out, frantically beating. The silver dragon slowly rose into the air. Nayev bunched his legs and sprang upward, his wings snapping out and beating steadily. Timbrel remained quiet, holding onto Nayev's saddle scale.

*She is not moving. Are you certain she is awake?* She recognized Krys' quiet voice, though she had never heard it in her mind before.

*Her body is awake, but her mind still sleeps, I think. The Melani caged her for three months.* Timbrel could feel the worry in Nayev's mind-voice.

*She resisted the mind-drugs last time, but she drank only a single dose. She came back to herself in familiar surroundings.*

*Will the elven court be familiar enough, or should I take her somewhere else? Is there a healer who can examine her? I can't even tell if she is hurt beneath the filth.*

Timbrel scratched at her head. Her fingernail, already torn and dirty, caught chunks of crusted grime. The girl stared at her finger in dismay. When had she gotten so dirty?

Aware of the dirt coating her skin and hair for the first time, Timbrel felt the need to wash. She glanced down as the dragons flew toward a mountain pass. A lake shimmered in the sunlight.

*Nayev.* She pushed her mental voice as loud as she could. *Nayev, I need to wash. Can we find a lake?*

*Of course, Timbrel. Hold on tight.* The golden dragon curved smoothly around and flew back toward the lake, Krys following behind.

Feeling her body again, Timbrel was keenly aware of the rhythmic pressure of the saddle-scale's ridge against her pelvis. Her newly awakened senses heightened the wisps of pleasure that grew with the rhthym. The beating of the golden dragon's wings as he hovered sent her into a moment of mindless pleasure.

The shock of icy cold water put an end to that. She surfaced in the lake, sputtering. She had fallen off Nayev's back.

The silver dragon shook, its abdomen spasming. Krys laughed at her. Staring at him, she caught a faint glimmer of his mind, enough to realize that Nayev had purposely twisted to dump her into the water.

She looked up at the golden dragon. His neck arched high, shaking with laughter. He peered down at her. *You're all wet.*

Timbrel's face twisted into a grin. "You have no idea." Leaving the puzzled dragon behind her, she swam to the shore. Shouldering her pack, she prowled the bushes along the edge of the lake.

*What is she doing, gathering flowers? We should hurry.* Timbrel could just hear Nayev's comments to Krys.

*You tell her, then. This is Timbrel. I prefer to let well enough alone.* Krys' voice faded out as the girl concentrated on the blooms she had gathered. She moved to a sandy area with a few thick willow bushes and laid out five rocks. She pounded part of her gathered soapwort into a slimy mess, using it to wash both her blue dress and her golden silk dance outfit. She hung the clothing out of sight of the dragons before setting to work on the rest of the soapwort. When the plants were thoroughly smashed, she massaged the broken plants into her hair along with a handful of wet sand. She mixed more sand with crushed violets, ready to scrub the crust from her arms and legs. She laid a few wild olives between the last two flat rocks, their oil dripping into a bowl-like depression on the fifth rock.

Violet petals and sand in her hands, Timbrel waded shoulder-deep into the water and began scrubbing. Clean sand from the lake bottom replaced foul as the grime began to slough off. The water swirled around her, the slight current carrying the dirt away. She stripped out of her filthy rag, rinsed it, then used it to scrub sand across her back. Her belly was next. When she could see pale skin, the dancer scrubbed at her hair again. It was a bright gold before she finished.

Both dragons watched her intently. She looked directly at Nayev, and then turned her back in a sharp movement. She could feel the dragon's rising interest suddenly drop to silence in her mind. Timbrel glanced back over her left shoulder. Nayev was dunking his head in the cool water, shaking it. The girl laughed.

Finally clean enough, Timbrel walked up the shore, dangling the rag between two fingers. The girl carefully kept her back to the dragons. She dug a hole in the sand with her foot, then unceremoniously dumped the rag in and buried it by kicking sand over the top. She marched up the beach, disappearing behind the bushes.

The gold dance outfit was dry, with a scattering of water spots that made her think of scales. Timbrel carefully folded the midriff baring top, the long skirt, and the long thin wing-style veil. She chose two straight branches from a willow bush, suitable for use as dowels, and placed them by her pack as well. She would slide them into the hems at the sides of the veil at a later time.

She looked through the rest of her pack, discarding most of the contents. She dumped a layer of crumbled leaves from her herb pouch on the shore. The few herbs left after Rockhold's war were withered from close contact with Shess and Gowell. There would be no bitter tea until the dancer found fresh ingredients.

Repacking only her dance clothing, willow switches, flint and steel, and her dance bells, she left her brush and comb out to work on her hair.

She discarded her few cosmetics as well. With pale skin from living weeks in the darkness, she needed nothing to brighten the contrast between skin and lips. Catching sight of her reflection in the water, she saw that her eyelids were still bruised with exhaustion, giving her a unique purple shade that highlighted the blue of her eyes.

Using a few drops of oil, the dancer combed and brushed her hair free of tangles. It shone like spun gold in the afternoon sun. She rubbed the rest of the oil into her skin. A glance at her fingernails brought the half-elf's steel back out from her fire kit, raggedly trimming them a short as possible. She could not remove a few smudges of dirt. *Besides*, she thought as she adjusted the blue dress for better fit, *no one will be looking at my nails*.

### 

*The Grand Ballroom at the Henin Palace*

Lady Kareni waved away a tray of sweets with a perfectly manicured hand, and sipped from her thirtieth glass of wine, already bored with her wedding. The early morning rites sealed her to Lord Jherik for the next seven years. The hours of the reception had been filled with well-wishers. The seemingly endless line of ambassadors and foreign dignitaries began to blend into each other after the third hour.

She stole a glance at the newly crowned Urramachi Matriarch. Lostaria sat with the human Baron of Rockhold, an obnoxious young man named Alexander who propositioned every female in the room by the second hour with no success. Lostaria's presence unsettled Kareni. When the golden-haired elf passed through the receiving line, Kareni thought it was Timbrel. Her heart skipped a beat. The two were similar in appearance though Timbrel's human features marred her beauty.

The half-elf was marred by more than that. Kareni sent out spies to learn about the woman who spoiled her Jherik for the wedding night. Jherik still insisted that nothing happened, though Kareni received many reports that assured her otherwise. The surprise of those reports, however, was that Timbrel spent her time in the human world *dancing*. She may have status among the elves as a distant relative of the Urramachi, but her status among the humans was that of a lowly *dancer*. When that news came out, Kareni knew that Timbrel would be forced to crawl back into the mud she came from. Even better, it would lower Lostaria's status. It galled Kareni that her own people's leadership, even the son of the Henin matriarch, acknowledged Lostaria as having a higher status. Her prince was a century older than the girl, and from just as long a line. Lostaria should be kneeling to *him*. Kareni hated the Ravali elves. How dare they be so friendly?

The new bride looked around the room. She successfully avoided the last several ambassadors to be announced. Nayev of the Daraga and party. Who in the world were they? Kareni had never even heard of the Daraga, though both Lostaria and Jherik ran right off to greet them. Even Alexander went in that direction. As if the latecomers were actually important.

The musicians struck up another slow tune. Kareni's feet throbbed. Apparently everyone else was just as tired of dancing. The floor emptied, leaving one couple. It looked like Lostaria finally found a partner, but who was he? Lostaria's blue dress flattered her. Kareni stopped. Hadn't the young Urramachi Matriarch been wearing green?

Kareni looked around in confusion. Lostaria stood to one side, still dressed in green, chatting with Alexander and a tall, silver-haired elf that looked like Jherik's friend Krys. Krys? Kareni's mood soured. The dancer must be Timbrel.

The music continued, the single couple drawing attention from the entire room. It wasn't fair, this was Kareni's day. No one else should get such attention. She watched the dancers for a moment before she recognized the dance. The *Akeni*, the ancient dance once used to signify betrothal to a life-match. It fell out of use generations before when the elves came to their senses about proper marriage lengths.

The dancers stopped, trying to talk above the music. When the music stopped as well, their voices rang above the silence of the watching crowd.

"You understand the significance of the *Akeni*?" The young man spoke in the human tongue.

"I do. It is a life-long marriage, as is the human custom. I accept." Timbrel's crisp tones were unforgettable. The two leaned together in a public kiss.

The floor suddenly filled with activity as the newly betrothed couple received congratulations. Lostaria held the couple's hands in the air, showing her acceptance of the match. Kareni sat in her chair, stunned at being forgotten. How dare that... that dancer... Kareni's anger flared, particularly when Jherik gave Timbrel a hug. The young bride stood, her chair tumbling to the ground behind her, and called for attention by rapping a spoon on her crystal wine glass.

The glass shattered, spattering Kareni with dark wine and bringing more attention than she wanted. Jherik glanced up at his wife and paled, his expression horrified before Kareni said a word. Lostaria merely watched her.

"I would like to congratulate the new couple-to-be," Kareni began. "What better place to arrange a wedding than at the celebration of one." The crowd muttered agreement, confounding Kareni. She had just pointed out a breach of etiquette. The crowd should condemn them, not agree.

378

"My husband's far-traveling friend has not greeted me yet, nor has she brought a gift." The crowds murmur turned darker. Kareni panicked a little when she realized the glances were aimed at her this time. "Timbrel, I understand you are acclaimed a dancer of quite some renown in the human world. I want you to dance for me as your gift."

The crowd went absolutely silent. Kareni had just insulted Timbrel, equating her to the lowest status an elf could imagine. Worse, she phrased the insult as a request, a request that could not be denied.

"Yes, cousin, dance for us." Lostaria's voice rose proudly. "It is true, you are quite skilled. I have seen you dance."

The crowd broke out in astonished murmurs. The Urramachi Matriarch proudly claimed what should have been a shameful secret. The crowd was curious now.

"She is indeed skilled," joined in Alexander. "I, too, have seen her dance."

Timbrel took a step forward. The crowd backed away. "I will dance. In ten minutes time, after I've spoken to the musicians and changed into an appropriate costume, I will dance for all of you."

Kareni motioned for a servant to pick up her chair. She sat on the embroidered cushions, a smug look on her face. The half-breed whore was found out.

### 

From the look on the elves' faces when Kareni made her announcement, Nayev understood that Jherik's bride insulted Timbrel. He was still thinking of a response when Lostaria and Alexander chimed in, turning an insult into pride. The crowd's hostile mood turned to curiosity, particularly when Timbrel agreed to dance.

The young dragon burned with curiosity, never having seen his betrothed dance alone. Others told him of her skill.

"I will dance for all of you," Timbrel announced in a loud voice, and then whispered to Nayev, "especially for you."

He was already more interested in the half-elven girl than he would ever admit. In spite of his years in dragon form, the girl's glances over her shoulder through half-lidded eyes excited him almost as much as his first elf-woman did. His hormone-laden perversions, as his fellow dragons called them, led to offspring the first time. He had control of his human urges now, though. He would not breed again unless the girl managed a mating flight, unlikely since she could not fly.

Nayev knew that Timbrel wanted him. Before they entered the castle, just after he shifted back to human form, she confronted him. "Are you a man who becomes a dragon? Or a dragon who becomes a man?"

Nayev stung with doubt. He liked Timbrel and planned to ask Lostaria for permission to marry the girl. Could his origins really matter so much to her?

She persisted. "Are you born man or dragon?"

"Does it matter?"

After too long a pause, Timbrel finally took his hand. "No," she whispered. Nayev caught a thought-glimpse of the overwhelming love she felt for him. She would be happy to be his bride.

Jherik's bride was the problem. The red-haired woman was drunk, so drunk that her new husband abandoned her to her cups and sought refuge from her tongue in the crowd. Nayev spoke to Lostaria while Alexander kept Timbrel busy on the dance floor. The Princess, now Urramach Matriarch, gave her blessing to his proposal long before the dance. She also admitted to Nayev that she sought to name Timbrel an ambassador. Kareni's loose tongue put that plan in danger, unless Timbrel could find some way out of the strange insult.

The musicians stood as if in salute and seated themselves. Timbrel walked out among them, her body draped in a borrowed cloak that dragged on the ground.

"I call this the Dance of the Skies," she announced. She nodded to the musicians. An elven melody began, a long piece that mimicked the sound of the wind in the mountains. Nayev had heard it before and liked it. It reminded him of his home.

Timbrel dropped her cloak. The crowd's reaction nearly drowned out the music. Nayev could hear appreciative sounds as well as outraged ones. Timbrel was draped in golden silk, very nearly the color of her hair. The torchlight shimmered on her skin like sunlight across scales as she slowly circled the room, crouching and turning very slowly as she walked. Her skirts flared slightly, emphasizing her slow spin within a spiral and showing her well-toned legs. Occasionally she nudged a chair to the side. Nayev watched her with interest.

The dancer circled the room a second time, this time leaping smoothly from chair to chair with bent knees and straight body. The crowd turned to her, entranced by the quickening movements. Nayev could hear the heartbeats of the men change, pounding in time with the half-elf's movements.

Her third circuit included the tabletops along one wall of the room, as well is the thin ledge that ran around the other side. She moved faster but appeared more fluid. After a moment, Nayev realized that she had unwrapped a thin length of material that extended her reach. The torchlight shimmered along the girl's oiled skin, reflecting the golden silk of her costume. Her body appeared made of gold.

At a sighing change in the music, Timbrel straightened completely, standing on her tiptoes and beating her veil quickly back and forth. She has wings, thought Nayev. He pressed closer to her, joining dozens of other young men around the table.

Hands reached for Timbrel's skirts, but she used her pulsing veil to somehow beat them away. Nayev's hand stung where the fabric touched it, and he recognized the willow switches she'd brought in her pack. The stinging on his hand excited him in ways he could not explain.

The girl spun suddenly, leapt to a higher table, and resumed pulsing her veil. Nayev found himself circling the new table, vaguely aware that the others followed him in a great circling dance. He focused on Timbrel, his heart beating in time with her veil. Urges swept through him, dragon and human both, and pounded through his blood.

One of the men stood on tiptoe, trying to reach the dancer's hem again. Nayev found himself in a similar pose, his arms at a precise angle and then falling away to clear the space at his sides. Timbrel continued her dance, her body twisting as she posed. The blood rushed to the wizard's head as his attention focused tighter and tighter on the girl.

The last chord of the music played and lingered in the air. Timbrel snapped upright, taking the same pose as Nayev and falling into his arms from above. He swung her to the ground, gripping her shoulders from behind and burying his head in the thick golden hair of her neck. He felt pressure against the back of his legs as Timbrel's veil wrapped around him. When she tilted her head back to rub her face along his own, his fists clenched. She spun from his grasp, leading him away from the floor by the length of her veil. He barely heard the thunderous applause that followed them.

Timbrel darted out a side door, Nayev in pursuit. He caught her at the stairs, veil fluttering. There was no spinning away this time. His hands caught her shoulders tighter than before. His need was magnified by the short chase. Caught up in his odd mating flight, Nayev took the willing dancer in the stairwell. By the time his first urges subsided, her short nails had scratched bloody furrows along the back of his thighs.

"You make a good dragon," he murmured as he rubbed his face alongside hers.

"I make an even better human," she whispered as she pulled him along the hallway, searching for an empty room.

###

*Allowei's Treehouse, Ravali*

Allowei greeted Timbrel in the lowest chamber of their treehouse. "Is this an official visit from the ambassador to the humans?"

"No. This visit is personal." Timbrel looked uncomfortable.

Allowei tried to calm her friend's fears. "You are always welcome here. I heard about your marriage. Congratulations." The half-elf still seemed nervous. "Why are you here?" She escorted the girl to a chair, and then took a close look at the odd reddish cast to Timbrel's cheeks. "What would you ask of me?"

Timbrel wiggled in her seat.

Allowei looked again at Timbrel's red cheeks. The flush of embarrassment had not touched the mask she had initially seen. There was a slight swelling of the dancer's abdomen as well. "You are pregnant?"

Timbrel nodded.

Allowei clapped her hands with joy. "How wonderful! Is the father your new husband?"

Timbrel looked down again, chewing on her lip.

The healer put a hand to her mouth. She had been mistaken. Apparently some of the rumors about her former roommate were true. The girl must have conceived outside her marriage.

"I am so sorry, I should not jump to such conclusions. The father is the problem?"

"My husband is the father, but there is a problem." Timbrel's eyes darted around the room, looking everywhere but the healer. "My husband is a hybrid of sorts, too."

"Is he? He doesn't have the look."

Timbrel bit her lip again. "He is a wizard. He can shift forms."

The elven healer looked Timbrel over carefully. "I can see where this might be a problem. I assume that your condition is not widely known?"

"Not even my husband knows yet. He is with his people right now. I... I just want to know what to expect."

383

Allowei thought about her options. "Lie down on the table." She leaned over Timbrel and put a listening horn on the half-elf's belly.

The heartbeat sounded odd. Allowei frowned as she moved the horn several times. "Oh, my."

Timbrel tensed immediately at the healer's words. "Is something wrong?" The dancer tried to sit up.

"Nothing, it is just..." The healer paused before continuing. "It is unusual. I think this has only happened once before in our recorded history."

"What is it? Tell me."

"I hear three heartbeats. You bear triplets."

The End

#

## ACKNOWLEDGMENTS & THANKS

There are so many people to thank that I'm sure to forget someone. You aren't really forgotten, I'm just terrible at remembering names.

First, special thanks to Jeanne Cavelos, Director of the Odyssey Fantasy Writing Workshop. I couldn't have gotten this novel into shape without your guidance.

Thank you to my classmates at Odyssey 2007, TNEO 2009, and TNEO 2013 for your excellent critiques and feedback. Also to the Odyssey Discussion Board - I may be mostly silent, but I do listen.

Thank you to my early Beta readers: Alaric Bishop, Cherish Hunter, Tarina Jameson, Chris McCallister, and Melissa Robbins. You each had your specialties for finding mistakes (Timing, Plot Holes, Grammar Police, City Uniqueness, and Character Personalities) that helped me keep everything consistent. Any leftover errors are mine alone.

Thank you to the Write On Joliet! critique group, especially Denise Unland and Tom Hernandez, for pushing me to publish.

To Abby Goldsmith, for showing me that villains were people, too.

To Susan Sing, who taught me how to really use dialogue.

To Susan Abel Sullivan, who showed me what passive verbs in my writing looked like. (Forty-seven times on the same page!)

To Diana Estell, who kept me sane when she helped me laugh at some of my mistakes and auto-corrects (uninformed vs. uniformed soldiers; one character telling another to "chew the caverns").

To William T. of Ocala, FL for reminding me to never make it easy on my characters.

To Sheila Kennedy of Lewis University for the encouragement.

And last, but certainly not least, Thank you to my husband Kirk for putting up with me when I ignored everything around me while writing. Love you! -CHR

# About the Author

Colleen H. Robbins has been writing since she was nine years old and holds a Bachelor of Arts degree in English Language and Literature from Lewis University. She has attended numerous workshops, including the Iowa Summer Writer's Conference in 2003, the six-week long Odyssey Fantasy Writer's Workshop in 2007, and TNEO in 2009 and 2013. Her stories, poems, essays, and articles have appeared under a variety of names in everything from small regional magazines to the rpg-gaming-oriented magazines Different Worlds and The Dragon, and have been included in numerous anthologies. She writes both mainstream (literary) fiction and genre (science fiction, fantasy, and horror).

Outside of writing, Colleen has lived in numerous (mostly coastal) states, and spent her childhood reading, primitive camping, hiking, skiing, and sailing in the northeastern United States. She became a member of the Society for Creative Anachronism [recreating Medieval and Ancient times], authorized in the broadsword and round shield fighting style, took up archery, bellydance [Egyptian-Turkish style, and later added American Tribal style], costuming, and motherhood while in the southeastern US. Further moving around the country allowed her to visit numerous caves and mines, fossil sites, and historical areas such as Gettysburg. She enjoys attending historical recreation weekends of a number of eras and cultures, and is a past member of the Historical Miniatures Gaming Society. She continues to add new experiences: during a 2017 trip to California she attempted to learn surfing, and one of her many mishaps while doing so will appear in the third book of the Daraga series (due in 2020). Many of her other experiences and travels find their ways into her writing.

Colleen has worked as a Paralegal, Medical Records Analyst, Bellydance Instructor, and Library Volunteer, among other jobs, and holds degrees from the University of South Florida [Tampa, FL], Joliet Junior College [Joliet, IL], and Lewis University [Romeoville, IL].

# Coming in 2019:

# The Daraga's Children

Family is everything, right? Then why do they have so many secrets?

When sixteen year old Nicholas Nayevson discovers he can shapeshift into a dragon, he can't wait to show off to his wizard father. When his father doesn't come home from a visit to the distant Daraga lands, a noble tries to force his sister into marriage and Nicholas' people struggle with dragon attacks. Nicholas recognizes that he must take action. Hoping to solve both problems and avert an all-out war with the dragons, he determines to track his father down.

Travelling as a dragon is tricky, but travelling as a human has its own challenges. Worse, Nicholas has no idea where his father's mysterious Daraga people live.

But what can Nicholas do when he discovers that the young man on the other end of his sword is his nearly identical brother--from his father's *other* family?

.

# Coming in 2019

## Stories of a Sheltered Suburbanite

A woman with "Too Many Kids."

A child watching the hero next door.

A toy saving lives on the battlefront.

Not everything is as it seems, particularly to the sheltered.

COLLEEN H. ROBBINS